CLOSE TO HOME

She made her way to the door at the end of the hallway that led to the narrow passage upward into the attic and beyond.

As she stepped through it, anxiety elevated her pulse. Since childhood she'd avoided these stairs, refused to step foot into the attic, but she could do so no longer.

Get a hold of yourself. There is nothing evil in the attic. Nothing.

She flipped on the light switch at the base of the stairs. It clicked loudly, but that was it. The steps and gaping area above remained dark. "Of course," she muttered and clicked on the flashlight of her cell phone to illuminate the stairs. Feeling her neck muscles tighten, she forced herself to climb the steep flight and ignored the beating of her heart and the fear that slid through her veins.

The temperature dropped as she stepped into the attic, where gaps in the shingles caused the wind to whistle and wail and allowed rain to slip inside.

She remembered being up on the widow's walk that night she'd gone to the attic. Frigid rain pelted from an obsidian sky. Her nightgown was soaked, her skin was wet, and a bitter wind cut through her as she shivered. But it was more than winter weather that caused the icy fear in the pit of her stomach. There was something malevolent out there, horrifying enough to make her mind block the memories.

But sometimes bit

Also by Lisa Jackson and available from Hodder

Standalones

Running Scared
Twice Kissed
Deep Freeze
Fatal Burn
Almost Dead
Without Mercy
You Don't Want to Know
Unspoken

The Montana Novels

Left to Die
Chosen to Die
Born to Die
Afraid to Die
Ready to Die
Deserves to Die

The New Orleans Novels

Hot Blooded
Cold Blooded
Shiver
Absolute Fear
Lost Souls
Malice
Devious

The Savannah Novels

The Night Before
The Morning After
Tell Me

About the author

Lisa Jackson's books are number one bestsellers in America. She now has over twenty million copies of her books in print in nineteen languages. She lives with her family and a rambunctious pug in the Pacific Northwest. You can visit her website at www.lisajackson.com, become her friend on Facebook or follow her on Twitter @readlisajackson.

LISA JACKSON

Close to Home

MULHOLLAND
BOOKS
HODDER

First published in Great Britain in 2014 by Mulholland Books
An imprint of Hodder & Stoughton
An Hachette UK company

This paperback edition first published in 2015

1

A CIP catalogue record for this title is available from the British Library

Paperback ISBN 978 1 444 79330 7
eBook ISBN 978 1 44479329 1

Printed and bound by Clays Ltd, St Ives plc

Hodder & Stoughton policy is to use papers that are natural, renewable
and recyclable products and made from wood grown in sustainable forests.
The logging and manufacturing processes are expected to conform to the
environmental regulations of the country of origin.

Hodder & Stoughton Ltd
338 Euston Road
London NW1 3BH

www.hodder.co.uk

Close to Home

PROLOGUE

October 31, 1924
Blue Peacock Manor

*H*elp *me! Dear Father in heaven, please!*

Angelique's heart was pounding, fear spreading through her bloodstream as she raced barefoot up the wide staircase. She had to find a way to save herself and her children. For the love of God, she had to save them.

Frantic, she gathered the torn hem of her tattered, grass-stained skirts in one hand, her legs wet and covered in mud.

And semen.

Proof the bastard had raped her.

Her stomach roiled at the thought as upward, ever upward she ran. Downstairs, near the parlor, her grandmother's ancient clock was ticking off the seconds of her life. Grasping the polished banister, she propelled herself upward, past the second floor still bathed in lamplight, its long carpets running down the corridor and onto the stairs leading to the upper stories of this monstrosity of a house, a home in which she'd once felt such pride.

Fool!

Run! Run! Run!

Don't let him catch you again!

Lure him away from the children.

Her breath was coming in short gasps, her lungs burning, her body heavy, the stays of her corset stretched. She reached the landing and thought she heard heavy footsteps below.

One of the children?

Or him?

Oh, God.

Sweat running down her back, she climbed to the third floor, where, gasping, she turned down the darkened hallway. Images of the children—the innocents—filled her head.

Help them! Mon Dieu, *please . . . HELP ME!*

If she were to die, so be it, but not the little ones. Tears filled her eyes as she thought of sweet Monique and chubby little Jacques and the others, older and yet suffering as well. Stalwart Ruth, sweet Helen, and Louis with the sad eyes . . . Her throat closed. This was all her fault, and the innocents would suffer, die hideously, because of her.

The woman who'd sworn to protect them.

She looked down the dizzying, curving staircase into the shadows below. Flickering lamplight gave off an eerie glow at the landing of each floor, and the darkness on the steps between made her blood run cold.

But she couldn't give in to the fear. Not yet.

Come on, you bastard. Follow me. Leave them be! Even as the thought crossed her mind, she knew he wouldn't let them go untouched. She knew that as well as anyone, didn't she? It wasn't his way. Didn't she have the scars to prove how cruel he could be, this man she'd once loved?

She heard the front door creaking open, then bang shut with a heart-stopping thud. She nearly tripped on her skirts as terror enveloped her. *Stay calm. You can outwit him. You must. Oh . . . God . . .*

His boots rang loudly across the wooden floor of the foyer to thud on the first step.

Her skin crawled, and she bit down hard on her lip.

Le monstre hideux was coming.

Just as she'd known he would.

She clutched the silver cross swinging from a small chain around her neck and dared look over the railing. His menacing shadow, a huge, elongated umber stretching to the ceiling, moved inexorably forward. He was carrying something in his hand. And then she recognized the axe for what it was.

Her insides shriveled at the thought of him swinging the sharp, heavy blade, his intentions to hack her to death all too clear. What chance did she have against his brute strength?

Belatedly, she realized she should have run to the stable. She'd discarded the notion as there wasn't time to ride her mare into the town five miles away through the fog and rain and muck of the road, across fields or through woods, to reach the gaslit streets of Stewart's Crossing. Even if she had reached the town, how could she possibly convince the sheriff that she hadn't gone stark, raving mad and return in time to save them all? Impossible. Recklessly, she'd run through the house and now regretted she hadn't veered to the stable, where not only the horses were housed, but in the attached shed a variety of tools—hatchets, hammers, and scythes—were stored.

She waited.

Her only hope was that when he followed her to the rooftop, she'd have a chance—a slim one, true—but at least a risky opportunity to turn the tables on him. If she couldn't save herself, at least she might be able to take the bastard with her.

And what of the baby? Can you sacrifice that new unborn life as well?

Tears burned her eyes.

Again she looked over the curved railing, catching a glimpse of him, now on the second floor, climbing to the third.

NOW!

She leaned over the railing and yelled at the top of her lungs, "Run!"

"What the bloody hell?" he snarled, glaring up at her, his eyes gleaming a malicious blue above his beard.

"Ruth! Helen!" she screamed desperately, hoping to warn the children. "Get the babies and run away as fast as you can!"

"They'll never get away," he warned, a smug look twisting the lips she'd once kissed with such ardor. How had she been such an imbecile? He laughed again, and the acrid smell of alcohol reached her nostrils. He was too close!

Whirling around, she dashed along the runner to the attic stairs at the end of the hall. The door was locked, as always.

"Harlot!" he yelled after her. "Goddamned whore, come back here!"

Never!

She sent up a silent prayer for the dear, sweet souls of the little ones.

Our Father, who art in heaven . . .

The clock in the lower hallway began to chime, counting out the hours in reverberating peals.

Hallowed be thy name.

His footsteps quickened, and she reached into the pocket of her voluminous skirts for the keys. She fumbled in the dark with the massive key ring, the metal clinking as she struggled to find the right one for the attic door.

Hurry!

Her pulse was pounding in her brain, her fingers slick with sweat, keys clanking. She dropped the ring only to retrieve it quickly.

Thy kingdom come.

Thy will be done.

On earth as it is in heaven.

The clock continued to strike off the hours, and along with the familiar peals came the heavy, determined tread announcing that he was following.

Her heart froze. Her breath stilled in her lungs for the briefest of seconds. She inserted another key.

Nothing!

"You think you can run from me?" he bellowed, his words echoing to the rafters, chilling her soul. "You really think you can get away?" His laughter was obscene.

Her throat closed in fear.

Hands trembling, she forced the key into its lock and twisted frantically. A glance over her shoulder confirmed he'd made the climb and was now smiling, walking slowly, unhurried, savoring these last few minutes when he could terrorize her for one final time.

Click!

The lock sprang!

She hurriedly shouldered open the door to the attic.

Let him come.

She was a clever woman and far from dead.

Yet.

Someway, somehow, with just an ounce of luck, she would save her children, if not herself. The air was thick and dank, smelling of dust. She slammed the door behind her, twisted the lock, then scrambled up the narrow, steep flight in all-consuming darkness.

She heard the unmistakable squeak of a bat and a flutter of disturbed wings, but she hardly noticed as she reached the attic floor.

Think, Angelique, think. Do not let him get the better of you! Her mind raced as quickly as her bare feet scurried across the cold floor. This was her chance to even the odds, to grab a weapon to protect herself. She didn't have much time. Up the last, winding stairway she ran to the small, glass-encased cupola.

Rain drizzled down the windows of the tiny room, and her trembling fingers worked feverishly on the latch of the door. *Please, please, please!* The lock gave way with little effort, but the tiny door to the roof was stuck, its sodden wooden frame swollen shut.

Gritting her teeth, she tried again, throwing her shoulder into the door and feeling the damp wood hold tight before finally giving way. He was closer now. She heard him at the base of the attic stairs, rattling the doorknob.

No!

Desperately she flung her weight into the door, and it finally gave way, opening in a *whoosh* as it was caught by the wind shrieking down the chasm of the river far below.

Frigid rain spit from the sky, clouds obscuring the moon, but she didn't pause to look, just quickly returned to the attic. If she could somehow lure him onto the roof, alone, and lock the door behind him, he'd be trapped.

Except he has an axe. He can chop his way back inside.

Damn!

Craaaack! Bam!

The door from the third floor gave way, splintering and crashing loudly against the wall.

She bit back a scream.

Noiselessly, she stepped farther into the darkness of the north wing. All the while, she searched the cold space by feel.

The attic stairs groaned under his weight. He was taking his time, either because he was afraid of an attack or because he was savoring every moment of the hunt.

Frantically, she made the sign of the cross over her bosom and forced her mouth shut so that he couldn't hear her panicked breaths. *Calm down. You can outsmart him. He's an oaf. Don't fall apart!*

Inching backward, her fingers scraping along the wooden walls and bare rafters, splinters catching beneath her fingernails, she bit hard on her lower lip, refusing to make a sound, even when the sharp points of the nails holding the roof shingles in place scratched her head.

Don't let him hear you.

Crouching, she eased backward, through an icy pool of water where the roof had leaked, her arms outstretched, searching for something, anything to protect herself, but she touched nothing that would help her.

She smelled him now, the odor of alcohol reaching her nostrils. She knelt, frantically feeling the floor and the crates stacked upon it. She touched an old picture frame, a trunk, a forgotten basket of needlepoint and moldy crates, but nothing hard or sharp, not even a damned rock. Scouring the area blindly, she prayed for some kind of weapon or shield.

There *had* to be something! Even a small shard of glass. A nail. A hanger. An old iron. Anything!

Thud!

The rafters shook.

"Son of a bitch!" he snarled as if he'd hit his head on a low-hanging rafter. She became a statue, not moving a muscle.

Swallowing hard, still huddled close to the floor, she worked her fingers around her skirts in a wide circle. Her fingertips brushed against cold metal, a rod of some kind. Her heart soared. Maybe a forgotten poker from the fireplace or . . . no! A candlestick! She almost cried out in surprise and relief.

"Where are you?" he said, his voice soft. Cajoling. "Come out, come out, wherever you are."

Her fingers clamped around the cool metal. It wasn't much in the way of weaponry compared to an axe, but it was hard and heavy. She grabbed it near the tapered end, so that she could swing it and strike with the base, hard enough to crack his skull. She heard him moving toward the stairs to the cupola. *Please,* she thought, sure she could lock him on the roof, then run downstairs and gather the children, leaving him up there as they took the wagon into town.

She sensed, rather than saw him start up the final short flight of stairs through the cupola to the widow's walk outside. She hardly dared breathe.

But he hesitated. As if he sensed a trap.

No! No! No! Keep going. Just a little farther. Please. Only three or four more steps onto the roof outside!

But he turned back. She heard the door to the widow's walk slam shut, then felt the vibration of the attic floorboards as he stepped into the garret once more.

"Angelique?" he called softly over the wind whistling around the gables. "I know you're in here. Come on out. You cannot get away."

Sick at heart, she knew there was only one sure way to get him onto the roof. She'd have to use herself as bait.

Ears straining, she heard his footsteps thankfully receding as he walked to the far end of the attic away from her. Dragging the candlestick from its resting place, she sprang, running up the steep, winding steps to the domed cupola again.

This time the door opened easily.

She tumbled outside, tripping on her own skirts and nearly dropping her weapon as she skidded across the slick, flat roof. A screaming wind tore at her hair. Rain lashed at her face, but here at least she had a chance.

Far below, the Columbia River churned, flowing swiftly westward, a wild dark ribbon cutting through the canyon walls on which this grand house had been constructed. Once it had been her pride and joy. Now it was a prison.

In her naïveté she'd named the imposing structure Blue Peacock Manor for the birds she so loved, but now the house was nothing but a death trap, perched high over the churning water, her lovely birds already slaughtered at his hand. Just this afternoon, she'd come across the body of the one she'd named Royal, his shimmering, sapphire-like feathers dripping in blood, an arrow's shaft jutting from his chest.

But she couldn't think of the senseless sacrifice now . . . not when the children's lives were at stake.

Drawing herself to her full height, she waited near the doorway. Her plan was to lock him up here and run away with the children.

Not good enough. You need to set this house ablaze. Trap him on this roof and burn the house beneath him. What good is this repulsive prison to you anyway?

"Father forgive me," she whispered, raising the candlestick high just as the top of his head appeared in the small opening. She didn't think twice. Throwing all of her weight into the blow, she struck.

Craaaack!

The bones in his cheek shattered, and he stumbled slightly, howling like a wounded wolf.

She swung again, but he moved, and the candlestick glanced off his shoulder.

He grabbed it, stripping it out of her wet hands as he shoved his way onto the roof.

She backed up as he swung. In one hand the axe, in the other the damned candlestick. "Whore," he said over the wind as he advanced with the infinite patience of a killer who knew he'd cornered his prey. "You think to hurt me? Kill me?" he said, his eyes narrowing as if he couldn't believe she had had the gall to turn on him.

"Maman?" a frightened voice called over the hiss of another slash of lightning, and Angelique glanced to the doorway, where ten-year-old Helen was shivering, hiding under the portico. "What is . . . ?" Helen, a waif, turned her round eyes to the monster. "No, wait!"

"Go back down, Helen!" Angelique ordered.

"But, Maman—"

"Just go!" Angelique met the girl's frightened stare for a split second. "And lock the door."

"No!" He turned toward Helen. "Don't lock anything!"

Angelique was desperate. "Run! Now!" She leaped forward, throwing her body against his and reaching upward, scratching his face and scrabbling for the axe handle.

"Whore!" he bellowed.

Somewhere behind them Helen screamed.

The axe glinted.

But his boots slipped on the tiles.

"Run!" Angelique shrieked to Helen as he started to topple. With all her strength, she kicked up swiftly, driving her knee hard into his groin and causing him to yowl and sway, the axe flying into the darkness.

Screaming in agony, he clasped one calloused hand around her throat as she kicked hard once more.

Together they tipped slowly, hesitated, eyes locked, then spun into the blackness of the night.

CHAPTER 1

October 15, 2014
Blue Peacock Manor

"God, Mom, you've got to be kidding!" Jade said from the passenger seat of the Explorer as Sarah drove along the once-gravel lane.

"Not kidding," Sarah responded. "You know that." Winding through thick stands of pine, fir, and cedar, the twin ruts were weed-choked and filled with potholes that had become puddles with the recent rain.

"You can't actually think that we can live here!" Catching glimpses of the huge house through the trees, Jade, seventeen, was clearly horrified and, as usual, wasn't afraid to voice her opinion.

"Mom's serious," Gracie said from the backseat, where she was crammed between piles of blankets, and mounds of comforters, sleeping bags, and the other bedding they were moving from Vancouver. "She told us."

Jade shot a glance over her shoulder. "I know. But it's worse than I thought."

"That's impossible," Gracie said.

"No one asked your opinion!"

Sarah's hands tightened over the steering wheel. She'd already heard how she was ruining her kids' lives by packing them up and returning to the old homestead where she'd been born and raised. To hear them tell it, she was the worst mother in the world. The word "hate" had been thrown around, aimed at her, the move, and their miserable lives in general.

Single motherhood. It wasn't for the faint-hearted, she'd decided long ago. So her kids were still angry with her. Too bad. Sarah needed a fresh start.

And though Jade and Gracie didn't know it, they did too.

"It's like we're in another solar system," Jade said as the thickets of trees gave way to a wide clearing high above the Columbia River.

Gracie agreed, "In a land, far, far away."

"Oh, stop it. It's not *that* bad," Sarah said. Her girls had lived most of their lives in Vancouver, Washington, right across the river from Portland, Oregon. Theirs had been a city life. Out here, in Stewart's Crossing, things would be different, and even more so at Sarah's childhood home of Blue Peacock Manor.

Perched high on the cliffs overlooking the Columbia River, the massive house where Sarah had been raised rose in three stories of cedar and stone. Built in the Queen Anne style of a Victorian home, its gables and chimneys knifed upward into a somber gray sky, and from her vantage point Sarah could now see the glass cupola that opened onto the widow's walk. For a second, she felt a frisson of dread slide down her spine, but she pushed it aside.

"Oh. My. God." Jade's jaw dropped open as she stared at the house. "It looks like something straight out of *The Addams Family.*"

"Let me see!" In the backseat, Gracie unhooked her seat belt and leaned forward for a better view. "She's right." For once Gracie agreed with her older sister.

"Oh, come on," Sarah said, but Jade's opinion wasn't that far off. With a broad, sagging porch and crumbling chimneys, the once-grand house that in the past the locals had called the Jewel of the Columbia was in worse shape than she remembered.

"Are you blind? This place is a disaster!" Jade was staring through the windshield and slowly shaking her head, as if she couldn't believe the horrid turn her life had just taken. Driving closer to the garage, they passed another building that was falling into total disrepair. "Mom. Seriously. We *can't* live here." She turned her wide, mascara-laden eyes on her mother as if Sarah had gone completely out of her mind.

"We can and we will. Eventually." Sarah cranked on the wheel to swing the car around and parked near the walkway leading to the entrance of the main house. The decorative rusted gate was falling off its hinges, the arbor long gone, the roses flanking the flagstone path leggy and gone to seed. "We're going to camp out in the main house until the work on the guesthouse is finished, probably next week. That's where we'll hang out until the house is done, but that will take . . . months, maybe up to a year."

"The guest . . . Oh my God, is *that* it?" Jade pointed a black-tipped nail at the smaller structure located across a wide stone courtyard from its immense counterpart. The guesthouse was in much the same shape as the main house and outbuildings. Shingles were missing, the gutters were rusted, and most of the downspouts were disconnected or missing altogether. Many of the windows were boarded over as well, and the few that remained were cracked and yellowed.

"Charming." Jade let out a disgusted breath. "I can't wait."

"I thought you'd feel that way," Sarah said with a faint smile.

"Funny," Jade mocked.

"Come on. Buck up. It's just for a little while. Eventually we'll move into the main house for good, if we don't sell it."

Gracie said, "You should sell it now!"

"It's not just mine, remember? My brothers and sister own part of it. What we do with it will be a group decision."

"Doesn't anyone have a lighter?" Jade suggested, almost kidding. "You could burn it down and collect the insurance money."

"How do you know about . . . ?" But she didn't finish the question as she cut the engine. Jade, along with her newfound love of the macabre, was also into every kind of police or detective show that aired on television. Recently she'd discovered true crime as well, the kind of shows in which B-grade actors reenacted grisly murders and the like. Jade's interests, which seemed to coincide with those of her current boyfriend, disturbed Sarah, but she tried to keep from haranguing her daughter about them. In this case, less was more.

"You should sell out your part of it. Leave it to Aunt Dee Linn and Uncle Joe and Jake to renovate," Jade said. "Get out while you can. God, Mom, this is just so nuts that *we're* here. Not only is this house like something out of a bad horror movie, but it's in the middle of nowhere."

She wasn't that far off. The house and grounds were at least five miles from the nearest town of Stewart's Crossing, the surrounding neighbors' farms hidden by stands of fir and cedar. Sarah cut the engine and glanced toward Willow Creek, the natural divide between this property and the next, which had belonged to the Walsh family for more than a hundred years. For a split second she thought about Clint, the last of the Walsh line, who according to Dee Linn and Aunt Marge, was still living in the homestead. She reminded herself sternly that he was *not* the reason she'd pushed so hard to move back to Stewart's Crossing.

"Why don't you just take me back to get my car," Jade said as Sarah swung the Explorer around to park near the garage.

"Because it won't be ready for a couple of days, you heard Hal." They'd left Jade's Honda with a mechanic in town; it was scheduled to get a new set of tires and much-needed brakes, and Hal was going to figure out why the Civic was leaking some kind of fluid.

"Oh, right, Hal the master mechanic." Jade was disparaging.

"Best in town," Sarah said, tossing her keys into her bag. "My dad used him."

"*Only* mechanic in town. And Grandpa's been gone a long time, so it must've been eons ago!"

Sarah actually smiled. "Okay, you got me there. But the place was updated from the last time I was there. Lots of electronic equipment and a couple of new mechanics on staff."

To her amazement, Jade's lips twitched as well, reminding Sarah of the younger, more innocent girl she'd been such a short while ago. "And a lot of customers."

"Must be bad car karma right now," Sarah agreed. There had been an older woman with her little dog and two men, all having problems with their vehicles; the little group had filled the small reception area of the garage.

"Is there ever such a thing as good car karma?" Jade asked, but she seemed resigned to her fate of being without wheels for a while. Good.

Until recently, Jade had been a stellar student. She had a high IQ and had had a keen interest in school; in fact, she had breezed through any number of accelerated classes. Then, about a year ago, she'd discovered boys, and her grades had begun to slip. Now, despite the fact that it might be a bit passé, Jade was into all things Goth and wildly in love with her boyfriend, an older kid who'd barely graduated from high school and didn't seem to give a damn about anything but music, marijuana, and, most likely, sex. A pseudo-intellectual, he'd dropped out of college and loved to argue politics.

Jade thought the sun rose and set on Cody Russell.

Sarah was pretty sure it didn't.

"Come on, let's go," she told her daughters.

Jade wasn't budging. She dragged her cell phone from her purse. "Do I have to?"

"Yes."

"She's such a pain," Gracie said in a whisper. At twelve, she was only starting to show some interest in boys, and still preferred animals, books, and all things paranormal to the opposite sex, so far at least. Blessed with an overactive imagination and, again, keen intelligence, Gracie too was out of step with her peers.

"I heard that." Jade messed with her phone.

"It is kinda creepy, though," Gracie admitted, leaning forward as the first drops of rain splashed against the windshield.

"Beyond creepy!" Jade wasn't one to hold back. "And . . . Oh, God, don't tell me we don't get cell service here." Her face registered complete mortification.

"It's spotty," Sarah said.

"God, Mom, what is this? The Dark Ages? This place is . . . it's *horrible*. Blue Peacock Manor, my ass."

"Hey!" Sarah reprimanded sharply. "No swearing. Remember? Zero."

"But, Jesus, Mom—"

"Again?" Sarah snapped. "I just said no."

"Okay!" Jade flung back, then added, a little more calmly, "Come on, Mom. Admit it. Blue Peacock is a dumb name. It even sounds kind of dirty."

"Where is this coming from?" Sarah demanded.

"Just sayin'." Jade dropped her phone into her bag. "And Becky told me the house is haunted."

"So now you're listening to Becky?" Sarah set the parking brake and reached for the handle of the door. The day was quickly going from bad to worse. "I didn't think you liked her."

"I don't." Jade sighed theatrically. "I'm just telling you what she said." Becky was Jade's cousin, the daughter of Sarah's older sister, Dee Linn. "But it's not like I have a zillion friends here, is it?"

"Okay. Got it." In Sarah's opinion, Becky wasn't to be trusted; she was one of those teenaged girls who loved to gossip and stir things up a bit, gleeful to cause a little trouble, especially for someone else. Becky cut a wide swath through everyone else's social life. Just like her mother. No doubt Becky'd heard from Dee Linn the tales that Blue Peacock Manor harbored its own special ghosts. That kind of gossip, swirling so close to home, just barely touching her life but not ruining it, was right up Dee Linn's alley.

Gracie said, "I think the house looks kinda cool. Creepy cool."

Jade snorted. "What would *you* know about cool?"

"Hey . . . ," Sarah warned her oldest.

Used to her older sister's barbs, Gracie pulled the passive-aggressive card and acted as if she hadn't heard the nasty ring to her sister's question. She changed the conversation back to her favorite topic. "Can we get a dog, Mom?" Before Sarah could respond, she added quickly. "You said we could. Remember? Once we moved here, you said we'd look for a dog."

"I believe I said 'I'll think about it.' "

"Jade got a car," Gracie pointed out.

From the front seat, Jade said, "That's different."

"No, it's not." To her mother, Gracie threw back Sarah's own words, " 'A promise is a promise.' That's what you always say." Gracie regarded her mother coolly as she clambered out of the backseat.

"I know." How could Sarah possibly forget the argument that had existed since her youngest had turned five? Gracie was nuts about all animals, and she'd been lobbying for a pet forever.

Once her younger daughter was out of earshot, Sarah said to Jade, "It wouldn't kill you to be nice to your sister."

Jade threw her mother a disbelieving look and declared, "This is so gonna suck!"

"Only if you let it." Sarah was tired of the ongoing argument that had started the second she'd announced the move two weeks ago. She'd waited until the real estate deal with her siblings was completed and she had hired a crew to start working before breaking the news to her kids. "This is a chance for all of us to have a new start."

"I don't care. The 'new start' thing? That's on you. For you. And maybe *her*," she added, hitching her chin toward the windshield.

Sarah followed her gaze and watched Gracie hike up the broken flagstone path, where dandelions and moss had replaced the mortar years before. A tangle of leggy, gone-to-seed rosebushes were a reminder of how long the house had been neglected. Once upon a time, Sarah's mother had tended the gardens and orchard to the point of obsession, but that had been years ago. Now a solitary crow flapped to a perch in a skeletal cherry tree near the guesthouse, then pulled its head in tight, against the rain.

"Come on, Jade. Give me a break," Sarah said.

"You give me one." Jade rolled her eyes and unbuckled her seat belt, digging out her cell phone and attempting to text. "Smart-phone, my ass—er, butt."

"Again, watch the language." Sarah pocketed her keys and tried not to let her temper get control of her tongue. "Grab your stuff, Jade. Like it or not, we're home."

"I can *not* believe this is my life."

"Believe it." Sarah shoved open the driver's side door, then walked to the rear of the vehicle to pull her computer and suitcase from the cargo area.

Of course, she too had doubts about moving here. The project she planned to tackle—renovating the place to its former grandeur before selling it—was daunting, perhaps impossible. Even when she'd been living here with all her siblings, the huge house had been sinking into disrepair. Since her father had died, things had really gone downhill. Paint was peeling from the siding, and many of the shiplap boards were warped. The wide porch that ran along the front of the house seemed to be listing, rails missing, and there were holes in the roof where there had once been shingles.

"It looks evil, you know," Jade threw over her shoulder before hauling her rolling bag out of the cargo space and reluctantly trudging after her sister. "I've always hated it."

Sarah managed to hold back a hot retort. The last time she'd brought her children here, she and her own mother, Arlene, had gotten into a fight, a blistering battle of words that precipitated their final, painful rift. Though Gracie was probably too small to remember, Jade certainly did.

Gracie was nearly at the steps when she stopped suddenly to stare upward at the house. "What the . . . ?"

"Come on," Jade said to her younger sister, but Gracie didn't move, even when Sarah joined her daughters and a big black crow landed on one of the rusted gutters.

"Something wrong?" Sarah asked.

Jade was quick to say, "Oh, no, Mom, everything's just perfect. You get into a fight with that perv at your job and decide we all have to move." She snapped her fingers. "And bam! It's done. Just like that. You rent out the condo in Vancouver and tell us we have to move here to a falling-down old farm with a grotesque house that looks like Stephen King dreamed it up. Yeah, everything's just cool." Jade reached for her phone again. "And there's got to be some cell phone service here or I'm out, Mom. Really. No service is like . . . archaic and . . . and . . . inhumane!"

"You'll survive."

Gracie whispered, "Someone's in there."

"What?" Sarah said, "No. The house has been empty for years."

Gracie blinked. "But . . . but, I saw her."

"You saw who?" Sarah asked and tried to ignore a tiny flare of fear knotting her stomach.

With one hand still on the handle of her rolling bag, she shrugged. "A girl."

Sarah caught an I-told-you-so look from her older daughter.

"A girl? Where?" Jade demanded.

"She was standing up there." Gracie pointed upward, to the third story and the room at the northwest corner of the house, just under the cupola. "In the window."

Theresa's room. The bedroom that had been off-limits to Sarah as a child. The knot in Sarah's gut tightened. Jade again caught her mother's eyes in a look that silently invoked Sarah to bring Gracie back to reality.

"Maybe it's a ghost," Jade mocked, "I hear there are lots of them around here." She leaned closer to her sister, "And not just from Becky. You told me you'd been doing some 'research' and you found out the first woman who lived here was killed, her body never found, her spirit roaming the hallways of Blue Peacock Manor forever."

Gracie shot her mom a look. "Well . . . yeah . . ."

"Oh, please," Jade snorted. "The second you step foot here, you see a ghost."

"Angelique Le Duc did die here!" Gracie flared.

"You mean, Angelique *Stewart*," Jade corrected. "She was married to our crazy homicidal, great-great-great-not-so-great-grandfather or something. That's what you said."

"I read it on the Internet," Gracie responded, her mouth tight at being corrected.

"So then it must be true," Jade said. She turned her attention to her mother. "The minute you told us we were moving, she started in on all this ghost stuff. Checking out books from the library, surfing the Net, chatting with other people who think they see ghosts. And she didn't find out about just Angelique Le Duc—oh, no. There were others too. This place"—she gestured to the house and grounds— "is just littered with the spirits who've come to a bad end at Blue Peacock Manor!" Jade's hair caught in the wind as the rain picked up. "Do you see how ridiculous this all is, Mom? Now she's believing all this paranormal shi . . . stuff and thinking we're going to be living with a bunch of the undead!"

"Jade—" Sarah started.

"Shut up!" Gracie warned.

"You sound like a lunatic," Jade went right on, then turned heatedly to Sarah. "You have to put an end to this, Mom. It's for her own good. If she goes spouting off about ghosts and spirits and demons—"

"Demons!" Gracie snapped in disgust. "Who said anything—"

"It's all a load of crap," Jade declared. "She's going to be laughed out of school!"

"Enough!" Sarah yelled, though for once Jade seemed to be concerned for her sister. But Sarah had enough of their constant bickering. Forcing a calm she didn't feel, she said, "We're going inside now."

"You don't believe me," Gracie said, hurt. She looked up at the window again.

Sarah had already glanced at the window of the room where she knew, deep in her soul, dark deeds had occurred. But no image appeared behind the dirty, cracked glass. No apparition flitted past the panes. No otherworldly figure was evident. There was no "girl" hiding behind the grime, just some tattered curtains that seemed to shift in the dreary afternoon.

"I saw her," Gracie insisted. A line of consternation had formed between her brows.

"It could have been a reflection or a shadow," Sarah said as the crow cawed loudly. Deep inside she knew she was lying.

Gracie turned on Jade. "*You* scared her away!"

"Oh, right. Of course it's my fault. Give me an effing break."

"She'll punish you, you know." Gracie's eyes narrowed. "The woman in the window, she'll get even."

"Gracie!" Sarah's mouth dropped open.

"Then you'll see," Gracie declared, turning to the front entrance and effectively ending the conversation.

"Here's the latest," Rhea announced as she stepped through the door of Clint's cramped office in the small quarters that made up Stewart's Crossing's City Hall. As city building inspector, he checked on all the jobs currently being constructed or renovated within the city limits and beyond, and contracted with the county for the outlying areas. "You might find one particularly interesting." She raised her thinly plucked eyebrows high enough that they arched over the frames of her glasses. "A neighbor."

"Don't tell me. The Stewart place."

"The Jewel of the Columbia?" she said dryly, shaking her head, her short, red hair unmoving.

His insides clenched a bit. "Maybe Doug wants to take this one."

"I thought you hated Doug."

"Hate's a strong word," Clint said. "He just wouldn't be my first choice to become my replacement." He wasn't sure why he didn't trust Doug Knowles, but the guy he was training to take over his job seemed too green, too eager, too damned hungry, to give each job its proper attention. There was something a little secretive about him as well, and Clint had a suspicion that Doug would take the easy way out, maybe let some of the little details slide on a job. "On second thought, I'll handle the Stewart project."

"Figured," she said, her red lips twisting a bit. "Oh, and wait!" She hurried out of the room and returned a few seconds later with a candy dish that she set on the corner of his desk. "Halloween candy for your clients with sweet tooths, er, teeth."

"I don't need these."

"Of course you do. It's that time of year. Don't be such a Grinch."

"I believe he's associated with Christmas."

"Or whatever holiday you want. In this case, Halloween." She unwrapped a tiny Three Musketeers bar and plopped it onto her tongue.

"Okay, so I'm a Grinch. Don't hate me."

Laughing, she gave him a wink as she turned and headed through the door to the reception area of the building that housed all the city offices. Built in the middle of the last century, the structure was constructed of glass and narrow, blond bricks; it had a flat roof and half a dozen offices opening into the central reception area. The ceilings were low, of "soundproof" tile, the lights fluorescent, the floors covered in a linoleum that had been popular during the 1960s. Now, it was showing decades of wear. "Just take a look." Rhea clipped away on high heels as a phone started jangling. She leaned over her desk and snagged the receiver before the second ring. She did it on purpose, he suspected, knowing he was still watching her as she gave him a quick glimpse of the skirt tightening over her hips.

"Stewart's Crossing City Hall," she answered sweetly. "This is Rhea Hernandez."

She had a nice butt, he'd give her that, but he wasn't interested.

Attractive and smart, Rhea had been married and divorced three times, and was looking for husband number four at the ripe old age of forty-two.

It wasn't going to be Clint, and he suspected she knew it. Rhea's flirting was more out of habit than sincerity.

". . . I'm sorry, the mayor isn't in. Can I take a message, or, if you'd like, you can e-mail her directly," Rhea was saying as she stretched the cord around the desk and took her seat, disappearing from view. He heard her start rattling off Mayor Leslie Imholt's e-mail address.

Clint picked up the stack of papers she'd dropped into his inbox. Plans for the complete renovation of Blue Peacock Manor, the historic home set on property that backed up to his own ranch, was the first request. No surprise there, as he'd heard Sarah was returning to do a complete renovation of the Stewart family home. The preliminary drawings were already with the city engineer for approval; these had to be renovations to the original plans. A helluva job, that, he knew, and to think that Sarah was taking it on and returning to a place she'd wanted so desperately to leave. He eyed the specs and noted that he needed to see what work had already been accomplished on the smaller residence on the property—the guesthouse, as the Stewart family had called it.

Until the mayor had hired Doug Knowles, Clint had been the only inspector in this part of the county and had checked all the work himself. Now he could hand jobs off to Doug if he wanted. Clint had already decided that was generally a bad idea. It certainly would be in this case, he thought.

But if he took on Blue Peacock Manor, no doubt he would see Sarah again.

Frowning, he grabbed one of the damned bits of candy, and unwrapping a tiny Kit-Kat bar, leaned back in his chair. He and Sarah hadn't seen each other for years, and if he were honest with himself, he knew that their split hadn't been on the best of terms. He tossed the candy into his mouth, then wadded up the wrapper and threw it at the waste can.

High school romance, he thought. So intense, but in the larger scheme of things, so meaningless, really.

Why, then, did the memory of it seem as fresh now as it had half a lifetime ago?

His desk phone jangled, and he reached for it willingly, pushing thoughts of Sarah Stewart and their ill-fated romance to the far, far corners of his mind.

CHAPTER 2

"That's it. I'm outta here," Rosalie Jamison said as she stripped off her apron and tossed it into a bin with the other soiled towels, aprons, jackets, and rags that would be cleaned overnight, ready for the morning shift at the three-star diner. She slipped her work shoes onto a shelf and laced up her Nikes, new and reflective, for the walk home. "I'll see you all later."

Located a few blocks from the river, the restaurant had been dubbed the Columbia Diner about a million years ago by some hick with no imagination. It was located at one end of the truck stop about a half mile out of Stewart's Crossing. Rosalie had spent the past six months here, waiting tables for the regulars and the customers just passing through. She hated the hours and the smell of grease and spices that clung to her until she spent at least twenty minutes under the shower, but it was a job, one of the few in this useless backwoods town.

For now it would do, until she had enough money saved so she could leave Stewart's Crossing for good. She couldn't wait.

"Wait!" Gloria, a woman who was in her fifties and perpetually smelled of cigarettes, caught up with Rosalie before she got out the door where she stuffed a few dollars and some change into Rosalie's hand. "Never forget your share of the tips," she said with a wink, then continued, "They keep me in all my diamonds and furs."

"Yeah, right." Rosalie had to smile. Gloria was cool, even if she continually talked about how long it would be before she collected

Medicare and Social Security and all that boring stuff. A frustrated hairdresser, she changed her hair color, cut, or style every month or so and had taken Rosalie under her wing when a couple of boys, classmates from high school, had come in and started to hassle her with obscene comments and gestures. Gloria had refused to serve them and sent them out the door with their tails between their legs. The whole scene had only made things ugly at school, but Rosalie had solved that by cutting classes or ditching out completely.

"If you wait a half hour, I'll give you a ride home," Gloria said, sliding a fresh cigarette from her pack as she peered outside and into the darkness. "I just have to clean up a bit."

Rosalie hesitated. It would take her at least twenty minutes to walk home on the service road that ran parallel to the interstate, but Gloria's half hours usually stretched into an hour or two, and Rosalie just wanted to go home, sneak up the stairs, flop on her bed, and catch an episode of *Big Brother* or *Keeping Up with the Kardashians* or whatever else she could find on her crappy little TV. Besides, Gloria always lit up the second she was behind the wheel, and it was too cold to roll down the windows of her old Dodge. "I'd better get going. Thanks."

Gloria frowned. "I don't like you walking home alone in the dark."

"It's just for a little while longer," Rosalie reminded her, holding up her tips before stuffing the cash into the pocket of her jacket, which she'd retrieved from a peg near the open back door. "I'm gonna buy my uncle's Toyota. He's saving it for me. I just need another three hundred."

"It's starting to rain."

"I'm okay. Really."

"You be careful, then." Gloria's brows drew together beneath straw-colored bangs. I don't like this, y'know."

"It's okay." Rosalie zipped up her jacket and stepped into the night before Gloria could argue with her. As the diner's door shut behind her, she heard Gloria saying to Barry, the cook, "I don't know *what* her mother is thinking letting that girl walk alone this late at night."

Sharon wasn't thinking. That was the problem. Her mom wasn't thinking of Rosalie at all because of crappy Mel, her current husband, a burly, gruff man Rosalie just thought of as Number Four. He was a loser like the others in her mother's string of husbands. But Sharon, as usual, had deemed Mel "the one" and had referred to him as her soul mate, which was such a pile of crap. No one in her right mind would consider overweight, beer-slogging, TV-watching Mel Updike a soul mate unless they were completely brainless. He owned a kinda cool motorcycle that she could never ride, and that was the only okay thing about him. The fact that Mel leered at Rosalie with a knowing glint in his eye didn't make it any better. He'd already fathered five kids with ex-wives and girlfriends that were scattered from LA to Seattle. Rosalie had experienced the dubious pleasure of meeting most of them and had hated every one on sight. They were all "Little Mels," losers like their big, hairy-bellied father. Geez, didn't the guy know about waxing? Or man-scaping or, for that matter, not belching at the table?

Soul mate? Bull-effin'-shit!

Sharon had to be out of her mind!

Rosalie shoved her hands deep into her pockets and felt the other cash that she'd squirreled away in the lining of her hooded jacket, a gift from her real dad. The jacket was never out of her sight, and she'd tucked nearly nine hundred dollars deep inside it. She had to be careful. Either Mel or one of his sticky-fingered kids might make off with the cash she was saving for a car. Until she could pay for the Toyota outright, as well as license and insure it for six months, she was forbidden to own one.

All around, it sucked.

Her whole damn life *sucked.*

As rain began to pelt, striking her cheeks, splashing in puddles, peppering the gravel crunching beneath her feet, she began to wish she'd waited for Gloria. Putting up with a little cigarette smoke was better than slogging through cold rain.

She couldn't wait to get out of this hole-in-the-wall of a town where her mother, chasing the ever-slippery Mel, had dragged her. Kicking at the pebbles on the shoulder, she envied the people driving the cars that streaked by on the interstate, their headlights cutting through the dark night, their tires humming against the wet pavement, their lives going full throttle while she was stuck in idle.

But once she had her car, look out! She'd turn eighteen and leave Sharon and hairy Mel and head to Denver, where her dad and the boyfriend she'd met on the Internet were waiting.

Three hundred more dollars and five months.

That was all.

A gust of wind blasted her again, and she shuddered. Maybe she should turn back and take Gloria up on that ride. She glanced over her shoulder, but the neon lights of the diner were out of sight. She was nearly halfway home.

She started to jog.

A lone car had turned onto the road and was catching up to her, its headlights glowing bright. She stepped farther off the shoulder, her Nikes slipping a little. The roar of a large engine was audible over the rain, and she realized it wasn't a car, but a truck behind her. No big deal. There were hundreds of them around Stewart's Crossing. She expected the pickup to fly by her with a spray of road wash, but as it passed her, it slowed.

Just go on, she thought. She slowed to a walk, but kept moving until she saw the brake lights glow bright.

Now what?

She kept walking, intent on going around the dark truck, keeping her pace steady, hoping it was only a coincidence that the guy had stopped. No such luck. The window on the passenger side slid down.

"Rosie?" a voice that was vaguely familiar called from the darkened cab. "That you?"

Keep walking.

She didn't look up.

"Hey, it's me." The cab's interior light blinked on, and she recognized the driver, a tall man who was a regular at the diner and who now leaned across the seat to talk to her. "You need a ride?"

"No, it's only a little farther."

"You're soaked to the skin," he said, concerned.

"It's okay."

"Oh, come on. Hop in, I'll drive you." Without waiting for an answer, he opened the door.

"I don't—"

"Your call, but I'm drivin' right by your house."

"You know where I live?" That was weird.

"Only that you said you're on Umpqua."

Had she mentioned it? Maybe. "I don't know." Shaking her head, she felt the cold rain drizzling down her neck. She stared at the open door of the pickup. Clean. Warm. Dry. The strains of some Western song playing softly on the radio.

"You'll be home in three minutes."

Don't do it!

The wind blasted again, and she pushed down her misgivings. She knew the guy, had been waiting on him ever since she took the job. He was one of the better-looking regulars. He always had a compliment and a smile and left a good-sized tip.

"Okay."

"That-a-girl."

Climbing into the truck, she felt the warm air from the heater against her skin and recognized the Randy Travis song wafting through the speakers. She yanked the door shut, but the lock didn't quite latch.

"Here, let me get that," he said, "Damned thing." Leaning across her, he fiddled with the door. "Give it a tug, will ya?"

"Okay." The second she pulled on the door handle, she felt something cold and metallic click around her wrist. "Hey! What the hell do you think you're doing?" she demanded, fear spreading through her bloodstream as she jerked her hand up and realized she'd been cuffed to the door handle.

"Just calm down."

"The hell I will! What is this?" She was furious and scared and tried to open her door, but it was locked. "Let me out, you son of a bitch!"

He slapped her then. Quick and hard, a sharp backhand across her mouth.

She let out a little scream.

"There'll be no swearin'," he warned her.

"What? No what?" She swung her free hand at him, across the cab, but he caught her wrist.

"Ah-ah-ah, honey. You've got a lot to learn." Then, holding her free wrist in one hand, he gunned the engine and drove toward the entrance to the interstate.

"Let me out!" she screamed, kicking at the dash and throwing her body back and forth, screaming at the top of her lungs. The heel of her shoe hit the preset buttons of the radio and an advertisement filled the interior.

Dear God, what was this? What did he plan to do to her?

Panicked, she tried to think of a way out of this. Any way. "I—I have money," she said, thinking of the cash in her pocket, all the while struggling and twisting, to no avail. His grip was just so damned strong.

"It's not your money I want," he said in that smooth, confident tone she now found absolutely chilling. His smile was as cold as the wind shrieking down the Columbia River Gorge. "It's you."

"Mom!" Gracie's voice rang through the house. "*Mom!*"

Sarah's eyes flew open. Her heart hammered. "Gracie?" she called, sitting bolt upright from her sleeping bag on the floor. The room was dark, dying embers of the fire casting a blood-red glow on the walls. "Gracie?" she said, one hand searching the flattened sleeping bag beside her, the other reaching for the flashlight. "Where are you?"

The bag was empty.

A shiver slid down her spine.

"Grace?" Scooping up the flashlight, she was on her feet in an instant. "Grace?" she called again, her heart hammering.

"Here!" was the panicked cry, and Sarah followed the sound, the beam of her flashlight sweeping the floor and hallway ahead of her, her heart hammering in dread.

"I'm coming!"

"Mom, hurry!" Gracie cried. "Up here!"

Sarah reached the stairs, flipped on the switch, and took the steps two at a time as the dim light from the sconces gave off a soft, golden glow. "Gracie! Where are you?"

"On the stairs," her daughter responded, and she sounded less panicked, more in control.

Sarah rounded the landing at the second floor and found her daughter lying on the steps leading to the third floor. Pale, shaking, eyes wide, Gracie was huddled against the wall, which was still covered in faded, peeling wallpaper. Her right hand gripped the railing over her head, as if she needed support to keep from sliding down the worn wooden stairs.

"Are you okay?" Sarah said, grabbing her child and holding her close. "What happened?"

"I saw her."

"Who?"

"I saw the ghost."

"The ghost?" Sarah repeated.

"Yes!" Gracie was insistent, and her little body quivered in Sarah's arms. "I got up to go to the bathroom, and I saw something up here, and I . . . I just followed."

"And it was a ghost?"

"Yes! I already said." There was a higher pitch to Gracie's voice, a desperation that Sarah didn't recognize. "She was dressed in white, a long dress, and hurried up the stairs. It was like she was flying. I . . . I followed her, and she disappeared and . . ." She sagged against her mother. "It was freaky."

"It's okay," Sarah said, her gaze traveling up the stairs to the third floor of the house, an area that she'd avoided most of her life. She understood about freaking out, about fears, and about believing in seeing a ghost on the premises.

"You don't believe me."

"Of course I do, honey. I know you saw something, but I'm not sure what it was. You have nightmares," she reminded Gracie softly, "and sometimes you sleepwalk."

"This was different."

"That's what you always say. Come on, let's go downstairs." Sarah helped her daughter to her feet, and Gracie dared to look over her mother's shoulder to the upper floors.

"She's real, Mom," she said, sounding more like herself. Normally, in broad daylight, Gracie was a kid who had few fears. A tomboy, she played sports ferociously and held her own in arguments, even with some of her teachers. "A bit of a loner," "definitely an individual," and "certainly knows her own mind" were some of the comments they had made, along with "stubborn" and even "refuses to take orders." If Gracie hadn't been such a good student who devoured books, those same traits would have landed her in trouble in school.

But at night, Gracie was sometimes plagued with insecurities and anxieties that made her seem younger than her years. Her nightmares seemed to have worsened since Sarah's divorce from Noel and his moving a continent away to Savannah.

Using the flashlight's beam, they made their way back to the living room, where they'd camped out for the night. As Gracie scooted into her sleeping bag, Sarah stoked the fire, adding chunks of oak that she'd found, along with split kindling, in the woodshed located just off the back porch. The firewood had been stored in the shed for years, probably since before Dad had died. Tinder dry, the chunks of oak and fir, dusty and covered in spiderwebs, ignited easily.

"What's going on?" Jade asked, lifting her tousled head and squinting as the fire began to crackle and pop, hungry flames giving off a flickering illumination.

"Nothing!" Gracie said.

"I heard you scream." Jade roused herself into a sitting position.

"I wasn't screaming. I just wanted Mom."

"Nightmare again?" Jade guessed, yawning.

"No." Gracie's jaw jutted forward.

"God, what time is it?" She glanced at her phone and then rolled her eyes. "One-thirty? That's all? I can't believe I fell asleep. So what happened?"

"Gracie got lost on her way to the bathroom," Sarah said.

"Got lost? How could . . ." Jade frowned. "Oh, God, don't tell me. Let me guess. You think you saw the ghost again, don't you?"

Gracie opened her mouth, then closed it quickly.

Jade said, "Oh, for the love of God. This place is pretty weird, Gracie, but there are no ghosts. Sure, people may have died here, and maybe there's a mystery or two, but no damned ghosts."

"Let's not talk about it anymore tonight," Sarah said.

"Just sweep it under the rug," Jade grumbled. "Pretend it's not a problem. Great idea, Mom." Jade cast her sister a final glance. "Don't be talking about this when you try to make new friends at school cuz they'll think you're a freak."

"Jade, enough!" Sarah said. "Go back to sleep."

"It's true," Jade muttered. She turned her back on her mother and burrowed deeper into her sleeping bag.

"Come on. It's late, and we need to get up early," Sarah said.

"Why?" Grace asked suspiciously.

"Lot of work to do."

"But no school," she reminded, making sure.

"Not tomorrow," Sarah agreed. "However, if you want to talk to your dad before he goes to work, we have to call early."

"It's three hours later in Savannah," Gracie intoned before Sarah could say the same.

Sarah nodded. "Right."

"Okay." Gracie plumped her pillow, then settled back and closed her eyes. Sarah edged her own sleeping bag closer to the old couch and propped her back against the cushions to stare at the fire. The house seemed to close in on her, good memories and bad. Goose bumps rose on the back of her arms, and the shadows in the corners of the room, those spots that weren't illuminated by the fire, reminded her of her own fears as a child. There was that "incident" on the widow's walk, one that was still locked in a forbidden part of her memory and one she wouldn't dwell on, at least not this night.

Shifting to view both her daughters as they slept, she chided herself for not being honest with Grace. She should have admitted that she too had seen what could only be described as a ghost on those very stairs, that for years she'd thought she'd been going out of her mind, taunted by the rest of her family for what they'd decided were nothing more than "bad dreams" or "silly fantasies." The worst remark had been a stage whisper made by her own mother. Arlene had confided to Dee Linn that she believed Sarah was only making up stories to draw attention to herself. "That's what she does, you know. And the sad part is that it works on your father." The stage whisper had been uttered just loud enough for Sarah to hear it. Unfortunately, the accusation had hit its mark, and Sarah had learned to never again speak of what she'd seen. Just as Arlene had intended.

Sarah only prayed she didn't make the same mistakes with her own children. Every once in a while she'd hear Arlene's words spewing forth from her own lips, and it made her cringe inside.

You are not like her. You know it. And you'll find a way to come clean with your daughters. You will. But only when the time is right . . .

She grimaced.

She was more like Arlene than she wanted to believe.

CHAPTER 3

Fortunately, Gracie slept through the rest of the night, and even Sarah finally dozed off around two. She'd awoken to the sound of her cell phone vibrating its way across the floor and, seeing that the caller was Evan Tolliver, hadn't answered.

Evan was one of the reasons she'd left Vancouver.

A big reason.

He'd been her boss and had been pressuring her to go out with him. She had. And regretted it. Almost from the get-go he'd wanted to, as he'd put it, "take our relationship to the next level." Sarah had pointed out they didn't have a relationship and there were no more levels, but he'd never really taken the hint, and her hours in the offices of Tolliver Construction had become uncomfortable, to say the least. As the son and groomed heir of the company, Evan had thought she'd find him irresistible. He'd been wrong. But so had she. Going out with him the first time had been a mistake, and she'd stupidly compounded the error by accepting another dinner invitation.

On the third date, when he'd brought up marriage, he'd winked suggestively and said he wanted to "tie her down." There had been something half serious in the twinkle in his eyes, and she'd told him right then and there that it wasn't going to work. She'd said flat out that she didn't want to see him again, which he'd taken as a challenge, trying to woo her, disbelieving that she would actually say no. So, after a month of weighing her options, she'd worked out a deal with her siblings and moved back to a town she'd sworn she'd hated and would never reside in again.

"Never say never," she told herself now as she pulled on her jeans and sweatshirt, then made her way around boxes and old furniture and far too many memories as she headed to the kitchen.

It was a disaster, like the rest of the house, but she was able to locate the coffeemaker she'd moved with her from the condo. She ran the water in the stained kitchen sink for several minutes while she found the bag of ground coffee and filters she'd purchased. Once they were located, she plugged in the machine. Thankfully, there was still electricity and running water in the house, though the ancient furnace had given up the ghost, so they were stuck with the fire until they moved into the guesthouse next week.

As the coffee brewed, she ran a toothbrush over her teeth, rinsed her face in cold water, quickly snapped her hair into a ponytail and caught a glimpse of her reflection in the mirror over the cracked pedestal sink. It wasn't pretty, she thought, noting the circles under her eyes and how pale she appeared from such a short night's sleep. She looked a lot like her mother in the morning light, which, she supposed, wasn't such a bad thing. Arlene Bennett had been a striking woman in her youth, and the Bennett genes were strong enough that each of her children, from both of her husbands, had taken after their mother. Sarah had been confused with her older sister, Dee Linn, and been told she was a "dead ringer" for Theresa, their half sister, the oldest. Sarah's chin was strong, her cheekbones high, her face framed with wild brown curls that she regularly tamed into a bun. She'd overheard that she had "haunted" eyes, but she dismissed that. Yes, they were large, and gray, while most of her siblings' were slightly bluer, but that whole haunted thing? Ridiculous.

The smell of coffee permeated the air, and as Sarah poured herself a cup, she decided the main house was in even worse repair than she'd first thought. Sadly, Jade's observation that Blue Peacock Manor was straight out of Hollywood's version of a haunted house wasn't that far off the mark.

Though she'd managed to find the main water main and get water running, the pipes creaked and groaned, and the hot water was lukewarm at best. Yes, there was electricity running to the home, and the old pump seemed to work, but there was nothing in the way of an electronic connection, which drove both Gracie and Jade nuts. They could use their iPhones and iPad by virtue of some wonky cell phone reception that worked in certain areas of the house, but until the local cable company hooked up the Internet, a telephone landline, and the much-missed television, they were "in hell," as Jade so eloquently referred to her life these days.

"No wireless? No cable? Are you kidding me?" Jade had said when she realized just how little service was running to the old manor. "You expect me to live in this mausoleum and go to a stupid parochial school, all without any Internet? Mom, what's wrong with you?" She'd gazed at her mother with wide hazel eyes rife with accusations. "This is crazy. I mean like really, really crazy."

"We'll just have to camp out for a few days," Sarah had said, crossing her fingers against the chance she might be lying. "And I'll make sure all the services are hooked up. I'm pretty sure that cell phones work here," though she teetered one hand up and down to suggest that the service wasn't all that great. "As for the parochial school, we already discussed this."

"You mean you handed down an edict," Jade corrected.

"Well, public school wasn't really working for you, now, was it?"

Jade had wanted to argue, and her mouth had opened only to snap shut. Taking a deep breath, she'd said, "Fine. Whatever. Think what you want," before storming off to the one bedroom that was livable on the main floor, only to later hunker down with her sister and mother in the living room, where the fire was giving off some warmth.

That was yesterday.

"Today's a new opportunity," she told herself as she sipped from her cup of black coffee, wishing she'd had the foresight to buy some creamer, and looked around the kitchen. A gray dawn was filtering in through the windows near the breakfast nook. She'd tackle cleaning up the kitchen later, she decided. For now she intended to give the house a quick look over, just to get an idea of the condition of every room, then once she had a general overview of the disrepair and assessed the priority of the projects, she'd go through each floor more thoroughly and make detailed notes about what needed to be cleaned, fixed, upgraded, or gutted, so she could report back to her siblings, her not-so-silent partners in the project.

Jacob and Joseph, identical twins who were day and night in personality, were on board with the whole renovation thing. However, Dee Linn hadn't been as eager to put up any money to repair the old place. "Walter will have a heart attack if I put one dime into it," she'd said vehemently when Sarah had called her at the end of the summer. Walter was Dee Linn's husband of nearly twenty years and definitely ruled the roost. "I . . . I just can't."

"Then I'll cover your share, but you'll owe me," Sarah had said.

"I don't see what good fixing that monstrosity is to me."

"It's an investment, okay? You own a quarter of it." And that much was true. Franklin's will had made it clear that the house and property were to go to his children upon his death, and though Arlene had been aghast at the idea, she hadn't had a legal leg to stand on. Still, she'd resided in the house after her husband's death. None of her children had wanted to force her to move until her health had declined to the point where she could no longer care for herself.

Unfortunately, she'd been unable or unwilling, or both, to keep up the maintenance of the house.

"I know, I know." Dee Linn had said. "I'm not trying to be unreasonable, but, seriously, Walter will kill me if I give you any money."

"All right, I'll have you sign a note to me. For your quarter of the place."

She'd hesitated, the silence stretching thin on the connection until she'd finally acquiesced. "Okay, Sarah, but this is just between you and me, okay? Don't tell the boys or anyone. If Walter found out . . ."

"Got it." Sarah had cut her off, sick of hearing about her controlling brother-in-law and hating the way Dee Linn seemed to be afraid of the man she purportedly "loved as much as life itself" or some such crap. Walter Bigelow, DDS, was as much a tyrant at home as he was at his dental practice. Everything was his way or the highway, and Sarah had hoped more than once that Dee Linn would find the highway and thus regain her smile and self-confidence. The woman was a registered nurse, for God's sake!

Then again, who was Sarah to judge? Her relationships with men had been far from stellar.

Dee Linn had let out a long breath, as if she were incredibly relieved. "Then it's settled. So, now, after you and the girls are all moved in, I want you to come over for a little get-together."

"Oh, I don't think I'll have time—"

"Of course you will," Dee Linn had said, cutting in and taking control, now that the conversation was on comfortable and familiar ground. "You know, for the family, and maybe just a few friends."

"All the family?"

"Of course."

"What about Roger?"

"Well, no. I don't think even his parole officer knows where our dear brother is, but the twins and their wives, of course, and Mom, if she can make it."

"Really."

"Don't worry, there's no way," Dee Linn said. "But if I'm inviting Aunt Marge and her family, I have to include Mom."

"I know. But it might be a little too much right off the bat," she'd said. This "get-together" was starting to sound like too much of a big deal, a Dee Linn extravaganza she and her children would hate. "Dee, I'm not sure about this."

But Dee Linn had been off and running. "I've scheduled the party for the Saturday before Halloween. That will give you about ten days to unpack and settle in."

"Barely. From what I hear from Jacob, the house is a mess, unlivable. So I figure we'll move into the guesthouse, but it'll take some time to get it fully functional." Sarah had been to Dee Linn's parties before; they were usually lavish and over-the-top and involved more than "a handful" of friends.

"It'll be fun! The girls will love it!" Dee Linn had predicted. "I know Becky's looking forward to it."

"What? Wait. She's already 'looking forward to it'? So it's already in the works?"

"Oh, sorry, Sarah. I've got another call coming in. Have to run. See you then! And remember, not a word to Walter or anyone about the money."

Dee Linn had been off the line before Sarah could protest, and Sarah had hung up feeling as if she'd been somehow manipulated by her older sister. That feeling resurfaced now as she glanced through the dirty windows in the dining room and toward the tree-lined banks of Willow Creek as it wound under the fence line that divided the land belonging to the Stewarts from the parcel belonging to the Walsh family.

Sipping her coffee, she ignored the familiar little tug on her heartstrings that she always felt when she thought of Clint, whom she knew was living next door.

"Water under the bridge," she reminded herself. "And a very old bridge at that." Of course, it was inevitable that she'd come face-to-face with him. And the fact that he was the local building inspector cinched it.

Truth to tell, she and Clint had unfinished business, and that was the upcoming topic that made her dread seeing him again. Their white-hot, teenage affair was long over, cooled by good sense, time, and distance. Her broken heart had long since mended, thank God. She'd sworn she never wanted to see his handsome face again, and, well, she still kind of felt that way.

"Enough," she said aloud, then swallowed the last of her coffee and set her cup in the chipped sink, which was large enough to bathe a four-year-old in. With an industrial-sized stove from circa 1940, a butcher block island, and cracked linoleum floor, the room was still cavernous. The refrigerator and dishwasher were missing, spaces in the old cabinetry indicating where they had once existed. She tried several switches and realized only a few of the lights worked. Little could be salvaged here or in the bathroom, with its stained toilet, cracked pedestal sink, and chipped, loose tile.

The other rooms on the floor were in better shape, though, so she gained heart. She ran her fingers over the pillars separating the parlorlike living area from the foyer.

Both her girls were still sleeping soundly in their sleeping bags in front of the near-dead fire, so Sarah moved on through the massive dining room and single guest bedroom. Off the foyer, a wide, hand-hewn staircase curved upward for two stories. Beneath the flight of stairs on the first floor, just off the pantry and mudroom near the back porch, was a locked door that led to a basement that had never been finished and was probably home to all kinds of creatures who had nested there.

Sarah had avoided the basement as a child, and just the thought of going down those rickety stairs to an old root cellar and what had once been a laundry area gave her a serious case of the willies.

"Stupid," she said as her phone rang; she saw a local number on the screen. "Hello?"

"Sarah?" a gravelly voice asked. "It's Hal down at the shop."

"Hi, Hal. What's up?"

"Afraid I've got some bad news," the mechanic said. "Looks like your daughter needs a new transmission."

Sarah felt her shoulders sag. "And how much will that be?"

He rattled off an estimate that would vary once they were inside and the parts had come in, but it was enough to give Sarah pause. Right now, with no steady paycheck, and every dime she had going into the house, she didn't need any big hits to her budget.

"I'll let you know more as I get into it," Hal promised, and Sarah hung up, hoping that Jade's car wasn't going to be the next money pit. This house was bad enough.

"Rosalie didn't come home last night." Sharon Updike was a little worried and a lot pissed. She'd gone upstairs, peeked in Rosalie's sty of a bedroom and seen no sign of her daughter. Nor was there any message or text on her phone explaining where Rosalie was. That girl! Why couldn't she just toe the line, Sharon wondered as she cradled a cup of coffee in one hand and stood in the doorway of the bedroom. "Did you hear me?" she said, a little more loudly to the lump on the bed that was her husband, who, despite the fact that the sun had been up for several hours, was still trying to sleep.

"Wha—?" he said, then cleared his throat.

"I said Rosalie didn't show last night."

"Uh. So?" He blinked open a bleary eye, snorted, and ran his hand under his nose. Pushing up a little on the bed, he found his glasses on the night table and in the process caused a pillow to tumble to the floor.

"She didn't call. Didn't text. Nothin'."

He looked as if he wanted to roll over and go back to sleep, but catching the expression on his wife's face, he changed his mind and threw off the covers. "Prob'ly just with a friend."

"Maybe."

"You worried?"

"Yeah, a . . . bit." More than a bit, but she was trying to rein in her concern.

"You call that Dixon girl, what's her name?"

"Debbie. Yeah, I left messages for both her and her mother." Not that Miranda Dixon would give a flying fig about Rosalie, who, Sharon sensed, wasn't good enough to be a friend to her little "innocent" princess. What a snob. Just because Miranda had been married to her husband forever and had a nice house? Big effin' deal. The way Sharon heard it, Miranda had been knocked up when she'd gotten married. Sharon didn't really care about any of that ancient history. Who was she to judge? But the woman's holier-than-thou attitude really rankled.

Now, though, she didn't want to dwell on all that; she just needed to know Rosalie was safe.

"What about that guy she was hanging out with? Y'know, the one you didn't like?"

"Bobby Morris?" Sharon pulled a face and took a sip from her coffee. She didn't just not like him; she detested the punk. He was always getting Rosalie into trouble. "That was over. Month or two ago."

"Humph."

"You don't think so?"

"Don't know."

"We should have let her get that car," she said, sipping from her coffee cup and trying to think straight. Where would she go? Who would she have taken off with? Was she hurt? No, she was okay. She *had* to be okay.

"Believe me, a seventies Toyota with two hundred thousand miles on it wouldn't have changed nothin'. Except maybe she would've took off earlier." Mel gave her a look.

"You think she just took off?" Sharon asked dubiously. Rosalie would never have done that, never taken off without saying good-bye, not for good, like Mel was suggesting.

"What? You think she was, like, kidnapped?"

"Good Lord, I hope not," she whispered. But her husband was tapping into her most primal of fears.

"C'mon, Sharon. She was probably just out partying with some of her friends and crashed somewhere."

Sharon sent up a silent prayer that her husband's assessment was somehow the truth. "She's not answering her phone."

"Maybe she's just sleeping it off."

She glared at him. "You're no help."

"You know, honey, you were a teenager once, and had your own share of trouble. Least that's what your brother says."

"Yeah, but this is different. I can feel it."

"You want me to do something? Is that it?"

"Yes!"

"What?"

"I don't know!" She heard the panic in her voice and hated it.

"Ah, hell." Mel rubbed a hand over his unshaven jaw, then reached onto the floor, found yesterday's jeans, and yanked them over his legs before standing, pulling them up so that they rode just below his belly. Sharon couldn't help thinking he'd gained more weight, but then who would be surprised? This man could down two bacon cheeseburgers, an order of fries, and untold beers at one sitting. She held her tongue about his weight, though, since he'd been quick enough to notice when she'd gained five lousy pounds last Christmas.

"So what'd'ya want me to do?"

Care, she thought silently, but said, "I don't know. Start looking for her, I guess."

"She'll show up."

"How can you be sure?"

"Cuz I remember what it's like to be a kid her age, even if you can't or won't." He yanked a T-shirt over his head and stretched it over his belly. "Give me a chance to piss and drink a cup of coffee, then I'll do whatever." He let out a sigh, saw how upset she was, and whispered. "Oh, for the love of God, Sharon." Walking around the foot of the bed, he reached the doorway, where he pulled her into his arms. She tried not to notice the foul odor of his breath. "We'll find her."

She almost broke down. Felt her legs go weak.

"Come on. It'll be all right."

If only she could trust his words.

"Look, I'll fire up the Harley, and you and me, we'll go out search-in'. But when we find that little girl, I'm tellin' ya, she's gonna be in big fuckin' trouble. Okay?"

"Okay," she whispered, grateful he was on her side and hoping be-yond hope that he was right, that she was freaking out for no reason. But try as she might, as he let her go and playfully swatted her be-hind to get her moving toward the kitchen, she couldn't shake the feeling that something was wrong. Terribly, terribly wrong.

CHAPTER 4

Sarah checked her watch. It was after ten in the morning, and the girls were still asleep. She considered waking them, then thought better of it. Moving had been difficult enough yesterday, and then the night had been interrupted by Gracie's bad dream, or ghostly encounter, or whatever.

As she mounted the stairs, she paused in the spot where she'd found Gracie clutching the rail. In the light of day, the staircase looked absolutely normal, with no hint of paranormal activity.

"Because there was none," she said aloud. She noted that one or two steps on the first set of risers probably needed to be repaired, but the old banister, the one her brothers had slid down on a daily basis, was still strong. She tested it, putting all her weight into trying to rip it from the wall, but it didn't move.

Good. Her intention was to keep as much of the charm and character of the house intact as she could.

On the second floor, the bedrooms were dirty, of course, and probably needed insulation, but they could remain as they were if they were cleaned and repainted and the wooden floors were revived. Dee Linn and she had had separate rooms, Roger his own while he was still there, and the twins had shared the largest room. The single bath on the floor would also need a complete overhaul, but she'd expected as much.

On the third floor, things changed. Here was the master bedroom suite, with its marble soaking tub and shower, both in passable shape. It had a commanding view of the river and took up half the third floor. The hall bathroom was also operational, the faucets tarnished but working, the stains in the tub and sinks minimal.

"Thank God for small favors," she said.

But there was still another room to view, the corner bedroom, the one where Gracie had sworn she'd first seen the ghost: Theresa's room. No one had occupied it in the thirty-odd years since she'd disappeared, and even now, as Sarah walked down the old patterned hallway runner to the corner bedroom, she felt a chill in the air, a slight shifting in the atmosphere.

All in your mind.

She reached for the doorknob, and when she turned it, she experienced a chill, a tiny frisson of ice that swept up her hand and arm. With the cold rush came a memory.

"Don't you go in there! Sarah Jane, do you hear me, you stay out of your sister's room!"

Arlene's voice seemed to reverberate down the empty hallway, her strict, demanding tone still echoing in Sarah's head, though that particular warning had happened when Sarah couldn't have been more than six or seven.

Theresa had disappeared years before, so Sarah had no real recollection of her eldest sister, and recognized her only from snapshots and pictures taken over the years before Sarah's birth, photos that ended abruptly when Theresa had been sixteen and disappeared for good.

Arlene's warning still hung in the air, the image of her twisted, pained face burned into Sarah's brain. *"You know better than to step foot in that room, so don't you dare!"*

Sarah, then, had let go as if the glass doorknob was white-hot, her mother's wrath palpable though she'd merely been a curious child who had just wanted a glimpse into her sister's private life, to understand more about the girl who'd become a saint in their mother's eyes. "She'll come back, you wait and see," Arlene had insisted time and again, becoming an avenging angel who guarded the sanctuary and eventual memorial to her eldest daughter with her life.

And a willow switch.

Arlene had used the snapping whip sparingly but effectively; she'd lashed Jacob's and Joseph's butts and the back of Sarah's hands when she'd deemed harsh punishment to be warranted.

Only Dee Linn had escaped their mother's fury. And Theresa, possibly, though Sarah had never really known. Theresa was an enigma to her, a ghost in the sense that she existed only in her very young memory, and even then, Sarah wasn't certain the images were real or just her subconscious coming to the fore. Roger was certainly more real, drifting in and out of the house—as well as jail.

"Troubled," Arlene had said, "so troubled." However, Sarah often had wondered if her mother's explanation for her eldest son's problems was an excuse for something darker, something that couldn't be cast aside with a simple excuse.

Standing in the hallway, Sarah imagined her mother's high-pitched voice reprimanding her, and for a second she paused, closed her eyes, and cleared her mind.

Get a grip. Arlene isn't in this house. She hasn't been for years. And Theresa never returned, did she? She escaped this prison of a home. As for ghosts, they don't exist except for inside your own weak mind. You know it, and you know when it started, don't you? The "incident" on the rooftop in the rain? You remember?

"No," she whispered aloud and realized her fists were clenched, the muscles in the back of her neck so tight they ached.

Mom can't see you now, Sarah, and just because Gracie thought she saw something in this room is no reason to buy into the idea of a ghost.

"Stop it," she warned herself. She wouldn't let all her fears and insecurities as a child creep back into her consciousness. Setting her jaw, she pushed on the door to Theresa's bedroom.

It didn't budge.

"Oh, come on." Again she tried, but the door was swollen and stuck. She rattled the doorknob, then threw her shoulder against the panels. With a groan, the door opened suddenly, and she nearly lost her balance as she half fell into the room.

The cold room.

Colder by at least five degrees.

An icy spot in the house.

Don't go there.

She saw the window on the north wall near the fireplace and noticed it wasn't quite shut. Naturally the room was cooler. Also, the damper could have been left open or rusted out in the flue. Though the marble face surrounding the firebox was intact, the wooden surround and mantel were cracked, the white paint wearing thin, a layer of dust covering the narrow shelf. On one knee, she reached into the blackened firebox, felt for the handle on the damper, and pulled. It screeched shut.

The room seemed more lifeless than the rest of the house, but Sarah shrugged off the feeling as she walked to the window facing the front of the old building and looked through the glass panes to stand where Gracie had been certain she had seen someone. There was no evidence anyone had recently been on this spot. The dingy, gauzy curtains were covered in spiderwebs, complete with dead, trapped insects, and looked as if they hadn't been disturbed in a quarter of a century. The sill on the window was dusty, as was the floor, and there were no footprints visible, no handprints on the grimy panes.

She tried to close the window, but it too was stuck, the casing swollen.

"No big mystery," she told herself, examining her older sister's room with an adult eye. It was older and time-worn. The faded, floral rug, mildewed and tattered, lay over the dark wooden floors. Dusty sheets were draped over a four-poster bed and a small night table. In the alcove a vanity was exposed, its sheet having slid halfway off the fly-specked mirror to pool on the floor near the small closet.

Theresa's retreat.

Arlene's memorial.

"Mom!" Gracie's voice rose to the rafters. "Mom! Your phone's ringing!"

Along with her daughter's voice, Sarah heard the faint sound of her cell's default ringtone. "On my way," she yelled, hurrying out of the room. Flying down two flights of stairs, she found her youngest daughter on the first floor, Sarah's cell in her outstretched hand.

"Evan."

"Oh."

"I didn't answer."

"Good thinking." She snapped up the phone, then shoved it into the front pocket of her jeans. "Hungry?" she asked, steering Gracie toward the kitchen.

Gracie shrugged.

"Sleep okay?"

"Yeah."

"No more bad dreams?" Sarah asked.

"It wasn't a . . . ," Gracie sighed. "No."

"Good."

"What were you doing up there?" Gracie hooked a thumb toward the ceiling.

"Inventory, I guess you'd say. Maybe reconnaissance."

Sarah searched through a couple of sacks she'd brought in last night. "Thought I'd just take a quick look to see what needs to be done before we get started with construction."

"Jade up?"

Gracie looked at Sarah as if she were as dense as concrete. "No way."

Sarah nodded. *Good. At least the battles won't start for a few hours.* For once, she was content to let her teenager sleep away the morning. All that would change come Monday morning, of course, when school started for the girls. Sarah couldn't imagine what a battle that would be. For now, though, there was a semblance of peace.

"Let's not wake the sleeping dragon, okay? So how about peanut butter and jelly . . . or jelly and peanut butter? We've got both."

"Mom . . . ," Gracie said, half amused, half embarrassed by her silly joke.

Sarah grinned at her youngest. Maybe things were going to be okay.

CHAPTER 5

"So I guess you heard that Sarah's back in town," Holly Collins said as Clint swiped his debit card through the machine. He was standing at the counter of Collins Lumber, an all-purpose supply store located in a warehouse that had survived two world wars, three generations of ownership by a member of the Collins family, and still stood just off Main Street.

"I heard," Clint responded, stuffing his card into his wallet.

"Of course, it's because she's planning on renovating that old wreck of a house." Holly waited as the machine chunked out his receipt. "She's single now, you know."

"Is that right?"

"C'mon, Clint, don't play dumb with me. I bet you've kept tabs on her. You two were pretty hot and heavy back in the day." She ripped off the receipt and handed it to him.

"Back in the day was a long time ago." After signing the receipt, he jammed his wallet into the back pocket of his jeans.

"I just can't imagine trying to bring some life into that old monstrosity of a house. The Blue Pigeon or whatever."

"Peacock."

"Right. Jewel of the Columbia, my father used to call it. Like eons ago. No one except the old-timers around here remember it or care. Except Sarah. Looks like you'll be neighbors again."

"Looks like."

"If you ask me, it's going to take a fortune to restore that old place. Most people with any sense think it would be best to bulldoze it down, get rid of that rotten old house, all the bad memories, and maybe a ghost or two in the process." She actually smiled more widely, warming to her idea. "Up there on the point, with that view of the river, a new place would be spectacular! Maybe a resort with a golf course and a spa? Can you imagine? Worth a king's ransom!" She jabbed a finger at Clint. "Now that would be a real jewel, y'know? It's just too damned bad no one asks me."

"A shame."

"And well . . . Sarah." She held his gaze as if they shared a private secret. "She always marched to the beat of a different drum, if you know what I mean."

He did, but he didn't like where this was heading.

"To each her own, of course," Holly added, and he felt a ridiculous need to defend her.

"Of course." He couldn't hide the sarcasm in his tone, not that Holly noticed.

"I just think it's a little weird to move now, with her kids still in school and all. Uproot them less than six weeks after the new school year starts? Who does that?"

"Apparently Sarah."

"Like I said, 'different drum' or maybe marching on another planet. Oh, well!" She threw him a "what're ya gonna do?" smile. "I guess I can't say too much about how weird the Stewarts are, as Cam's kind of related to them," she admitted, mentioning her husband. She leaned over the counter, getting closer. "But I think it all started with Maxim, the one who built that damned house. The way Cam's grandfather tells it, Maxim was a real piece of work. Beat the crap out of both his wives and all his kids. Sick stuff. Cam's grandpa was just a boy, of course."

"How could he have known Maxim? Maxim disappeared about a hundred years ago," Clint said.

"Cuz that old coot was nearly sixty when Cam's dad was born, or something like that. Gramps had himself a much younger wife."

Clint had heard enough. He glanced at his watch. "Gotta run," he said, hoping to cut off any more gossip about the Stewart clan. "On my lunch break."

She nodded. "Course."

Clint rained a smile on Holly and saw something in her melt inside. He'd known she'd had a thing for him all those years ago, and it hadn't completely gone away, not even with a fifteen-plus-year marriage to Cameron, the owner of the store, and four stepping-stone sons.

She clicked on an ancient walkie-talkie. "Clint Walsh is on his way down to pick up his order. You got it ready?" she almost screamed into the receiver before releasing the "speak" button. Static and a crackling "Yep" confirmed the message had gotten through to the loading area. To Clint, Holly added, "Cam'll have your order 'round back, in the lower lot. As always." She winked at him, and he was reminded of the girl she'd been in high school, sassy and smart, quick with a come-on smile and captain of the cheerleading squad.

"Thanks." Clint was already near the front door, his boots heavy against floorboards that had weathered over the course of a century under the tread of farmers, loggers, ranchers, and builders. At this "feed and more" store you could buy anything from lumber to penny nails, livestock feed, landscaping tools, and the like. In the spring baby chicks were kept in a special pen complete with water, feed, and heat lamps. For a few weeks, they peeped loudly enough to drown out the country music that played over tinny speakers hidden near the exposed rafters.

Outside, he zipped his jacket against an unseasonable cold front, then climbed into his truck and was greeted by Tex, his half-grown dog of indeterminate heritage. With black and white bristly hair and a long nose, the slightly hyper pup had shown up one day and just stayed. Clint hadn't minded. "I missed you too. Now sit," he ordered, and the dog obeyed, happily sticking his head out the open passenger window. The pickup he'd named the Beast started on the third attempt, its engine finally sparking and coughing before catching.

Driving down a steep hill, he put any lingering thoughts of Sarah Stewart, or whatever her name was now, out of his mind. The less he thought about her, the better it was for everyone, Sarah included. She'd gone to the local Catholic school, and he the public high school, but as Holly had said, they had been neighbors and known each other since childhood. As they'd grown and Sarah had changed from a tomboy who kept to herself to a gorgeous woman who could give as well as she got, he'd looked at her in a new way. Theirs had been a blistering attraction, but it had also been a mistake.

Nosing his truck into the gravel lot, he then backed up so the bed of his truck was only inches from the raised loading dock of the feed store.

Cam and his oldest boy, Eric, were already waiting with his order: ten sacks of feed, a new shovel, and five fence posts to replace those that had rotted near his machine shed. "Stay," Clint said to Tex. The mutt watched through the open window as Clint climbed out of the truck.

Together Clint, Cam, and Eric loaded the bed of the GMC with his purchases, and then he was off, waving to the man who'd been brave enough to marry Holly Spangler, who had also been known as the biggest flirt in Wasco County.

From the parking lot, he drove up the sharp hillsides of the town that had been named for Sarah's ancestors and was jokingly referred to as "a poor man's Seattle" because of its steep terrain. With the Beast's engine grinding, Clint took the back county road into the hills to his own spread, a hundred and eighty acres of ranchland and timber that he'd inherited from his old man. The ranch sprawled across the foothills of the Cascade Mountains, bordered government land on three sides, and was only half a mile down the road from Blue Peacock Manor, which he, along with most of the locals, called the "the Stewart house."

His fingers gripped the steering wheel a little more tightly, and though he told himself that it was over, had been for half his life, he wondered about Sarah. What did she look like? Who were her friends? Was she really single . . . ?

"Trouble. That's what she is," he confided to the dog as he remembered Sarah's mysterious smile, the sparkle in her eyes, her not-so-innocent laugh, low and sexy and free. He told himself that back then he was a horny kid, that she'd just been a fling. However, she was like a burn that had gotten under his skin when he was twenty and, he suspected, had never quite died.

"Son of a bitch," he muttered under his breath. Though their affair had been over ages ago, he still thought of her now and again . . . well, probably, if he were completely honest with himself, a lot more often than that, but he'd let go of the fantasy of reconnecting with her a long time ago.

"Water under the bridge," he said as he turned off the county road, then drove down the long, winding lane to the farmhouse where he'd grown up. Through stands of pine and fir and over a short bridge that spanned the creek, the truck bounced along rocky ruts that could use a new load or two of gravel. The lane curved as the forest gave way to dry pasture where horses and cattle grazed. Farther ahead, the homestead house anchored the ranch, outbuildings spaced around a huge parking area filled with a dozen or more potholes. Yeah, before winter really set in, he'd have to order that gravel.

He parked near the barn. "Come on," he said, whistling to the dog. Tex eagerly bounded out of the truck and ran to the nearest fence post, where he sniffed before lifting his leg. "Yeah, a lotta good you are." He hauled the sacks of grain up the ramp to the lower level of the barn, under the hay mow, where he stacked them near the old open bins.

This time of day the cattle and horses weren't inside, but their smells assailed him, the acrid odors of manure and urine mixed with the scents of dusty, dry hay and oiled leather—smells he'd grown up with.

Glancing up at the hay mow, he remembered more than one summer night when he and Sarah had climbed the old metal rungs to lie on an old blanket and make out for hours. It's not that the mow was special; they'd also spent hours on the shore of the pond on her parents' property and high on the ridge above the river. For no good reason, he climbed upward and stood on the wooden floor before the bales stacked to the high, pitched ceiling. It was pretty much the same as it had been all those years before, the small round window at the apex of the roof line cracked open a bit. He remembered breathing hard, holding her naked body close, the scents of dusty hay, sweat, and sex mingling as his hands tangled in her hair. He'd stared through that same round window and seen hundreds of stars strewn across the night sky.

He shook his head and mentally chastised himself before climbing down the ladder again. No need for nostalgia right now, Sarah or no Sarah.

None whatsoever.

"Hey, Sleeping Beauty, join the party," her mother said.

Jade opened a bleary eye to find Sarah standing over her. "It's afternoon, and I let you sleep in today," she went on, "but now it's time to get up and get going. We've got a lot to do."

Jade groaned and rolled over in her sleeping bag, pulling it over her head.

"You can start with the garbage sacks that Gracie and I've filled." Her mother's voice was muffled but firm. "I'm serious, Jade, let's go!"

"Great," Jade mumbled and knew she couldn't argue when Mom adopted that "I'm in charge" tone.

With a dramatic effort, Jade dragged herself out of the sleeping bag and saw that Sarah had left and, to judge from the noise emanating from the kitchen, was already hard at work.

Sighing, Jade got to her feet and found a pair of flip-flops near the hearth. She shuffled into the sty of a bathroom, peed, splashed water over her face, and tried to wake up. After Gracie had made all the commotion about seeing a damned ghost and waking her, Jade had been too hyped up to go back to sleep, though she'd tried. Really. Finally she'd given up and discovered both her mother and sister were dead to the world, so she'd started texting Cody, begging him to come and rescue her as she was still without a car.

She'd been up most of the night until she'd fallen asleep sometime around five in the morning, so she wasn't all that interested in any projects her mother might dream up. Ever since Sarah had come up with the crazy decision to move back here, Jade's life had been on a downward spiral that she was certain was heading straight to hell. Hauling out garbage was just one more task confirming her suspicions that some greater force was punishing her and making her life miserable.

"Okay, let's get moving," Sarah yelled again. "We need to clean this place up as best we can."

"We?" Jade said and cringed as her mother had obviously heard her from the other room.

"Yes, we. Like it or not, we're all in this together."

"I don't. Like it."

"I know. Today, your vote doesn't count."

"That's not fair," she shouted, but knew she was fighting a losing battle.

"Probably not."

Grumbling under her breath, Jade, in one of Cody's T-shirts and pajama bottoms, made her way into the kitchen, where Gracie and Sarah were already scurrying around, trying to clean up the filthy room. The old counters were covered with jars, boxes, utensils, and all kinds of garbage.

Jade flopped into an old chair at the table.

Her mother was already sweeping the uneven, cracked linoleum or whatever it was that had once covered the floor. "We'll start here and clean out everything that we don't want or need or can't be restored." Gracie, the suck-up, was filling trash bags with stuff Mom had already pulled out of the gross-looking cupboards. Tall and narrow, the cabinets and shelves stretched to the ceiling. It looked like they'd once been painted a soft green, but now the doors and boxes were dirty and dingy, the hinges rusting, the glass panes of a sideboard nearly opaque with years of grease and grime.

Still tired, Jade wasn't into this at all, but as she opened her mouth to suggest putting a lit match to the place, she caught the warning look on her mother's face and knew she should stop arguing.

"Oh . . . yuck . . . ," Gracie wrinkled her nose as she read the label of a box of baking soda. "Nineteen ninety-eight."

"Grandma was never one to throw things out. 'Waste not, want not' was her credo," Sarah said dryly.

"And a good way to get salmonella or ptomaine or whatever," Jade pointed out.

"No kidding." Gracie quickly tossed the box into a bag she was filling.

"Where is she anyway?" Jade asked, hauling one of the full bags off an old table and tying the plastic cords. She saw her mother's back stiffen slightly.

"Grandma? She's in Pleasant Pines, remember?"

"Pleasant Pines. God, could they name it any more like a funeral home?" Jade muttered.

"Will we see her?" Gracie asked, and for once Jade and her mother shared a knowing look. Jade remembered the last time she'd seen her grandmother, and it wasn't exactly the kind of warm and fuzzy recollection you wanted to keep in your memory bank. Jade had never witnessed her mother so upset, so out of control, as she had been with Grandma Arlene.

"Sure, we can go up there," Sarah said, but there wasn't a lot of conviction in her eyes.

Gracie asked curiously, "Don't you want to?"

The nerd just didn't get it. Time to straighten her out. "Mom and Grandma hate each other." End of story.

Sarah stopped sweeping. "That's not true. Hate is too strong a word." She shot her eldest a warning glare. "We don't see eye to eye, and never have, so we've never been very close, but no one hates anyone."

Gracie picked up another jar from the cupboard and examined it cautiously. "That's sad."

"I guess." Sarah had picked up the broom and now swept a pile of grime into her dustpan with a little more force than necessary. "It's just the way it is."

Jade yawned. "Grandma can be a bitch."

Sara turned on her daughter. "Don't, Jade."

"Just because she's in some kind of nursing home doesn't make her nice," Jade retorted.

"It's a care facility," Sarah said shortly. "Assisted living."

"She's still the same person she always was." Jade looked around the room. "Why are we even doing this? I thought we were going to live in the guesthouse. Isn't cleaning this up like a waste of time?"

"Just get to work." Sarah pointed at the filled bags that were propped against the lower cabinets.

Grudgingly, Jade got to her feet and hoisted the first heavy plastic trash bag to her shoulder. "Where do you want these?"

"The back porch. A Dumpster is being delivered tomorrow, and we'll start filling it with them."

"Great," Jade said without an ounce of enthusiasm. She felt as if she were in prison.

"It'll be fun."

Like, sure.

She started hauling the bag of trash to the back door when she heard the rumble of a car's engine and looked out the window to see a silver vehicle roll to a stop near the guesthouse. Before the engine died, the passenger door opened, and Uncle Jake stretched out of the sedan and started toward the house. A second later Uncle Joe, stuffing car keys into his pocket, jogged to join his twin.

"We've got company!" she yelled and wished to high heaven she was spying Cody and his old Jeep rather than her uncles climbing up the porch. If only he would come and take her away from here before she started school at Our Lady of the River.

She hated the idea of being the "new girl" and having the whole damn school scrutinize her.

The thought was terrifying. Nearly paralyzing. Tears threatened her eyes, but she fought them.

No one could know how she really felt, how scared she was.

Not even Cody.

"What now?" Sheriff J. D. Cooke asked as he looked up from the pile of papers covering his desk. His newest detective, Lucy Belli-sario, was walking through the door to his office in the hundred-year-old building that housed the Sheriff's Department. When she showed up, it usually spelled trouble. Built like a dancer, with a temper that matched her fiery red hair, she was also one of the smartest women he'd ever met, and she knew it. Lucy had been raising her hand to rap her knuckles on the pebbled glass of his door, even though it was ajar. "Don't tell me," he said, leaning back in his chair before she'd breathed a word. "More bad news."

"So now you're psychic?" she asked, pushing open the door.

"Doesn't take any ESP to see trouble on your face."

"On top of the budget cuts and deputies out sick, the rash of cat-tle rustling, and the group of antigovernment types taking up resi-dence and riling up the public, the weather service is predicting one helluva storm heading our way. Straight down from Canada. But that's not all . . ."

J. D. made a growling sound.

One corner of her mouth actually lifted as she stepped all the way inside. "And good morning to you too. Geez, look who woke up on the wrong side of the bed today."

He winced slightly. Ever since Sammi-Jo had left him two months ago, he had been a bear to work with, and he knew it, but he couldn't seem to shake himself out of his funk. He placed his elbows on the desk he'd inherited along with this pain-in-the-neck job and said, "Let's start over. What's up?"

"Missing person," she said and slid into one of the uncomfortable chairs across the desk from him. "Seventeen. Rosalie Jamison. She's a classmate of my younger sister's, and so I know her mom, Sharon, kind of." She tipped her flattened hand up and down to indicate that it was an "iffy" relationship. "We've met each other at some school functions. Anyway, Sharon called me this morning beside herself. Rosalie's missing. Been gone more than twelve hours. I know, I know. Not twenty-four, but hear me out. She works at the Columbia Diner."

He knew the place, had frequented it himself on occasion.

"So she left work around midnight, clocked out at eleven fifty-three, but never made it home."

"Runaway?" he asked.

"Possibly." Lucy's eyebrows drew together the way they always did when she was tasked with a problem she couldn't figure out. "She's had some trouble at school, but Sharon called around and the people who worked with her saw her leave, walking. One of the other waitresses, Gloria Netterling, offered to give her a lift, but the girl declined. Decided to walk."

"Last night," he said, thoughtfully and tapped his fingers on his desk. "Bad weather."

"Yeah." Bellisario was nodding, her hair catching fire in the light from the overhead fixtures. "It's about a twenty- to twenty-five-minute walk, so she should have been home by twelve-thirty at the latest. Her mom and stepdad, Mel Updike, were already at home, in bed, with the TV on. They figured she'd come in, and only the next morning did they realize she hadn't come home. Sharon didn't push the panic button because it had happened before, but by afternoon, she was worried and started calling around to Rosalie's usual haunts. Drove to the diner and back, talked to everyone there, then called all her friends. No one had seen her since she walked out the door of the diner."

"Boyfriend?"

"None currently, though Sharon said Rosalie had mentioned a boy she'd met online. Sharon doesn't even know his name, only that he claims he's from around Denver, where her ex, Rosalie's dad, lives."

"Online? How the hell does that work when you're a teenager?"

"I don't know, but probably the way it does for adults."

"What about a car?" he asked.

"She didn't own one. Used her mom's Chevy when she needed one, or walked, sometimes hitched."

Cooke locked gazes with Bellisario. The hitchhiking thing was a flag.

"There are other vehicles in the house. Updike has a truck and motorcycle, and they're all accounted for."

"Siblings?"

"None who live with her. And only half siblings at that, a couple of 'em. Live with their dad. Updike's got a handful, also. None of whom are in state."

"What about her dad?" He held up a hand and clarified, "I mean the biological father? The guy in Denver. She call him?"

"Mick Jamison. Yeah, she called him. Woke him up. He lives with wife number two, a woman Sharon doesn't like or trust."

"Does the first wife ever trust the second?" he asked rhetorically, the wheels in his head turning. "The dad and online boyfriend, both in Colorado. What're the chances of that?"

"Maybe they know each other."

"Check 'em out. Both of 'em."

"Already started."

Cooke rapped his fingers on the desktop. He didn't like the sound of this one little bit. "You got pictures?"

"Sharon supplied me and Missing Persons with a couple of recent shots, along with the pic and info on her driver's license. We've already put a BOLO out on her and, considering her age, an AMBER Alert."

"So much for the twenty-four-hour waiting period."

"She's a kid, Sheriff. And I'm going with my gut on this one."

"Okay." He too had a bad feeling. "Start checking with friends, work with Missing Persons, look into the stepdad and old boyfriends, as well as the kid who's supposed to be in Denver. If she met him online he could be anywhere. Maybe even just down the road. Someone who knows she's got a dad in Colorado and is using it as bait to get close to her. You know, an opening. For that matter, the online guy might not be a teenager at all. Could be an adult. A poser." He let out a long breath and thought of his own teenaged kids, who lived in Portland with their mom. He knew how it felt when one didn't show up when they were supposed to, though he'd lucked out and Hallie and Ben had always been okay. "Let's just hope she has a rebellious streak, took off, and has a change of heart. That way she'll come home on her own."

Lucy Bellisario's gray eyes met his. "That would be best," she agreed, but she didn't look as if she had much hope of that particular scenario happening.

Neither did he.

CHAPTER 6

The ghost had been trying to communicate with her—Gracie was sure of it as she stood just on the other side of the wall to the dining room, eavesdropping on the conversation between her mother and uncles. She'd been terrified on the staircase, never expecting such a close encounter, but the woman in white had been trying to tell her something. And Gracie had been too scared to realize it until now.

It hadn't been a dream.

She hadn't imagined the ghost.

But in the light of day, having had time to think about it, she realized that the spirit of Angelique Le Duc was reaching out to her.

She'd blown it and now had to do something about it. She'd read enough history about Blue Peacock Manor to know that Angelique might not be the only ghost haunting the place; lots of people had lived and died here, and many of them were interred in the family plot somewhere on the property. Gracie had already been researching the people who had lived in the house and around the area.

But she had to keep what she was doing to herself. If she was to communicate with the ghost, maybe help her spirit cross over— which was what all ghosts seemed to want to do—then she would have to keep her mouth shut. Otherwise, her mother would haul her back to see the psychologist again, just as she had after the divorce. No thanks. Gracie wasn't nuts, she knew that much; she just sensed more things than most people, which freaked out her mother but made Gracie feel somehow complete.

She just had to figure out how to use this gift she'd been given.

* * *

"Just so we're on the same page," Jacob said, always one to clarify a situation. He was the more nervous of her twin brothers, and that's how a lot of people told the two men apart. Their faces were nearly identical, their hair a dusty blond, their eyes sky blue, their builds athletic and broad-shouldered. But Joseph usually presented an easy smile, while Jacob's forehead was already lined from years of pulling his eyebrows together. Today, there were more obvious distinctions, as Jacob's hair was clipped and short, while Joseph's was longer and disheveled, his jeans worn, his shirt with a few wrinkles, the sleeves rolled up. Jacob, on the other hand, was wearing a polo shirt and crisply pressed khakis and appeared ready to step onto the first tee of a country club. "Once the renovations are complete, we sell this thing."

"Or you lease it to me, until I can buy it." She eyed both her brothers. "That was the deal, remember? That we wouldn't sell as long as Mom's alive."

Jacob's eyes darkened. "That could be decades!"

"We can only hope," Joseph said, "Geez, Jake."

"It's not that I want her dead. Come on, you both know that. Even though, face it, Mom's always been a pain in the butt." He looked from his twin to his sister. "Oh, what? You don't think so?"

Rolling her eyes, Sarah said, "Fine," and caught a bemused glance from Joseph.

"I mean it, Sarah," Jake said, "I'm not the one with a problem with Mom."

Joseph held up both hands. "We *all* have a problem with Mom."

"Enough! You guys didn't come out here to badmouth Mother, so let's get back on track, to the renovations," Sarah said. "So here's what we've got." Sarah flattened the rolled plans across the table and secured the corners with dusty books she'd found in the library area of the parlor. A worn edition of *The Exorcist* by William Peter Blatty held one corner fast, while a gnawed copy of Louise May Alcott's *Little Women* anchored another.

"Here are the original plans," she said.

"Seriously?"

"Look at the date. Nineteen twenty-one." The brittle pages were yellowed, grimy, and covered in pencil notes. Smudged fingerprints and stains of undeterminable origin discolored the drawings. With great care, Sara stretched the fragile, often unintelligible pages. "The original house was pretty amazing, especially for the time. It had running water and electricity, which was huge. It wouldn't have been such a big deal in a large city like San Francisco or even Portland, but out here that was a real accomplishment. Remember, the highway, I mean the old historic highway, wasn't completely finished until nineteen twenty-two." The faded architect's plans showed the house as it had been built by Maxim Stewart, Sarah's great-great-grandfather. "Maxim was an autocrat, by all accounts, and always got his way."

Jacob caught the mention of their ancestor. "Maxim? Isn't that the old coot who killed his second wife? Angeline or something."

"Angelique," Sarah corrected. "That's the story."

"You see her ghost running around yet? Isn't she the one who's supposed to haunt the place?"

Sarah felt a chill that started at the base of her spine and crawled upward, but she thought she'd keep Gracie's ghost sightings to herself. "Rumors," she said. "People in a small town like to talk, live vicariously, or, better yet, exaggerate and make up stories."

Jacob said, "Yeah, but even you said you saw her."

"I was a kid," Sarah snapped, a little too quickly. Her daughter's panic attack from the night before was still too fresh. "Now, come on, we've got work to do." While Jacob shrugged, dismissing the ghost, Joseph's gaze lingered thoughtfully on her. She ignored them both and rolled out the second set of plans, dated 1950, and pointed out the addition of a bathroom and expansion of the kitchen. Finally, she spread architect's drawings from 1978, which included yet another kitchen remodel, more electrical panels, the addition of a patio off the back porch, and a master bathroom that cut into an existing walk-in linen closet.

Joseph studied each set. "Just about as many reincarnations as there have been generations."

"Not quite," Sarah said.

"And now we have to do it all over again." He grimaced, then gave a cursory look at the place. "Isn't this just cosmetic?"

"I wish. I've only looked over the first two floors, still have the third, attic, and widow's walk to check over and the basement."

Joseph's brows lifted. "You're going down there? Seems to me you were deathly afraid of it."

"Maybe because you two jerks locked me down there."

Jacob pulled a face. "Sorry."

"If I remember right, we paid," Joseph said, and Sarah inwardly cringed as she recalled the lashing the boys had gotten from Arlene when she'd discovered Sarah, age six, trapped and crying on the top step of the long staircase leading to the basement.

"Yes, I'm going down there and take inventory," Sarah said.

"And the widow's walk?" Jacob said. "Who are you and what have you done with my sister?"

She actually smiled. "I'm not the same little girl you teased and bullied."

"So it seems." Jacob actually smiled. The twins too had grown up, and she saw no reason to go into the trauma she'd endured at their hands, though the incident on the roof had not had anything to do with them, or so they'd sworn over and over again. Rather than dredge it all up now, she said, "As for everything just being cosmetic, Jacob, look at the size of this house. Cosmetic costs. And, unfortunately, it runs a little deeper than just a tiny face-lift."

Jacob's smile fell away.

"I think I hear the sound of a bulldozer's engine revving up in his head," Joseph said. He leaned in and added, "I'm a little clairvoyant, you know, with him. It's a twin thing."

"Oh, shut up." Jacob stared out the window to the grounds outside. Rolling pastures butted up to forested hills on one side; on the other lay the wild Columbia. "But, you know, the value of the property is the land. The house is a mess, falling down. Maybe Joe's right."

Joseph threw up his hands and took a step backward. "I didn't suggest tearing down the house. I just mentioned I figured that's the route you'd want to go."

"It's the most practical," Jacob encouraged.

"This is history, Jake," Sarah cut in, jabbing a finger at the original drawings before the two could start teasing and arguing and going into what she considered their "twin schtick," an act they'd perfected since birth. "And this is our home, a beautiful home where we were raised. It just needs a little TLC." Jacob's eyebrows raised. "Okay, *a lot* of TLC. But I've got the time, the skills, and the connections in the business." She looked up. "You know that, Jake, or you wouldn't have agreed to it." She didn't go into the fact that after college she'd first worked as an architect's assistant or that she'd spent the last five years of her life as a project manager for Tolliver Construction in Vancouver. Remodeling had been her specialty. "Besides, who's going to tell Mom we bulldozed down the house?"

Neither twin volunteered.

"I thought so. So I'll give all the floors a cursory look again and come up with some more fabulous ideas. I've already sent the plans and some ideas to the architect, and he's come out with an engineer for preliminary measurements and to look the place over. I've been e-mailing back and forth with the firm for months. Thankfully, I hired a local guy to oversee the guesthouse renovation, and it's almost ready for us to move in. Once it is, we can really get started on this house."

Jacob stated the obvious. "Sounds expensive."

"Of course it is; we already talked budget," she pointed out to both of them, "and signed our lives away at the bank."

"Don't remind me," Jacob said, in a tone that suggested he wished he could take it back.

"Hey, you've got to be with me on this. Both of you. This," she tapped the open plans with two fingers, "is a big project, a major renovation, but it'll be so worth it."

"Okay," Joseph said, shrugging. He'd never been the serious opposition Jacob was. "Go for it."

"I am. I've already moved my family here, and, trust me, there are heel marks all the way from Vancouver to this hill because Jade didn't want to come. But there's no backing out now." She turned her attention to her other brother. "Right, Jake?"

Jacob hesitated, then caught a glance from his brother and nodded. "Okay." A lift of one shoulder. "Sure."

"Good," Sarah said, relieved.

"We better roll," Joseph said to his brother just as his cell phone rang. "Gotta get this." He started for the front door. "Don't forget about Dee Linn's party."

Sarah cringed inside. "That's still happening?"

"Didn't she call you?"

"Eons ago. I haven't talked to her in, I don't know, maybe three weeks. I've been busy with moving, and now that we're here, cell phone reception is spotty at best. Jade seems to think I dragged her here, away from her friends as part of my long-term, devious plan to make her life miserable."

Joseph grinned. "Didn't you?"

"You're not helping," Sarah charged, but returned his knowing smile. "So Dee Linn's party is on?"

"You think she'd change her mind?" Joseph asked, lifting an eyebrow that told her she needn't have posed the question.

"Her mantra is 'Never miss an opportunity to show off what you've got,'" Jacob reminded. "The whole fam-damily is invited."

"Mom?" Sarah asked and hated the way her back muscles tensed at the thought of seeing Arlene.

"I'm sure if she can, she will," Jacob said. "Guess you haven't seen her in a while, or you'd know."

"What?" Sarah felt a little pinprick of guilt, her conscience jabbing her again. She had visited her mother twice. Both times Arlene had slept and never woken up, so the visits had been wasted. She'd hung around for several hours each time and wondered if her cantankerous mother had been feigning sleep, then had felt awful on the drive home for thinking Arlene would be so devious.

"Anyway, she's not up for that kind of gig, or maybe any kind of to-do. Probably never will be again, not that they were ever her thing," Jacob said. "But the rest of them are supposed to be there. Aunt Marge is coming, along with her kids." Marge was Arlene's younger sister; her daughter, Caroline, was Sarah's cousin. "At least, I think that's what Danica said," he added, mentioning his wife, "but don't quote me."

"I'll call Dee tonight," Sarah promised as her brothers left and the house closed in on her again.

"Hey, girls," she said, walking into the kitchen and finding it empty, then locating her daughters in the living area. "Get ready, we're going to visit your grandmother."

"You've got to be kidding, right?" Jade, looking up from the cell phone where she was either texting or playing a game, turned horror-filled eyes in her mother's direction.

"That's right. It's the last chance we'll have before you're both in school next week and I'm all wrapped up in the renovations, so come on, get it together. "Head on out to the car."

"I'm not even dressed yet!" Jade protested.

"Not my problem. It's afternoon and we're leaving in five, so get it together."

As her mother drove through the open gates of Pleasant Pines Retirement Center, Jade eyed the facility with a jaundiced eye. So far she'd been in Stewart's Crossing not quite twenty-four hours, and each and every minute had been torture. From the ridiculous lack of Internet and TV reception to Gracie's claims of seeing a ghost, the place had been awful. And now they were visiting Grandma Arlene in this place, a modern building with a huge portico that stretched over a circular drive. A leaf-strewn lawn and a few shrubs completed the landscape around the main building of three stories, each with banks of windows punctuated with air-conditioning units.

Jade hated it on sight, but then, she hated just about everything that was her life these days, and seeing Grandma Arlene wasn't going to improve her mood. The drive here had been tense; her mother had been silent, and that hadn't ended when she'd wheeled the Explorer into a vacant parking space.

As Gracie got out of the backseat, Jade climbed out of the front, only to feel the chill of raindrops upon her bare head.

Great. Just fabulous.

She wrapped her ankle-length coat more tightly around her and forced her hands deep in its pockets as she followed her mother and sister inside. For some unknown reason Gracie didn't seem to notice how lame this visit was.

For a second, Jade felt the sting of guilt for her thoughts, then quickly dismissed that emotion as totally undeserved because she really wanted to like her grandmother, but it was impossible. She had friends who thought their grandparents were the absolute coolest. Cody's grandpa was a kick, a man Cody loved and respected. His grandma, Violet, was a sweet thing who baked cookies, and knitted, and took in stray cats whom she adored. Violet had a collection of old vinyl records she loved to play for Cody as his grandpa showed him the arsenal of weapons he kept in a special locked room with the skins and heads of animals he'd "nailed"—everything from a stuffed alligator placed near the stone fireplace to a cougar crouching on one of the crossbeams of the vaulted ceiling. That part was kind of gross, she thought, as she walked through the glass door of the building to feel a blast of heat as hot as the very fires of hell. She really didn't like the fact that Cody's grandpa took great pride in killing the beasts, but Gramps's arsenal of old guns and knives was pretty cool. Cody loved it all, especially the old World War II German Luger, and a machine gun complete with ammo belt that Gramps kept in his "war room" in the basement.

Despite the old man's affinity for warfare and hunting, both he and his "bride" of fifty-plus years were fun and loving and had the laugh lines to prove it.

Jade hadn't been so lucky. She'd never met her father's parents, which was no surprise as she'd never met her biological father, a mythical male beast who had impregnated her mother and apparently had no name. As far as her adopted dad, Noel McAdams went, his parents were in Savannah, where he now resided after the divorce. She'd met them only a few times, so they hardly counted anymore. Sarah's father, Grandpa Frank, was long dead, so that left Jade stuck with Arlene, a crotchety, mean-spirited old woman who seemed to blame the world for her fate.

Today, Jade figured, would be no exception.

After signing a guest registry and receiving badges at a reception desk, they were escorted by Mrs. Adele Malone, a cheery-faced, plump woman who chatted incessantly. She led them past a room filled with floral couches and chairs, where some of the residents were reading the paper or watching TV, then past an empty dining area, to a wide corridor where she smiled and waved to several women pushing walkers.

"Here we go," she announced at an elevator flanked by fake plants that looked suspiciously like marijuana. They probably weren't, but Jade preferred to believe that some twisted decorator had thrown them into the decorating mix as a joke.

On the third floor, Mrs. Malone, still chatting on and on about the great things that were happening at Pleasant Pines, guided them to a room and knocked softly on the door.

The whole place gave Jade a major case of the creeps. Oh, it was nice enough; most of the residents greeted them in the hallways, some with walkers or wheelchairs, others walking slowly, but happy enough. They were all so happy that Jade secretly wondered if they were all on some kind of antidepressant.

All that changed when Mrs. Malone rapped her knuckles against a closed door and said in a singsong voice, "Mrs. Stewart? You have guests."

When there was no response from inside, Mrs. Malone knocked again, gently opened the door, and popped her head inside. "Your daughter and granddaughters are here to see you, Arlene."

Again, nothing.

Undaunted, the caretaker swung the door open and stepped inside a compact suite. "Come on in," she said, waving one hand quickly behind her to usher the small group inside.

Sarah stepped inside while Gracie and Jade hung back, huddled around the open door.

"Mrs. Stewart?" Mrs. Malone said again, more loudly. "You have company."

"Go away," was the sharp response.

"It's your daughter and granddaughters," Mrs. Malone repeated as she approached an overstuffed couch where a frail woman sat surrounded by pillows and a stuffed rabbit. Not quite white, her hair was thinning and straight. Owlish glasses were propped on the bridge of her nose, a chain securing them around her neck, should they fall off.

"Wait here a second," Jade's mother said quickly over her shoulder as she approached the couch. "Hi, Mom! How are you?" She bent to take her mother's hand and brush a kiss across her cheek, but Grandma Arlene visibly recoiled. Her bony face twisted in revulsion.

"You?" she accused in a low, raspy voice. "What're *you* doing here?"

Undaunted, Sarah straightened. "The girls and I moved back into the house, you know that, to renovate it. But we took a break to visit you."

"What girls?" Arlene demanded, her angry eyes sliding in their sockets as she trained her gaze to the doorway, where Gracie and Jade stood, half in, half out of the room. "Why are they here?" Arlene's thin lips were bloodless, her cheeks creased deep with wrinkles, her eyes a blue so pale they appeared ghostly.

"We wanted to visit you," Sarah explained.

Arlene's lips quivered. "I thought you were dead."

Mrs. Malone's hand flew to her chest.

"What? Mom, no." Sarah was shaking her head, her pasted-on smile wavering slightly. "I know it's been a while. I've been by, but you were sleeping."

"Why in heaven's name would you let me think you were dead?" The old woman's fury exploded, her fingers, already bony, gripping the arm of the faded couch as if they were talons. "What kind of daughter does that to her mother?" Her voice was rising, her arms visibly shaking. "I should have known with you! The nuns told me that you had strayed. They warned me. Don't you know that the Madonna is the key to your salvation? The Holy Mother? She's the key. Are you a heathen?"

Mrs. Malone stepped in. "Arlene, Sarah just brought her girls by for a visit."

"Sarah?" the old lady said, her breath coming out in a rush.

"Yes, your daughter."

Arlene blinked rapidly and her mouth worked. "My daughter is Theresa!" The fire that had flashed so hot seemed suddenly doused, and her lips trembled as if she might break down. "You're not . . . ?" She looked down for a second, gathering herself, and Jade actually felt sorry for her, for her obvious confusion. Anxiously, Arlene rubbed the back of one age-spotted hand with the other. "I . . . I don't understand. Where's Theresa? Where's my baby?"

Sarah had crouched down beside the chair. "We don't know, Mom. We still don't know."

"I think she's with John," Arlene said suddenly.

"John? John who?" Sarah asked.

"Or was it Matthew?"

"Mom, who's Matthew?" Sarah didn't understand.

"Maybe they were friends of your sister's," Mrs. Malone suggested softly. "Or family members."

"They'll keep her safe," Arlene said. "I know they will." The angry woman was completely gone, leaving in her wake a dazed, broken old lady who started mumbling gibberish as she blinked behind the lenses of her oversized glasses.

"Maybe this isn't a good time," Mrs. Malone said, her forehead lining with worry.

Well, duh! In Jade's estimation, this might be the worst time in the world. Poor Grandma.

The caretaker added, "Perhaps you could come back another day?"

"Mom?" Sarah asked, but Jade knew it was over. Whoever or whatever had been possessing this shriveled shell of a body moments before had shrunk away and was now hidden. Jade just hoped it would be forever.

They stepped into the hallway again, and Mrs. Malone said, "Sometimes she retreats. If you'll just give me a sec—" She pulled out some kind of walkie-talkie from her pocket and called for help. "You can go if you'd like and I'll call you later," she said as a tall woman with thick graying hair scraped into a bun at her nape and an expression that said she was all business hurried toward them.

Dressed in blue scrubs with a name tag indicating she was an RN, she drew Mrs. Malone aside for a quick, hushed word, then stepped through the door of Grandma's room.

"Is this normal?" Sarah asked.

"She has her good days and bad days." Mrs. Malone glanced at the half-open door, where the nurse was already trying to communicate with Arlene. "Obviously this isn't one of her best."

The woman was just full of understatements. God, how did she hold down her job?

"We'll come back," Sarah said, and for that Jade was relieved. The sooner she was out of this place, the better.

Outside she finally felt as if she could breathe again and didn't care about the rain pummeling from the dark sky.

"That place is awful!" she declared as her mother hit the remote for the door locks and Jade dashed across the parking lot to flop into the Ford. Her sister and mother were quick to follow, and as Gracie clicked her seat belt, Jade slid a hard look at Sarah. "Just for the record, Mom. I'm *never* going back to that place."

"Of course we are, to see Grandma—"

"Why? She's horrible. And she didn't even recognize you. She even thought you were dead. How weird was that?" Jade fiddled with her own seat belt, securing it before Sarah dived into the same old boring lecture about safety.

"She just confused me with my older sister, Theresa, that's all," Sarah said.

"That's all?" Jade flung her head back against the headrest.

"She's sick, had a stroke, and there's some kind of dementia going on."

"She's lost it. Okay. Fine. I get it. She's got Alzheimer's or whatever," Jade said. "I feel sorry for her. It's sad, okay? But this is just too out there for me, Mom. I don't even know her, and she obviously doesn't want to know me, either. I'm *not* going back there."

"Me, neither," Gracie said from behind her sister. "Jade's right." For once, she was actually in Jade's corner. Hard to believe. "She's all kinds of crazy and—"

"Enough!" their mother snapped in frustration as she started to back out of the parking space, only to slam on the brakes as the car across from them was backing out as well. "Come on, girls! She's *my* mother. *Your* grandmother. Show a little respect and some compassion for a sick woman."

Jade said, "Why? She obviously doesn't want us here. Any of us. And I just don't get why you keep trying to make it seem like it's better than it is."

Sarah closed her eyes a second as the rain drizzled upon the fogging windshield.

"Uh oh," Gracie whispered, and Jade could almost hear their mother counting to ten in her head as she gripped the steering wheel so hard her knuckles blanched. Finally, calmer, she drew in a deep breath and shook her head before backing up again. "She's my mother," Sarah said again, softly. "She raised me."

"Explains a lot," Jade said, then saw a flash of hurt cross her mother's face. Inwardly Jade squirmed, but she set her jaw.

Sarah said, "She wasn't always like this."

Finally, they were headed down the long lane to the main road.

"Mom, Grandma's always been weird. You know it. Anyway, I'm sorry that she's your mother, but that's on you. I'm . . . I'm just saying she's like a witch or something."

"Jade . . . ," she murmured.

Jade wasn't about to back down. "Mom, face it, Grandma's evil."

"For the love of God, she's ill. That's all. Try to dial back the drama."

"That's not all. You keep lying to yourself about her, and other things too. When everything doesn't turn out perfect you're surprised." She saw her mother flinch at that one, but it was just too bad.

"Let's just be nice to Grandma, okay?" Sarah slowed and let a huge truck rumble past, then turned onto the road that led into the heart of Stewart's Crossing. "Show some compassion and empathy. If we're lucky enough, we'll all get to be her age someday."

Like in a million years!

"Okay," was the grumbling assent from the backseat.

"Sure," Jade finally agreed. She did feel a little bad about how harsh she was, but still . . . she remembered Grandma Arlene and what she'd been like as a younger woman. "I'll be as nice to her as she is to me."

"Fine," Sarah said, her eyes steadily forward. If Jade didn't know better, she'd think her mother might actually be agreeing with her.

CHAPTER 7

It was cold. So damned cold.

And dark, the blackness complete.

"Let me out of here!" Rosalie yelled, but her voice was raw, her tone pleading, and though she pounded on the locked wooden door, no one responded. It was as if she was alone in the world, and she wanted to burst into tears again, though falling apart hadn't helped the situation so far. She was locked in a barn of sorts, her "room" a stall with sides so close she could nearly touch each wall if she stood in the middle. The only light that came in was through a window nearly eight or nine feet above the wooden floor. But now, it was dark again, sometime in the early evening, she thought, her stomach rumbling from lack of food.

More scared than she'd ever been in her life, she searched for a way out of this place, just as she had from the second she'd been dumped here. She'd fought and kicked and screamed, furious and terrified all at once. Her voice was raspy, her face felt puffy from crying, and her hands, bound together with tight cuffs in front of her, were bleeding and scraped from pounding on the door. Even her legs hurt; she'd kicked the solid wood panels so hard she'd sent a jarring pain up her right leg.

"Damn it all!" With her two hands clasped together, she rubbed her leg now, but it still ached.

She didn't know where she was, but not horribly far from Stewart's Crossing, she guessed. The entire ride in the truck, from the moment she'd been abducted and driven through the woods and hills, had taken about half an hour, and was less than twenty miles from the diner. She'd kept an eye on the clock and odometer during her abduction to this isolated building in the middle of the woods.

Gone were his sexy smile and cowboy demeanor. The friendly man who'd left great tips and always made pleasant conversation as he'd sipped his coffee had vanished completely, replaced by this stone-faced freak.

Probably the nice man hadn't existed at all; that good-guy façade that had helped trick her had slid off his face to reveal a monster she was certain was capable of murder.

Her mind traveled along dark roads of thought as she considered what he might do to her, and she was nearly physically sick. So far he hadn't touched her, except to bind her, but all that could change, and the thought of what might be her future caused her blood to turn to ice.

You have to stay strong, to be smart, to find a way to change your destiny. Shivering, she swallowed back her fear.

She'd been a fool, she realized. Mentally berating herself, for what had to be the millionth time, for her stupidity in climbing into his truck, she slid down the door to sit on the floor.

Once she'd realized he was kidnapping her, she'd expected him to rape her or torture her or kill her, but so far he'd only hauled her kicking and screaming into this frigid, stark room. A small cot had been pushed into one corner, along with two bottles of water and a bucket to pee in.

"All the comforts of home," he'd said cruelly as he'd dumped her onto the cot with its faded sleeping bag and musty pillow and left her there, still in the damned handcuffs.

She'd spent all night pacing and kicking at the door, alternately crying and screaming, but all the while trying to figure out how to escape and wishing fervently that she'd taken the ride Gloria had offered, that she'd walked straight home and hadn't gotten in the truck, that she'd done anything other than let herself be lured into this awful trap.

"I hate you!" she yelled, and her words almost echoed back at her. She was certain she was alone. All alone.

Would her mother ever find her?

Would that jackass Mel convince Sharon that she'd just pulled her same old trick of staying out all night? Would they start searching?

Please, please, please, she prayed to a God she'd sworn she didn't believe in. *Let someone find me!*

Surely even Mel would start to believe this was serious. Oh, God, she hoped they were searching for her, that someone had seen her get into the jerk-off's truck, that someone recognized the creep, or had taken down the numbers from his license plate or . . .

Oh, it was useless, she thought as she got to her feet and felt tears rain from her eyes again. She crumpled into a heap on the stupid cot and drew the sleeping bag up around her shoulders. It had been a long time already, long enough that she was really hungry as well as scared to death. The bastard wouldn't just leave her here, would he? To starve to death? He wouldn't have left two water bottles if he wanted her to die of thirst. Her mind spun with all kinds of horrid scenarios, and she wondered if something awful had happened to him, and though she hoped it would, who would know where to find her? Maybe she'd just die in this stinky, moldy sleeping bag.

Oh, dear Jesus, she *had* to find a way out of here. Had to! Tears rolled down her cheeks, and with the cuffs digging into her wrists, she brushed them aside.

Mom will find you. She will. You know that.

The trouble was, Rosalie *didn't* know it . . .

She didn't know it at all.

So far she wasn't exactly batting a thousand in the mother department, Sarah thought as she climbed the creaky stairs to the third floor. Her older daughter was brazen and uncaring enough to call her grandmother evil, and her younger daughter was convinced she'd seen a ghost in the premises. Twice. So much for family stability.

Guiltily, Sarah wondered if she'd unwittingly engendered both. She certainly hadn't been particularly kind about her mother, and she too had thought she'd seen an unhappy spirit in this very house. Had she unwittingly said as much to Gracie and exacerbated her younger daughter's fears? Whereas Jade had always been independent and outspoken to a fault, Gracie had been more introverted and experienced difficulty making friends. Sarah crossed her fingers that this move would be a positive change for not only herself but her girls as well.

At the landing she paused. She'd been through all the rooms on this floor and had decided that, once again, the bathroom would have to be taken down to the studs; the master bedroom needed total refurbishing too. The entire house could use new wiring and plumbing, insulation and an overhaul of the heating system.

It would cost a fortune.

"But it'll be so worth it," she reminded herself as she passed the room where her sister had lived. Her footsteps slowed a bit. "Later," she told herself when she had more time. Right now she had to face her own damned demons, so she made her way to the door at the end of the hallway that led to the narrow passage upward into the attic and beyond.

As she stepped through it, anxiety elevated her pulse. Since childhood she'd avoided these stairs, refused to step foot into the attic, but she could do so no longer.

Get a hold of yourself. There is nothing evil in the attic. Nothing.

She flipped on the light switch at the base of the stairs. It clicked loudly, but that was it. The steps and gaping area above remained dark. "Of course," she muttered and clicked on the flashlight of her cell phone to illuminate the stairs. Feeling her neck muscles tighten, she forced herself to climb the steep flight and ignored the beating of her heart and the fear that slid through her veins.

The temperature dropped as she stepped into the attic, where gaps in the shingles caused the wind to whistle and wail and allowed rain to slip inside.

She remembered being up on the widow's walk that night she'd gone to the attic. Frigid rain pelted from an obsidian sky. Her nightgown was soaked, her skin was wet, and a bitter wind cut through her as she shivered. But it was more than winter weather that caused the icy fear in the pit of her stomach. There was something malevolent out there, horrifying enough to make her mind block the memories.

But sometimes bits came through.

She knew that Roger had been here with her.

Or was that later? Had she been delusional, as Arlene had repeatedly told her?

But even now she thought she could recall the calluses on her half brother's hands, fingers that were work-roughened as they closed over her arms. He'd been in his late teens, then, nearly a man, and he'd whispered into her ear. "Everything will be all right." But it had been a lie.

Remembering his hot breath against the shell of her ear, she shuddered. Fear pulsed in her brain. She needed to remember, yet that same mind-numbing dread kept the memory at bay, or so the psychologist she'd seen years before had explained. "It's your subconscious, Sarah, your brain's way of keeping you safe," Dr. Melbourne had said in her soft, dulcet tones. "It's protecting you."

"But I need to know!" she'd insisted as she'd sat on a corner of the couch in Melbourne's office, two rooms in an old house made to look homey, as if in hopes of giving her patients the illusion of a safe haven. Subtle lighting, comfortable furniture, even a hand-knit afghan and a quietly ticking clock, created a feeling of home and hearth. Still she hadn't felt safe and had clenched her fists as she'd tried hard not to hyperventilate. "I have to know what happened to me before I get married." She was desperate not to take her fears into her marriage to Noel McAdams.

"The block will erode. When you're ready. Trust me," Dr. Melbourne had said.

"But I need it gone now," Sarah had insisted.

The doctor had been unable to offer any further assurances, however, so she'd entered into her marriage with Noel, still unclear what her brain was trying to save her from. Since then she'd decided Dr. Melbourne's theory was just so much bullshit . . . until recently, when she'd decided to return to this old house, and a few tiny bits of recollection had begun to break through.

Now she wondered if she were ready for the truth. "Better than not knowing." Or was she kidding herself? Steadying herself at the top of the staircase, she fought the urge to run back down, to close her mind to that dark night.

Why had she been up here? What had she been doing with Roger?

Murky images slithered through her mind, like picture frames that moved too quickly to catch.

"Sarah," Roger had whispered, his voice tight, "don't be frightened . . ."

But she had been. Not just scared, but virtually paralyzed with fear. He'd been too close. She'd smelled him, the sweat, the maleness of him underlain with a hint of alcohol. He'd held her near, and his beard had scraped her cheek as his hand found their way under her legs to carry her . . .

Dear Mother Mary . . .

Now, she tried to grab hold of something, anything that would help her remember, but the images that had been blooming quickly withered into the void once more.

"Son of a bitch," she whispered. She couldn't let this cripple her. With an effort, she pulled herself together and tamped down the feeling that something evil had happened on the roof that night.

"Come on, Sarah. Get over it," she said and shined her phone's tiny beam over decades worth of junk stored under the eaves, where she suspected bats roosted and who knew what else called home. This dark area with its peaked, dripping ceilings, rough rafters, and dusty floors was a perfect hiding spot for all kinds of rodents.

Her skin crawled a little, but she kept on, fanning the beam over old trunks, piles of forgotten books, broken furniture, crates, and stains on the floor that indicated where the roof had leaked.

Picking her way carefully, she made her way to the final stairs and upward, into the cupola. Two of its glass sides were cracked, which was no surprise, but she tried the door and found it swollen shut.

She almost turned back. The old fears had returned, and the excuse that it was a little nuts going out onto the widow's walk in the rain and the dark had a lot of appeal.

But she'd come this far.

"Just do it," she told herself, her hands clammy, her nerves stretched tight. She intended to step outside, onto the widow's walk to stand in the very spot where Angelique Le Duc Stewart had stood nearly a hundred years earlier when, as legend had it, she'd faced her attacker and they'd both fallen to their deaths, their bodies never recovered.

It was the very same spot where Roger had sworn he'd found her, wandering and delirious in the storm. He'd carried her downstairs to the living room, where her father was seated before the fire. Sarah had been five at the time. A child. She'd vowed she didn't remember how she'd ended up there, and her father had been kind, holding her close in his big La-Z-Boy while the rapid click of Arlene's heels on the wooden floor announced her arrival.

"What were you doing up there?" Arlene had demanded as she'd furiously scooped Sarah away from her father. "You know better!" She'd given Sarah a quick little shake, then, catching herself, yanked her daughter close as she'd started to cry. "You scare me, Sarah Jane," Arlene had choked out, her voice cracking, her eyes gray. "Don't you know, you scare me to death!"

She'd smelled of some kind of perfume tinged with the scent of smoke from a recent cigarette. She'd dropped onto the couch, still clutching Sarah as if she were afraid the girl would disappear. "What were you doing up there?"

"I don't know," Sarah answered truthfully.

Arlene hadn't believed her, but Sarah had insisted she had no memory of how she'd ended up on the widow's walk.

Finally her mother gave up. "Well, thank the good Lord that Roger found you!" Arlene had said into her daughter's wet curls as Sarah shivered. "I hate to think what would have happened to you if he hadn't. Now, come on, let's get you in a hot bath to warm you up. Then we'll get you some dry pajamas."

Had she seen a ghost that night? It seemed so. Or had it been something more terrifying, something more visceral? The experience had been terrifying, traumatic, and never resolved, so here she was, in the attic years later, feeling those same cryptic emotions claw at her, even though she'd told herself over and over that whatever had happened up here was long buried.

Arlene, who refused to even consider a resident ghost or anything unexplained, insisted whatever had scared Sarah was all in her mind—the result of a fever or bad over-the-counter drugs coupled with a child's overactive imagination.

Until today Sarah had never passed the door to the upper staircase without the skin on the back of her arms breaking out in goose bumps, a visceral warning, while a tenebrous childhood memory shifted in the nether regions of her brain.

Now, she pressed her forehead to the cool glass of the cupola and closed her eyes for a second, taking in a deep breath.

Forget it. Let it go. You're a woman now. A mother. Not a scared little girl.

With renewed determination, she tried once again to open the door to the roof.

"Come on, come on," she said, pushing hard until at last the door burst open and she fell forward, catching herself before she did a face plant on the slick widow's walk.

The air outside was heavy and moist, with rain falling and wind rushing through the gorge that surrounded the river far below.

Using her flashlight, she examined the roof tiles and railing, but it was much too dark to make a valid assessment.

The roof around the flat widow's walk was pitched and gabled with steep dormers and chimneys, and the dome of the cupola spiked upward. Venturing to the railing, Sarah stared across a sloped area of the roof to look straight down to the cliff on which the house was mounted. Though it was too dark to see the Columbia River, she heard it roaring as it pursued its swift path westward.

What had happened to Angelique Le Duc Stewart that night nearly a hundred years earlier? Her body had never been found, nor had anyone seen her husband, Maxim, again. There were rumors of a horrible fight, a story said to have started with Maxim's daughter, Helen, who had witnessed a horrifying struggle between them on this very roof.

It had been theorized by the townspeople of Stewart's Crossing, and confirmed by Maxim's children, that Angelique and Maxim, locked in a stormy marriage, had clashed in their final battle high on this rooftop, only to fall to their deaths in the icy, furious river.

Sarah's skin prickled again at the thought, her blood turning cold. She understood about fury within a relationship, anger and fear and, yes, even violence, with those you most loved, but still she felt a darkness in her soul, and when she looked westward, following the river's swath through the gorge, her mind's eye saw Angelique and Maxim, wrestling here—each with a weapon, according to legend— fighting on this slippery rooftop with its short railing.

According to stories passed on by generations, Maxim had been after her with an axe, had chased Angelique ever upward until she had nowhere to go but over the edge. Had she jumped for her life? Tried to escape? Or been thrown over the railing and fallen to her death?

She heard a scrape of something—a footstep?—over the howl of the wind and looked back to the open door to the cupola. No way. She was alone up here. No sane person would want to be up here in the storm, though of course she'd climbed those last few steps, hadn't she?

Nerves strung tight, she glanced over the nightscape of the roof and, of course, saw no one. No person. No ghost. Nothing.

Get over yourself. Sheesh! No reason to be jittery.

Blinking against the rain, she peered over the edge of the railing and squinted, searching for the river she could hear and smell but, in the pitch-black night, could not see.

She envisioned a beautiful woman tumbling through the darkness, white dress billowing around her, dark hair flying wildly, the roiling water below ready to swallow her—

Bang!

The loud sound ricocheted off the roof.

Sarah jumped.

Her feet slipped.

Biting back a scream, she caught herself with one hand on the top rail.

From the corner of her eye, she saw a flutter of white, that very same billowing white dress!

The ghost! Again! Just like before . . .

Pulse pounding in her ears, she turned, half expecting to catch a glimpse of a specter disappearing like smoke into the darkness.

"Mom?" Gracie's scared little voice reached her just as she recognized her daughter shivering in the rain—just as she had done thirty years earlier.

Oh, sweet Jesus. Sarah nearly collapsed, the sense of déjà vu overwhelming.

"Gracie?" she whispered, having trouble finding her voice. Gracie's face was ghostly white, her hair in wild, wet ringlets. "What're you doing?" Sarah's voice was a little sharp, an edge of panic to it. She hurried toward her daughter. "Let's go back inside."

"What're you doing?" Gracie echoed. She was in her nightgown, her feet bare, again, much the way Sarah had been nearly thirty years earlier.

"Checking out the roof."

"In the middle of a storm? At night?"

"Not my smartest move. Come on, let's get out of the rain." She decided that she wouldn't mention anything about facing down her own fears, not just yet. After shepherding Gracie inside again, she yanked the door to the cupola shut behind them, then followed her daughter down the spiral staircase leading to the attic. "You're soaked," Sarah said, one hand on Gracie's shoulder as they followed the bluish beam of the flashlight through the maze of clutter in the cold garret.

"So are you!"

"I'm wearing a jacket."

"Big deal."

"Hey, it's something." Over Gracie's shoulder, Sarah shined her bluish beam from her phone down the next steep flight downward. "You don't have a flashlight?" Her panic was subsiding, the spike in her adrenaline declining. She finally regained her equilibrium as they reached the steps to the third floor.

"Nah."

"How did you find your way? It's a rabbit warren of junk up here."

Gracie lifted a shoulder. "Dunno," she said as they stepped onto the worn floorboards of the upper hallway and, after Sarah secured the door to the attic, started toward the main stairs. That's how it always had been with Gracie. Sometimes it was as if she possessed some kind of heightened precognition; other times she was a regular kid.

"You've got to be freezing," Sarah said, trying to usher her daughter toward the main stairs.

But Gracie stopped dead in her tracks at Theresa's room and grabbed the doorknob. "Something happened in here."

Sarah's newfound equilibrium took a hit. "Of course things happened in there," she said. "Just like in every room. The house is nearly a hundred years—"

"I mean something *bad* happened in here." Gracie was shaking her head.

"What do you mean?"

"I'm not sure." She turned the knob, and as the door creaked open, she stepped into the bedroom.

"Gracie, no. Let's go," Sarah said, wishing her kid wouldn't do this kind of thing, that Gracie would just play soccer, or be attached to her smartphone as if it were a lifeline, or hang out with friends . . . just not be such a loner. "Have you talked to your dad? Told him about the move?"

But her daughter wasn't listening. Nor did she bother to snap on the overhead light. "It's cold in here," she whispered, and her breath actually fogged a bit.

"Of course it is. There isn't any heat and you're soaked."

Sarah flipped the switch, and pale light filtered from one of the two bare bulbs from the broken fixture overhead. "And the window doesn't seal, and the damper in the fireplace is probably broken, causing a draft."

"That's not what I meant."

Sarah paused, then gave up. "Yeah, I know."

Biting her lower lip, Gracie walked to the fireplace and touched the mantel, her gaze traveling to the cracked mirror. "What happened here?"

"I really don't know. It was my sister's room."

"But not Dee Linn's, right? She was on the second floor with you and Uncle Jake and Joe."

"That's right." They'd discussed some of this before. "It's Theresa's room. You never met her, and I don't really remember her, either."

"Huh." Gracie picked up a small figurine, a statue of the Madonna that had been standing alone on the mantel for decades. "Kind of weird." Gracie blew the dust from the tiny statue. "And no one knows what happened to her?"

"Everyone says she ran away."

"Do you believe that?"

"I don't know what to believe. Mom says she's alive somewhere, that Theresa ran away because she couldn't follow the rules of the house, that my father was too strict."

"Was he?"

"Not with us, but he might've been different with Theresa and Roger. They were older, his stepkids."

"Where was their dad?"

"Dead. He'd died a year earlier, I think. Mom was a widow when she married Dad. We can talk about this downstairs, after you're changed."

But Gracie seemed a million miles away as she rotated the little statue in her hands.

"Honey?" Sarah prodded, feeling a chill that had nothing to do with the temperature in the room.

"You think she's dead?"

Oh, Lord. "Maybe. I hope not." Feeling as if she were walking across her sister's grave, Sarah crossed the short distance to Gracie and plucked the ceramic Madonna from her fingers.

"But, Mom, something happened here, didn't it?" Gracie pressed, turning her white face to her mother. "Something really bad." Sarah's blood turned to ice, as her words from a world away echoed in her mind.

"What happened in here?" Sarah had demanded after Arlene had caught her snooping. "Something bad."

Arlene's response had been instantaneous. She'd clamped her fingers around Sarah's arm and dragged her youngest daughter into the hallway. "Don't you ever go in there again. Do you hear me? If I catch you, Sarah Jane, I swear, I'll make you stay in your bedroom for a month! How would you like that?" she'd threatened as she'd closed the door to Theresa's room and found her key. Her jaw had been set, her color ashen, her fingers quivering as she'd locked the door.

Once the room was secure, she'd let out her breath and leaned against the oak panels. Seeing that her fingers were still gripping Sarah's arm, she'd let go immediately, almost as if she'd been burned. Tears had welled in her eyes, and she'd knelt before her youngest. "Oh, honey, I'm sorry," she'd whispered, nose to nose, as light from the lower floors illuminated the stairwell. "I don't know what got into me."

Sarah hadn't bought that. She believed to this day that Arlene had understood her motives clearly.

With one hand, her mother had pushed a lock of hair off her forehead and glanced at the ceiling, as if she were waging some inner battle with herself. "But you mustn't go into Theresa's room again, all right?"

"Why?" Sarah had demanded, the handprint on her upper arm still visible.

Arlene's gaze had traveled from the mark on Sarah's arm to her eyes. She must've seen some kind of defiance or even a spark of hatred in them because she'd grabbed Sarah then and held her tight, the smells of her perfume and last cigarette still lingering. "I just want you to be safe, baby, that's all," she'd said, and it had seemed heartfelt, her voice cracking. When she'd held her daughter at arm's length to impress upon Sarah how sincere she was, Arlene had even blinked against tears shimmering in her eyes. "Believe me, I just want to keep you safe."

Now, standing in the very bedroom she'd been warned to leave alone, Sarah wanted desperately to say the same things to her own child.

Instead, she'd cleared her throat and said, "Come on, let's get downstairs and make some hot chocolate. Tomorrow's a big day. The last one before you start school."

"I know. Ugh." Gracie was less than enthused, but at least she didn't argue. As Sarah shepherded her daughter out of the room and snapped off the light, she saw the peaceful little Madonna statuette upon the ledge, and just for a second, she was certain the serene little Mary stared right back.

CHAPTER 8

Rosalie threw back the top of the musty old sleeping bag. She was sick of lying here in this miserable horse barn, sick of crying her eyes out, and really sick of feeling so damned helpless. What was it her Gram had always said? "The good Lord helps those who help themselves." That was starting to make a lot of sense.

She'd spent the last two days covered on her cot, wishing her mother or the police or *some*-damned-body would show up to rescue her, and so far, it hadn't happened.

He'd returned for all of five minutes, scaring the crap out of her as she'd heard an engine, the outer door creak open, and the ring of his boots along the old floorboards, louder and louder with each purposeful stride.

She'd cowered in the corner, holding her sleeping bag to her chin, her eyes following his every move. He'd stayed near the door, blocking her escape, and had dropped off a microwave meal that had been heated but was by then cold, then emptied her crude chamber pot and left a couple more bottles of water.

When he'd tried to engage her, she'd kept a stony silence, and that had really pissed him off.

"Better learn some manners, girl," he'd said with a knowing smile. "Real quick." Then he'd slammed the door shut and disappeared.

She shivered at the memory.

How could she ever have trusted him?

Now, the barn was silent. Not even the sound of quick thuds and scurrying footsteps of squirrels disturbing the silence. *Do something. Anything.*

You have to get out of here, Rosalie. Just because he hasn't raped or tortured or killed you yet, doesn't mean he won't.

Tamping down the fears that had been her constant companion since he'd kidnapped her, she decided to make use of the few hours of daylight that illuminated this prison cell of a room. She rolled to her feet, and tried the door again. Of course it was locked tight. She didn't bother with screaming or yelling as her voice was already raw; she'd exhausted herself trying to get someone outside to hear her by banging on the walls and shrieking at the top of her lungs for what seemed like hours.

All to no avail.

Think, she told herself now. All she had were her wits, and though her grades in school had never shown her intelligence, she knew she was smart. Hadn't those IQ tests she'd taken shocked the socks off of Mrs. Landers, the school counselor who'd about written her off as a total loser?

So now she had to use those brains to her advantage. Since screaming and threats hadn't moved her captor, she thought she should pull out her acting skills, make him think her spirit was broken, that she'd become docile, and go along with him so that he would trust her and she could find a means of escape.

At the very thought of playing the weak little girl she actually gagged. She couldn't play meek and malleable when all she wanted to do was rip the guy's throat out, cut off his balls, and gouge his eyes for doing this to her. The thought of hanging her head and pretending to curl up in fear at the sight of him galled her.

No effin' way was that going to happen.

She'd find a way out of this prison or die trying.

She looked through the room again, searching for some way out or at the very least a weapon.

Nothing at first glance.

And the window was too high. Even if she managed to tilt the cot up on its end, she wouldn't be able to climb it and reach the window and slip through. The old glass was probably thin and might break easily, but it was made up of small panes surrounded by a wooden frame. The door was solid. She'd already tried.

However, the walls of the stall didn't reach the ceiling. There was about two and a half feet of open space between the sides of the box and the beams running overhead. If she climbed up on the cot to hoist herself over the wall, she could land on the other side and maybe get out that way. Unless that stall was locked as well. But why would it be? It was empty.

She eyed the opening. She'd have to balance the cot against the wall and reach up to loop her hands over the edge. They were cuffed, but not useless. If she managed to pull her body to the top of the stall, she could peer into it, see that it was safe, roll over and drop down on the other side.

It was worth a try, right?

Except that the cot was lightweight, with a thin aluminum frame that wouldn't support any kind of weight when it was turned on end. The legs were short and folded inward for storage. Trying to balance on them would be tricky.

"Nothing ventured, nothing gained," she said, quoting Grams again.

It was now or never.

After pushing the fabric side of the cot against the wall, she tried to climb onto the legs. *Bam!* She fell immediately, landing hard on the floor. Pain rocketed up her spine, and the tiny bed tumbled backward to land upside down on her.

"Damn it!"

Not good.

But she wasn't giving up. Once she'd caught her breath, she turned the stupid cot onto its end again and, gently, being careful with her weight, attempted to rest her body on it. Once stable, she slowly dragged her feet under her. She managed to plant one foot on the short leg, then slowly draw her other foot up the side and—

Thunk!

Down she came again.

Her head banged hard against the floor, and the damned cot fell atop her once more.

"Shit!" she cried in frustration, and tears filled her eyes. "Shit, shit,

shit!" She kicked the flimsy bed to one side and lay on the floor staring upward at the rafters high above. Her head throbbed, and her back ached. She was no better off than she'd been when she started. In fact, she was worse, considering her injuries.

Rosalie wanted to cry, to break down in bitter tears. She hoped her mother would come for her, but she knew deep in her heart that she was on her own. She'd have to rely on her own wits and agility to save herself.

Or else, most likely, she would die.

Our Lady of the River was even lamer than it sounded.

Jade thought she'd prepared herself, that she'd formed a pretty good idea of how bad it would be before she ever pushed open the wide glass doors with the name of the school and two angels etched into them, but she'd been wrong. The place was positively archaic, with its stained-glass windows, shiny linoleum floors, and pictures of saints decorating the walls.

But she was stuck.

At least for a while.

Hiking up her backpack, she headed toward the school offices. She hated transferring schools and being the new kid all over again. It had happened twice before in her lifetime and it sucked big-time. As a junior she wondered how she'd survive this place, with its already established cliques and social strata.

Maybe she didn't want to know.

Now, the hallway was empty, its floors gleaming, a beat-up bank of lockers flanking one side, floor-to-ceiling windows letting in light on the other. Deep down, she knew that this was the first day of what would be the school year from hell. She'd be the new kid again, taunted, teased, maybe bullied and alone for at least a while—until some nerd or geek or worse took pity on her and tried to welcome her into a pathetic circle of the socially unacceptable.

Rather than dwell on the inevitable, she texted Cody again and told him she wanted him to visit her here. She'd rather drive to Vancouver, of course, but with her car on lockdown in the shop, that was impossible.

She found a sign pointing her toward the counseling offices, and she headed in that direction, grateful that for once, her mother hadn't insisted on joining her, even though Sarah had made noises about escorting her into the school and introducing herself to the counselor.

Inwardly Jade shuddered. She'd made Sarah drop her off a block down the street and had entered through a back door near the cafeteria, where the smells of tomato sauce battled with an underlying odor of pine-scented cleanser. There was just no need to have another reason for the kids to make fun of her. They'd have plenty already. And though Sarah had seemed a little wounded about Jade's refusal, she'd acquiesced. After all, she'd done enough damage by registering Jade at this freaky old school, the very high school where Sarah had been a student.

Just effin' . . . perfect.

Of course Jade had been forced to wear the Our Lady of the River uniform, and it was about as bad as it could be: Plaid skirt to her knees, white blouse, uncomfortable navy blue jacket.

Save me, she thought as she walked past a huge mural of a Crusader astride a white horse. A red cross was emblazoned upon his white tunic, and he wielded a long, deadly-looking sword in his right hand. The painting was immense, filling an impossibly tall wall near the gym. Jade stared at it briefly, then wended her way past the athletic department and through a rabbit warren of offices that, aside from the computers, looked like they were straight out of the 1800s.

The counselor was waiting for her in a tiny office filled with notebooks and stacks of papers and smelling of invisible, hundred-year-old dust that couldn't be hidden by any amount of room freshener. For the next hour Jade tried not to slouch in an uncomfortable plastic chair while the sickeningly pleasant Miss Smith, a redhead with doe eyes, receding chin, worry lines creasing a huge forehead, and a patient smile "worked out the kinks" in Jade's schedule. While her fingers flew over the keyboard of a computer, she kept talking about boring extracurricular activities and clubs she was certain Jade would "just love."

Worse yet, the slim woman was obviously as nervous as she was. Miss Smith's fingers shook a little on the computer keys when they weren't hooking and rehooking a wayward lock of hair over her ear.

The minutes crawled by while they were tweaking the schedule until, in the end, Miss Smith declared it perfect.

Yeah, right. Nothing about this place comes close to perfect, Jade thought, climbing to her feet.

"Wait!" the counselor called out to her, getting up from her chair. "I need to get you a hard copy."

"Oh."

"Also, at our Lady of the River, each new student is assigned an 'angel' to help with the first week or two of school. You know, to help out and show you the ropes, so to speak."

"Why? So they can hang themselves?" It just slipped out. Jade was tired and cranky and nearly sick to her stomach at being here, but she knew immediately from the way Miss Smith's face shut down, she'd goofed. "Sorry," Jade mumbled quickly, "just a joke."

The prim counselor cleared her throat. "In any event, we like every new student to feel included and make friends. You might not yet know it, but recently a local girl went missing, so we're doubling our efforts to make sure no one is ever alone at Our Lady."

"Isn't it safe here?" Jade asked.

"Of course! But, um, you can never be too safe, can you?"

For once Jade held her tongue. She didn't blurt out another smart-ass quip about God watching over the hallowed halls of this school because she was stuck here for now, and it didn't make sense to make things any worse than they already were.

"So," Miss Smith went on, as the printer purred and spat out Jade's "final" schedule, "Mary-Alice Eklund, your personal angel, should be arriving shortly. Her friends call her Mary-A."

Oh joy. Jade could hardly wait.

Miss Smith stepped into another office to retrieve the documents and returned with a pasted-on smile and several pages. Appearing as relieved as Jade that their meeting was about over, she straightened the pages that held Jade's schedule, map, and student rights information, then crisply tapped the edges on her desk and slid them into the stapler before pounding it with her fist. "Oh, here's Mary-Alice now." Miss Smith's grin widened as a fresh-faced blond girl wearing the standard Our Lady uniform, lips shiny with gloss, and a perky ponytail nearly bounced into the small room.

"Hi!" the blond girl enthused. She was petite, had perfect skin, and a cute little smile that didn't quite touch her eyes. "Welcome to Our Lady!"

Jade forced out a "thanks" she didn't mean.

"Trust me, you're gonna love it here."

Jade merely lifted her brows.

Quick introductions were made, and before Jade could scream, "Let me outta here," they were off, out of the claustrophobic office and back into the wide hallway. From inside her hot-pink purse, Mary-Alice's cell phone rang. Without breaking stride, she checked the screen, frowned, then dropped it back into a pocket and just kept on talking.

Mary-Alice was a senior and captain of the dance team as well as "on student council and a member of honor society," she'd said, almost as if she thought Jade might be impressed by her résumé.

Jade was marched quickly through the maze of hallways, Mary-Alice chattering on about the benefits of attending the private school. "This is the social science wing, where you'll have American history." She pointed to an offshoot of the main corridor. "And the library is upstairs. Watch out for Sister Donna. She's kind of old school. Thinks no one should utter a word and is always shushing everyone." She tossed Jade a knowing grin before bouncing down the halls and introducing Jade to a few of the teachers. Most of them weren't nuns, but they all had the same enthusiasm about the school that Mary-Alice exuded.

It was enough to make Jade consider running for her life.

Worse yet, they ran into a priest walking in the other direction.

Oh, great. She hated trying to make small talk with priests or monks or anyone in the church, for that matter.

"Father Paul!" Mary-A waved and was quick to gain his attention.

Jade wanted to disappear.

A stooped man in gray slacks and matching jacket, the priest wore a black shirt with a clerical collar. His was one of those bland faces with a practiced, oh-so-patient smile. Father Paul had to be eighty, maybe older. His hair was thick and snowy, his face a craggy landscape that suggested his life, or priesthood, hadn't been easy.

"This is a new student, Jade McAdams," Mary-Alice introduced.

"Hello," he said and took Jade's hand, holding it in both of his a little too long. "Welcome. I hope you like it here." She didn't say a word, just nodded and pulled her hand out of his warm clasp as soon as she could. "You know, Our Lady of the River is an excellent school with a wonderful, caring staff and a student body of good, Christian children."

You bet, Padre.

"Wait a second. You're Sarah's daughter, right?" he asked.

Jade froze. He remembered her mother? "Yeah, er, yes."

His thoughtful expression didn't change. "I knew her when she was just a girl and I was the assistant priest here. Years ago. In fact I remember your grandfather too."

"They attended Mass?" This was news to Jade. She couldn't imagine her grandmother, head bowed, hands clasped as she prayed on a kneeler in the large church attached to this school. Maybe her grandfather came alone, or with his kids?

Father Paul wagged his hand in a "maybe yes, maybe no" motion. Jade tried to keep her face as emotionless as Father Paul's. She'd never heard about any member of the family attending Mass, except maybe at Christmas and sometimes Easter. Not that it mattered.

"I don't know if your parents shared this with you, Jade, but Angelique Le Duc Stewart actually started this school. She donated the funds for the original building, which was much smaller than this, of course, but the point is, she's the reason Our Lady of the River is here today." He spread his hands and finally his grin seemed sincere. "What incredible foresight she had."

Jade hadn't heard this before, didn't know if he was telling the truth or just jerking her around, but the good news was there was a tiny bit of horror showing on Mary-Alice's perfect features.

"Really?" Jade asked.

"Absolutely. The town may have been named after her husband, Maxim, but this school owes its very existence to his wife."

Mary-A looked as if she'd just been shot. "Jade's great-grandmother?"

"A few more greats than that, I think," the priest said, and Jade didn't bother to mention that she wasn't related to Angelique, that her great-great-great-grandmother was Maxim's first wife, Myrtle.

"That can't be right," Jade's "angel" finally said, obviously upstaged, and Jade decided not to correct the priest. Let them all think what they wanted. Who cared?

"I assure you it is." The priest was firm, and for the first time gave Jade a look that almost convinced her he knew how awkward she felt. More sincerely, he said, "I hope you enjoy your time at Our Lady, Ms. McAdams." And then he was on his way.

For a few seconds, Mary-Alice was struck silent, her gaze following his figure as he rounded a corner at the far end of the hall near the gym.

Through no fault of her own, Jade realized she'd trumped the girl assigned to make her feel welcome and fit in. Assessing the spark of annoyance in Mary-Alice's eyes, Jade decided this bit of information probably wouldn't serve her well, at least not with Mary-A and her crowd.

"Okay, so let's get going," Mary-A suggested. "More to see." Her voice was a little curter, a little less friendly as she lifted her pointed chin a notch and started leading Jade toward a back staircase. "By the way, just a heads-up here: You should really answer 'Yes, Father' when any of the priests talk to you."

"I did."

"Nuh-uh." Mary-A arched one of her neatly plucked brows as they took a flight of steps down to a lower level, their shoes clattering on the stairs.

"I think I said—"

"No," she shook her head, blond ponytail wagging. "Trust me. You said, 'Yeah,' when he asked about your mom."

"Whatever."

"I'm just giving you the protocol."

"Maybe I don't care about protocol."

Mary-Alice's eyes slitted for a second. "Don't you want to fit in?"

Reaching the lower level, Jade lifted a shoulder. "Not sure it's gonna happen." People like this prim girl with her hair pulled back and round, innocent eyes bugged the crap out of Jade. " 'By the way, got a cigarette?"

"What?" Mary-Alice looked appalled, though Jade had spotted a pack of cigarettes in her bag when Mary-Alice had been checking her phone. "No! Why would you think I smoked?"

"Saw the pack."

Color rose on the older girl's cheeks. "Those are Liam's."

"Who's Liam?"

"My boyfriend."

"Don't tell me." Jade said, mimicking her guide's snarky tone. "The quarterback."

Mary-Alice's face tightened. "Has anyone ever told you that you're not as clever as you think you are?"

"Oh, maybe a few hundred times."

"Maybe you should rethink your attitude."

Jade actually smiled, loving that she'd gotten the suck-up's goat.

"And just to set the record straight, Liam Longstreet doesn't play football. He's into soccer."

"Same difference."

Mary-A rolled her eyes before letting out a long-suffering sigh. "If you're so smart, you'd know that 'same difference' is an oxymoron."

"Oh, I know a moron when I see one."

"You're a—" If she hadn't seen a nun, her long habit billowing around her, just then, Mary-Alice might actually have sworn and slapped the grin off Jade's face. Instead she forced a smile over locked teeth. "Hello, Sister Millicent," she said to the nun, but the heavyset woman was marching past, obviously on a mission, her rosary clacking with each stride; she either didn't hear Mary-Alice's greeting or chose to ignore it.

"Guess she's busy," Jade observed dryly.

"Come on, let's go back to the library and I'll show you—"

"Forget it. The tour's over."

"But it's my job—" Mary-Alice feigned surprise.

"Screw your job. Better yet, just leave me alone. I'm firing you."

"You can't fire me!"

"Sure I can. Go be somebody else's angel." Jade started walking in the other direction.

"You're making a big mistake."

"I've already made a lot of them." Jade had met a dozen Mary-A's at previous schools. She started to turn away but stopped. "And, you know, you might 'rethink' your choice of boyfriends."

"What's that supposed to mean?"

"Serious athletes don't mess with their lungs, and if they ever did, they probably wouldn't smoke some old lady brand." She paused. "Virginia Super Slims?" she asked. "Really? What is this, the nineteen eighties?"

"You're such a piece of . . . work," Mary-Alice said, her façade finally slipping completely, her mask of ebullience giving way to straight-out scorn.

"Probably."

"But you won't get away with it, you know. God's going to punish you!"

"Trust me, he already has," Jade said, looking around the empty hallways of a school that Angelique Le Duc had started. To Jade they represented the nine circles of hell.

"It could get worse," Mary-Alice warned.

"Could it?"

The blonde bristled, about to explode, when she caught herself and let out her breath slowly. "Oh, Jade," she finally said, as if she really cared, "you just don't want to know."

"You're right. I don't."

Mary-Alice opened her mouth to say something more, changed her mind, then turned her back on Jade and stormed off, an "angel" with her jaw set, her fists clenched, her ponytail swinging with each determined stride, and no sign of a halo to be seen.

CHAPTER 9

Sarah saw Gracie nearly trip as she got off the bus. Fortunately, she caught herself, but not before a ripple of ugly laughter slipped through the closing doors. The faces of several kids were pressed against the bus windows, mingled breaths fogging the glass, wide nasty grins mocking as one of the boys pointed a fat finger at Gracie.

"Rough day?" Sarah asked, hating the fact that her child had to go through the social trauma of being the new kid. The big yellow behemoth rumbled off, belching exhaust.

"It was okay," Gracie said without any inflection, then sneaked a glance over her shoulder as if to make certain the bus and its load of students was well out of earshot.

God, kids could be so cruel, the bullies ready to pounce on the weak. It really bothered Sarah, but she didn't spout off. Yet.

"Do you like your teachers?"

"Miss Marsh for homeroom is fine, I guess." Again, no interest as they picked their way along the twin ruts of pebbles, dead weeds, and potholes that were the private drive leading from the county road to the house. A stiff wind was blowing, the smell of rain heavy in the air, though no drops had yet fallen.

"What about the others? Is the jury still out?" As usual, getting her daughter to talk about what happened during her day was like pulling teeth.

Gracie shrugged.

"Meet any new friends?"

"Maybe Scottie," Gracie said, then added quickly, "she's a girl."

Shifting her backpack to her other shoulder, she glanced up at Sarah with eyes that knew far more than most twelve-year-old's. "I asked why she had a boy's name, and she said her dad wanted a son so her mom came up with the name. Cuz her dad's Scott."

"Makes sense."

"Maybe." Gracie kicked a rock out of her path, and it flew into the brush flanking the drive and startled a bird. Gracie watched the finch flutter from one tiny branch to another higher in the leafless canopy overhead.

"But you like her, right? Scottie?"

Gracie wrinkled her nose. "Don't really know yet. She sits by me in homeroom and is sorta friendly."

"Well, that's good."

No response, and for a second Sarah wondered if her daughter had even heard her. Finally she said, "Gracie, everything went okay, right?"

Gracie's eyebrows drew together, and Sarah felt that familiar twist to her stomach, a feeling that came over her whenever she sensed things weren't going well with either of her kids. "It just takes time," she said as much to herself as her child.

Rounding the corner, they walked out of the shelter of the trees to the clearing where the house and outbuildings dominated the landscape and they could hear the sound of the river rushing far below. Gracie glanced up at the house and Sarah tensed.

Please don't tell me you see a ghost. Please.

"Mom?" Gracie asked.

Here it comes. "Yeah?"

Her face was clouded. "Nothing."

"Something's bothering you, isn't it?" Sarah asked, bracing herself as a breeze rustled the remaining leaves.

"Maybe."

Sarah's gut tightened a little bit more. "What is it?"

"Scottie says that our house is haunted and that everybody knows it."

"People talk."

"She said a woman was murdered in it. Not just died, but was killed. She's talking about Angelique Le Duc."

"We've been over this."

"Yeah, but I didn't know that you saw her too. Scottie's mom said that everyone in town knows that *you* saw the ghost when you lived here with Grandpa and Grandma."

Sarah didn't know Scottie's mom, but at that moment she wanted to strangle the woman.

"Why didn't you tell me you saw the lady in the white dress too? Why did you let Jade make fun of me and—"

"No, I didn't do that, Gracie. Listen to me," she said, grabbing her daughter's shoulder, only to have Gracie spin away from her.

"Yes, you did, Mom. You let me think that I was wrong. That I didn't see what I know I saw, and *you saw it too*." She started running toward the house.

"Crap," Sarah muttered under her breath. She'd bungled it. She took off after her daughter, catching up to her at the front steps when Gracie stopped short. "I was just trying to protect you."

"By lying to me?" Gracie said. "By letting me think that I might be going crazy and imagining it when I knew I really did see it?"

She mentally kicked herself. "I didn't mean to make a mess of things." Her daughter glared at her. "Okay, so I did, and yeah, years ago I thought I saw a ghost too."

"Where?"

"In my room."

"In *your* room?"

Sarah nodded. "Sometimes I'd wake up and I'd think she was there, and then nothing. I thought it might be dreams. Once I was on the roof and"—how could she explain what she didn't understand herself?—"that time I don't really know what I saw. I couldn't re-member. But I was on the widow's walk when they found me."

You mean you were up there with Roger.

Tiny, icy fingers seemed to crawl up her spine when she thought of her older half brother.

"But it was the lady in the white dress. That's her, isn't it? The one who was killed by her husband? Angelique Le Duc?"

"I assume so . . ."

"It is her. I know it is. Scottie said she—Angelique—was chopped to death with an axe up on the roof, and there was blood everywhere, running down and gurgling in the gutters to spill out all around the house. She said that my great-great-great-grandpa did it, he killed her and cut off her head and—"

"Wait! Whoa!" Horrified, Sara was shaking her head. "Slow down, okay? This is all crazy talk. No one knows what happened, but I'm sure it wasn't something so gruesome."

"Well, someone must know how she died," Gracie charged. "They have to."

"How?"

"Don't *you?*"

"No. Of course not."

"Scottie said her body floated down the river and over the falls and disappeared and that someone found the head on the banks right around the spot where that diner is now."

"Oh, for the love of God. No. That's all a lie." Sarah placed a reassuring hand on her daughter's shoulder, only to have Gracie shove away from her. "It's fiction woven with fact, Gracie. You've read what happened in books and on the Internet? None of those awful rumors were ever substantiated."

"So, it's not true?" Gracie wasn't letting her off the hook.

"People love to talk and make things worse than they are. And I'm sorry I fudged a little about telling you the truth."

"It wasn't 'fudging,' Mom, it was lying."

"I won't do it again," she said. Rain was beginning to fall in earnest, running down Sarah's neck. "What are we doing out here?" Together they climbed the three steps of the porch. "And just one more thing, Celilo Falls, when they existed, were upriver from this house. There's no way a body could float upstream."

Gracie thought that over silently.

"Angelique disappeared, and no one knows what happened to her. That much is true."

"And to her husband?"

"Maxim went missing too. Some people think they ran off together."

"And just left all their kids?" Gracie said incredulously. "They had five of them. At least he did, with his first wife. I already researched it. So, no, I don't think they just ran off. What kind of parents would do that?" she asked before her face fell and Sarah realized her daughter was considering the actions of her own father. After the divorce, Noel McAdams had taken the first flight out of the Northwest to Savannah, Georgia.

"I guess we'll never know." She unlocked the front door, and they stepped inside, where it was a few degrees warmer and dry, if still gloomy and depressing.

"I think he killed her," Gracie decided, shrugging out of her backpack and dropping it onto the marble floor of the foyer. "Like in a fit of anger like you see on *CSI*."

"A crime of passion?" Sarah asked as Gracie peeled off her jacket. "Maybe you should be watching something else."

"Like what? *Teen Mom* or *Here Comes Honey Boo Boo* or maybe one of those real housewives shows? That's what Scottie likes. She watches them with her mom."

"Okay, rewind. Forget I said that."

Gracie said, "I think once Maxim realized what he'd done, that he'd actually killed his wife, he went on the run. Maybe jumped into the river and swam to the other side. Went to Canada somehow, or followed the river to Portland and caught a freighter or a train. Just disappeared so he wasn't caught and hanged. They did that then, you know. Hanged people. I've seen pictures."

Sarah shook her head. Gracie was only twelve, too young, she thought, to be dealing with these kinds of issues. But there it was.

"Don't let the kids at school get to you. What happened here nearly a hundred years ago is a mystery that will probably never be solved."

"Not unless someone cares. That's why I think the ghost appeared to me. She wants me to find out what happened." Gracie walked into the dining room and draped her jacket over the back of a chair.

"You know, Stewart's Crossing is a small town, and it was a lot smaller back then," Sarah reminded her. "Sometimes people in a place this size just like to talk and speculate. Make more of something than there really was."

"I did see her, Mom," Gracie said, on her way into the kitchen.

"Gracie, I know you saw something, but—"

"Don't!" Gracie turned quickly and glared at her mother. "You're doing it again—messing with the truth. *You* know what I saw!"

Sarah regarded her uneasily and finally conceded, "Okay. I *thought* I saw something. Years ago. I was a lot younger than you. But the truth is that I'm not sure anymore what I saw, or even if I did. At the time I was convinced. Was it a ghost? I don't know. Probably not. A bad dream? A shadow? Again, I'd only be guessing. But whatever it was, whether a figment of my imagination or a shadow or something unexplained, it certainly wasn't malevolent, or . . . evil or anything. It was just there. So I don't think we have anything to worry about. There's nothing malevolent haunting the place."

"I'm not worried," Gracie stated matter-of-factly. "I just don't like being teased."

"Is that what Scottie did? Tease you?" Immediately Sarah's protective-mother feathers were ruffled.

"No, not really. Like I said, she's friendly, but some of the boys overheard her."

"And what?"

"They just called me a ghost whisperer and laughed like hyenas." She rolled her eyes. "Morons."

"I bet they were trying to get you to notice them."

"I did," she said once they were in the kitchen. "I noticed that they were big, fat losers."

"Forget them. How about a fiber bar or a fruit snack? I'm afraid that's all I've got."

"I don't care what they think or what they say," Gracie said, showing her grit again. She found a box of fiber bars, picked out a peanut butter one and climbed onto a kitchen stool. "I know Angelique's going to keep haunting this place until we find out the truth so that she can pass over."

"Okay," Sarah said, trying to lighten the mood, but Gracie was having none of it.

"Don't humor me," she said. With deft fingers, she opened the fiber bar and announced, "I'm going to help her."

Before she could ask how, Sarah's cell phone vibrated. Retrieving it from her pocket, she saw her sister's name and profile picture flash onto the screen.

"Hi, Dee," she answered.

"Sarah. Have you heard?" Dee Linn's voice held a tremulous note of panic. "A local girl's gone missing. I saw it on the news. Rosalie Jamison; no one Becky hangs out with, thank God, but still . . ."

"What do you mean 'missing'?"

"She was working on Friday night and never came home. I heard the girl has been in trouble. Parents divorced, new spouses and step-siblings in the mix. Nothing stable."

"I'm divorced," Sarah pointed out. "It's not a sin. Or a recipe for disaster with your kids."

"Oh, I know! I wasn't talking about you, but, you know, when no one's in the home, the kids get into trouble."

"Mom was home. We still got into plenty of trouble."

"Don't be so defensive. This isn't about you. But I was sure you'd want to know, and I thought maybe you didn't have your television hooked up."

"You're right," Sarah said, glancing out the window as the rain began coming down in sheets. She listened as Dee Linn explained what she knew of the circumstances of the missing girl.

"I suppose she could be a runaway," Dee Linn finished up. "Look, I've got to go, but I thought you should know. And I wanted to remind you about the party. You and the girls are coming, right?"

"Wouldn't miss it for the world," Sarah said, turning to find Gracie staring at her and silently accusing her of the lie. "Can I bring anything?"

"No—I've got everything handled," Dee said before hanging up.

"You don't want to go to the party," Gracie said as soon as Sarah was off the phone. She wadded up the wrapper from her snack and tossed it into an open garbage bag propped against the table. "Why don't you just admit it? What is it with you and the lying?"

"There's lying and there's lying. I guess I'm trying to protect people from getting hurt."

"You don't like it when Jade and I lie."

"You're right, I don't. So we'll all work on it together. Now, come on, we've got to get going. We have to pick up Jade in about half an hour."

"*That* should be fun." She was already walking into the hallway searching for her jacket, and her voice carried back to the kitchen. "Jade's been in a bad mood for a long time."

"She didn't want to move here."

"She didn't want to leave Cody," Gracie said from the foyer.

"Same thing."

"No, it's not." Gracie, pushing her arms down the jacket's sleeves, walked back into the kitchen, where she sent Sarah a look that accused her of being obtuse, or just plain naïve. "It's all about Cody with her."

"She's only seventeen."

Gracie gave her a *look*. "You never thought you were in love in high school?"

Dear Lord, when did her twelve-year-old turn forty-five? Sarah had been a complete lovesick fool over a boy when she was Jade's age. "Okay, point taken."

As Sarah scooped up her keys from the kitchen counter, Gracie finished shrugging into her coat. "He doesn't love her, you know. Not like she loves him. She's going to get her heart broken."

"And you know this, how?"

"I just do. I know a lot of things."

CHAPTER 10

He parked a block from the school on a side street, the nose of his Prius not quite to the corner of Crown Boulevard, where the sprawling campus of Our Lady of the River was situated. The side street was actually closer to the church itself and the parsonage, but it provided a great view of the school through the peppering rain. Eyes on the front doors, he slid the window of his Prius down and tossed his cigarette butt out the window; it sizzled and died in the wet grass. Checking his watch, he knew it was only a matter of minutes before the final bell, and then he would have his chance. The camera he'd mounted on his dash was small enough to hide in the palm of his hands, but the lens was strong enough that pictures from this distance would be clear.

He'd have to work fast. Though he was fairly certain Our Lady of the River wasn't fitted with security cameras that would reach past the school parking lot, he needed to be careful, get his business done quickly.

The Jamison girl had been an easy target, but now, with the Sheriff's Department on alert, he would have to be doubly careful and strike quickly, get in and get out before that dolt of a sheriff realized what was happening. He hoped to shut the operation down and move on just after Halloween. Unfortunately, it wouldn't take long before the authorities understood that Rosalie Jamison wasn't a runaway. For a while, they'd be on the wrong track, thinking she'd taken off on her own, but that would change.

He smiled thinly, one hand scrabbling in his pocket for his pack of cigarettes before he decided he'd wait for another smoke. He'd already taken shots of the public schools, had matched pictures with those in last year's yearbook with Facebook and Twitter accounts, but he hadn't taken any new shots from Our Lady until today. He mentally kicked himself for ignoring a perfect hunting ground.

Better late than never, he told himself.

He kept the engine running quietly, the defroster blowing warm air to keep the windshield clear, because he only had one shot at this. Rain was falling, but he still should be able to get some good shots. He didn't like taking chances, but risks were a part of his obsession, so he waited and watched as a line of cars formed, mommies picking up their little darlings.

Just as he'd hoped.

"Love them up tonight," he whispered as if the drivers of the cars could hear him. "It might be your last chance."

The final bell rang, and almost immediately the doors of the school opened. He hit a button, and the digital camera, pointed straight at the glass doors, began snapping off shots, one after the other, as students streamed out. A lot of the photos wouldn't help; there would be pictures of boys as well, but he should get enough to sort through and choose. He felt a thrumming in his bloodstream, a spark of adrenaline at the thought of those he would abduct: perfect, beautiful specimens. A redhead caught his eye, one with long legs and big tits. Yeah, she'd do, and then there were several blondes who were potentials. He needed a blonde or two, and a brunette, who should be slim and athletic. He saw three who might be perfect.

A girl he recognized emerged and seemed to be alone, without a friend. She was wearing a long, black coat, hiding her uniform, and she looked uncomfortable, maybe even a little pissed off. Jade. He smiled, remembering that she had more than decent boobs. Her eyes were big and serious, her lips full and pouty, her black hair a little too dark for her white complexion, but that could be fixed.

"Oh, honey, have I got plans for you," he whispered as he watched her hurry down the steps of the school toward an older Ford Explorer pulling up. Jade's mother. Again, he grinned. If she only knew.

Jade started down the steps, and he thought of what she'd be like in bed. Naked. Did she have big nipples? Brown or rosy? And what color was that patch of hair down under. He'd bet not the black of her hair . . . but he'd find out soon enough. See for himself, maybe touch the tuft and smell it. He licked his lips, his pants growing tight as his cock started to stiffen.

Oh, what he could do to her.

He took in a long, calming breath.

Not now . . . not here. He heard his mother's voice ringing in his ears, "You stay away from those kinds of girls!" she'd hissed, the smell of gin on her breath. "They'll ruin ya, you know. Tease you. Make you want them. Make you feel that if only you could fuck them, you'd find ecstasy. It's a lie, son. Your body lies to you. Remember that."

"Go away, Mother," he whispered now, returning to his fantasy of Jade spread upon his bed, writhing as he nipped at her, begging for him as he ran his dick up her flat abdomen, promising so much more—

Something moved in his peripheral vision.

What the hell?

A kid of around twelve flew by on his bike, then hit the brakes suddenly, nearly clipping the car's mirror as he screeched around the front of his vehicle, rounding the corner without bothering to stop. Close enough that he could have dented the front panel.

"Hey!" he yelled before he thought about it and shut his trap. The kid flipped him off as he sped down the road.

Shit! Now he'd been spotted.

His good mood withered away along with his hard-on, and he thought briefly of running down the biker and clipping him back, sending him flying into the ditch, where he could break his stupid neck. He fingered the gearshift lever, then slowly let out his breath through clenched teeth.

He had to let the biker flee.

He couldn't ruin this opportunity.

The kid on the bike probably wouldn't remember him.

Trying to focus on the task at hand, he decided he'd taken enough pictures, that somewhere in the digital camera roll, he'd found his next victim.

Could things get any worse?

Jade couldn't believe it when she saw her mother's SUV idling in the line of vehicles collecting the younger students at Our Lady's front doors. Mom had agreed to meet her down the street, out of sight, but here she was, the Explorer inching forward as the car in front of her collected a group of girls who had to be freshmen.

Just great.

It had already been a horrible day at this hellhole of a school, and Cody hadn't texted her since late last night. She was starting to get pissed at him. And then there was the rain—buckets of it pouring from the sky, as if God had decided to punish her too.

Ducking her head, Jade dashed down the wide front steps and saw that her sister had already claimed shotgun by stealing the front seat.

The perfect ending to a perfect day, she thought dismally as she yanked open the back door, slid into the seat, and yanked the door to slam behind her.

"I thought you were going to park down the block!" she greeted her mother.

"It's raining." Sarah glanced over her shoulder.

"It *always* rains. It's Oregon."

"And there's a girl gone missing."

"Yeah. Rosalie somebody. We heard about her in seventh period. She didn't go to Our Lady. And it doesn't matter anyway. You said you'd be down the block."

"Well, you're here now," Sarah said, driving the car forward, then stopping to allow another vehicle to merge in. "How was your first day?"

"How do you think?" Jade didn't need her mom to start prying. Not now when the whole school was dumping out, students rushing through the front doors and down the steps to waiting vehicles. Through the window she saw several faces she'd met in her classes and, of course, Mary-A, along with two other senior girls who threw her superior glances as they hurried down a long covered porch to the designated parking area for students near the gym.

God, this was hell.

Jade slid farther down in the seat, though she caught Mary-Alice's smirky smile as the senior tossed one last glance over her shoulder.

Ugh!

"Can we just go now?" When her mother didn't immediately step on the gas, she added, "Please."

"Just waiting for traffic to clear."

Jade just wanted to disappear. The day had been pure torture, being "introduced" in every class, as if she were in third grade, for God's sake. She'd wanted to drop through the floor. The only good news was she'd found a way to skip lunch so that she didn't have to suffer through Mary-Alice's company and have all the rest of the student body staring at her.

Instead, she'd left campus and wandered around the surrounding blocks, showing up ten minutes late for the next class and really pissing off Mary-Alice, who'd been apparently waiting for her at lunch. She'd blasted Jade for missing the first safety announcement because of the girl who had gone missing. *Everyone* was to have heard it, and Mary-A took it as a personal insult that Jade hadn't appeared on time, the teacher taking note and reminding Mary-Alice of her responsibility to her new charge.

By the time Jade had reconnected with her, Mary-Alice's cheeks had been wildly red, her anger palpable. "You go ahead and mess up your own life if you want," she'd blasted Jade in the empty stairwell, her voice echoing, "but don't screw with mine!"

"Just leave me alone," Jade had suggested with a dismissive shrug.

"I wish I could. But I'm in a senior college-prep program, and getting you oriented is part of my project, so move it!" She'd steamed up the stairs, her heels clipping angrily as Jade had sauntered after her.

Now, though, Jade wondered if she'd erred in taking Mary-Alice on. Had she never met the senior, Mary-A wouldn't have known she existed, but as it stood, they'd become mortal enemies in one school day.

Finally, her mother eased out of the circular drive and pulled away from the school.

Jade could finally breathe again.

Sarah said, "So, what happened?"

"Nothing."

"Wanna talk about it?"

"I said it was nothing!" She stared out the fogging side window as they drove through the small town of Stewart's Crossing. All the older buildings looked like something out of the Wild West, with false façades and long porches. The newer structures too were designed in that same Western style. In Jade's opinion it was all kind of phony. Like Stewart's Crossing was Dodge City or something.

Sarah's cell phone beeped loudly.

"I'll get it." Gracie retrieved the cell from their mother's purse and checked the name on the small screen. "Evan."

Jade's heart sank. She hated that guy. "He's a perv."

"He's not a perv. Let it go to voice mail," Sarah said, not taking her gaze from the road.

"Okay." Gracie dropped the phone into her purse, and it finally quit ringing. "Why won't you talk to him?"

"It's not a good time."

"Will it ever be?" Gracie asked perceptively.

"Nope. They broke up," Jade said, leaning forward. "It's over, but Evan is such a dumb-ass, he hasn't figured it out yet."

"But we moved," Gracie pointed out.

Jade rolled her eyes. "I didn't say he was smart, did I?"

"How about we grab a pizza and a salad for dinner while we're in town?" Sarah cut in. "It's not very imaginative, but until we get the kitchen up and running we're kind of forced to eat takeout."

She didn't want to talk about Evan, either. Good.

"Cheese and pepperoni!" Gracie declared, like the suck-up she was.

Jade closed her eyes. She couldn't believe this was her life now.

It seemed as if the entire world was against her. Even Cody. Why hadn't he called or texted? Maybe he was already moving on. She gazed out the window at the funereal sky, the darkness reflecting her own mood, her watery image visible in the glass. She'd always heard she was "interesting-looking," "intriguing," that she had "classic features" and "haunted eyes." All a bunch of crap and a way to hide the fact that she wasn't pretty or even cute. Cody had called her "beautiful" and told her that he loved her, but that was always because they were making out. Sometimes she'd caught him looking at other girls.

Gracie said, "Actually, I want Hawaiian."

"Sound good?" Sarah asked as she braked for one of the few stop lights in the town.

Jade couldn't have cared less, but she said, "Fine," because she knew that the subject wouldn't be dropped until she acquiesced. Of course, they didn't go straight to the restaurant as Mom had to run some errands. Sarah had Gracie phone in the order and rattled off the number without even checking her cell phone.

"You know the number?" Jade asked.

"It hasn't changed in twenty years," Sarah informed her.

Jade and Gracie waited at the bank, grocery store, and post office as Sarah finished her errands, and it was nearly five before she pulled into the parking lot of a strip mall, complete with the obligatory Western façade, where Giorgio's Real Italian Pizza Parlor was located. The asphalt was old and bumpy, the lines indicating parking slots nearly invisible.

Gracie was already unbuckling her seat belt as Sarah pulled her keys from the ignition and asked, "Coming?" She opened her door just a crack so as not to hit the monster pickup in the next space.

"I'll pass," Jade said, but her mother was having none of it.

"Oh, come on. I used to work here after school," Sarah insisted. "Maybe they're hiring. And you could use the gas money."

"If I ever get my car back." Reluctantly, she climbed out, slammed the door, and followed Gracie inside, where the Western theme literally crawled off the walls. A false wooden roof covered the salad bar, while open barn doors led to the "video corral" near the soda machines. With a nod to the whole "Real Italian" part of the name, flags of Italy had been strategically hung next to wagon wheels, and picks and axes were mounted on the walls. Kind of a weird combo, just like the "pizza special of the week," which was an "infusion" of Italian sausage and barbequed chicken.

"Bizarre," she whispered to herself as her mother paid for and picked up a large pizza box and a plastic carton of green salad.

"I'll carry the pizza," Gracie offered just as, deep in the pocket of her coat, Jade's cell phone vibrated. She slipped it out and read the text.

From Cody! Finally.

Be there Sat nite. Miss you.

Her heart melted, and all her anger at him faded with those six little words. Jade stared at Cody's text and felt tears burn the back of her eyes.

How could she have doubted him?

Quickly texting back, she followed her mother and Gracie to the door and nearly ran over Gracie. "What the . . . ?"

"Hey!" Gracie cried.

Jade looked up from her phone to see that her mother had stopped dead in her tracks and was staring at a tall dude in jeans who'd just walked inside.

"Sarah!" A slow grin slid across his jaw, as if he was happily surprised to damn near literally run into her. Oh, great! Just what she needed. Her mother to run into an old friend and stop to catch up. Now they'd be here *forever*.

But that's not how it played out.

Sarah actually seemed at a loss for words for a second, like she was stunned at the sight of him. Then she caught herself. "Oh. Hi." She quickly hid her surprised expression as she motioned to Jade and Gracie. "Girls, this is Clint, er, Mr. Walsh."

"Clint," he corrected quickly and seemed amused that Sarah was so flustered. What was *that* all about?

"He's our neighbor," Sarah added, then kept right on talking, "We grew up next door to each other. His place and ours share a fence line."

Jade narrowed her eyes as she looked at her mother. Why was she making such a big deal out of it, explaining so much?

"Mr. . . . Clint was friends with your uncles. They were in the same class in school," she went on, then introduced, "These are my daughters. Jade, my oldest, just had her first day at Our Lady." She pointed to Jade, then quickly motioned toward Gracie. "And this is Gracie. She's at the junior high."

"Nice to meet you, girls," he said, his gray eyes crinkling at the corners, as if he really meant it.

Jade mumbled a stilted "hi" while still trying to size him up. In beat-up jeans and a work jacket, he was more than six feet tall, she guessed, his hair deep brown, the shadow of a beard darkening a strong jaw. He was kind of a cowboy type, with sharp, pronounced features, and he looked like he spent a lot of time outdoors; he naturally fit into the whole Western theme. His smile when he flashed it was a little crooked, kinda sexy cool. For an old dude.

"I see you're planning to renovate," he said to Sarah. "The plans came across my desk. Just today." He glanced at the girls and explained, "I'm the building inspector for this part of the county, so you might see me walking around and checking things."

"The place should be condemned," Jade blurted, and when her mother turned horrified eyes in her direction, she decided not to back down. "Come on, Mom, it's a wreck, barely has running water, for God's sake. Don't act like you don't know it."

"You're living in the house?" He seemed taken aback.

Mom launched into her story about the guesthouse and making it livable, as if that were possible.

The whole situation was really awkward, but a couple of teenaged boys whom Jade didn't know, each holding a skateboard in his hand, came through the front doors and broke up their little weird group. For once, Mom seemed anxious to wrap up the conversation and said, "We've got to go; the pizza's getting cold."

"Good to see you again, Sarah." He actually touched her, and his gaze met Sarah's for the briefest of instants before skating to Jade and Gracie. He dropped his arm and nodded. "See you all around."

And then Mom hustled them outside and into the Explorer, which was just fine with Jade. Sarah threw the SUV into reverse, nearly scraping the behemoth of a pickup parked near them, then took off, tromping on the gas a little harder than usual.

"That was kind of weird," Jade said.

Sarah glanced at her daughter before checking the rearview mirror, as if trying to catch a final glimpse of the guy. Or maybe just checking traffic? "It's been a while," she said.

"He seemed to be glad to run into you," Jade observed.

"And that's weird?"

Jade couldn't really explain it, the vibe she'd sensed. "He just didn't seem the type to hang out with Uncle Joe or Uncle Jake."

"Mainly Joe. He and Jake didn't get along." Sarah's hands were holding the steering wheel in a death grip as she pushed the speed limit, which in and of itself was odd, as if running into the neighbor had set her nerves on edge.

"I think he likes you," Gracie piped up from the backseat.

Sarah laughed, but it sounded forced, and she actually blushed. Jade noticed the color crawling up the back of her neck. Really? Sarah and that Clint dude? Jade twisted in the seat to catch another glimpse of him out the back window, but the pizza parlor and strip mall were long out of sight.

"Clint and I were friends, because he hung out with my brothers," Sarah said.

"Nuh-uh. You liked him too," Gracie insisted.

"So now you're an authority on people's love lives?" Jade asked, sending her sister an "I don't believe it" glance before settling into her seat again.

"I just know."

"Great. Maybe you can add psychic love expert to your abilities," Jade muttered.

Gracie sniffed. "Make fun all you want, but that guy really likes Mom. A lot more than Cody likes you."

Jade whipped around so fast her seat belt restrained her. "Cody loves me."

"If you say so." Gracie actually smiled in that secretive way Jade found kind of scary.

"Girls! Don't."

Mom was obviously jittery, so Jade let it go. "Yeah, what does *she* know?" she asked and went back to staring out the window. But she was bugged. Gracie's barb about Cody had hit her where she was the most vulnerable. Deep down, she sometimes wondered if she loved Cody way more than he loved her. Closing her eyes, she decided not to think about it and wouldn't give her sister the satisfaction of knowing she'd hurt her.

Instead, she said to Sarah, "You dated that guy or something?"

Sarah cranked the wheel and hit the accelerator again as the county road wound upward through the surrounding hills. "Or something," she said in a voice meant to shut down the conversation.

"Told ya!" Gracie nearly crowed over the whine of the engine.

Jade ignored her. God, Gracie could be so irritating. Sometimes Jade wished she'd never had a sister. "So what happened?" she asked her mother. "He dump you?"

Mom was gazing out the windshield, driving as if by rote, as if she were thinking of something else. "We kind of . . . drifted apart. He headed back to college in southern California."

"And that was the end of it?" Jade asked and saw how tight her mother's face was.

"Yeah. Just about."

"Sounds like a dick."

Sarah's mouth opened and closed, as if she were really going to defend the loser who had left her in this godforsaken town while taking off for the bright lights of L.A. or wherever. "It . . . was mutual."

Didn't seem that way, and Gracie was all over it. "Mom, I thought you weren't going to lie anymore."

"It's not a lie, Gracie," Sarah said, and Jade wondered about that conversation, but before she could ask, as her mother turned the Explorer into the lane for the old house, Jade heard her phone again. Quickly, she slid it out of her pocket and her heart did a triple axel.

Cody was texting her again, which just went to prove how wrong Gracie was about him.

Dead wrong.

He loved her. As much as she loved him. Maybe more . . . she hoped.

CHAPTER 11

You're an idiot.
Pure and simple.

Tossing the empty pizza carton into an open bag of trash in the kitchen, Sarah berated herself for the hundredth time. She'd told herself she would be prepared, that running into Clint Walsh was inevitable, that it was no big deal. What else could she expect in this small town? She'd heard he was the building inspector, and of course, he'd lived on the neighboring property most of his life, so naturally she'd come face-to-face with him.

But she hadn't expected it to happen so quickly or that she would react like a teenage girl with her first damned crush.

"Ridiculous," she muttered under her breath as she walked into the old woodshed with the wood carrier, pulled on a pair of gloves that were far too big, and began stacking chunks of oak and fir into the same leather tote her father had used for years. Split and stacked neatly decades ago by her father and brothers, the wood was bone-dry, dusty, and infested with spiders, their webs and egg sacs clinging to the bark and heartwood.

Fortunately she wouldn't have to make too many more trips out here as, according to the contractor she'd hired, the smaller but more modern quarters of the guesthouse would be ready for occupancy soon despite several construction delays.

Which didn't solve the problem of Clint Walsh.

Somehow she'd have to find a way to deal with him, especially if he would soon start showing up at the house to check the progress of the renovations, probably unannounced.

"Great," she muttered, hauling the load from the woodshed, along a short path and up the back stairs to the mudroom.

She hoped she'd looked and sounded a lot cooler than she'd felt when she'd nearly stumbled into him at the pizza parlor, because being that close to him was akin to being thrown into some strange time warp in which she'd once again become a tongue-tied adolescent.

Stupid, stupid, stupid!

Somewhere in the middle of her sophomore year of high school, she'd overcome her shyness and her feelings of being different or odd, she thought as she carried the wood through the kitchen. That's when she'd come into her own and decided it was okay if she wasn't what people expected her to be. Her mother hadn't liked the "new," stronger Sarah, and neither had Dee Linn, who had considered her younger sister an embarrassment of epic proportions. Sarah hadn't cared. By the time she and Clint had started dating, during her senior year, she'd found herself.

Until today, when she'd dissolved into the kind of insecure teenager she'd once been. "Just because you were blindsided," she told herself as she wended her way through the blankets and sleeping bags still strewn across the floor and set the carrier near the hearth. At least now the ice had been broken, and she wouldn't have to run into him again for the first time.

But that's not what's worrying you, is it? You knew you could handle facing him again, didn't you? It's Jade that's the problem.

"You say something?" Gracie asked as she appeared near one of the matching pillars that separated the parlor from the entry hall.

"Just talking to myself."

"That's the start of it, you know," her youngest informed her. "Insanity."

"No start. Already there." Yanking off her gloves, she straightened. "That's what having two daughters does to a sane woman."

"I heard that!" Jade called from somewhere near the dining room. She appeared, phone in hand, texting with the dexterity of those who grew up with electronics.

"It's true," Sarah said.

"Should I ask Grandma?" Gracie asked. "About you and Aunt Dee driving her crazy?"

"Go ahead. She'll confirm it." Sarah said, dusting her hands as bits of bark dust had worked through the ancient gloves. "Though she'll probably tell you that the boys did their part as well. Sons are no picnic."

Without looking up, Jade said, "I don't think Grandma can confirm anything."

Sarah stared at her daughter, head bent, dyed black hair falling over her face, and her throat tightened. Running into Clint had brought everything to the fore.

What had she been thinking?

That Jade wouldn't ask again?

That her eldest didn't have the right to know about her father, her heritage, and her genetic makeup? That Clint Walsh would never know he'd fathered a child?

Sarah had acted like a scared rabbit, and now she was paying the price, which was only going to get steeper. Like it or not, she owed Clint Walsh and Jade the right to know they were father and daughter. Each would probably ice her out. Completely.

She should have been forthright from the get-go, the first time her daughter had asked about her father.

Sarah still remembered the day Jade had come home from preschool with the question. "Everybody else has a daddy," she'd announced at the dinner table. "Where's ours?"

And so the lie had started, one that had grown over the years and now wasn't going to be just a simple answer, but would have to come with all kinds of explanations and, most likely, accusations.

Though she had been adopted by Noel McAdams, Jade had known that he wasn't her biological father and had asked for the truth. Sarah had hedged, admitting only that her real dad didn't know that he'd fathered a child and that she hadn't wanted to burden him with a family, as they'd both been young. That much had been true, but she'd never really named Clint because she'd seen no point. They'd broken up before Sarah had realized she was even pregnant, and by the time she'd worked up the courage to tell him, he'd already moved on and was dating someone else. No way would she have ever tied him down or burdened him with a child.

So she'd guarded her secret, even though her mother had said to her once, "You can lie to everyone else about this, Sarah, but you can't lie to yourself. That Walsh boy has the right to know he's fathered a child. You're cheating yourself and him and, most of all, your own daughter." Arlene had guessed the truth, but kept it to herself; all the rest of her family thought Jade had been fathered by a boy she'd met soon after entering the university.

That argument with Arlene had been the last time Clint Walsh's name had ever been brought up, and as the years had passed, the secret had grown until it had seemed to have taken on a life of its own. When Jade had asked about meeting her biological father, which hadn't been often, Sarah had always said, "We'll contact him when the time is right."

The last time they'd had that conversation was when Jade was about twelve. One of her friends had discovered by accident that she was adopted and had been shattered. Jade had demanded answers, but since Sarah and Noel were splitting up around that time, Sarah had once again decided to keep Jade's paternity to herself.

However, she had known then that everything would come full circle, and now the "right time" appeared to be at hand. Whether she liked it or not.

First she would tell Clint. She owed him that.

And then, after gauging his reaction, she'd confide in her daughter. *After* Jade had settled into her life here.

As if sensing her mother staring at her, Jade looked up. "You okay?" she asked.

"Sure. Why?"

"Cuz you seem worried or something."

If you only knew.

Jade had so much potential. She was smart—as proven by intelligence tests, if not by grades—and she was beautiful, though she didn't seem to know it yet. With wide hazel eyes, even features, high cheekbones, and thick hair, the girl was stunning, though she tried to hide it with oversized clothes, heavy makeup, and hair dye that had turned her natural light hair a flat black color.

"I'm fine," Sarah lied as she bent to the fire again and added some logs. "How about you?"

"Okay." Jade slid her phone into her pocket, then threw her sleeping bag onto the couch and flopped onto it.

"And you, Gracie?" When her younger daughter didn't look up from her tablet, Sarah repeated, "Gracie?"

"Huh? What?" she asked as she moved a page on the electronic reader. She settled herself cross-legged on the floor in front of the fire.

"Did you call your dad about your first day of school?" When there was no immediate response, she said, "Gracie? Put that thing down while we talk, okay?"

Her daughter reluctantly slid the tablet onto the table. "What?"

"Your dad wanted to talk to you," Sarah reminded.

"I texted him."

"I think he'd really like to speak to you."

Gracie reached for her tablet again. "I will."

"It's later in Savannah. Maybe you should take care of that now."

"Okay, fine," Gracie snapped, searching through the pile of blankets surrounding her. She finally found her phone and began to call.

Sliding a glance at Jade, Sarah asked, "What about you?"

"I already texted Dad," Jade said, her gaze following her sister as Gracie, phone to ear, walked out of the living area. "And don't tell me 'it's not the same' like you did with Gracie. I know it's not, but it's what we do now."

"I know."

"Good. Because I don't need a lecture."

"I wasn't lecturing," Sarah said.

"You were going to, though, right? And I've heard it all before." There was a pause as if Jade expected an argument. All that could be heard was the crackle of hungry flames consuming the dry wood, and Sarah let the moment pass.

Jade's phone beeped, indicating she'd gotten a text. "I'll call him when there's something to talk about," she assured her mother. "Something good," she added, a touch of irony in her words as if she didn't expect that to happen anytime soon.

Rosalie heard the rumble of an engine before she saw the wash of headlight beams high overhead, barely permeating the dirty glass.

Oh, God, he was back! The perv who had captured her had returned.

She almost threw up.

For a second her tiny room was illuminated, and of course, there was no place to run, nowhere to hide.

Her heart hammered wildly, and she wished there was some way she could escape. Her hands were still cuffed in front of her, which allowed her to eat and clean herself clumsily, but that was about it. She'd fantasized about somehow getting the drop on him, leaping onto his back when he'd turned away, and wrapping the short chain linking her handcuffs over his head and neck. Then she'd squeeze and pull hard, using all her weight as he frantically tried to buck her off. If she were lucky and strong enough, she might be able to crush his windpipe and cut off his air supply, strangling him as she'd seen on TV and in the movies.

It was all she could think of to save herself.

After her failed attempts at trying to climb over the stall wall, she'd searched the enclosure for a weapon. She was certain this stall had once held horses; it still smelled of dung and urine. She'd hoped there would be something like a nail from a horseshoe wedged into the floorboards or a forgotten currycomb tucked into a corner. She'd spent hours scouring the stall, running her fingers over the floor until they were raw and testing any crack in the flooring or walls to see if there was something that would inflict bodily harm.

The fruits of her labor had been puny at best: A small pebble with sharp edges that had been overlooked in the corner under her cot and a hook for hanging tack. It was within her reach, but it was screwed tight to the thick board on which it had been mounted. She'd tried to dislodge it, using her broken fingernails as a screwdriver, to no avail, then pulling hard against the smooth curve of the hook and yanking with all her strength. She'd even hung from it, hoping her hundred and ten pounds would loosen it.

It hadn't so much as budged.

Despite the chill in the air, she'd been sweating by the time she'd given up and flung herself onto her cot to contemplate another avenue of escape.

She'd found none.

Now, hearing the roar of the pickup, she backed onto the cot and waited. Ears straining, heart thudding, nerves strung as tight as bowstrings, she scrambled to come up with a plan. Maybe she could lure him all the way into the stall, even going so far as to offer him sex, and then, when his pants were down at his ankles, she'd kick him in his exposed balls and use the little rock to blind him, before racing out and locking *him* inside. It would serve the bastard right!

Could she do it?

Would it work?

Her pulse was skyrocketing in fear, her mouth dry of all spit as she contemplated the idea of seduction and, if possible, murder.

Her skin crawled at the thought of it, but she was running out of options and didn't believe for a second that he would, out of the goodness of his heart, suddenly let her go. No, he would kill her and God only knew what else.

The engine died. She waited, gripping the tiny stone until it cut into her fingers. Counting her heartbeats. Finally, she heard the familiar jingle of his keys and the muted click of the keyed lock giving way before the sound of a dead bolt scraping open and the creak of the door being pushed open announced his arrival.

You can do this, Rosalie. You can!

Oh, God, help me, she silently prayed.

Relax. You have to look scared, not ready to fight. Like you're too frightened to do anything he doesn't expect.

Her grip loosened on the pebble, and she swallowed hard as she heard the steady thud of his boots on the floor . . . but wait! His gait was off, the sound bouncing off the walls. It was as if—

"Got her in here," he said loudly enough that she heard him distinctly.

And then she knew why his footsteps weren't normal. He wasn't alone.

He'd brought someone with him.

Her heart dropped, and a new fear curdled through her blood.

She scooted back on the cot. Why would there be someone with him?

For no good reason, she was certain.

Huddling more tightly into the corner, she wrapped her arms around her body as hard as the damned handcuffs would allow.

"Locked up tight?" Another male voice, higher-pitched and nasal, inquired before breaking into a horrifying bout of laughter that ended in a cigarette-induced coughing spate.

"You'll see," her abductor assured his companion.

Rosalie wanted to die.

"Just one, though?"

"For now."

Again, the sniggering, ugly chuckle that made her skin crawl.

What did that mean—just one for now? There were going to be others? Why? Who?

"We have to move fast, be finished by Halloween."

Finished? She froze. *Finished with what?*

"I'm thinkin' the weekend, there'll be easy opportunities. Maybe a twofer."

"Twofer?" the new man asked.

"Two fer one." A note of disdain was audible in the monster's voice.

"Oh. Sure." Once again he chortled, this time over the jangle of keys and the heart-stopping click of a padlock springing open.

Oh, God, now what?

Nearly frantic, she watched as the door swung open and two shadows lengthened in the swath of light that poured through the doorway and into her cell. Pressing her back into the corner, she tried to crawl into the woodwork, but she was trapped. Her heart was thudding crazily with fear, her body shaking. No longer did she have to pretend to be afraid.

Using a switch on the outside of the doorway, the bigger of the two men snapped on the overhead light. She winked and blinked at the sudden illumination flooding her room, and she saw him take a step inward, his hand raised. For a terrifying second, she thought he had a gun and was going to shoot her right then and there in front of a witness. She started to scream, her mouth open wide as her eyes started to finally focus again, and she realized it wasn't a small pistol in his hand, but a smartphone. "What?" she asked, then heard a series of soft clicks and realized he was taking pictures of her.

"Stop!" she cried.

The smaller man, who was no longer in shadow, studied her hard. Unshaven, his hair a scraggly, red-blond mop, his jean jacket tattered, and dirty, his blue eyes cruel as they appraised her, he was making a face of distaste. "She don't look much like her picture."

"Just needs to be cleaned up."

What picture? This dickhead had been photographing her? For what?

"Let me go!" Rosalie burst out, jumping off the cot. She couldn't just cower here and let them do whatever they wanted to her.

The little guy held out his hands. "Whoa there, missy!"

"Don't call me that!" she spat out before she bit her tongue and turned to the taller man, the one she'd so foolishly trusted. "How could you do this to me?" she demanded. "Let me go! Now!"

"Not just yet," he countered, rubbing his jaw.

"When?"

The smaller man chuckled, which again rippled into a coughing fit that made him nearly double over for a second. She noticed his jeans were dirty, matching a flannel shirt that was visible through his open jacket, and his boots were sturdy but worn.

She took a step toward her captor and tried to keep her voice from trembling. "Get out of my way."

If she'd thought she could bully him, she'd been wrong. A slow, cold smile crawled across his lips. "You'd best learn to behave," he said, and some hideous little spark leaped in his eyes—a warning that if she pushed him too far, he might react and hurt her. Worse yet, he would enjoy it.

"I said, 'Get out of my way.' "

"Get back on your cot, Star," he ordered.

Star? The name nearly tripped her up, but she held her ground.

"Now!" he warned. "Unless you want me to make you behave." He reached for the buckle of his belt, and his smaller compatriot nearly danced with glee at the thought of a whipping or a rape or both.

She held her ground. "I need to go home."

Sssssss! His belt was ripped from his pants with a snakelike hiss. The vicious gleam in his eye caused her blood to turn to ice. "Hold her down." he ordered through barely moving lips.

No!

With sickening enthusiasm Scraggly Hair lunged forward, grabbing at her.

She kicked hard, landing a blow to Scraggly Hair's shin that sent him howling. She tried to wedge through the door, but her attacker blocked the entrance. Scraggly Hair managed to grab her again. She whirled instinctively, twisting and aiming for his crotch. Bam! She nailed her kick, driving her foot deep between his legs.

"Oooowwwwww!" He went down with a scream, thud, and clunk. His howls shook the rafters.

"What the hell?" the big man growled, turning, belt in hand as she squeezed past him and raced through the rest of the huge barn. Spurred by adrenaline, she ran by blurry images of old machinery and bins for feed, tools on the wall.

"Come back here!" he roared. "Son of a bitch!"

She heard his heavy footsteps as he started chasing her. *Run. Faster! Don't let him catch you!*

Impeded by her shackled hands, she sped past old sawhorses and dusty cots to the door. It was still open, thank God! Darkness beckoned beyond.

"Shit! Stop!" he commanded.

If she could just get outside, she'd have a chance!

"Don't!" he warned, but she kept going, racing fast as she leaped through the doorway, her shoes landing on sparse gravel. Cold night air hit her full in the face, rain slanting down from a black, stygian sky. Her breath fogged as she sped, feet flying over the uneven ground. Jesus, it was dark.

Good. Maybe you can get away. Hide somewhere.

She ran to his truck, but as she reached for the door, she remembered she'd heard the chirp of its automatic lock when he'd arrived. Instead she took off, flying down the long lane.

She only hoped he was as blind as she was in the all-consuming darkness.

Run. Run. Run!

Breathing hard, she raced down the lane that she could only hope led away from this godforsaken place, her feet slipping a little in the wet grass and weeds. How far was it to the main road, a place she might be able to find someone to help her? A quarter mile? Maybe a half? More?

Don't worry about it, just run!

Her mind was spinning, adrenaline propelling her. If she stayed on the roadway, he'd find her, so she needed to veer off, hide in the dense forest that, she remembered from the ride to this isolated hell-hole, surrounded the lane. She'd seen it as he'd driven her here, the beams of his headlights washing against the trunks and branches of trees before landing on the barn and attached lean-to, with its sagging roof, a car hidden beneath the rotting rafters.

Was there a fence?

She didn't remember seeing any kind of enclosure, but she couldn't be certain of anything right now.

Behind her she heard the sharp beep of a keyless lock and caught a glimpse of lights flashing as he unlocked the doors of his truck. *Damn!* Angry shouts and heavy metal doors slamming shut rolled over the land. Oh, God, they'd catch her for sure, she thought as the soul-numbing roar of a large engine sparked to life.

She swerved off the lane just as bright headlights switched on, beams reflecting on the wet gravel and washing over her as she ran. She saw the fence just before she slammed into it and hurtled, head-first over the top of the worn, rusted mesh.

Searing pain sliced through her abdomen. Toppling to the wet ground, she landed hard, her head cracking against the edge of a post. "Ooof."

For a millisecond, the world shrank. Unconsciousness threatened, the warm black void tempting. Her mind swam, and in that moment when she was teetering toward the depths, she saw her mother's worried face.

"Mom," she whispered as the headlights bore down on her.

Blinking hard, she pushed the hallucination away and scrambled to her feet.

Go! Go!

Slipping in the grass and mud, she propelled herself forward, her abdomen aching, her head pounding, the pickup's headlights illuminating the area. Scurrying, she ducked under branches that were visible in the eerie glow and dodged through the trees, deeper and deeper into the surrounding forest, heading downhill, all the while hoping against hope that she would find a way to escape.

The rain lessened in the canopy of fir branches, and the smell of dank earth was heavy in her nostrils as, spurred by adrenaline, she ran. Her arms were outstretched, hands splayed to protect her from running into a tree as she cut and wove her way ever deeper through the woods, wet cobwebs clutching at her, branches slapping her arms and face.

The light from the truck's headlights grew dimmer, hidden partially from the thickets of pine and fir.

Good.

Darkness leveled the playing field.

Downward, nearly tripping, her toes hitting rocks and roots, she propelled herself forward and listened to the sound of the truck's engine.

It was still too close.

Keep running, Rosalie. Go! Don't stop!

Her legs were wobbly, her stomach, where she'd scraped it going over the fence, ached; her lungs were beginning to burn.

Tires screeched.

She glanced over her shoulder, to see a bit of light high on the hill where the truck had stopped.

Keep moving!

"Over there!" Her abductor's voice echoed through the darkness, and she caught a glimpse of him jumping out of the truck, its cab illuminated by the interior light.

Shit!

"I seen her!" Scraggly Hair. He too jumped from the pickup, and fear was a stone in her throat.

Faster Rosalie ran, slipping and sliding through needles and leaves, deeper into the forest, ever downward, hoping she would find the county road that would lead her to civilization or even a passing motorist.

Don't run in a straight line!

Zigging and zagging, she had no idea which direction she was running, only that the hill was getting steeper and somewhere she heard water running. A river? Creek? Her legs were wobbly, her breath coming in gasps, but she forced herself forward, weaving between the huge trees and saplings, hoping beyond hope that she'd find the main road and that a passing motorist, a Good Samaritan, would find her—

From the corner of her eye she saw a flash.

Her heart leaped.

Her prayers had been answered! A car's headlights—No! Oh, God, no. The bobbing beam wasn't from the vehicle of a would-be savior, but from a flashlight as one of the men had circled around. It faltered a bit, and she heard "Fuck!" in that nasal tone belonging to Scraggly Hair as the beam fell downward, as if he'd dropped his flashlight.

Good.

Where was the other guy? Her abductor. Was he back in the truck waiting or . . . oh, crap, she noticed the other pinpoint of light in the trees above her. He was holding his flashlight steady. Unmoving. As if he were focusing on a thicket far to her left.

Good.

She started downhill again, but wondered. Why was he just standing there with the beam of his flashlight burning evenly? Like a friggin' beacon.

- Did he think Scraggly Hair would drive her back to him?

Something was wrong here. She sensed it, but all she could do was run. Away. Fast.

She veered right, away from the bobbling light of Scraggly Hair, away from the steady motionless beam.

Why was it not moving, not coming closer?

Senses heightened, she ran into a fallen log, scaled it, and jumped down on the other side, her feet slipping a little.

Scraggly Hair was closing the distance between them, the wobbling beam of his flashlight brighter.

Damn!

The other light didn't move.

That wasn't right, was it? Her kidnapper wasn't the kind to just let her go and hope his partner would drive her to him. He loved the hunt, the abduction, to be in control . . .

Wait a sec—Oh, God, oh, God, oh—

"Gotcha!" From behind a nearby tree the bigger man jumped, his arms surrounding her.

She screamed and tried to twist away, but it proved impossible. Soaking wet, she was wriggling like an eel, but he held her fast, his arms like steel bands, nearly squeezing the breath from her lungs. The smell of him, his rain-dampened skin and wet hair, was rank in her nostrils.

How had this happened? Were there now three men? Two with flashlights and this monster who was restraining her?

"Let me go!" she yelled, squirming, hitting at his head with her joined hands, scraping his face with her handcuffs but unable to inflict any serious damage.

"Got her!" he yelled. "Let's go!"

Breathing hard, Scraggly Hair appeared. "That worked out good, huh? Shinin' the light on her shoes."

What? What about her shoes? She was still struggling as Scraggly started with his crazy-sounding laugh-cough.

"That's what she gets fer wearin' those 'spensive kicks."

And then she got it. Her running shoes had reflective bands to make her visible when she walked home late at night from the diner. Bright strips that caught the beams of headlights and flashlights. Sick to her stomach at her stupidity, she flung herself hard, swinging her clasped fist and striking her abductor on his nose.

Crack! Cartilage broke, and blood, warm and sticky, spurted out in a stream, spilling over his chest and her hair.

"You little bitch!" he snarled.

"Don't hit her!" Scraggly came to her rescue. "No bruises! At least none visible! Remember."

"Fuck!" The big man restrained himself, every muscle tense as he hauled her, kicking and screaming, to his shoulder and started trudging upward through the wilderness. The light from Scraggly's flashlight led the way back to the spot where he'd planted his, her tethered fists beating on his back, her legs pummeling the air, the rain lashing through the forest, coming down in cold, hard pellets.

Rosalie was crying now, and she knew that when he got her back to the barn, he would punish her. Her insides shriveled at the thought, and at that point she gave up fighting, just let him haul her up the hillside, across a short field, and over the wire mesh to his waiting, idling truck, a black beast that appeared malevolent, headlights like eyes, burning through the night. Into the cab she was flung, and there Scraggly held her down. His face a pale mask of fury in the light from the dash, her abductor climbed behind the wheel, slammed his door shut, and threw the truck into reverse. Gunning it, swerving in his wrath, he drove crazily backward.

"Hey! Careful!" Scraggly screeched.

Rosalie didn't care. She figured she was dead.

Except that Scraggly had said, "No bruises."

That couldn't be good.

Her kidnapper stood on the brakes, and the truck slid to a shuddering stop. He opened his door, hauled her outside, and without a word carried her straight to her room, spinning around just once to order Scraggly, "Be sure to close and lock the door, for shit's sake." In that moment, she got a view of the area where she was being held. Yes, it was a stall, the first in a line of boxes with doors and padlocks. Over each door the name of a horse had been etched in thick black letters. In her case, the former occupant of the stall had obviously been named Star.

No wonder he'd called her that. She caught a glimpse of the next stall, which was named for Princess, and the third was Stormy. There were others, as well, too far away for her to read in that one quick glance.

"You just lost dinner," her captor told her and kicked her water bucket so hard, the contents sloshed over the side and the bucket clattered against the wall, "and you're damned lucky to be alive!" He tossed her onto the cot, then stalked out, slamming the door behind him so hard the whole barn shook. "Let's go," he said to his companion as the padlock clicked into place. "Let the little bitch think about what she's done."

The footsteps faded, any bit of light sliding under the door extinguished, the exterior door thudding hard before the sound of a dead bolt sliding into place and a lock turning met her ears.

Rosalie fell into a puddle of desperate tears.

She was alone again.

CHAPTER 12

Gracie had to be careful and really, really quiet as she descended the steps to the basement. Her mom didn't like her poking around in the unused portions of the old house, but then Mom was always overprotective, and besides, whether she admitted it or not, this old house freaked Sarah big-time. Gracie could tell. She just had a sense about those kinds of things, nothing she could put her finger on, not really, but a heightened awareness that she took for granted and other people apparently weren't blessed with.

She'd tried to describe her ability to Jade once, to prove to her skeptical sister that she was for real, by informing Jade that Dad was just about to call right before the phone rang. That had only made things worse because when Jade had answered and heard Noel McAdams's voice, she'd glared at Gracie as if she thought the call was some kind of elaborate trick concocted by her sister and father.

When they'd both insisted they weren't in cahoots and Jade had finally believed them, instead of being impressed, Jade had said, "I don't get you," and slapped the phone into Gracie's hand.

After that Gracie had kept her mouth shut. When Jade had been searching all over the house for her phone and Gracie had known it was under the seat in the car, she'd stayed mum. And she hadn't told Jade about the time when Jade had been complaining that Cody hadn't called and Gracie had the very distinct feeling he was with someone else. Maybe a girl, maybe one of his friends, she couldn't tell which, but she did know that he sure wasn't thinking about Jade. The vibe she'd gotten from Jade's boyfriend was that he just wasn't as into

Jade as she was into him, but telling Jade that wasn't going to win Gracie any points. In Gracie's opinion, Cody Russell was a low-life loser, but she kept that opinion to herself. Mostly. The few times she'd voiced her thoughts, Jade had gone ballistic, so it was better to just keep quiet. At least for now.

While Mom was in the middle of a bunch of phone calls and paperwork in the dining room, and Jade was wrapped up in something on the Internet, Gracie used the keys she found hanging on a hook near the back door, grabbed a flashlight from a shelf in the mudroom, then slipped around the staircase and unlocked the door to the basement. The flashlight's batteries were low, its beam a sickly yellow, but she didn't have much time anyway, so she hurried down the stairs.

The dusty steps creaked loudly, and cobwebs caught in her hair, but she didn't stop because she knew her time was limited. Soon Mom would look for her, and she didn't want to have to explain herself.

How could she? Who would believe that she was actually communicating with the ghost of Angelique Le Duc? She'd been frightened at first and nearly fainted on the stairs that first night she'd felt the ice in the air and seen the spirit form vanish as swiftly as it had appeared, but she was less afraid now. She'd since realized that the apparition hadn't been trying to scare her, just reach out to her.

Most of this information had come in the form of a dream Gracie had experienced the second night she'd been at the house. She was certain it wasn't just her subconscious, that Angelique was talking to her, begging her to solve the mystery of her death, so that she could pass over to the other side.

It sounded weird, even to Gracie herself, but then life and death were inexplicable. She was just going to go with it, and it made her feel special and kind of important.

She reached the bottom step and swept the wimpy beam around the cement floor. Stepping into near darkness, she tried to ignore the sound of tiny claws scratching on the floor. Rats, probably, disturbed that she was down here. She imagined seeing their beady little eyes as she moved deeper into the basement, which was really several very large rooms divided by bookcases and shelves that held a century of forgotten junk. Exposed pipes climbed up the cement walls and ran between the joists overhead. In one corner an ancient washer and dryer were rusting near an even older wringer-washer. At least that's what she thought it was; she'd read about the contraptions in historical novels. Cords were strung from wooden pillars, and on one cord wooden clothespins were still attached.

It was like stepping back in time, she thought, as she made her way through piles of junk. What hadn't been stored in the attic had found its way down here—broken lamps, old books, empty jars, and discarded picture frames. There were tools as well, handsaws and hammers and wrenches and the like, along with furniture that had been carried down here and forgotten. Lawn chairs, of course, but interior furniture as well. A broken rocker and a chaise with the stuffing exposed were pushed into a corner with old desks and bureaus, all of it slowly deteriorating.

As she walked to the corner of the basement, the temperature seemed to drop. One second she was comfortable; the next she was so cold goose bumps rose on the back of her arms. For the first time since stepping through the doorway at the top of the stairs, she felt as if she wasn't alone.

She swallowed hard, forcing herself to be brave.

"Are you here?" she whispered, her breath fogging. Would someone answer her? Biting her lip, she waited, listening to her own heartbeat, hoping she wouldn't scream if she heard a voice. She held the flashlight so hard she was sure her fingers had turned white.

Nothing.

The basement was eerily silent; even the rats had quit moving around. "I—I want to help."

Slowly she shined her light over the area again.

"Angelique?" Her voice shook a little, and she felt a little foolish calling out to the ghost. If Jade ever found out, she'd never hear the end of it.

Still there was no response, and she was running out of time. Swinging her flashlight over the furniture, she found what she thought was the oldest dresser and opened the drawers, but they were all empty. A carved wooden desk that also appeared to have been built in a previous century sat next to it. Inside the top drawer were artifacts from another century. Faded black-and-white postcards, a fountain pen, colored pencils, and a sharpener lay amid the mice droppings. The second drawer down was stuck closed, almost as if it were locked and no amount of tugging would open it. Inside the third drawer was a sheaf of yellowed stationery covered in dead insects.

Nothing that would help.

And yet she felt as if she was close to something. Why else the cold presence?

"There must be something," she whispered as she heard muffled footsteps on the floor overhead. Gracie swept the beam of the flashlight to the crossbeams and figured her mother was walking into the kitchen from the dining room. If Sarah searched for Gracie and couldn't find her, she would wonder where her daughter was, and Gracie didn't want to try and explain herself.

Reluctantly she started up the staircase.

Whoosh! Creeeaaak!

Her heart nearly stopped as she felt a breath of wind pass through her. Icy cold, it caused her insides to tremble. Certain she would be nose-to-nose with the wispy lady in white, she forced herself to turn around and held the flashlight in a death grip. It was one thing to talk about confronting a ghost and helping a spirit, but to actually see one? Would she be able to stand her ground or flee up the stairs?

"H-Hello?" she whispered, seeing nothing but pitch black in the lower rooms. "Is anyone there?" She swung the beam of her light over the basement's interior.

Nothing.

No sound.

No flimsy wraith flitting under the old furnace's huge vents.

And yet . . . *Something* had made that noise and passed through her body.

She felt an urgency to return upstairs, but she stepped back into the shadowy basement once more and noticed that her flashlight's beam wavered; her hand was shaking. The air seemed thin but suddenly odorless.

Gracie swallowed hard, telling herself she was being a ninny.

There was nothing to be scared of.

But her heightened senses disagreed, and as she swung the beam from her light over the stacks of junk and bookcases, she braced herself, certain some horrid ghostly creature would lunge out at her.

The basement remained still.

As if drawn by a magnet, she returned to the old desk and saw that the second drawer, the one she'd tried so hard to open, was now slightly pulled out, the dark opening beneath the lip of the desk beckoning.

Every hair on the back of her neck lifted as she stepped closer. Poised to sprint in the opposite direction, she shined her pale light at the drawer. She reached out and pulled on the handle, but again, as before, it wouldn't budge. It would go backward, but not forward all the way, as if . . .

And then she knew.

Dropping to her knees, she pulled out the third drawer and shined her light on the bottom of the stuck second one. Sure enough something was adhered to the bottom of it, tacked into a purse of sorts.

Again, the floorboards overhead creaked as her mother stirred around on the first floor.

Hurry!

She reached inside and pulled. The small bag shredded and its contents, a slim book, fell into her palm, the word *Journal* scrolled across the leather binding in faded gold letters. She flipped it open, and though many of the thin pages stuck together, she saw the fluid intricate script and realized she had stumbled upon Angelique Le Duc's diary.

"Gracie?" her mother's voice seemed to ricochet down the huge ducts.

Gracie slid the diary under her sweatshirt and climbed up the stairs as silently as possible. She didn't know why, but she knew she had to keep her find a secret—for now. Mom wouldn't approve of her snooping through the basement, nor would she understand.

Quietly she slid into the darkened hallway, tiptoed to the mudroom, and hurried outside, where fresh rain was falling. Once her hair was damp and the shoulders of her sweatshirt showed drops, she returned to the house and found her mom walking down the hall, just a step in front of the doorway to the basement.

"Where were you?" Sarah asked, her brow knotted in concern.

"Outside."

"I can see that, but why?"

She shrugged and felt the diary slide beneath her sweatshirt. "Just needed to get out for a minute."

"Really?" Her mother eyed her skeptically, and Gracie noticed that she hadn't completely latched the door to the basement. It was hanging slightly ajar, and if Mom turned around she'd wonder why it wasn't locked.

"Yeah, I, uh, didn't feel so good."

"You didn't?"

"I'm okay, though. I just think I need something to drink."

"Water? Seven-Up?" Sarah asked and headed back into the kitchen.

"Whatever." Gracie gently pulled the door to the basement closed and hurried after her mother, feeling relieved until she caught Jade standing on the other side of the staircase watching her every move.

"What're you doing?" she whispered, and Gracie held up a hand and shook her head.

Now, all she could do was hope that Jade wouldn't blow her secret. At least not until she had a chance to look at Angelique's journal.

"It's as if Rosalie Jamison just disappeared off the damned earth!" Deputy Bellisario declared, trying to keep up with Sheriff Cooke's longer strides as he walked briskly through the offices of the department on Tuesday. Rosalie had now officially been missing since midnight on Friday.

"Can't argue that."

The sheriff himself was working the missing girl case with her, as the department was a few deputies down. Montcliff was recuperating from an accident where a drunk driver had T-boned his county-issued cruiser, Zwolski was on vacation somewhere in Mexico, and Rutgers was just starting her maternity leave. Today, after talking to Ray Price, whose prize bull had been stolen, they'd been called to the Delanys on yet another domestic disturbance. The night before had been no better, as they'd had to break up a near-brawl at the Bend in the River Tavern that had included a few of the antigovernment types who'd migrated into Stewart's Crossing and started mixing it up with some local boys. Now Bellisario and the sheriff were headed to the lab to see what progress, if any, had been made with Rosalie's iPad and computer, which a deputy had picked up twenty-four hours before.

"Someone knows where she is." Cooke held the exterior door open.

A blast of late-October air hit Bellisario in the face, and she zipped up her jacket to her neck. Together they headed past the flagpole where Old Glory was snapping, the chains rattling in the stiff breeze screaming down the gorge. "We just have to find that particular someone."

"Needle in the haystack time."

"Right."

They reached the Jeep just as the first drops of rain fell from an ominous sky. By unspoken agreement, Bellisario slid behind the wheel. She'd already buckled up and started the engine by the time the sheriff dropped into the passenger seat and slammed his door shut.

"I interviewed her coworkers," she said. "Gloria Netterling, another waitress at the diner, is beating herself up that she couldn't convince Rosalie to wait for a ride. She and the cook, Barry Daughtry, were the last people to see her that we know of. Only people left in the diner that night."

"No customers?"

"The last two were a couple. A man and woman in their forties. They left ten, maybe fifteen minutes earlier. We're checking credit card receipts, trying to locate customers who might've seen something, and before you ask, no, the Columbia Diner doesn't have security cameras either inside or in the parking lot."

"Too bad," he said thoughtfully, reaching into his pocket for a nonexistent pack of cigarettes; he'd given up the habit a few years back. "You talk to the dad?"

"Several times." She backed out of the parking slot, then shoved the gear-lever into drive. "I think Mick Jamison and his new wife are on their way here from Denver. He didn't know about any new boyfriend in the area, online or off."

"What have you found out about the mom's boyfriend?"

"He couldn't have done it, not unless the mom is lying, as she's his alibi, and no, I don't think so." She fiddled with the heater, cold air blasting for a few seconds before it warmed.

"What about Rosalie's boyfriend?"

"Bobby Morris?" She shook her head, then eased the cruiser into the flow of traffic. "Rosalie's mom, Sharon, swears it was over, and so does Morris."

"You talked to him?"

"Oh, yeah." Sliding the sheriff a knowing glance, she added, "Let's just say the kid didn't have any kind words for her." In fact, he'd called her a slut, a bitch, and worse. Bellisario hadn't liked him on sight. Bobby Morris was a snarly-faced twentysomething with a scruffy beard and eyes that never quite met hers when she'd caught up with him at a skate park. He'd been hanging out with some other less-than-motivated types and obviously hadn't appreciated a face-to-face with a cop. Most of his friends, upon spying her county-issued vehicle, had drifted away from Bobby. Hoodies over their heads, some wearing sunglasses on a dark day, the scent of marijuana strong, they'd rolled off on skateboards, wheels rasping against the concrete.

"I got nothin' to do with that cu—bitch," Bobby had insisted when she'd asked about Rosalie. Lighting up a filter tip, he'd stared insolently through the smoke at Bellisario, as if all the problems on his scrawny shoulders were her fault. "I broke up with her."

"She's gone missing," she'd said, and he'd shrugged.

"Ain't got nothin' to do with me." Cigarette pinched between his lips, he held up both hands and took a step back. "She's probably out fucking some new dude."

"And who would that be?"

"I don't know, and I don't care," he said, taking another drag. Then, as if the notion had suddenly come to him, he added, "Some guy from Colorado or somethin'. An online thing. Not that I give a rat's ass. I hope she fucks her brains out."

She'd fought back a retort, reminding herself not to engage with him. Glancing around the park, she wondered about his friends, who had somehow disappeared during the conversation.

The one who'd remained had given her a weak alibi of sorts. "Kona" had confirmed that he and Bobby had been together at a local club called Trailhead.

"Talk to the bouncer if you want," Bobby had sneered. "He'll tell ya that I was there. Most of the damned night. Until he drop-kicked me outta the place. I should sue."

"I will," she'd assured him and had made good on her promise, heading directly to Trailhead.

The huge bear of a guy manning the door, his shining, tattooed pate in direct opposition to the beard covering his chin, had nodded when Bellisario had shown him a picture of Bobby Morris.

"Yeah, he was here. Wasted as usual. Had to toss his butt onto the street."

"What time was that?"

"Near closing. He was with that skinny kid with the Hawaiian name."

"Kona?"

"That's it."

"What time did they arrive?"

"Not sure, but I think they were here most of the night. Came in around ten, maybe. Security cameras would show."

And they had. Rosalie could have made a detour after work, hooked up with someone, then met Bobby later, she supposed, but according to her mother, her pattern was to come directly home to clean up even if she did go out after working her shift.

Bellisario hated to admit it, but she thought Bobby Morris might be telling the truth and in the clear.

As she slowed for a red light, she said to Cooke, "Bobby thinks she ran off with the guy she met online, the Colorado dude, who is like a ghost. So far, even with the Denver P.D. and Colorado State Patrol's help, we haven't located him. I'm not sure he even exists."

Cooke scowled. "Check it out. Again."

"Already all over it." Her fingers tapped an anxious tattoo over the wheel as the light took its sweet time turning from red to green. She eyed the computer monitor on the dash. "Just haven't been able to root him out yet," she admitted, flipping on her wipers as the rain started in earnest. "We don't know his name, Sharon only recalls her saying something about Leo or Leonardo. She isn't sure if that's the guy from Colorado or someone local. There's no one who goes to her school with either name."

"Could have met him at the diner."

"Or, as the mom suspects, online. Lately Rosalie had been making a lot of noise about moving to Denver to be with her dad, and Sharon thinks this Leo has something to do with it." The light turned, and Bellisario hit the gas.

"We didn't give the Colorado cops much to go on," Cooke muttered.

"I know. I'm still waiting for the info on her iPad and cell."

"Doesn't her phone have a GPS on it?"

"Disabled. Seems as if Rosalie didn't want her mother tracking her down."

"Perfect," he said, with more than a trace of sarcasm.

"I should hear from the carrier soon and get all the info off it. If he exists, she probably texted or called him."

"Let's hope. We need a break." The sheriff leaned against the passenger window and pointed at a small coffee kiosk located on the edge of a parking lot. "Pull in here. I could use a cup. Large or venti or whatever the hell they call it. Sixteen ounces. Coffee. Black."

"Sure." The windshield was starting to fog, so Bellisario flipped on the defroster and rolled down her side window as she drove up to the single window as a dirty silver van pulled away. "Two grande coffees," she said to a barista who looked to be about fifteen. "One black, the other with cream and sugar."

"Grande," the sheriff repeated from the passenger seat as the wipers scraped against the windshield. "Why the hell can't they go with small, medium, and large and make it easy?"

"Cuz we're living in enlightened times."

"Shee-it."

She grinned, and he shot her a disparaging glance but handed her some cash.

"My treat, smart-ass."

Minutes later, after dispensing with the exchange of dollars for cups, she was driving off again, the interior of the vehicle filled with the aroma of hot coffee.

"What about knowns?" he asked, taking a sip of his coffee.

"As in known sex offenders?"

"To start, but we may as well lump in the ex-cons who haven't walked the straight and narrow. You know, our A-listers."

"Pretty big list, but we're winnowing it down. Williams is on it," she reminded, referring to Tallah Williams from their office.

"Good. Let's check with her when we get back."

"Will do." She was already one step ahead of him and had asked Williams to pull files on several of the area's worst offenders. Jay Aberdeen, Calvin Remick, and Lars Blonski were the first to come to mind; all had alibis that had yet to be double-checked. And then there was Roger Anderson, a local man who just couldn't keep his nose clean. He wasn't in the same category as the first three, all of whom had been convicted of serious crimes against women, but Anderson was like the proverbial bad penny; he kept showing up, getting into trouble, claiming his innocence, and either doing time or fading away for a while, only to appear yet again. Trouble usually ensued.

At the parking lot for the lab, Bellisario nosed the Jeep into an empty spot and cut the engine. Hoping to high heaven that the techies inside had found something that would help them locate Rosalie Jamison, she grabbed her cup and kept up with Cooke as he strode toward the wide glass doors. She had the unwelcome feeling they were running out of time.

CHAPTER 13

"I figured since you're playing the part of a pioneer woman, you might not know what they're saying about that girl who has gone missing," Dee Linn said, and Sarah, glancing out the window, felt chilled to the bone. It was early evening, and twilight was darkening the land; a few lights on the main floor of the old house gave off just enough illumination to keep the nearest shadows at bay.

"They still don't know what happened to her?" she asked her sister.

"Not that I know of, but it's been all over the news today. I think she went missing on Friday, but there was an initial thought that she was a runaway. I saw the AMBER Alert on the news yesterday but didn't think about calling you until I realized you don't have a television and probably don't get the paper."

"Not yet." Sarah was worried and walked into the living area, where Gracie was huddled over her laptop and Jade was walking down the hallway from the bathroom. "Cable's supposed to come the day after tomorrow, I think."

"Well, I don't know if it's something to be too concerned about. At least not yet. As I said, it's still undetermined if the girl left on her own or not, but I thought you should be aware."

"Thanks."

"Okay, then, I'll see you on Saturday," Dee Linn said. "Aunt Marge told me that Caroline and Clark are definitely coming."

"Good to know," Sarah said, though she and her cousins had never been close. Caroline, an outrageous flirt, and Dee Linn had been classmates, so they'd had a closer bond, while Clark, nearly ten years older than Sarah, was a little more reserved than his younger sister and one of the few people in the family who had connected with Roger.

As if reading her mind, Dee Linn said, "I asked Clark if he knew how to get hold of Roger, not that I really want him there, but he is family, and Clark said he hadn't heard from him, which is a little odd as he's the one person in the family Roger would try to reach, I think. I swear, Walter told me one of his patients had seen Roger in town."

"I, um, I thought that Roger had disappeared again and that even his parole officer couldn't locate him." The thought that Roger was anywhere nearby was worrisome, and not just because of the incident on the widow's walk all those years ago. No, there was more, a lot more. Roger's whole life, after Theresa had disappeared, had spiraled downward to the point where he'd become a felon. Roger was the last person Sarah wanted around Jade and Gracie. Jade had already had her share of run-ins with the law for truancy and underage drinking, and Gracie was too young and impressionable to have to deal with an uncle who was a criminal.

In a way, Sarah blamed Roger and Theresa for her own disconnect with her mother. It was as if Arlene had lost both her children with Hugh Anderson when Theresa had disappeared, and her relationship with her other four children—and with their father, Franklin Stewart—had deteriorated as well. Of course, it wasn't really Roger's fault, but Sarah had always felt that if he'd pulled himself together after Theresa had disappeared, Arlene too would have been less emotionally shut down and perhaps had a closer kinship with the children she'd had with Franklin.

Then again, maybe not.

"Oh, well," Dee Linn was saying, "Maybe the patient was mistaken or Doctor Walter misheard. That happens, you know, more often that he'd like to admit. It's difficult for a patient to keep a conversation going when the dentist has mirrors and fingers and equipment in his mouth. Walter, bless him, never has understood that."

Along with a lot of other things, Sarah thought, but kept it to herself.

"Anyway," Dee Linn said cheerily, "I'm hoping it turns out to be a fun party."

"I'm sure it will," Sarah said, though she didn't believe it for a minute. "So is there anything I can bring?"

"Just the girls!"

"Okay. It's at seven, right? I'll see you then." She hung up, and Jade, hearing the tail end of the conversation, announced, "I'm not going!"

"To Dee Linn's party?"

"That's right. No way." Jade was emphatic as she stood in the archway leading to the parlor. She folded her arms across her chest, almost daring Sarah to thwart her.

"Of course you're going," Sarah said, as if there were no discussion to be had. She could match her older daughter's stubborn streak with her own. "Why wouldn't you?"

"It'll be boring."

"No excuse. It's a family get-together to welcome us to Stewart's Crossing. Since we're the guests of honor, we have to attend. Besides, your aunt has been working on it for weeks."

"I barely know any of them, except for Becky, and I don't really like her."

"It's time to change all that. I'm sorry we didn't keep in better contact with all of them, but that's water under the bridge. We can make up for lost time."

"Save me," Jade said, leaning against the pillar.

"Have a positive attitude for once, and look at this as an opportunity to get to know your relatives."

"*You* don't even like any of them."

"Of course I do."

"You think Dee Linn's husband is some kind of monster or pervert or something."

"I said 'male chauvinist'," Sarah declared.

"And what about Aunt Danica? You're not exactly BFFs with her, either."

Jade's assessment of Sarah's relationship with her sister-in-law wasn't far off. Jacob's wife was a snob as well as a drama queen. Danica wore her superior attitude with the flair of a self-involved, has-been movie star.

"It's just that they've had some rough patches in their marriage," she hedged. Jake and Danica were currently "back together," though they'd recently been separated again over rumors of Jake's infidelity and Danica's excessive spending. Who knew the truth? Sarah tried to stay out of it and had learned long ago to keep her mouth shut each time Jake swore he was getting a divorce because inevitably he and Danica made up and got back together, rekindling their passion for each other, then acted as if they were the poster children for being "in love."

"I *know* you're not cool with Uncle Roger. You said yourself that he can't stay out of prison, but you and Aunt Dee were talking about him."

"Yes. Yes, we were," Sarah admitted; her true feelings for her older half brother were murky. She hadn't seen Roger for a long while and found that oddly comforting. "I don't think Roger will be there," she said to Jade. He'd been out of prison for six or seven months; his most recent run-in with the law was for domestic abuse, though the woman who'd called 911 had appeared less harmed than Roger, whose lip had been split from a punch and cut from her ring. He hadn't fought the charges, which Jacob had said "was an idiot move" and had instead worked a plea deal. The woman had landed in prison six months later for a drug charge, and Roger was now out, supposedly walking the straight and narrow—aside from not keeping in touch with his parole officer.

He was definitely under the radar, so who knew?

Jade hadn't finished with her list of complaints about the family. "Then there's Grandma. Wow. She's a lot of fun."

After their last visit to Pleasant Pines, Sarah couldn't argue about her mother. "Point taken. But give her a break, okay? Grandma's ill, and she had a hard life."

"Haven't we all?"

It wasn't the same, Sarah thought, knowing her mother had been an orphan who had married twice, never happily, buried both husbands, and lost a child.

"Fine," Jade said, arching an eyebrow that silently called her mother a hypocrite. "I'm just saying they're all weird. Everyone in the family."

Sarah actually laughed. "You mean weirder than us?"

"Oh, Mom!" Jade was not amused. "You want me to go to a costume party, really?"

"It's almost Halloween."

"Big freakin' deal." Jade's face was pulled into a serious pout, and she looked absolutely miserable, but Sarah was having none of it.

"Look, I don't even like to dress up. You know that. But it's Aunt Dee's thing."

"Well, it sucks."

"Maybe so, but too bad. Besides, I thought you were into the whole Goth thing."

"That's different, that's my style," Jade said, scowling.

"Okay." Tired of the argument, Sarah left Jade digging into her jeans pocket for her phone and headed into the kitchen.

Sarah understood how her daughter felt. She too would have liked to have opted out of what was sure to be an over-the-top extravaganza. Sarah's sister didn't know the meaning of small, quiet get-together. In Dee Linn's estimation, a party was a P-A-R-T-Y, with several exclamation points following the capital letters.

Though Sarah would never admit it, she didn't blame Jade for not wanting to go to the party. The last thing they needed to do was gear up for a big event when they had barely begun to find their pajamas, dishes, or bedding. No one here was in the mood for Dee Linn's Halloween gala.

The kids had been going to school, Gracie with a little enthusiasm, Jade with zero; she'd also complained about her car still being in the shop, but there was nothing to be done about that until her Honda was operational, and Hal, if not speedy, was meticulous.

The family's belongings had shown up in a portable moving container that had been dropped off near the guesthouse, so finally they were officially out of Vancouver. Now if only they could move into the guesthouse. "Soon," she told herself, crossing her fingers that the meeting with her contractor would confirm what he'd promised before they'd moved.

Leaning over the sink in the kitchen, she peered through the window into the darkness beyond. The smaller house, like its larger counterpart, seemed dark and forlorn. Abandoned. She'd already walked through it without the contractor. The real tour of the main house was scheduled for later in the week, but at least she now knew that the guesthouse was close to being livable. The plumbing and electrical adjustments had already been completed; now it looked like they were waiting for a heating inspection.

Probably from Clint, she reminded herself.

No big deal. Right?

Then why did the thought of seeing him again make her nervous? She knew the answer to that one, of course. She just dreaded the meeting.

She started to retrace her steps to the living area and was skirting a stack of boxes marked KITCHEN when her cell phone jangled. Scooping it from the counter where she'd left it, she eyed the small screen. Evan's number appeared.

Her heart sank.

She did not want to speak to him. Not now. Not ever.

But Gracie had made a good point earlier. It was time to quit being a coward by dodging his calls. She picked up on the third chirp. "Hi, Evan," she said.

"Wow, a real voice," he said, and she inwardly sighed at his sarcasm. "I was beginning to think you weren't alive."

"Still kicking," she said, sitting on the second step of the staircase. She glanced through the long windows flanking the front doors. Outside, night had descended completely beyond the glass, a dark void. She felt, rather than saw, that someone was watching her, which was of course nuts. "Just busy."

"So you say."

"What's up?" She conjured his image in her mind. Over six feet, with the body of a football running back, Evan was handsome and fit, his eyes a frosty blue, his gaze hard and sharp. He could turn on the charm when he wanted, then have it disappear in a flash; his temper was quick, hot, and deadly. He'd grown up rich and privileged and was used to getting his way.

Now he was turning on the charm. "I thought I'd take you to dinner."

"I'm in Stewart's Crossing."

"I realize that, but I was heading across the mountains to Sun River anyway. I planned to spend the weekend there, what with it being the holiday and all."

"It's too far out of your way." Sun River was a resort south of Bend on the eastern slopes of the Cascade Mountains.

"I've got some suppliers in The Dalles, you know, so lots of times I shoot down 84 all the way to The Dalles before hitting the road south. I can do some business in The Dalles and also avoid a lot of the skiers heading to Mount Hood Meadows."

"It's not winter," Sarah pointed out.

"I'm just saying, I'd like to see you again."

Here it comes, Sarah thought. *The blame.* She braced herself and felt her back muscles tighten.

Evan didn't disappoint. "Listen, honey, I know we didn't leave on the best of terms, and I want to change that." She heard the bit of a wheedle in his voice, and she ignored it.

"Not a good idea, Evan. And I'm not 'honey'."

"You are to me."

Her insides ground. Why had she ever caved and dated him?

"I thought I made myself clear. It's time for me to move on. You too. It's over, not that there was anything to begin with."

A beat.

Was he angry? Seething? Hurt?

"I love you," he said with the barest undercurrent of anger in his words. "You know that. I wanted—well, still want—to spend the rest of my life with you."

"Evan, seriously. We went out . . . what? Three, maybe four times? It wasn't a relationship."

"So I was right," he said with a little less restraint, his trigger-quick anger sparking. "There's someone else."

"Someone else," she repeated. "Where did you get that? There's no one."

"Why don't I believe you?" His voice was cold.

She felt herself growing angry. "Even if there was someone else, that's my business. I think it would be best if you didn't call me again," she stated firmly. "And don't stop by. We're done, Evan." She hung up just as Gracie cruised by on her way to the kitchen.

Immediately the phone started ringing again. Evan's name and number flashed onto the screen. She clicked her cell off as she knew he wouldn't give up. He'd call back over and over again, leaving messages, each a little more demanding, and inevitably he would end up reminding her of all he'd done for her while she was an employee at Tolliver Construction. He'd already twisted history enough to believe that it was because of him, not her own abilities, that she'd been promoted by his father before Bill retired and made his son president.

"Evan?" Gracie asked.

"Evan," she agreed.

"He's a dipstick."

Though Sarah agreed, she held her tongue. "Let's not think about him right now."

"But he's here, isn't he?"

Sarah gave her daughter a long look. "Here?" she repeated, the warning hairs on the back of her neck lifting a little. "What're you talking about?"

"Evan was at the pizza parlor when we were there."

Sarah was slowly shaking her head. "Of course not."

"Not inside," her daughter clarified as Sarah told herself this was all a big mistake. "His truck was parked outside, across the street."

"You're sure?"

"Uh-huh."

Gracie wasn't one to make a mistake like this. "I was gonna say somethin', but we ran into that neighbor guy and I forgot."

Sarah's mind was turning in circles. If Evan really was in Stewart's Crossing, why hadn't he said as much on the phone?

"Did Evan see us?"

"Well, he was sitting right there. I looked at him, and he looked down, like he was texting or something. He was wearing his Mariners baseball cap and sunglasses."

"So he saw us talking to Clint? The neighbor?" She thought about the way Clint had touched her on the shoulder. Familiarly. As if they shared something, which, of course they did, a past she'd never mentioned to anyone outside of Stewart's Crossing.

"I don't know how he could've missed it." Gracie shrugged as Sarah's heart did a nosedive. That explained the comment about her seeing someone else. "Evan's weird, Mom, I'm glad you told him to leave us alone."

"Me too," Sarah said with new-felt conviction. Not for the first time, she wished she hadn't ever agreed to go out with him. She should've known better. Now, though, it was too late for self-recriminations. What's done was done. She only hoped that this time he got the message.

And what if he hasn't? What if he truly was in Stewart's Crossing and saw Clint touch your shoulder the other day? Out of the corner of her eye she glanced at the windows, where the darkness beyond was almost palpable. Even if he had been in town, and that was un-likely, what were the chances he'd stuck around?

Don't borrow trouble. He's not lurking outside, not peering through binoculars at the windows, trying to catch a glimpse of you, not plotting some bizarre revenge. He's not psychotic or some kind of sociopath. He's just a narcissist.

"Bad enough," she said under her breath as she walked to the dining room and dimmed the lights. There were no blinds to snap shut, no curtains to pull, no drapes to close. No, for the present, the windows that existed were bare, and they would be until the place was renovated. As for the guesthouse, she decided at that moment she'd spend the money and buy cheap blinds just to ensure her family's privacy.

Don't let the seeds of paranoia grow. Nothing good will come of it.

No longer backlit, she stepped closer to the windows and peered outside again. Pale moonlight washed the landscape, flimsy clouds unable to hide the luminescence of a nearly full moon.

No one was outside.

Nothing evil skulked in the shadows.

Still, goose bumps rose on the back of her arms.

She leaned closer to the window, placing the tips of her fingers on the cold, watery glass and squinting into the darkness. Surely they were alone. Surely they were safe. Surely—

Thud!

Sarah nearly jumped from her skin.

What the devil? Instinctively, she glanced to the ceiling. One of the girls must've gone upstairs, she thought. She looked in the living room and found both Jade and Gracie huddled beneath blankets around the iPad. "Is the cable ever going to get hooked up?" Jade asked, looking up through the fringe of long bangs. "I mean real cable. So we can watch TV?"

"In a couple of days, in the guesthouse."

"God, it's like forever!"

"You guys hear anything?" Sarah asked.

"What?" Gracie raised her eyes, lifting her gaze from the screen.

Jade ignored her.

"Nothing." No reason to freak out the girls just because of her overactive imagination. She'd let Evan's call and the isolation of the night get to her, which was just plain stupid.

Nevertheless, after grabbing a flashlight from the kitchen, she climbed the stairs to investigate. On the second floor, she yanked open the door to the first room, the one that had belonged to her twin brothers, and shined her flashlight over the barren interior. The room appeared the same as it had earlier: cobwebs and draped furniture, a few old basketball posters falling from the walls, twin bed frames pushed against the closet. Nothing was out of place.

The same went for the rooms across the hallway, including hers. The twin bed that she had occupied growing up, lying sleepless on hot summer nights, eyes focused on the ceiling as she dreamed of Clint Walsh, was intact, its mattress wrapped in plastic. Her unoccupied desk was pushed into a corner, and faded awards for riding gathered dust on the old bulletin board. Everything was still. Motionless.

Dee Linn's room, still painted a faded pink, was nearly empty of furniture. The oversized bathroom and walk-in storage closet felt cold and dusty from disuse.

On the second floor, everything looked untouched, just the way it had the last time she'd been up here, earlier in the day. But then, deep down, she'd known it would.

Tamping down her dread, she mounted the stairs to the third floor. Her fingers skimmed the worn banister, and she forced her feet to step quickly up the remaining steps. At the landing, she flipped the switch for the hallway, and the lightbulb in the old fixture popped, flashing bright before dying completely.

"Great." Turning on her flashlight, she passed by the closed door to the master bedroom suite, which consisted of the bedroom, a dressing room, a private bath, and a study. The suite was one more area that had been off-limits to her as a child. The door had always been closed, and she'd heard the fights that had emanated through the solid wood, her mother's accusations and shrieks, the harsh slapping sounds of flesh meeting flesh. She suspected her parents had fought as violently as they'd made love, with a blinding, hostile passion that Sarah had yet to understand. For most of Sarah's life, Arlene had seemed angry, while Franklin, a kinder soul, had often been distant to his children.

For the moment, she ignored that closed door to her parents' fortress and trained her flashlight's beam along the hallway and on the door of the room near the attic stairs. Theresa's room. Another spot that was forbidden.

Sweeping the flashlight's beam over the floor, Sarah sensed her heartbeat quicken, a cold dread growing within.

Gritting her teeth, she walked to the room. At the doorway, she imagined she heard sobbing from within, but, of course, that was impossible. Heart beating light and fast, she twisted the knob and pushed on the panels. For once the door opened easily, swinging into the cold room.

Stomach tight, Sarah stepped carefully inside and chided herself for the overwhelming sensation that someone or something was waiting inside, ready to lunge from the darkness.

The room was still.

The moaning she'd conjured was just the whisper of the wind blowing through the crack in the window.

Nothing sinister.

Nothing unworldly.

Just the sough of a breeze.

No one was inside.

Nothing was wrong.

Everything from the cracked mirror to the half-draped vanity was just as she'd left it.

She let out her breath as the flashlight's beam swept over the floor.

Standing in front of the fireplace stood the little Madonna statue.

Sarah's heart stilled.

Impossible!

If the statue had fallen, it would not have landed on its base and would have cracked or splintered into a thousand pieces.

With icy talons of fear climbing up her spine, she stepped backward.

Suddenly a gust of wind, heavy with the smell of the Columbia, raced into the room. The curtains fluttered wildly, twirling in a gauzy, macabre dance.

Sarah bit back a scream as the door to the hallway slammed with a hard, loud *slam*.

Whirling, she shined the light over the door and walls, then stepped back, knocking the Madonna over and nearly tripping.

"Leave us alone!" she hissed through gritted teeth, addressing the ghost that she purported not to believe in, the spirit of Angelique Le

Duc. "Do you hear me?" she said and heard the desperation in her words. "Leave me and my family the hell alone!"

She half expected some apparition to whip by her, a hollow, mind-numbing laugh trailing after it, just as she'd seen in Hollywood horror movies.

Instead she saw and heard nothing, not even the faintest sough of the wind any longer. Inside the room there was only an aching, nearly palpable silence.

CHAPTER 14

"**M**om?" Gracie's voice accompanied the creak of the opening door to the third-floor room. "Are you okay?" Her daughter stood in the dark hallway. "I heard you talking to someone."

"Just myself," Sarah said quickly, mentally kicking herself for letting her case of nerves get to her. She must've sounded like a lunatic, railing at imaginary ghosts. Quickly she scooped up the tiny statue and set it back on the mantel, where it had stood for years. Luckily it was still intact. *Stay,* she mentally ordered it, staring into the Madonna's beatific face.

"What're you doing in here?"

"I thought I heard something. Turns out, the little Madonna statue fell off the mantel, probably from a gust of wind from this damned window." She walked to the faulty jamb and tried to force the panes downward, but the glass was stuck and wouldn't budge. "Something we'll have to put up with until the windows are replaced," she said. "Come on, let's go downstairs. I could use a cup of hot chocolate." *With a significant amount of liquor tossed into it.*

"Did you know that there's a cemetery on this property?" Gracie asked once they were in the kitchen again and the ghosts of the past remained upstairs.

"Of course." How often had she and Clint gone riding on the pastureland abutting the small fenced plot? As a child, she too had been fascinated with the family graves and had wandered through the graying headstones, as she'd marveled at the names and dates carved into each marker. Children younger than herself had been laid to rest there, along with her ancestors, some of whom had lived to be over a hundred.

"And a lot of people died here?"

"A lot of people who lived here were buried there."

"No, I mean they died *here!*" Gracie pointed emphatically at the floor. "Not in the kitchen, but in the house or on the property. I looked it up. Not just Angelique and maybe her husband."

"Maxim."

"One of the ranch hands hung himself out in the bunkhouse," Gracie said.

"That was just a rumor."

"What about Grandpa?"

"My dad was sick a long while, and he wasn't young. It happens, honey. People die." Where was this going?

"It seems like there have been lots of 'em." She angled her face up to stare at Sarah. "You probably know Angelique Le Duc has her own tomb too?"

Nodding, Sarah found a box of cocoa mix and pulled out a packet. She dumped the powdery contents into a cup she'd brought from Vancouver and heated the concoction in the ancient microwave, the only kitchen appliance that still worked.

"You never told me about the cemetery and the tomb," Gracie said.

"I never really thought about it."

"So have you been inside?" she pressed. "I mean, is it locked or open? There's nothing in there, right? Since Angelique was never found. No other dead bodies?"

"None that I know of."

"Has anyone checked?"

As the microwave dinged, Sarah shook her head. "Maybe." She opened the microwave to pull out the mug, but one touch and she realized the ceramic cup was too hot. "I think my brothers talked about it once, but that's all it was—just talk. You know how boys are," Sarah said, though as a child she'd wondered if maybe there was something in the tomb. If not the bones of Angelique Le Duc, maybe the skeletons of others who had gone missing over the years. She'd even thought about her older sister, Theresa, but had never breathed a word of it as the subject of Theresa possibly being dead was taboo. No one ever mentioned it. Ever.

Using a dish towel as an oven mitt, she carried the mug to the table, where it steamed, giving off a warm, chocolate scent. "It's hot. Let it cool."

Gracie ignored the cocoa as she climbed onto a battered stool near the counter. "Is it sealed?"

"I . . . don't know." Sarah shrugged, feigning disinterest when really the crypt, with its intricate biblical carvings, had always fascinated and frightened her. Angels and scriptures had decorated the tomb—winged, spiritual creatures and banners, with short passages from the New Testament, carved into marble that had chipped and darkened over time. She'd touched those cool walls, traced the chiseled words of scripture with her fingertips and yes, often wondered who, if anyone, lay within.

"Can we get inside?" Gracie asked.

The thought was petrifying, if a little inviting. Yes, she was curious, but if a dead body were inside, wouldn't it be best to let it rest in peace? *Not if it would solve a family mystery.* "Why would you want to?"

"Maybe there's some clue to what happened to Angelique."

"In the vault?" Jade asked, walking in on the end of the conversation. "How morbid." She too pulled up a stool near the counter and pushed aside a box of old cookware Sarah hadn't yet sorted through. "You're obsessed."

Gracie threw her a "who needs you?" look. "At least it's a better obsession than yours."

Jade looked at her sister as if she'd gone mad. "I'm not obsessed with any—"

"Cody Russell?"

"That's not obsession. It's . . ."

"What?" Gracie cut her off. "Love?"

"Oh, get over yourself," Jade tossed back. "What do you know about it?"

"Enough!" Sarah declared. She was sick of the bickering, and her case of nerves hadn't completely abated. "Jade, do you want some cocoa?"

Jade glanced at Gracie's cup. "Sure, why not? Got marshmallows?"

"I really doubt it." Sarah started the instant hot chocolate process all over again, using the last packet. "Oh, wait . . ." She found an unopened bag of miniature marshmallows that she'd put in one of the few food boxes they'd hauled from Vancouver. "Your lucky day," she told her older daughter and was rewarded with an eye roll.

"I'll take some," Gracie said, and Sarah dropped a few of the not-so-soft white bits into her younger daughter's cup.

As she heated Jade's cocoa, Sarah relaxed a little and told herself she'd overreacted earlier. So the statue had fallen off the mantel and landed upright. So what? It *could* happen. And if Evan were really in Stewart's Crossing, yeah, okay, it was odd that he hadn't mentioned it, but not a big deal, right?

But what about the missing teenaged girl? That is *something to worry about.*

"You know," she said over the quiet hum of the microwave's slowly rotating turntable, "I've been thinking that Gracie's right."

"About what?" Jade asked, looking faintly horrified.

"About a dog. Maybe we do need one." *A big dog,* she silently added, *a guard dog.*

"Mom, are you serious?" Gracie jumped off her stool, she was so excited.

"Um-hm. And the sooner the better, I think. Let's go to the shelter tomorrow after school and pick one out."

A wide smile stretched across Gracie's face. "A puppy?"

"Let's start with a mature dog," Sarah suggested. "One that's at least house-trained."

"Okay." Gracie was beaming as Sarah found the pot of this morning's coffee and poured herself a cup. She retrieved Jade's cup of hot chocolate, then put the mug of coffee on the turntable in its stead and, with a push of a button, once again started the microwave.

"You're giving in?" Jade asked, lifting her brows.

"Uh-huh." Sarah added a handful of marshmallows and placed the warm cup on the counter in front of her eldest. "Gracie's right, 'a promise is a promise.' "

Jade thought that over. "Can I ditch school so we can go earlier to get the dog?"

"I said, 'after . . .' Oh."

Sarah shot her a look but saw that Jade was teasing, which was nice. Glimpses of the younger daughter she remembered, hidden behind makeup and attitude, were rare but gave Sarah hope that, after these trying teenage years, Jade would come around again, show an interest in school, and realize that she was smart and pretty and could do anything she wanted.

As Jade blew across her cup, she said, "Seriously, Mom, I think public school would be a better fit for me."

"You've only been to Our Lady a few days."

"I can already tell it's not going to work."

"Can we give it the rest of this year, which, by the way, is already paid for? Our Lady is a great school. If you still feel this way after the end of the school year, then we'll discuss."

"But I hate it," Jade grumbled.

"Just give it a shot, okay?"

"You don't know what it's like."

"I didn't want to go there either when my folks sent me," Sarah said. The microwave dinged loudly, and she grabbed her cup carefully, using the dish towel again. "I hated leaving my friends from junior high. Thought I'd die. In fact, I think I even told my parents that I would. Dad would have let me pull out and go to the public school. He was kind of a softie where we girls were concerned. We could get away with murder with him. But let me tell you, there was no way my mother would hear of it." She took a tentative drink of her coffee. "You know, I really hate to admit it, even to this day, but Mom was right. I ended up with tons of new friends as well as keeping the old ones that I made in elementary and junior high school."

"My 'old ones' are in Vancouver," Jade pointed out.

"Which is less than a hundred miles away. You won't lose them. Not the real ones."

"You don't know that," Jade charged.

"Let's not argue," Gracie cut in as she retrieved her spot on the scarred stool. "We're getting a dog! And that's like the coolest!"

"It is," Sarah agreed and said, "Let's have a toast," then clinked her cup to both her daughters'. "To Rover."

Jade groaned loudly. "*Not* Rover. Geez, Mom, you're ridiculous!"

"Then Fifi. Or maybe Spot or Fido," Sarah teased.

"God, Mom, you're the lamest." But Jade actually chuckled.

Sarah smiled. "Okay, we'll wait until we meet him."

"Or her," Gracie said.

"Right, or her," Sarah agreed. "Now, everyone who has homework better get at it."

This time Jade's groan was sincere, though Gracie, anxious to please lest Sarah change her mind about the dog, scrambled off her stool and headed for the dining room, where she'd tossed her backpack earlier. Jade's phone vibrated loudly enough that Sarah heard it. Climbing off her stool, Jade began texting like mad as she too left the room.

Alone again, Sarah sipped her coffee in the kitchen and told herself she'd been irrational earlier.

There were no ghosts haunting this old house.

Nor had there ever been.

But as she carried her girls' cups to the sink, she caught a glimpse of the marshmallows melting in Jade's remaining cocoa—streaming, white, phantom-like strands of sugar—and Sarah knew she was kidding herself.

The ghost of Blue Peacock Manor had roamed these hallways for nearly a century and wasn't about to stop anytime soon. Sarah had always known it at some level. The question was: what could she do about it?

Lying on his stomach in the brush, his elbows propped on a fallen log, he stared at the old house through night-vision goggles. He hadn't been here in a long while, and even in the darkness it was obvious the house was in sad repair, not that he cared. He was just surprised that anyone would want to live in it. Especially because he'd been told that the place was haunted with restless spirits, that unthinkable acts had occurred within the walls of Blue Peacock Manor.

All the better, though.

For his work.

Ever since he'd spied Jade on the steps of Our Lady of the River, he'd decided to place her on his list of candidates. He only hoped she was more malleable than Rosalie, who had turned into an A-one bitch. He had the war wounds to prove it after her attempted escape. Shit, she'd almost gotten away, and that really pissed him off! But, he reminded himself, he needed a couple of girls with fire. A meek one would be necessary, of course, and he'd already chosen her, but Jade, with her sultry attitude and haunted eyes, would be a nice addition.

Adjusting the vision, he froze as he saw movement in his field of vision, then relaxed when he realized it was only a coyote wandering across what had once been the front lawn. The animal looked directly at him before skulking away. Once again he concentrated on the windows of the house, where lights from inside backlit anyone moving within. But he saw nothing, and even when he slid the night-vision lenses off and used his binoculars, training them on the glowing patches of light, no one appeared.

They were there, though; the Explorer was parked near the garage.

"Come on," he whispered, wanting just one more glimpse, a little peek, and then he lucked out. As if someone inside had heard him and heeded his calling, a shadow appeared in the window. Not Jade, with her pouty mouth, big eyes, and pointy little chin, but the other one, the younger girl, who was not quite a woman, maybe twelve or thirteen, an innocent . . . a virgin?

Probably.

Oh, *that* would be good. Very good. He almost peed himself with delight at the prospect. Yes, yes!

The wheels in his mind began to whir as he considered, once more, the prospect of taking both girls. It would be tricky, probably not accomplished at the same time . . . no! One would become bait for the other. Oh, yeah, that would be it.

The scenario played out in his mind, and he smiled to himself. He would have to work fast; capturing this pair would become his ultimate goal, and then he'd move on. But if he found a way to lure the little one, certainly big sis would follow.

The light snapped off, and the girl in the window was no longer there. He took his time getting the lay of the land, making note of the outbuildings and lane, the cliffs, forest, and property lines, the river on one side, the Walsh property on the other, the county road bisecting the parcel, and government land backing up to the rest.

And while he waited, not one car came down the lane.

This would be an ideal place to nab them and far enough away from the stable to be safe.

Slowly he scooted away from the log, packed up his gear, and began jogging back to the spot where he'd hidden his vehicle on a forest service road. Through the brush and around a small, fenced-in plot was a cemetery, complete with overgrown headstones and a bigger tomb. The fence was falling down, nearly useless in places, but he skirted the graveyard anyway, not out of any respect for the dead, but because he didn't want to disturb any lingering spirits. He told himself ghosts didn't exist, that demons and witches and the lot were all created to keep people in line, but deep down the idea of spirits frightened him, and he wasn't certain they weren't real. How many times had he thought he'd seen a wraith or ghost, here, on this property? Hadn't the people in town insisted that Blue Peacock Manor was haunted? And hadn't his own mother warned him that malevolent spirits were about, existing among the living, and, of course, collecting in boneyards? Lucifer himself, she'd insisted, had visited the wooded plots surrounding the old house with its peculiar family. "Take a look at them," Mother had advised. "Everyone who lives there. They're touched in the head, I tell you. All a little bit off, and it's because of the demons within."

So now, as always, he gave the ancient cemetery a wide berth and made his way to his waiting truck.

It was time to step up his plans.

Rosalie's eyes felt gritty from lack of sleep when finally the first streaks of dawn filtered through the grimy windows high overhead. Shivering from the cold, her body aching, she felt as if she would never escape.

So it was another day.

Rosalie silently prayed that this was the day that somehow her family would find her.

As if.

Her heart sank, and despair clutched at her as she stared at the dusty rafters supporting the ceiling. She'd seen the bruise developing beneath a long scrape on her side and abdomen where she'd fallen on the fence during her ill-fated escape attempt.

If only she'd gotten away!

She'd spent the hours since then lying on her cot, replaying the scene over and over again, wondering how she could free herself.

It was impossible she decided, tears filling her eyes. Whatever the jerk wanted to do with her, she was doomed. Yanking the sleeping bag closer to her chin, she couldn't stop herself from shaking with the cold. Sniffing and angry with herself, she dashed the tears from her eyes as she recalled the ignominy of being hauled over the dickhead's shoulder like a damned sack of potatoes.

If she could, she'd kill the bastard.

Instead she was stuck here, lying on the stupid cot, feeling sorry for herself, watching as morning light chased away the shadows and gloom of this sorry barn.

Get up. Do something. Anything. Do not let yourself become a victim! You're not dead yet, but you damned well will be if you let this goon do what he wants to do to you!

Sniffing back the last of her tears, she tried to think. To plan. To find a way out of this horrible place, away from the monster—no, make that monsters, plural. The dickhead had Scraggly Hair, a man whom Rosalie instinctively knew was weaker, the follower. Maybe she could get him alone, plead with him . . .

Stop it! Neither of these jerkwads is going to let you go! Get real. You've seen their faces, could ID them. Haven't you watched enough cop shows on cable to know that criminals, at least those with any brains, leave no witnesses?

Her stomach tightened, and fear crawled through her blood. Just because they hadn't killed her yet didn't mean they weren't planning it. And not just her; they'd mentioned others.

Do something, Rosalie. Don't count on Mom or stupid Mel or even Dad to show up. This is on you.

Her bladder was about to burst, so she had to get up. With an effort, she kicked off the sleeping bag and rolled off her cot, only to wince as she straightened. Lifting her sweatshirt, she viewed the bruise. Bluish with green edges, it had spread along one side under her ribs. What if she were bleeding internally? Is that what this meant? Oh, Jesus, that sounded really bad.

Gently she touched the darkened skin and flinched when pain shot through her. Not a good idea to poke it much, especially since the shallow scrape was still raw. She decided to just take care of her bucket business and lie back on her bed of sorts to plot her escape. There had to be a way out of here. *Had* to.

First things first.

She used the damned bucket; after emptying her bladder, she straightened and pulled her pants over her hips with difficulty because of the handcuffs. Working the zipper was worse, and when it was finally up, she let out her breath and scanned the room again, catching a glimmer of something on the floor, something that shined briefly in the weak rays of light. "What the hell?" She took a step forward, saw the glimmer tucked deep into the corner near the doorway to the stall. Across the tiny room in an instant, she bent down and discovered a bit of metal wedged into the crack between the wall and floorboards.

Quickly, she tried to pry it from its resting place, digging with her already-broken nails, attempting to loosen the slim, flat piece with her cuffed hands. "Come on, come on," she whispered. What the devil was this metal strip that she could barely get her finger under? Biting her lip, she dug at the thing and eased it slowly and gently from its resting spot. Finally, it came loose and slid into her palm. A tiny little nail file, no longer than her pinkie, it had a hook on one end and a minuscule hole on the other. She turned it over in her hand and wondered where it had come from. Surely she would have noticed it before now.

Wait! Suddenly she remembered her struggle with her captor's sidekick, Scraggly Hair. This must've fallen out of his pocket during the fight. It wasn't much, but . . . used the right way, into an eye or ear or voice box, the little strip of metal could do some serious damage.

Revived, she started looking around the floor, hoping that something else had fallen out of the little man's pockets and was rewarded with the actual clippers, in pieces, and a tiny chain. Again, they weren't the best weapons, not much really, but they would have to do. For now.

With the element of surprise on her side, the clippers might just be enough for her to get in one good shot and wound her abductor long enough to get free. Next time she wouldn't run blindly, but jump into his truck and drive like a bat out of hell. She remembered that when he'd brought her to this godforsaken place, he'd hauled her inside and left his keys in the truck. He hadn't made that mistake when she'd tried to escape, but hopefully it was his habit to leave the keys in the ignition.

If so, she'd damn well take advantage of it.

Slipping all the metal pieces into the front pocket of her jeans, she felt slightly better than she had since her thwarted run for freedom.

For the first time since she'd been thrown back into this horrid prison, Rosalie felt a tiny ray of hope.

CHAPTER 15

Though it was obvious that Mary-Alice loathed her as much as Jade detested the two-faced "angel" she'd been assigned, Mary-A was impossible to shake. No matter which corridor Jade used at Our Lady of the River, the blonde appeared, always with a cheery, pasted-on smile, and she hung out with Jade as much as possible between classes. It was enough to make Jade sick, so she decided they needed to have it out.

"Look," Jade said as Mary-Alice tagged along while Jade was on her way to her next class. "I don't need a babysitter."

"It's not like that."

"Sure it is."

"I don't know why you have to be so nasty all the time."

Here we go. Jade started down the stairs toward the math wing, where all the classrooms faced the student parking lot. "I'm just used to having my space, that's all."

"No, that isn't all. You're rebelling because you think it's cool."

Jade thought about it half a second and decided maybe honesty was the best policy with Mary-Alice, who was just half a step behind her. "Maybe, but having you puppy dog after me is creepy." From the corner of her eye, Jade saw Mary-Alice's lips tighten at the corners and her eyes flare a bit. "So you can just leave me alone and we'll be cool."

Mary-Alice kept up with her as they wended their way down the staircase teeming with kids hurrying to the second floor, the clatter of footsteps echoing in the stairwell. "I can't. You're my assignment."

Ugh. Of course. They'd reached the first floor and were near the restrooms outside the auditorium. "You mean like you get an 'A' or something if you hang out with me?"

"If I introduce you around and, you know, get you interested in extracurricular activities or clubs or whatever, it goes on my permanent record, and so it's something I can refer to when I apply for college."

"Are you insane?" Jade demanded. "Clubs? No! I'm not—oh, for the love of God!" Before she could think, Jade wrapped her fingers around the other girl's skinny arm and dragged her into the women's washroom.

"What the hell do you think you're doing?" Mary-Alice gasped.

Jade propelled her around the privacy partition blocking the doorway to the area around a row of stainless steel sinks. Paper towels littered the floor. One sink dripped. Hastily written crude comments and/or vows of love covered the back side of the partition and the walls around the mirrors. Cozy, it was not. Jade didn't care. It was time for Mary-Alice to hear her out. "Permanent record? Really?" She dropped Mary-Alice's arm. Mary-A quickly took a step back, rubbing her upper arm and glaring at Jade as if she were the devil incarnate. "I'm not joining any clubs or going to be on some stupid dance committee or whatever it is you think I might get into. I don't like one thing about this school, and I *really* don't like being someone's 'project,' so don't start talking up drama club or pep band or whatever it is you do around here. I'm not interested, and it's not happening. I'm *not* your project, so get over it. Find someone else to mold into a little mini-you, cuz it's not gonna be me."

Mary-A crossed her arms under her chest. Her cheeks were flushed a vibrant angry red. "You have a horrible attitude."

"That is a fact," Jade agreed.

"You just don't care!"

Jade took a step closer to the popular girl, and though she knew she should shut up and quit while she was ahead, she was so irritated and frustrated and just plain mad that she couldn't stop her tongue. "You know what else is true? You're a fake, Mary-Alice. A back-stabbing, smile-to-your-face fraud."

For a second Jade thought the other girl might slap her, but Mary-Alice gathered herself.

"You'll be sorry you ever said that," Mary-Alice hissed in true drama queen fashion.

"Yeah?"

"I can make your life miserable here at Our Lady."

"You mean more miserable?" Jade didn't doubt it, but lifted a shoulder as if she didn't care. "Bring it on. I don't give a shit."

"You're dead at this school."

"Dead. Okay. That sounds sort of like a threat," Jade observed.

"I mean it. I can . . . I can . . ."

"What?" When Mary-A couldn't seem to complete her thought, Jade said in a tight voice, "So, here's one back at 'cha. I have friends in low places."

"You're threatening *me?*" Mary-Alice squeaked.

A toilet flushed, and a stall door swung into the sink area. A plump, worried-looking girl Jade didn't recognize stepped into the area near the sink. She had to have heard the entire exchange.

"Not a word of this, Dana," Mary-Alice warned her with a deadly smile.

"Of what?" Dana blinked innocently. "I didn't hear anything." She ran her fingers under the hot water, stripped a paper towel from the dispenser, and stared into the mirror, where she caught Jade's gaze. For a second she seemed anxious and ready to shrink away, but somehow she managed to get her case of nerves under control. Flipping her streaked hair over one shoulder with forced confidence, she twisted pink lips into a photo-ready smile that was as practiced and phony as Mary-Alice's. "No," she assured the more popular girl, "I didn't hear one thing."

After tossing her towel into the overflowing bin, Dana hastened around the graffiti-laden partition to the swinging doors to the restroom.

In those few moments Jade's irritation had cooled slightly, and she realized she'd said more than she should have; that was the trouble with her temper. "Okay, let's not get crazy. Just back off. Your duty, or whatever you call it, is over. I can find my way around the school by myself, and I don't need your help making friends."

"That's where you're wrong."

"Don't care." Jade hiked the strap of her bag over her shoulder.

"I was just trying to help," Mary-Alice insisted and, like a chameleon, changed her colors, going from fury to contrition.

"You were just hoping to make yourself look good."

"You're seriously twisted," Mary-A said angrily.

"Probably." Jade lifted a shoulder in indifference.

"I don't know why I bother," Mary-Alice said.

"For your permanent record," Jade responded, but Mary-A, as if deciding another second with Jade was too much, had already rounded the partition and shoved through the doors.

Jade figured that the minute she stepped into the hallway Mary-Alice was probably texting all of her friends, maybe the whole damned student body about what a loser Jade was.

Who cared?

You do. More than you want to admit.

Closing her eyes, Jade leaned on the counter where the sinks were mounted. What was she doing? It was one thing to avoid her "angel," but making an out-and-out enemy of Mary-Alice Eklund was just plain stupid. She let out her breath slowly and opened her eyes to catch her uniformed image in the mirror. She just wasn't cut out to be an Our Lady Crusader. She just didn't buy into the whole allegiance-to-my-school thing. Never had. Never would. Didn't her mother know that? Why did Mom insist on punishing her?

Leaning over the leaky faucet, she splashed some water over her face and told herself to cool off, to not let Mary-Alice get to her. She yanked down a paper towel and for the first time noticed posters on the walls inside the restroom urging the football team to win the big game this weekend.

Really?

In here? So that as you came out of the stall or were combing your hair or adding lip gloss or whatever you'd feel some sense of rah-rah for Our Lady's football team.

Jade leaned closer to the mirror and brushed a bit of fallen mascara off her cheek. Another poster caught her eye, black and white with a picture of Rosalie Jamison front and center, a reward offered for evidence leading to her safe return. Fleetingly she wondered about the missing teenager, who, according to what she'd heard in the hallways, hadn't gone to Our Lady.

"Lucky," Jade said, then regretted the word the minute it slipped out because it seemed that this was serious.

Bracing herself for the rest of the day, Jade hiked her backpack higher on her shoulder and was starting to text Cody again as she pushed open the swinging door of the restroom. Head bent, she ran into a tall dude who was talking to his friend while half running in the other direction. "Hey!" she cried as her cell phone slipped out of her hand to skid across the polished floor and smash into a radiator. "Watch where you're going!"

"Me?" He swung around, skidding to a stop, and she was about to lay into him when she recognized him. Liam Longstreet. Of all the rotten luck! Mary-A's boyfriend and a jock with an athletic swagger and killer smile.

Perfect.

His friend was shorter, thicker, with red hair and a smattering of freckles across the bridge of his nose.

Other than these two idiots, the long corridor was empty.

"Whoa," Liam Longstreet, who needed to shave or get serious about that beard shadow, stared down at her from somewhere around six feet two inches. He held out both his hands, fingers splayed, and took a step back. "Sorry. Didn't see you."

She scrambled for her phone, but it had slid closer to him, so as she reached for it, her boots slipping a little, he snagged it from the floor. "Give me that!" she ordered.

In a second her life flashed before her eyes. What if he kept it? Saw her pictures and her texts to Cody? Read everything she'd ever written? Saw her in various states of undress and posted those pics on Instagram or Twitter or wherever? What if he called or texted the friends on her contact list? Panic crawled through her as she realized that, with her phone, he could do to her what Mary-Alice, his girlfriend, had threatened.

"Said I was sorry." But he still didn't release the phone.

"So prove it." She held out her hand defiantly, palm up, while inside she was crumbling. Desperate. There were photos of her and Cody kissing and touching and . . . oh, crap! "Give it back." Oh, God, was her voice actually trembling?

She hadn't even noticed that Liam's friend was taking in the exchange with a twisted smile on his face and a glint in his eye.

"Let's take a look," the friend suggested, "See what she's got in there." He took a swipe at the phone, but Liam's fingers curled around it.

Jade said, "That's private property."

The tardy bell rang loudly, echoing down the empty hallway. Great, she was late. Again. "If you don't give it back to me, I'm going to tell Father Paul that you stole it from me." The threat about going to the priest had worked with Mary-Alice, so maybe . . .

"Don't do it, man. She's fuckin' freakin'! Doesn't want us to see what she's got on it," the friend advised. "Oooh, this could be good."

What a Neanderthal! Jade's stomach curdled. "You steal private property, you're off the team and probably expelled from school," she said, lifting her chin. "Now, give it back." Her arm was still out-stretched, and somehow she wasn't visibly shaking, even though she was trembling inside.

"Don't do it," Redhead advised again.

Liam shook his head. "I said I was sorry." Without so much as a glance at his friend, he placed the phone in her open palm.

Relieved beyond belief, Jade wrapped her fingers over the phone and dropped it quickly into her bag, but to add insult to injury, she felt her cheeks flaming. The big dumb-ass. His friend, shorter by three or four inches, still had a stupid smirk plastered across his freckled face. "What're you laughing at?" she demanded, bristling.

"You. Who the hell are you?" he asked.

"No one you need to know." Jade started to move away from them.

"You got that right," he agreed, shaking his nearly shaved head. "Jesus, Longstreet, that was a mistake. You *had* her, man. You had her." Throwing another superior glance at Jade, he sneered, "But, hell, what would you want with her? Come on, Longstreet. Let's roll."

"Good idea," Jade said and turned on her heel, feeling two sets of eyes watching her backside.

"Crazy bitch," the shorter guy muttered, and Jade wanted to turn and face him, yell back that he was an A-one dick, but decided she'd done enough damage for the day.

"Grow up, Prentice," Liam muttered.

So now he was playing the nice-guy role? Oh, sure. The guy who was hooked up with "Angel" Mary-A? Not likely. Really, could life really get any worse?

"You're a fuckin' asshole, Longstreet," Prentice retorted. "Just an observation. Don't take it personal."

Jade caught a glimmer of why her mother hated it when she let an f-bomb fly. Maybe she'd quit swearing. Or at least try to, though it was hard not to swear a blue streak at dicks like Longstreet and Prentice. At the stairs, she cast one curious glance over her shoulder and saw Longstreet's friend catch her eye, only to flip her off.

Grow up, she mouthed and if looks could kill, she'd already be six feet under. Prentice looked positively psychotic, but Liam was already walking away, rounding a corner, probably having already forgotten the incident.

"Losers," Jade said under her breath and hurried quickly toward her next class.

Longstreet couldn't be that great if he hung out with that jerkwad of a friend. From the corner of her eye she saw that the red-haired dirtbag was laughing now. She knew that she'd made another couple of enemies.

So far she was batting a thousand.

"What's that?" Scottie asked when she and Gracie were walking to the cafeteria for lunch and she caught a peek inside Gracie's backpack. She was looking at the journal Gracie had found in the basement. Gracie had slid it into a plastic freezer bag to protect it and kept it with her all the time.

"Nothing." So far she'd told no one about the old book she'd found in the basement, but she would have to soon. Because she needed an interpreter. The pages were so old and frail they almost cracked when you leafed through them, and the writing, a fluid feminine style, had faded with time but was still legible. The only problem? The whole diary was written in French, and though Gracie had tried typing in some of the phrases, using an online translator from French to English, she'd barely made out any of the content.

She knew the year was 1924, but other than that she hadn't made out much.

"Do you know French?"

Scottie shook her head, her brown hair shifting across her shoulders. "No. But my aunt Claudette does. She used to live in Paris."

"Does she live around here?"

"New York. Why?"

"I need someone who can read French." Other kids were filling the hallways, talking, laughing, and cursing, carrying books and checking their cell phones. Couples hung on each other, while packs of friends clogged the corridors. Gracie and Scottie had to wend their way through the throng and yell over the cacophony of voices and clang of slamming lockers.

"You're a dick, Carter!" one boy yelled over his shoulder as he jogged toward the cafeteria.

"Bite me, Maloney!" was the response.

"Why do you need a translator?" Scottie asked as they rounded the final corner to the cafeteria and the smell of tangy pizza sauce reached Gracie's nostrils.

Should she tell the other girl? Scottie was genuinely interested, but Scottie was a bigmouth. You just couldn't trust her with a secret.

"Oh, it's just something my dad wants me to do," Gracie said. "Because, he, like, wants to take me to Paris and the French Riviera, and he thinks it would be best if I knew the language."

Scottie pulled a face. "I would do it then. To go to France. My aunt Claudette, she used to be Claudia before she moved over there, she says it's fabulous. No, wait." Scottie paused and lifted her head at an angle, as if she were posing. "Paris, the City of Light is *très magnifique!*"

"I thought that was L.A."

"No, that's the City of Angels." She frowned. "Or maybe lights, plural." She shrugged. "Anyway, Aunt Claudette thinks you should do anything short of killing to get to Paris."

"All I need is a translator." She knew that Jade had taken a little French, but not that much, and besides, she couldn't trust her sister with a secret like this—not Jade, who didn't believe in anything and thought Gracie was an idiot, or worse. Gracie was pretty sure her mother could speak some French too, but no way was she going to ask Mom. She would utterly flip.

"So what about Miss Beatty?" Scottie suggested. "You know, the music teacher? She splits her time between here and the high school."

"So?"

"She teaches French too. My cousin had her last year."

"Can your cousin read it?"

Scottie shook her head. "She got a D one semester, and Uncle Ned flipped cuz he wants her to go away to school. In my family, Aunt Claudette is your best bet." Her gaze moved away from Gracie as it always did. Scottie was one of those people who always expected someone more interesting to show up. "Oh," she said, "There's Rita! You *have* to meet her. She's like super fun and is going with a sophomore at Our Lady." Scottie lowered her voice. "Her parents don't know. She sneaks out to meet him behind their backs." Her eyes glinted a bit as she shared the gossip, and Gracie decided for sure that Scottie didn't need to know about the journal.

No one did.

Not even Jade, who so far hadn't mentioned that she'd spied Gracie coming out of the basement. What was up with that?

Gracie crossed her fingers that Jade wouldn't spill the beans to Mom, or anyone else for that matter. Not until she had somehow managed to get the journal translated and then, hopefully, help Angelique Le Duc cross over.

CHAPTER 16

At the dining room table, Sarah was making notes to the plans, caught in thoughts of somehow adding a master suite on the main level. She was having trouble with the position of the existing plumbing. She'd talked to the head of a demolition crew, as well as an excavating contractor, and reminded herself she really needed to go down into the basement and look for water damage or any cracks in the foundation, and also check the old behemoth of a furnace, which, no doubt, would have to be replaced. So far she'd avoided descending the hundred-year-old stairs to the unfinished rooms beneath ground level—what had once been a root cellar, laundry, storage, and place for the original wood-burning furnace before it was replaced somewhere around 1960. She'd been reluctant to explore that dark, spider-infested area where she'd been trapped as a child.

But wasn't that exactly one of the reasons she'd come home? To face her old terrors and lay them to rest, to restore this house to its original grandeur as she repaired some of the deepest cracks in her soul?

Her cell phone rang and she answered, "Hello?"

"Sarah, it's Aunt Margie! I heard you're renovating that dreadful old house, and that you've moved in."

"Temporarily, but yes, the girls and I are here."

"Fabulous. I'm on my way."

"What? You mean now?"

"Absolutely. I'll be there in five and I've got a surprise for you!" She clicked off, and Sarah was left sitting at the table, holding her phone and thinking she really didn't need any more surprises. But that was Aunt Marge, or Margie, as she called herself, as different from her older sister, Arlene, as night to day.

"They're the yin and yang of the family," Joseph had said once, years ago, when Sarah had been about ten. On Thanksgiving, when the family had gathered together at this very table, Aunt Marge, drink in hand, had flitted and smiled and flirted with all the men while Arlene had dutifully served everyone. Not to be outdone by her younger sister, Arlene drank as well, the gin and tonics flowing. But as Aunt Marge had become more gregarious, Arlene had turned sour and glum.

"Those two are more like good and evil," Jacob had observed. The Stewart kids were all in the kitchen, running errands for their mother, making certain the holiday was perfect, at least in their mother's eyes. Jacob and Joseph were supposed to be hauling in more wood for the fire, but as usual, they were slacking off, while Dee Linn, in a bit of a snit, was checking on the pies cooling on the counter. The kitchen was warm and smelled of spices and roast turkey, the crystal glasses spotless and glittering, but the day had felt false to Sarah, a display without any true meaning. They'd prayed and given thanks, and there was a bale of hay and fat pumpkins and squash decorating the front door, but the feeling she'd thought should be a part of the holiday was missing. At least for her.

Cousin Caroline, not expected to do any work as she was a guest, had escaped the dining room and was leaning over the counter, playing with the extra salt and pepper shakers. It had seemed she was making sure her cousins caught a glimpse of her very visible cleavage. "Aunt Arlene is really on a crusade today, isn't she?" She'd picked up a basket of rolls that Sarah had taken from the oven where they'd been warming. "What a witch . . . or is she more of a bitch?" Caroline had been fifteen at the time and had wrinkled her nose, trying, as always, to be cute around the twins, or any boy for that matter. A flirt like her mother, she was pretty, with nearly black hair and a flawless olive complexion, but in Sarah's estimation, Caroline was a real pain.

"Don't!" Sarah had said. Her mother had instructed Sarah to bring the basket to the table, but Caroline had plucked a roll from beneath its orange napkin and taken a bite.

"Don't call your mother what she is?" Caroline had teased, her eyes sparkling.

"Don't . . . take a roll, yet," Sarah had clarified. "They're for dinner."

"But you don't care if I call your mother a b-word?" Caroline pushed, just as Clark had walked into the room and heard the end of the exchange.

"Quit picking on her," he'd said as the swinging door shut behind him, cutting off the sounds of conversation from the adults at the table. "She's just a kid."

Sarah had been thankful for the interruption but hadn't liked being reminded that she was the youngest.

Clark added, "Aunt Arlene wants us to take our seats."

"Oh, my. A royal command. We'd all better hurry and obey," Caroline said airily, again with an eye roll. She tossed her hair over her shoulders, timing things so that as she pushed through the swinging door to the dining room, then released it, it nearly hit Clark square in the face.

"So, who's the real bitch," he muttered, just loud enough for Sarah to overhear.

"Mmmm," Caroline had said, but her eyes had shot daggers at Clark. She and her older brother had always been at odds, and it had spilled over to adulthood as well, Sarah knew.

The memory faded just as Sarah heard a car arrive. Marge hadn't been kidding when she'd said they would be right over. As she walked out the door to meet her, she saw not just Marge, but Caroline and Clark too, all of them getting out of an older model Mercedes. Marge was still tall and slim and walked steadily, without so much as a cane for support. She was wearing a sweater and a hip-length jacket over slacks. A long scarf was wrapped around her neck. She'd slowed down, of course, but there was still a bit of spring in her step, and she greeted Sarah with a bear hug. Caroline and Clark, both bundled in long coats, looked on a bit uncomfortably, Sarah thought.

"Surprised?" Marge asked.

"Very much so, yes." Sarah stepped out of the doorway. "Come in."

Marge bustled forward, and her children, not nearly as enthusiastic, each muttered a brief "hi" as they passed by. Sarah pulled the door closed behind them.

"Oh, my," Marge said, eyeing the inside of the house, walking slowly from the foyer to the living room/parlor and hallways. "So dark in here. I just had to see for myself, and I was hoping the place was in better shape on the inside than out. I haven't been here in years," she admitted. "You know, your mother and I . . . well, it was always complicated."

"You hated each other," Caroline said, unbuttoning her coat.

"No, it was just—"

"Don't lie, Mom. We all remember how it was," Caroline insisted flatly.

Some of the gaiety went out of Aunt Marge's eyes. She wore glasses now, and her once-auburn hair was lighter and blonder. Her children too had aged. Clark had filled out, become a tall man with broad shoulders. Caroline was still trim, but her hair was shorter and streaked to hide the beginnings of gray that were invading her once-dark locks.

"Come into the parlor," Sarah offered. "I have coffee—"

"Oh, no, don't bother. I really just came by to see the place and ask if you'd seen Arlene."

"Once," Sarah admitted. "I hope to go back to Pleasant Pines soon."

Marge made a big point of visibly shivering. "Dreadful place. So institutional. Take note, kids. I do *not* want to end up there."

"Is it that bad?" Sarah asked.

"No," Caroline was quick to reply. "Mom's just sensitive about it."

"As any sane person would be. And poor Arlene. She can't drive anymore, well . . . I guess she's beyond all that now, of course," Marge admitted.

They walked into the living room, where the fire had died, and Marge propped herself on the couch against a faded cushion while Clark shifted from one leg to the other and checked his cell, presumably for the time or a message, while Caroline couldn't help wandering around the first floor, her footsteps fading past the staircase.

"I'm worried about Arlene," Aunt Marge said, still eyeing the interior of the house. "I, um, I'm afraid she might not last much longer. She's confused, you know."

"Some of the time," Sarah agreed.

"She probably doesn't make good decisions."

"Probably not."

Caroline returned to the living area and stood near one of the posts. "Just get to the point, Mom. We do have other things to do. Clark and I have jobs, you know, and family duties."

Sarah gazed at Marge, who cleared her throat. "Okay, fine," she said. "Sarah, I wanted to talk to you alone."

"Alone?" Sarah repeated.

"Oh, brother." Caroline was getting impatient.

"Well, I mean, before Dee Linn's extravaganza," Marge explained. "From what I hear, she's invited half the town."

Sarah looked from Marge to Caroline.

"She wants to know about your mother's will," Caroline explained, while Clark sighed and pretended interest in the far wall, where old wallpaper was peeling.

"Well, yes. Yes, I do," Marge said, slightly flustered by Caroline's bold statement.

Sarah steeled herself, wondering, for the first time, if all the comments Arlene had made over the years about her younger sister being envious of her were true. Arlene had forever insinuated that Marge, left in poor financial straits after her husband divorced her, had been jealous that Arlene had "married well."

"I mean, I don't understand." Marge looked to Clark for support, but he was having none of it. "The house was your mother's, Sarah. How can you just start renovating it? I would have thought all of the acres and buildings would be a part of Arlene's estate, but, of course, she never confided in me."

"Which really pissed you off, didn't it?" Caroline said with a sigh. "I told you that I talked to Jacob and he told me how it worked. Arlene doesn't own it any longer."

"So you bought it from her? You and your siblings?" Marge asked Sarah.

"Yes . . . essentially. I'm not trying to be secretive or coy, but I can't really discuss it."

"Arlene had always indicated that I was going to be left something when she passed," Marge said, cutting to the chase. "I . . . well, I'd hoped it would be enough to . . . make me more secure. You know that when Darrell left me and the children, things were tight." All of a sudden tears filled her eyes. "Oh, my . . . for the love of God," she whispered, digging through her purse until she found a tissue. "That man!"

"Mom," Clark warned, long-suffering.

Marge sighed, "Oh, I know he was your father—"

"Is, Mom," Caroline cut in. "He *is* still our dad." All traces of the flirty girl Sarah had once known had fallen away. She turned to Sarah. "I'm sorry. This is inappropriate, but she insisted. Clark and I didn't want to come."

"I'm just letting Sarah know what Arlene intended," Marge defended herself. "I know my sister's a little . . . confused . . . now, but when she was in her right mind, she wanted me to be secure. Comfortable. We talked, you know. She didn't have an easy time with her husbands, either. First that dreadful Hugh, and then Franklin . . . Oh, I know he was your father and you loved him, but the man was a philanderer, a player. Trust me, I know. He came on to me more than once and even cornered Caroline that time by—"

"Mom! Stop!" Caroline's mouth dropped open, and her skin turned red. To her brother she said, "I knew this was a bad idea."

Clark scowled. "So what were we going to do?"

"Say no, that's what." Caroline was shaking her head and cinching the belt of her coat more tightly around her.

Clark reminded, "She would have just made a scene at Dee Linn's."

"Don't talk as if I'm not in the room. Okay, I'm sorry!" Marge got to her feet and lifted her chin a notch. "I thought you were different from your brothers and sisters, Sarah. That you would be more compassionate, being a divorced woman and a single mother. That you would understand what happens when a marriage crumbles and the financial underpinnings, not to mention the emotional support, are stripped away. Your mother always mentioned that I would inherit something . . . I mean, even that little cabin that we used to rent from your father, or—"

"Let's go." Clark, suddenly in charge, took his mother by the crook of her elbow and propelled her out of the living room and through the foyer.

"I'm sorry," Caroline whispered again as Sarah got to her feet too. "I guess we're saying that a lot. Don't mind Mom. She's just bitter."

"I heard that!" Marge declared as Clark opened the front door with his free hand.

"You were meant tó, Mom." Caroline shook her head. "Bye, Sarah," she said as they all walked to the front door. "I'll see you at Dee Linn's extravaganza, I guess. Unfortunately, we'll all be there."

"See you there," Sarah said, and felt a welling disappointment that it had all come down to money with her aunt. She watched as Aunt Marge's aging Mercedes drove away, leaving a trail of blue smoke and sadness in its wake.

At lunch, Jade discovered her phone had sustained a major crack and barely worked, but fortunately Mary-A and her gang left Jade alone to down a Diet Coke and sneak outside. She thought about a cigarette but didn't have a pack and really wasn't that into it. Using the cell was a real pain now; reading texts was nearly impossible, and she found herself wanting to strangle Liam Longstreet and his loser of a friend.

The rest of the day didn't get any better, but she suffered through until last period, when, still avoiding her "angel," Jade made her way to the science wing, with its 1950s charm, ancient labs, and acrid smells that wafted into the hallways. Without saying a word to anyone, she slipped into an empty seat at a lab table in the back. Though most of the students in biology class sat in pairs, two lab partners at each table, she had, as yet, not been assigned a partner, so the other chair at the table was vacant.

Which was perfect.

After opening her book and pretending to read, she reached for her cell again but stopped when Sister Cora's high-pitched voice commanded everyone's attention.

"I have an announcement," she said, standing at her desk in gray slacks and a sweater, a silver cross swinging from a chain at her neck. "There are going to be some changes."

"It's about Antonia."

Jade turned a deaf ear. Antonia Norelli was another friend of Mary-Alice's and the TA for this class, so Jade barely listened to Sister Cora's long-winded explanation that Antonia had come down with a serious case of mono. At the end of her diatribe, Sister added, "Luckily, at least for me, I've found a replacement," she said, scrawling down the name of Antonia's replacement on the white board.

Jade glanced up, and her heart sank as she read Liam Longstreet's name in the teacher's flowing hand.

She couldn't believe it. What were the chances that Longstreet, a senior and a jock, would be assigned to this class? Jade wanted to die a thousand deaths—no, make that a million deaths. This was just too much. She even sent up a prayer that there had been some colossal galactic mistake. Surely God, if there was one, wouldn't do this to her.

But He did.

Ten minutes after Sister's announcement, Liam Longstreet, six feet plus of arrogance, sauntered in, dropped his backpack, and while Sister Cora taught the lesson, appeared to listen to the boring lecture on plant reproduction. Jade stared at the clock, willing the hour to pass. It seemed that he didn't notice her. Either that or he was ignoring her, which was just fine.

But that changed near the end of the period when he looked up and their gazes finally met.

He smiled.

Oh, this wasn't good!

She'd been certain he would say something to her, something harsh, but he merely nodded at her, his near-black hair falling over his forehead for a second before he grabbed his backpack and, five minutes before the final bell sounded, walked out of the room.

Somehow she'd gotten a reprieve from another confrontation.

For now.

Seeing him every day, though, in this class would change all that.

Talk about bad luck.

Automatically she started to text Cody before she saw the crack in the screen of her iPhone again. "Awesome," she muttered under her breath before realizing that her texts were going through, even though her screen was nearly impossible to read. Frantically she texted Cody once more, then spent the next forty minutes being bored to death in Algebra. Though cell phones were forbidden in class, she kept hers handy, in her pocket, the volume turned off. She checked the screen every five minutes while the teacher, a lay woman, frantically wrote equations on an old-fashioned chalkboard. The teacher was so interested in her work that it was easy for Jade to check her phone. She wasn't the only one. A boy who sat nearby, Sam Something-or-other, was totally into his as well, either texting or playing a game.

She caught a glance from that Dana chick who'd been in the restroom, and the girl sent her a frosty glare, but Jade tossed her a "what're you looking at" stare and Dana looked away. Good. Jade was more upset with Cody than anything. He hadn't shown up as he'd promised and had texted again that he was coming, just wasn't sure when. She'd called him, and he hadn't picked up nor called back, so her faith in him was waning. Not for the first time, she wondered if he already had another girlfriend.

What would she do then?

All her bravado with Mary-Alice and her claims that she didn't need anyone at this lame-ass school would be hollow.

Her phone vibrated, and her heart leaped as she glanced down at the text, but it wasn't from Cody. Nope. It came from a number she didn't recognize.

Wanna go out sometime?

What? Was this some kind of joke, a sick prank by Mary-Alice or Longstreet or one of their stupid friends? She didn't respond.

It's Sam. I'm trapped here too. With Ms. Sprout.

She glanced over at Sam's desk. He was kinda cute. Sure enough, his phone was in his lap, hidden, while he pretended to watch the teacher and check the book lying open on the desktop.

Go to the fb game?

No way. And how the hell had he gotten her cell phone number? Her finger hovered over the keypad as she formed a response in her head, but before she could type in a letter, the phone silently vibrated and a text from Cody came in.

Miss you.

Her heart melted.

Miss you too, she wrote, tears of relief glazing her eyes.

C U soon.

When?

OMG, did he mean now? Her heart soared. Maybe he was coming to surprise her! Quickly she brushed her tears away and ignored the other texts from Sam.

As the last bell sounded, she was out of the room in a shot and nearly ran to the staircase, where from the balcony she had a view of the student and teacher parking lots. Hoping against hope, Jade searched the vehicles. Cody's Jeep was glaringly absent. She walked to the opposite side of the landing and peered through the high windows that overlooked the front of the building and the streets nearby. Still no sign of him.

What had she expected?

Just because he'd texted her that he'd missed her hadn't meant he'd hopped into his Cherokee and driven here. She'd just hoped, deep down, that he couldn't stand being apart from her and had driven the hundred miles to just catch a glimpse of her. Her heart pounded at the thought. God, she loved him. She wanted to spend the rest of her life with him, and the sooner they could be together, the better. She peered at her cell phone, where his number was attached to a photo she'd taken of him: startling blue eyes, thick brown hair that fell over his face, and a firm jaw. He rarely smiled, but there was a certain brooding-actor quality to him that she found fascinating. Roguish. "Don't give a damn" attitude. "Very James Deanish," her mother had once commented, though Jade hadn't known who that guy was until she'd Googled him. Not hardly. Cody was so much better-looking.

She believed he loved her and couldn't stand being apart from her, and told herself he wasn't making excuses but really couldn't have gotten away any earlier. But, as he only worked part-time, she'd kind of expected him to show up, to surprise her. Before Saturday.

It could be that to make the surprise complete, he'd driven another car, but as she looked through the windows she knew she was grasping at straws, making excuses. A few days ago, she'd been elated, certain he wouldn't be able to wait until Saturday and was on his way to spirit her out of this hellhole. But she'd been wrong.

And she couldn't go to see him without her car. *That* really made her furious. How long did that cretin Hal have to keep it? She had his number in her phone, so she called and waited while the phone rang and rang. Certain she'd get a recording, she was about to hang up when a gravelly-voiced woman answered. "Hal's Auto Repair."

"Hi. This is Jade McAdams. You have my car," she said, then launched into why she needed it back ASAP. She must've been a little pushy, because the woman on the other end of the line responded with, "I'll have Hal call you, but we do have other vehicles to work on, you know."

"But this is important," Jade pressed, phone held to one ear as she tried to hear over the din of the students filing up and down the stairwell.

"I'm sure all the other clients want their vehicles as well."

Jade wanted to scream. Oh, she'd seen the other clients. One was the older woman with a dog, who'd pointed at her white Chevy Impala that had to have been from the 1960s. "In pristine condition," she'd told Hal with a nod and a smile, "and I'd like to keep it that way. Did you know it's only got thirty thousand miles on it? Well, of course *you* do. We always drove Randolph's car when he was alive, God rest his soul." Jade had thought she'd go crazy with that one, and there were others as well, a couple of guys who brought in their vehicles. That's what happened in a town this small. Hal's Auto Repair was the only game in town.

"But I need my car," she pleaded with the woman on the line. "Really, really badly." Surely her urgency was more dire than the old lady and her dog.

"The parts have been ordered and shipped, but they're not here yet. Once we've got 'em, Hal'll take care of you."

"You don't even have the parts yet?" Jade couldn't believe it.

"It's an older Honda. We don't keep parts for every make and model, but you'll get the car back soon."

Not soon enough, Jade thought, deflated. She descended the stairs and turned in the direction of her locker. Any thoughts that she could somehow get to Cody had been dashed. No way would Mom let her borrow her car. So she'd have to wait for Cody to show up here. If he even decided to come.

Don't give up on him. He's coming. You know it. You just messed up thinking he'd meant he was coming that night.

Not so, she realized. Maybe he would never come. But he had to! She couldn't suffer through many more excruciating days as the new kid at Our Lady of the River. She just couldn't.

CHAPTER 17

Scowling into the tiny mirror mounted near the door of his office, Sheriff Cooke adjusted his tie, tightening the damn thing and noticing that his salt-and-pepper hair was leaning a lot more toward salt even though he wouldn't be forty until the spring. His mother's genes. All of her family had been blessed with jet-black hair that started turning gray before they reached thirty. By forty-five or fifty most had hair that had turned snow-white, and he figured he was on that path. At least he wouldn't lose it, if, as it appeared, he took after his mother's family and not his father's. All the men and some of the women on his paternal side were bald long before they'd been laid to rest.

He would make sure the press conference wouldn't last long. After all, there just wasn't that much to say that hadn't been reported. There were no new leads in the case. Rosalie Jamison was long gone. In the wind.

And it scared the hell out of him.

He squared his hat on his head just about the time there was a quick rap of knuckles against his door. Before he could say, "Come on in," Lucy Bellisario had popped her head inside.

"Showtime, Boss."

He nodded curtly. He hated being put on display. Even though he wanted to portray a stern, solid leadership in a department that protected the citizens of this county, he detested the folderol that came with it. "Any news on her laptop or cell phone?"

"Nothing substantial. All the leads to that boyfriend in Colorado have led nowhere. It's as if he never existed."

"All in her mind?"

"Maybe. They haven't given up and are working with the cell phone company and the Internet provider."

"Hopefully they'll come up with something. You double-checked all the resident scumbags' alibis?"

"Still working on several. Lars Blonksi, for example. Something's not quite right there. His friend—and I use the term loosely—keeps changing his story. Gonna talk to Lars again and Jay Aberdeen's 'wife,' who's really an ex-girlfriend and lives in Cincinnati."

"Once a liar," he said.

"Yeah, and I've heard that there are sightings of Roger Anderson in the area, just local gossip, really, but I talked to the bartender at The Cavern, and he thought Anderson had been there. So far, he hasn't connected with his parole officer."

Cooke harrumphed his disgust.

"I've got a call in to the officer, and I'll check with Anderson's family and friends, but it's a long shot."

"Doesn't he have a cell mate from this area?"

She nodded. "Saw it in his file. Drifter named Hardy Jones. Already looking for him."

"Find him and talk to Lars and his alibi-buddy again."

"Will do," she said.

"Good." Cooke glanced in the mirror again and gave his tie one last tug. "Let's go."

They'd set up a podium outside, under the portico near the front door, by the flagpoles, where both Old Glory and the flag for the state of Oregon were snapping in the wind. Thankfully the storm that had been predicted had died before it reached this part of the country, but it was still cold as hell. Camera crews from a local station, as well as from Portland, had set up, their vans parked across the street. Reporters with microphones had gathered, along with people who lived in the area—the curious, who were being surreptitiously filmed by people in his own department with the wishful thinking that if someone had indeed kidnapped Rosalie, he or she might take great pleasure in watching the police scramble and squirm. Coming to the press conference for an up close and personal view might be top on their list.

Cooke hoped so.

"Thank you all for coming," he said once the initial screech of feedback from the microphone had passed and the tech in charge of the system had made some quick adjustments. Thankfully the sharp noise had died an instant death. "I'd like to give you all a quick update on the case involving the disappearance of Rosalie Jamison," he began, then launched into a brief description of what had transpired so far which, of course, wasn't very much.

Cooke explained that they were exploring all leads and hoped, as was promised by the local television station, a direct number to the department would be flashed across television screens across this part of Oregon, Washington, and Idaho in the hope that anyone who saw something suspicious would phone in a tip. There was already a reward offered, so hopefully even the most reticent informant would come forward. Cooke wasn't sure.

The reporters were eager and the questions rapid-fire.

"Any new leads?" one man, barely in his twenties, asked.

"Nothing substantial. As I said, we're exploring all avenues in this investigation."

"Has the FBI been called in?" a black woman, dressed to perfection, dark eyes serious, questioned.

"Not yet. Miss Jamison's disappearance hasn't been proved to be a kidnapping."

"You think she left on her own volition?" The female reporter was clearly not buying it. "Does she have a history of running away?"

The flag chains rattled with a sharp gust of wind.

"As I said, we're unclear as to what happened to her, but the investigation is continuing. We hope to have more substantial evidence and leads that will take us to her soon."

And on it went for ten minutes until he cut it off. Then, against his better judgment, but at the demand of the higher-ups, it was the family's turn. Sharon Updike, appearing defeated and older than her years, made a heartfelt plea to anyone who had information about her daughter to come forward. Her message was brief, and as her voice cracked before giving out completely, she whispered, "Please,

please help us find our daughter. If someone"—her voice broke and she cleared it—"if anyone has our daughter, please release her. Give us back our Rosie. And . . . and . . . Oh, God . . . Rosalie, if you can hear me, I love you. Your father loves you. Please come home." And then she fell into the waiting arms of a dry-eyed Mel Updike, while Rosalie's biological father, weary from a long drive from Colorado and the pain of his daughter's disappearance, stared bleakly from behind rimless glasses. Mick Jamison's face was somber and wary, his eyes sorrowful as he stood by a much younger woman, his wife, Annie, who kept squeezing his hand.

All in all, it was an ordeal that, to Cooke's way of thinking, hadn't accomplished much.

But there was always hope that someone who had seen the news report would remember something and call in, or that Rosalie, on the run, would hear her mother's pleas and return, or that the kidnapper, if there was one, was cocky enough to have joined the small crowd that had assembled.

If that were the case, Cooke silently vowed he'd nail that son of a bitch and slam his ass behind bars. One way or another he would find out what had happened to Rosalie Jamison.

By the time her mother pulled into the parking lot of the dog shelter, Jade was over being upset that Cody wasn't around. In fact, she was kind of bummed about it. Sure he was coming, but it was almost as if she had to beg him to come and see her, and that just wasn't right. Not if you really loved someone. And then there was her car. She *needed* the Honda back and pronto. She felt trapped without it. Worse yet, she was royally pissed about her damaged phone, which didn't begin to touch how Mom would go off the rails when she found out about it. And Dad? Jade didn't want to think about what her father would say. He'd bought the thing for her and put her on his plan so that they could communicate since he was in Savannah.

Explaining that it was pretty much trashed would be tough.

"Okay, let's go," Sarah said as she found a parking space near the front doors of Second Chance Animal Rescue and cut the engine.

Gracie took off like a shot and was inside before Jade had even opened her door.

"Guess she's excited," Sarah said, pocketing her keys

"Isn't she always?" Jade asked, but her mother was already out of the car. Gracie was like that, sometimes acting like she was closer to seven than twelve, other times surprising Jade with her deep, almost spooky, insight. Today, she was the kid. Jade followed into a wide reception area, where fluorescent fixtures reflected on shining tile floors. Leashes, collars, and harnesses decorated one wall, while metal shelves were piled high with bags of dog food, beds, and crates on another. Close to a reception counter, a long display board was mounted, and tacked up on it were pictures and information about each animal available for adoption. Gracie was already scouring the listings, while a three-legged tabby cat, obviously the shelter's unofficial greeter, perched along the top of the long board, his reddish tail ticking a bit as he eyed the newcomers.

"There are so many," Gracie said as she viewed the selection of dogs and cats ready for adoption.

"But we only need one," their mother reminded her.

"Maybe a cat too?" Gracie pointed to a picture of a black-and-white tuxedo kitten.

"One. Dog."

A glass door behind the counter opened. "Hello!" A plump woman who was barely five feet tall and dressed in jeans and a purple hoodie bustled in. "Sorry." She sounded breathless as if she'd been running. "I was in the back cleaning up, and I didn't hear the bell. So, welcome to Second Chance. I'm Lovey Bloomsville, the manager here, well, and the owner."

Sarah made quick introductions and said, "We're looking for a dog. Mature. Housebroken. Good with kids." She added that they wanted a midsize dog, finishing with, "A pet primarily, but a guard dog would be nice."

"Guard dog?" Lovey repeated slowly.

Jade gave her mother a look. Really? A guard dog?

"We live out of town and are pretty isolated," Sarah said. "The property's pretty vast, so it would be nice if the dog would bark when people showed up. I'm not talking about a dog that bites or even snarls, or that I have to put up a Beware of Dog sign for, just one that will give us fair warning that someone's around."

"Oh. Well. I'm pretty sure we've got that covered." Lovey waved a dismissive hand in the air. "Of course, we don't have any vicious dogs, though, if you ask me, it's the owners, not the dogs, that give some of the breeds a bad name. All that legislation against the pit bulls, for example. Nonsense! I've got two of my own, and let me tell you, they're lovers, wouldn't hurt a flea! Not nearly as feisty as my pug. She's in trouble all the time and rules the roost at my house, bosses the pits around, and they let her.

"So now . . . ," Lovey motioned to the pictures of the animals. "All of our dogs have had temp tests to see if they're good with cats or young children or other dogs or whatever. We work with them every day and know if they're shy or the least bit aggressive on the leash or around food or whatever. They all have different personalities, you know. Anyway," she said, clasping her hands together. "I'm sure we can find you the perfect pet. A midsize to large dog, you said?"

"I was thinking fifty or sixty pounds maybe? Even sixty-five, but not much bigger. We really don't care about breed."

Lovey took a sweeping glance at the posters on the wall just as the door to a back room opened and a thin twentyish guy walked into the lobby area. A cacophony of barks, yips, and howls rose to the rafters until the door shut behind him. Lovey took the noise as a cue. "As you can hear, finding an alarm dog shouldn't be a problem. Come on, let me show you around and we'll meet a few candidates. Then you can think it over as you fill out the adoption papers. Jared," she said to the skinny guy who'd picked up a broom, "can you bring Henry, Shogun, Brawn and, oh, maybe Xena, one at a time to the meet-and-greet room?"

"Sure thing, Ms. B." Jared was already heading through the door again.

"Perfect." To Sarah and her daughters, Lovey said, "I'll give you a quick tour of the place while Jared rounds up the most likely candidates. If you see any dog that appeals to you, just let me know."

Explaining a little about her rescue work and the health and well-being of the animals in the shelter, Lovey led them deeper into the interior, where smaller dogs were kept in one area, larger ones in another, and cats separated into a space of their own. A pot-bellied pig

Esmeralda ("Ezzy") was kind of the mascot. She trotted along after Lovey, snorting a bit, but a happy part of the entourage.

Gracie's face was alight as she watched the dogs playing and romping in the open area. Lovey Bloomsville chattered away as they walked, but Jade didn't really catch all that Lovey was rambling about as her phone kept vibrating. Sam, the phone geek from Algebra wasn't giving up, and Jade's cousin Becky had left her a message about her mother's Halloween party.

U coming? was Becky's question.

Mom says we have to, Jade texted back. Zero options.

Always options, Becky replied.

Hmm. Jade considered. Even though she acted like she didn't, she kind of liked Becky. But Becky was sort of two-faced, a little like Mary-Alice, though Becky had a darker side that appealed to Jade. Can we leave? Jade texted.

Not if we ask.

Jade almost laughed.

Becky wrote, I'll call you later.

K.

Jade was feeling better by the minute. The party was scheduled for Saturday night, right before Halloween, and just happened to be the night Cody had said he would show up. Yes! Finally it seemed things might be falling into place. Jade couldn't help but smile, and Mom probably thought it was because she was into the dogs.

Lovey Bloomsville showed off bouncing teacup Chihuahuas and Yorkies and finally a huge, droopy-faced mastiff that was the size of a pony. "No one wants Bubba here," Lovey said, gazing lovingly at the huge dog, "but he's an absolute love. I guess he'll just have to be our shelter dog, won't you, boy?" She patted his broad head, and Jade wondered who weighed more, the dog or the woman. Silently, she bet on Bubba.

All the dogs came closer, and while Gracie was literally in "doggy heaven," Sarah seemed a little overwhelmed. "This is going to be tougher than I thought," she said.

"It always is," Lovey commiserated. "And it's not any easier with the cats, let me tell you." With a shake of her head, she threw up her hands as if her workload were impossible. "A good thing I love ani-

mals. Now, here are the ones that I think might work best for you."
She pointed out the four dogs she'd tagged as possible pets, then
ushered them into a small room partitioned by glass, where they met
each one individually. Henry was a shy border collie mix, Shogun
some kind of shepherd, while Brawn was a purebred husky, and
Xena, the only female, was a blond mutt with Lab and pit bull traits
visible.

"Can't we take them all?" Gracie asked their mother in her most
angelic tone.

Sarah choked out a laugh. "I think we need to start with one dog."

Gracie looked them all over. "Xena," she finally decided, but she
was clearly torn.

"Okay with you?" Sarah asked Jade.

Jade was honest. "I like Brawn."

"Well, great," Sarah said, heaving a sigh. "Guess I'm the deciding
vote." She glanced up at Lovey. "Xena, it is."

Jade couldn't help saying under her breath, "Big surprise," and
caught a warning glance from her mother, which was probably
earned. Truth to tell, she was being bitchy about the whole thing.
The dog was for Gracie, and she should be able to pick it out. "Xena's
okay," she said. "No, I mean it. I like her." She was nodding her agreement, and Mom seemed relieved.

Lovey actually clapped her hands together. "This is a great fit.
Xena's a shelter favorite. Such a sweet girl." Then she heard herself
and added to Sarah, "But she's got a big voice."

"Good," their mother said.

"So let's get that paperwork rolling!" Lovey was already leading
the way to the reception area where the same man who'd shown up
at the pizza parlor, Clint Walsh, their neighbor, was waiting, a leash in
one hand, and a wallet and bag of dog food on the counter.

Jared had set aside his broom and was running a credit card.

Walsh glanced up as the door opened and they walked through.
His smile was less tentative than before, a crooked grin slashing
across his face. "Hey, Sarah," he said as the machine chunked out a
receipt.

Jade's mother forced a smile. "I guess I forgot what a small town
this really is."

"I say it's bite-sized," Lovey chimed in.

Walsh nodded at Jade and her sister.

"You two know each other?" Lovey asked.

"I grew up here," Sarah explained, looking slightly uncomfortable. "Clint was, is a neighbor. We kind of grew up together."

"Neighbors then. Neighbors now." He slipped his wallet into the back pocket of his worn jeans.

"How 'bout that? What goes around really does come around," Lovey said. Clint gave Sarah a look that could have melted steel, and she turned away quickly.

There was definitely something going on between them, Jade thought.

"See ya around," Walsh said as he hauled the bag of food onto his shoulder and, with the leash in his other hand, walked out the door.

Jared, at Lovey's urging, left to locate Xena.

Meanwhile, the wheels in Jade's mind cranked furiously to that spot she usually avoided. Was it possible? Nah . . . no way . . . but she couldn't help doing the math surrounding her birth. It was a game she'd played with herself ever since she was old enough to understand sex and gestation and the fact that it took around nine months from conception to birth. She'd done the calculations and figured her mom got pregnant soon after graduating from high school. Mom had always mentioned a crush she'd had in college, but that didn't necessarily preclude this neighbor, did it?

Clint Walsh, with his strong jaw, rangy build, and gray eyes, was about the right age.

Mom was acting pretty damned weird, and the "neighbor boy" and "friend of her brothers" was someone Sarah had known in high school. Mom had gotten pregnant right after graduation, the way Jade figured it, so . . . ?

She couldn't help but stare at the man as he walked out the door. Could it be?

Her throat went dry at the very thought that she'd just been face to face with the man who had sired her, and she walked to the window to watch him get into his truck.

After tossing the bag into the bed of his truck, he opened the driver's side door, then shooed his dog from behind the wheel to the passenger seat. A cowboy? Rancher? And building inspector?

Jade had always imagined her dad was someone famous, like the lead guitarist for a rock band or a movie star or something, a person with whom Sarah had somehow had one glorious, unforgettable night of passion that conceived Jade.

But the neighbor kid?

Friend to Uncle Joe and Uncle Jake?

Where was the romance and fantasy in that?

She watched as the truck's taillights faded away into the dark afternoon. Did he know about Jade? Had he rejected Sarah when he found out she was pregnant with an unwanted child? He was handsome for an old dude, in great shape, but he didn't look much like Jade at all, not that she could see. Then again, she didn't much resemble her mother either.

"Handsome devil, isn't he?" Lovey asked, and Jade jumped, realizing that she'd been caught staring.

"He's an old dude," she dismissed quickly. She glanced at her mother, but Sarah seemed to be purposely looking at the wall with the dogs.

Lovey said, "Kinda keeps to himself these days, though. Tragic what happened to him." She turned to Sarah, "Who can survive the loss of a child? I know I couldn't."

Sarah just nodded, never taking her gaze off the wall, but Jade keyed in on Lovey. Clint Walsh *was* a father? There had been another child? A . . . a potential sibling? "What happened?" she asked.

"Car accident," Lovey said sadly. "His wife was at the wheel." Shaking her head, she added, "Single car and the boy . . . well, he didn't make it. It wasn't much of a surprise that the marriage crumbled and Andrea moved back home, somewhere in California, I think." As if she realized she was gossiping, Lovey looked toward the door behind the counter just as Jared reappeared, this time leading Xena, who was pulling at the leash, straining to get to Gracie, who was already on her knees, arms spread wide to hug their new pet. "Yes, well, let's get to it, shall we? Jared, why don't you help Gracie and Xena get acquainted with the leash and crate and all, while we finish up the paperwork."

Sarah and Lovey started going through the adoption process while Gracie petted and walked Xena around the interior of the building.

Jade could barely breathe. She had questions. A million of them. All about Clint Walsh. But she couldn't ask them here, not in front of Lovey or even Gracie, so she held her tongue, though it damn near killed her.

CHAPTER 18

Clint dropped the bag of feed near the back door, hung his jacket on a peg, then walked into the kitchen and to the cabinet over the refrigerator where he kept his booze. His dad and grandfather had used this same cupboard as a liquor cabinet, and he figured some of the dusty bottles inside were as old as he was. He found a bottle of Jack Daniels, eyed the contents, and decided a drink was in order. " 'Bout that time, isn't it?" Clint asked and leaned down to scratch the dog behind his ears. Tex's tail whipped wildly back and forth, and he placed his front paws on Clint's jean-clad knee in order to reach Clint's face with his tongue.

"Yeah, yeah, I know. I love you too," he said, then grabbed a couple of ice cubes and poured a healthy shot of whiskey into his glass before taking a long swallow. Twice within a week he'd run into Sarah.

The two face-to-faces were just the tip of the iceberg. It was only going to get worse as he'd be up at Blue Peacock Manor, inspecting the construction work for God only knew how long. He took another long swallow of his drink and once again considered pawning the job off to Doug Knowles, but Clint knew, deep in his gut, he wouldn't go through with it. Then there was the matter of their co-owned fence line. He took another swallow.

The truth was that he actually liked seeing Sarah again. He'd found her fascinating in the past, and, he'd recently learned, his interest in her hadn't completely dissipated, no matter what he'd told himself over the years. "Idiot," he muttered and crunched on an ice cube.

Tex, looking up, eagerly whined to be fed.

"Yeah, I know." Using the pocketknife his dad had given him, he sliced the bag, measured out a ration for Tex, and as the dog devoured the morsels, poured the rest of the sack of feed into a big plastic bin.

All the while he was thinking of Sarah Stewart. No, wait. Sarah McAdams. She had an ex-husband tucked away somewhere in the South, if he'd heard right. He'd tried not to pay attention, convinced himself that she was out of his life forever, but now that she had returned to Stewart's Crossing and was once again living in the property abutting his, he'd been thinking about her more than he wanted to admit.

He deliberately set thoughts of her aside for the moment as he carried the remainder of his drink into the den, took a seat at his desk, paid some bills online, and checked his e-mail in case anything had come across his desk after he'd left for the day. His hours at the office weren't eight to five, as he was often on a jobsite and could do some of his work from home.

Nothing important.

Good.

Finished with paperwork, he decided it was time to check on the livestock. Night wasn't that far from falling, and the cattle would soon let him know that they wanted to be fed. He glanced out the windows to the barn where the three horses he kept were herded together. Beyond the outbuildings and pasture was a tract of old-growth timber that no one in his family had ever wanted to cut. Farther up the hill, toward the cliffs rising over the river, the third story, roof, and cupola of Blue Peacock Manor were just visible.

"A long time ago," he reminded himself as his gaze dropped to the desktop again and landed on a picture of Brandon, his son, age five, astride a painted pony. Against a backdrop of a blue sky and the dry grass of summer, Brandon was wearing a Stetson that was several sizes too big, a cowboy shirt complete with pearl snaps, a kerchief around his neck, and rawhide chaps over his little, jean-clad legs. He squinted toward the camera's eye and still managed to grin, showing off teeth that appeared too small for his freckled face.

Clint's throat grew hot, and his jaw tightened as he picked up the 5x7 in its silver frame to stare at his son's image.

I miss you, boy.

His heart twisted, and that familiar ache came over him again, a wound that never quite scarred over but still cut through him. Normally, in order to keep his sanity he tried hard not to review every detail of the tragedy, but just now he wanted to. Maybe it had something to do with seeing Sarah again . . . old friends and relationships. Whatever the case, he let himself remember.

Brandon had been gone for just over five years, the result of Andrea's lead foot and a faulty car seat. She'd survived the single-car accident when her Chevy had slid off the road and hurtled into an ancient fir tree; their son and marriage had not. Clint stared at the photo for a second; then, as was always the case, he set the picture back in its place on the dusty desk. He'd never get over his son's death, he knew that now, but he needed to keep living.

Though he'd consoled himself with the simple fact that Brandon had died instantly, he couldn't help replaying the hours leading up to the accident in his mind. If he, instead of Andrea, had taken Brandon into town—that was the plan, until the pump had stopped working and he'd made an emergency phone call—if he'd tossed Andrea the keys to his truck, newer than her sedan by a decade, if he'd hung up the phone as they were leaving and given his son a hug or a thumbs-up, or if he'd done any damn thing, changed even a second of that day, maybe Brandon would still be alive.

But, of course, he hadn't done any of those things, and that terrible, fateful day had played out, destroying his reason for living. Despite prayers and sympathy from friends, and regardless of more than a year of grief counseling, he'd never come to peace with what had happened.

He remembered arriving at the accident scene, where the first responders, firefighters and cops, the lights on their vehicles strobing the woods, were already prying open the door to the Chevy. The car was mutilated—metal twisted, glass shattered. The still, summer air had been pierced with shouts and orders from the men and women trying to save a boy who had already died. Those shouts, along with the soul-numbing screams and violent sobs of his wife, still echoed through his brain.

The EMTs had restrained her as she tried to scramble back to the car, where, he'd seen, the limp form of his son was being pulled from the wreckage. Blood. There had been so much blood. Clint had hurtled from his idling truck and ignored the shouts of rescue workers. Some cop had tried to hold him back, but he'd thrown the woman off to plow forward to his son's lifeless body.

He recalled falling to his knees, his own screams ringing in his ears, and then there had been a dead space, a void, no images in his mind until the grim doctor at the hospital confirmed what he already knew.

"Jesus," he whispered now.

Squaring his shoulders, he told himself, as he had a thousand times since that day, that he would just have to deal.

Somehow.

Brandon would have been eleven this coming December, a boy starting into adolescence, had he survived. The kid would have been learning to handle the cattle and shoot a rifle, would probably have gone skinny-dipping in the creek, been working hard to perfect a shot beyond the three-point line on the basketball court, been having his first real crush on a girl whose teeth were in braces—

"Damn," he gritted out, leaning hard on the desk as he forced himself to get a grip. Once the thoughts and memories rolled out, it was hard to hold back the tide, and as Clint struggled, Tex gave out a low, worried growl from his bed in the corner.

"It's okay," Clint said to the dog, his words hollow. Tossing back the few remaining drops of his drink, he heard the sound of a truck's engine. Tex, with a low, quick woof, was on his feet, trotting expectantly toward the back door, where Clint found Casey Rinaldo, the man who helped Clint with the chores and livestock. With a nod to Casey, he said, "Okay, let's go," then yanked his jacket off its peg. Slipping his arms through the sleeves, he added to the dog, who was already out the door, "We've got work to do," silently locking up the haunting memories once more.

Sarah finally began to relax as she drove along the rutted lane leading to the house. Though Xena, the Warrior Princess canine, didn't seem much like a guard dog, her pure size might be a deterrent to anyone who was thinking about casing the house or causing trouble.

Except for ghosts. No dog was going to scare away any other-worldly beings who happened to occupy Blue Peacock Manor.

There are no such things as ghosts, despite what Gracie says or what you may have imagined as a child. Nothing.

But her fingers gripped the steering wheel a little more tightly. As the trees gave way to fields, she noticed the wintry grass undulate in the wind that rushed down the gorge. Not for the first time, she felt as if someone were watching her, that unseen eyes followed the SUV as it emerged from the forest.

"Oh, crap! What's this?" Jade asked, straightening in the front seat as the Explorer rounded the lane's final curve and the house came into view. A white utility van with a metal sign slapped on the driver's door was parked in front of the guesthouse.

Sarah said, "The guy I hired to oversee some of the subs. He's hands-on and does a lot of the framing and trouble-shooting himself."

"Longstreet?" Jade asked, almost slithering down in the passenger seat.

"Yes. Keith Longstreet. Why?" Sarah parked in her usual spot. The minute the Ford stopped, Gracie and the dog bounded out of the back, the two already fast friends.

Jade, however, didn't move.

Sarah asked, "Do you know him?"

"No, no. Of course not." Jade peeked her head up and sneaked a look through the passenger window. "Does he have a son?"

"Yeah, a couple, I think. Maybe a daughter too."

"Great," she mumbled.

"So, you know Keith's boy? You met him?"

"No. I mean, not really. He goes to my school. He's just some hot-shot soccer player, I think. Oh, God!"

The passenger door of the van opened, and a tall, lanky boy of about eighteen in jeans and a sweatshirt with "Crusaders" emblazoned boldly across the front walked up to Keith.

"I take it that's the boy in question," Sarah said dryly. A good-looking kid with an athletic build and even features, the boy glanced at their car as he flipped his hood over a mop of thick brown hair.

"Yeah."

"And you have a problem with him?" Sarah guessed.

"No problem."

"Then why do you look like you just died a thousand deaths?"

"He doesn't know me."

"So he's not bullying you?"

"God, Mom, no!"

"Then you like him," she decided, adding, "He's kind of cute."

"Stop!" Jade shot up in the seat and grabbed the handle of her door. "Why do you always do this? Jesus, *nothing's* going on!" Jade was almost yelling, and she must've heard herself because she lowered her voice. "He and I don't know each other, okay? He's just the temporary biology TA!" She blew out a harsh breath. "Forget I said anything!" Then she was out of the car in an instant and storming up the front path, her long coat billowing in the breeze.

Bemused, Sarah climbed out of her Explorer. Keith raised his hand in greeting, and his son, cell phone in hand, watched Jade's backside as she stormed up the steps to the porch.

"Sorry I'm late," Sarah called, zipping her jacket. Damn, it was cold.

"No problem. We just got here. Hey," he said to the boy when he caught him texting. "What'd I tell you about that? Put that danged thing away. We're on the job now."

The kid slipped his cell into the front pocket of his battered jeans. "Give me a sec, Dad." Then he yelled to Jade, "Hey, wait!"

Sarah smothered a smile. So much for not knowing her.

Jade, hand on the doorknob, froze for a second, then slowly turned. Her demeanor as he took the steps two at a time was cold fury.

"What the hell is that all about?" Keith wondered aloud.

Though Sarah couldn't make out their brief exchange, she saw the kid holding out a hand with his fingers splayed, as if he was trying to explain something to Jade, who was having none of it. Her jaw was set, her lips flat over her teeth, and she glared up at him in anger. He said something more, and she shook her head. A snippet of the conversation reached Sarah's ears: ". . . and just keep that freak away from me! Got it?" Before he could respond, she yanked open one of the double doors, stepped through, and slammed it behind her.

For a second the kid stood stock-still. Then, hands in his pockets, nose red from the bite of the wind, he turned and jogged back to the area of the driveway where Sarah and Keith were waiting.

"What was that all about?" Keith demanded.

"Nothing," the boy said.

"Didn't look like nothing."

His son shifted from one foot to the other.

Longstreet dragged his gaze from his son and said, "This is my boy, Liam. He works with me once in a while. I'm hoping that he'll learn the business. Liam, Mrs. McAdams."

The kid actually met her eyes and shook her hand with a firm grip. "Nice to meet you," he said quietly.

"You too, Liam."

"You're Jade's mother?" His gaze slid back to the house.

"Yes. You go to school with her, right?"

He was nodding, his Crusader sweatshirt confirming the obvious. Liam cast another quick glance at the main house as if to catch another glimpse of Jade.

"Your daughter goes to Our Lady too?" Keith asked, and before Sarah could answer, he added, "Great school. Terrific athletic program. You know, Liam here is the star striker of the soccer team."

"Dad," the kid warned, shaking his head.

"Well, you are," his father bragged. With a knowing smile, he punched his son on the arm. "How many goals have you scored this season?"

"I don't know," Liam said and blushed.

"Fourteen and counting." Keith sent a "how about that?" look in Sarah's direction. "A school record already, and the season isn't over. He scored the winning goal against Molalla last week."

Liam looked pained. "Aren't we here to work?"

"Course we are. But I just had to talk you up a bit, y'know. That win was critical to get us into the playoffs."

His son sent him another embarrassed look, and Keith finally got the message. "Okay, okay," he said, lifting a hand as if to stave off further arguments. "Time to get down to the reason we're here, I suppose. Daylight's fadin'."

He was right on that count. Twilight had started to roll over the land, softening the shadows, warning of an early night. A trumpeting blast of wind rushed down the gorge again, rattling the branches of the cherry tree and reminding Sarah of the isolation of this place she called home.

Clearly relieved that the conversation had turned away from his athletic prowess, Liam pulled his phone from his pocket, glanced at it, then slid it away again.

Sarah wondered about him and the argument with Jade, but let it go. She motioned to the guesthouse, "So, how's the project going?"

"Better than expected." Keith nodded, as if silently agreeing with himself. "Really coming along." Suddenly the older Longstreet was all business. He opened the door of his van and pulled out a clipboard with a pen and legal pad attached. On the first yellow page was a handwritten list of the repairs they'd discussed earlier. "First of all, we replaced the gutters and downspouts that couldn't be fixed and used some old shakes we found in the garage to patch the roof. Also we took care of the rotten board on the porch." He pointed out a new board with his pen, the fresh lumber in stark contrast to the older, weathered planks that made up the floor. "The steps, railing, and rest of the floorboards are okay."

"Good," she said, relieved that they hadn't discovered more rot.

"Windows are scheduled to be delivered on Monday, and we'll install on Tuesday. Shouldn't take too long. Half a day, maybe. And that's it for the exterior."

They walked inside, where Longstreet referred again to the list on his legal pad and pointed out a few quick updates to the plumbing and electricity. The old furnace had been repaired, a rodent problem had been dealt with, and new wallboard had already been cut into the bedroom walls to cover up a couple of massive holes. The kitchen appliances were ancient but functional after a few repairs.

"Saved a little there," Longstreet observed, then led her to the bathroom, where a toilet and sink from the main house had been used to replace the cracked fixtures in the guesthouse. All things considered, the little cottage would be livable by the middle of next week. Sarah had already decided she and the girls could paint and clean over the weekend, then move in.

In the living room, Longstreet said, "I thought we could take one of the old fixtures in the main house and put it in here." He pointed his pen at the broken light dangling from the ceiling. "There's one in the foyer that would work pretty well, I think. About the right size. That is, unless you want a new one."

"No, let's reuse anything we can," she agreed.

They discussed the larger house for a few minutes before Longstreet and his son climbed into their van and drove off as darkness descended. The van rounded a corner, the rumble of the engine fading, taillights winking bright red through the trees.

The wind had died.

The isolation and darkness felt as if it was seeping into her soul.

Surely, though, that sensation was temporary. When the guesthouse was fully functioning again, the power, water, and heat hooked up, she wouldn't experience this sensation of being cut off from the world.

A wisping fog had started to creep across the fields, obscuring the trees and filling the gorge, wrapping tendrils around the corners of the guesthouse. The main house, barely discernable in the darkness, did appear sinister in the night.

Rubbing her arms, she made her way to the Explorer, popped the back door open, and pulled out the large sack of dry dog food for the new addition to the family. Juggling the bag, she pushed the back door of the SUV closed.

Once again the world went dark, the night black.

Only a bit of illumination from the windows of the first floor.

Enough, though.

She just needed to join the kids inside and push aside any ridiculous notion that there was someone watching her. Following her. Ready to do harm. Those lingering feelings had to be locked away and—

Craaack!

A dry twig snapped.

She whirled to face the sound.

Her eyes scanned the darkness, imagining movement in the umbra near the garage. That's where the noise had come from.

Or was she mistaken?

Had it come from beneath the cherry tree, where a brittle branch that had fallen to the ground could have been stepped on?

Or had the sound emanated from the nearby field? Glancing at the fence line, she saw nothing, only the barest hint of once-white rails. Her skin crawled as she peered through the wisps of fog to the night beyond. Ears straining, eyes narrowed, she backed up, one step at a time, toward the house. Surely she was alone out here. What she'd heard was probably just an animal—skunk, rabbit, even a deer.

Or the dog.

Maybe the rambunctious dog had never made it into the house.

So, where was Xena?

And the kids . . . God help her, they were surely in the house.

For a second Sarah was certain she wasn't alone. That someone or something was nearby, watching her every move.

You're being silly. There is no malevolent presence.

She remembered shouting out to the "ghost" upstairs and felt foolish, but her fears at that time had been real enough that they'd propelled her into adopting a dog. This was ridiculous. Of course there were wild animals out here, but so what? She'd grown up with them, whatever they were.

Lifting the bag to her shoulder, she faced the house again, and as she did, her eyes strayed to the third-floor window of Theresa's room, and there, through the thin layer of fog and watery glass, she saw movement, the flimsy image of a woman in a white dress.

Stumbling, she dropped the sack. It hit the corner of one of the flagstones and split open. Tiny kiblets sprayed over the grass and stones, but Sarah barely noticed. Her eyes were drawn to the window and the image behind the gauze of the curtains.

The ghost?

No way.

Her back tensed, and the hairs lifted at her nape.

In a second the image disappeared, but not before Sarah thought she recognized her daughter.

Jade?

She let out her breath slowly.

This was no otherworldly being, no specter, but it might be her daughter exploring around. Since it was too dark to clean up the mess, she left the spilled kiblets to whatever night creatures would come along and hauled the rest of the bag to the house.

In the kitchen, Gracie was trying to teach Xena to "shake" on command. So far the lesson wasn't going all that well. "Use some of these," Sarah suggested, dropping the bag onto the table. "Maybe you can find some plastic bin to pour it into, as the bag is toast."

Gracie dug into the torn sack for a few morsels. All the while Xena's eyes watched her every move.

"Jade?" she called up the stairs.

"What?" But the sound came from the living room, where she found her eldest daughter wrapped in a quilt and multitasking by texting on her phone and watching something on her iPad.

"What were you doing on the third floor?" Sarah asked.

Jade didn't bother looking up. "I wasn't up there."

"You were in Theresa's old room. Just a few minutes ago."

Finally, Jade's gaze moved from the screen to meet Sarah's eyes. She shook her head. "I said I wasn't up there."

"But I saw you."

"You didn't!" Jade declared. She stared at Sarah as if she'd gone crazy. "Wait. You actually think you saw me up there? In that room where Gracie saw the ghost?"

A frisson slid down Sarah's spine. "You weren't upstairs?"

"No." Flinging off the quilt, she gathered up her electronic equipment and stood up. "Why would I go up there?"

"I don't know. Maybe to watch Liam Longstreet and not be seen."

Jade made a choking sound. "Oh, God. He just came up to apologize for breaking my iPhone, and yeah, it's cracked!" she said, holding the screen up for Sarah to see. "It barely works."

Sarah nodded, gazing at the phone and trying not to think of the ghost. "I think your dad bought insurance." Swallowing, she added, "I thought maybe you and Liam might be friends."

"Friends? He's got an ogre named Miles Prentice for a 'friend,' and he goes with Mary-Alice Eklund, the biggest two-faced snob at the school. I hate her."

"Hate's a pretty strong word."

"Yeah, Mom, I do! She's making my life miserable, and I really don't need any help in that department."

"Jade, if you give it time—"

"I'm not taking any more advice from you," she said.

"What do you mean?" Sarah shook off her distraction and keyed in fully on her daughter.

"Because you haven't been honest with me."

"About what?"

"My father."

"Your father. Jade," she began, her tone weary.

"Is the neighbor my dad?" Jade asked flatly. "Clint Walsh. Were you dating him and broke up when you found out you were pregnant or something?"

Sarah opened her mouth to answer, but it felt as if she'd been hit in the gut. She wanted to lie her way out of it, but could do nothing more than stand in frozen shock, and that was enough.

"I did the math, Mom." Jade's chin lifted a bit, and she looked so young, so vulnerable. "Don't even think about lying."

"I've been meaning to talk to you," she said unevenly.

"Oh, Jesus. It's true. I knew it! Oh, God. That guy—that *man* I've never met before, he's my . . ." She was shaking her head, backing up. "Why didn't you just tell me? All this time? Why did you make it a big secret?"

"I didn't know how to tell you," Sarah admitted.

"Does he know?" Jade demanded. "You said he didn't know."

"He doesn't. No one knows . . . well, your grandmother guessed, but that's it. I was able to keep it from the family as I was away at college." Sarah had never felt such remorse. She was dying inside, wishing she could roll back the years, wishing she had come clean the first time Jade had asked about her father. "I'm sorry. It was wrong. I know."

"That's all you can say now?" Jade charged, her eyes brimming with unshed tears. She swiped at them furiously.

"Jade . . . ," Sarah tried to move a step closer, but Jade shrank back.

"When were you going to tell me? And don't say 'when the time was right' because that's the problem, Mom. It's never the right time to admit that you've been lying for years!" She was nearly shouting, her voice tremulous, her features distorted with her pain.

God, this was a mess, one she'd created and made worse with every passing day that the truth was hidden.

"You're right, Jade. I should have been honest with you and with Clint from the get-go."

"Why weren't you?"

"Because he and I were already split when I found out. It's not like it is today, that you can take a pregnancy test the same week as . . . as conception." She gathered herself. How could she explain that not only had they been broken up for several months, but that they'd gotten together one final time and it had been a mistake? That they'd tried to rekindle something that was gone? That they'd both felt awful; he was dating someone else, and it felt like they'd both cheated? "He was with someone else, and I didn't want to make him think he had to come back to me or marry me."

"It wasn't the nineteen fifties!"

"I know. I had plenty of opportunities over the years to tell you. You asked me, and I evaded, and that was wrong. And the longer it went, the harder it was to admit the truth. I didn't want to hurt you."

"Or yourself."

"I suppose. Yes." She took a step forward. "I'm sorry. Really."

Jade shrank away, and Sarah wanted to die inside. "So," Jade sniffed, "he doesn't know?"

"No."

"Are you going to tell him?"

"Think I'd better," she said and pulled her phone out of her pocket to punch in the number she'd memorized in her youth.

"Now?" Jade looked shocked just as, out of the corner of her eye, Sarah saw Gracie come in, with the dog trotting behind her.

"No time like the present. Hope he still has the same number."

"What's going on?" Gracie asked, sensing the tension running like a wild current of electricity through the room.

Sarah held up a finger.

"Gracie, this is none of your business," Jade said.

Gracie asked, "What isn't?"

The phone connected and started ringing. Sarah took in a deep breath. She'd thought about this moment a thousand times over the years, planned for it, but now that it was here, she had no idea what she would say.

One ring.

Two.

"Wait!" Jade said suddenly. "Maybe we should wait—"

Three rings that ended with a distinctive click, and then, "Hello." Clint's voice.

"Hi," she forced out, her insides quivering as she held her oldest daughter's gaze. "Clint, this is Sarah. I need to talk to you." Her legs went weak, but she somehow stood.

"About the house?"

"Something else. I'd really like to see you in person." Jade was shaking her head frantically, trying to stop what she'd started. Gracie's eyes moved from Jade to Sarah and back again, while the dog, sensing the tension, slunk into the living room to settle in by the fire.

"Okay," Clint said slowly.

"Would now be okay?" Sarah suggested as she drew in a long, calming breath. "I can come over to your place . . . or, if you'd rather, you can come here."

Jade was holding up her hands and waving, frantic to change the course of what was about to happen, backtracking like mad, no longer demanding the truth. "No!" she mouthed. "Mom! *No!*"

"Is something wrong?" Clint asked, the concern in his voice touching her.

"No," she said, her voice softer than she'd hoped, and she cleared her throat. "Nothing's wrong," Sarah insisted, as Jade continued to freak out, "but it really would be best if we talked in person."

"I'll be there in fifteen." He hung up, and Sarah, letting out her breath, finally fell into the old rocker.

CHAPTER 19

Her ponytail called to him.

Fiery red and swinging behind her, the thick, straight thatch of hair tempted and teased with each of her footsteps as she hurried down the sidewalk through the fog.

He eased up on the accelerator, ensuring that his hybrid was traveling slow enough to stay in the electric-power range so that the vehicle nearly made no sound as it rolled along the street. With the headlights off and the fog encroaching, the hybrid was virtually undetectable to human ears or eyes. Not that she would notice even if it was broad daylight and he was gunning the engine of a hot rod. She was either talking on her cell or texting, her mind anywhere but on the deserted street.

Still, he had to be careful. He didn't want to nab her when she could scream or text for help to whoever was on the other end of her connection. That wouldn't do. No. She would have to be disabled, and so would her phone. Immediately.

This would be tricky. Easing down the street, his foot barely on the accelerator, he felt every muscle in his body become tense. Using his own phone, he texted his partner again. The guy was a bit of a moron, but necessary if he wanted to finish this job. And he did. Badly.

Heading N on Claymore. X st. Dixon. B ready.

This would only work if his friend came through. Thankfully, there were no storefronts or cameras on this side street, and traffic was pretty much reduced to cars from the neighborhood.

God, she was a beauty. He knew. He'd found her picture in a yearbook left in a local coffee shop. He'd swiped it and used it to peruse more pictures and narrow his hunt, then with the names and personal information in the yearbook, he'd gone onto the social media Web sites and learned more. When he searched for a girl outside of the public high school, he used facial recognition software and applied it to Facebook and Twitter and Instagram until he found the girl he wanted and downloaded her information.

There were so many to choose from, but he had to pare down his list. He'd sworn to himself that he would wait another day or two, letting the heat from Rosalie's disappearance cool a bit. He'd also waited in order to pluck two or more at a time, but he believed in fate, and it was as if God had placed this perfect specimen in his path for a reason.

He needed more girls, and he felt the clock ticking, time running out.

This one, Candice, filled the bill in so many ways: long legs with great calves, thick hair, nipped-in waist, nice tits, high cheekbones, and a smile just recently released from braces. She was smart, a good student, but quiet and, more important, deeply religious—a nice balance to the wild, foul-mouthed Rosalie. Candice would be the meek one.

He craved a cigarette but made himself wait until afterward, when she was cuffed and shackled. Then he could relax a little. Enjoy a smoke. Maybe a drink. *After* she was tucked safely in her new home, a stall labeled Lucky because he thought he'd been lucky finding her.

In fact, he was surprised to find her alone.

Now that one girl had gone missing in Stewart's Crossing, the town had been warned and was taking note. He'd seen the posters tacked on bulletin boards and telephone poles, witnessed the AMBER Alert aired on the local news when he was watching his television, and heard the chatter in the local coffee shop.

Everyone in Stewart's Crossing was on edge and a little warier than they had been. Rosalie Jamison's disappearance had not gone unnoticed, and his hopes that people would think she was just another teenaged runaway had died. Even that buffoon of a sheriff had made a plea on television just this afternoon for information about her. And her parents, losers though they were, had come forth as well, the mother breaking down before the cameras, the father from Colorado looking shell-shocked as he'd tried to comfort his weeping ex-wife.

So he should lay low.

Wait it out.

Let the story die.

But he couldn't. He was quickly running out of time, and obviously the hype over Rosalie's disappearance wasn't dying down as rapidly as he'd hoped, so he'd have to risk another abduction. Then maybe he could take a few more on Halloween. After that, get the hell out of Dodge.

But for now, opportunity was knocking, and he was about to respond.

A reply text came in: **See her.**

His heartbeat increased, and he wrote: **Let's do this.**

In position.

Wait til she's off the phone then it's go time.

He inched the car closer and was amazed she didn't sense the vehicle.

Too wrapped up in her conversation.

As if God were on his side again, she suddenly pocketed her phone and started to cross the street, then realized for the first time that his car, with its lights off and making no sound, was within a few feet of her. She looked in his direction. Panic rose on her face, and she leaped back as he flashed on his lights, blinding her, just in time for his friend to grab her.

She started to scream, but it was too late as a big hand was suddenly over her mouth and squeezing her nostrils closed as she was pushed toward the car.

Perfect!

He rammed the Prius into park, threw himself out of the vehicle, and rounded the rear end within seconds. Opening a back door, he allowed his friend to wrestle her inside, where the handcuffs and gag were waiting. She struggled, fighting and kicking, but it was no use. His friend climbed into the back with her, subduing her and enjoying every second of it. He could see the light of anticipation, the thrill of overpowering the girl, register on the smaller man's face.

"Don't hurt her," he warned as he slammed the door shut. Once behind the wheel again, he took off, keeping to the speed limit on the side streets, avoiding as many other vehicles as possible, and finding the road that led upward through the hills. "Did you hear me?" he snapped, glancing back. "You know the rules. No bruises."

"But she's soooo nice," the other man breathed, no doubt sporting a boner that wouldn't quit. He was still lying atop her, and he was grinding.

"Don't touch her."

"But—" His voice was raw, breathless, and she was mewling, trying to scream despite the gag.

Shit. "Just don't!" He stopped the car on the hillside, set the emergency brake, and once again rounded the car to open the back door. Sure enough, his friend was on top of the girl, humping like crazy, sure to mess his jeans. "Get out!"

"But—"

"Now!"

"Oh, fuck!" As the traumatized girl quivered and cried, he climbed off her. "I was just—"

He kicked the door shut, and it locked automatically as he grabbed the lapel of his partner's dirty jean jacket in his fists and slammed him up against the car. "You were just gettin' your damned rocks off! Jerking off on her! That's *not* part of the deal." He yanked hard on the lapels and tossed the idiot against the car. "Leave her alone. All of them. We've got a job to do." Then, in disgust, he added, "Get in the car."

"Jesus, man . . ."

"Do *not* use the Lord's name in vain again!" he hissed, then as the guy started for the door, kicked him hard in the ass.

"Hey! Watch it!" He stumbled forward but caught himself and had a wounded look on his face as he glanced over his shoulder.

"We don't have time for this shit!"

So angry he thought he could snap the half-wit's neck with his bare hands, he climbed behind the wheel. Fortunately, the girl was so traumatized she hadn't figured out that she could have crawled over the seats and sprinted away. He yanked the door closed and hit the gas while the damned seat belt alarm dinged. "Buckle the fuck up!" he yelled, and for once, thankfully, the idiot listened.

*   *   *

Sarah stared out the window. Jade, furious, had wound herself into a sleeping bag and was icing her out by taking up residence in the one bedroom on the first floor. For once, Sarah decided to give her daughter space. Jade had wanted the truth but wasn't ready to deal with it, and Sarah had been a little rash in picking up the phone and calling Clint. It was a relief that the burden of the secret would be off her back, but now she had other demons to deal with. She was certain anyone who'd ever taken Psychology 101 would tell her she'd blown it, big-time. But there it was. The biggest secret of Sarah's life, one she'd guarded for nearly eighteen years, out.

She'd been blindsided by Jade and reacted. Probably stupidly. Forcing a mammoth, emotional confrontation that would probably only make both Jade and Clint hate her, at least for a while, though time, she hoped, would be on her side.

She didn't want to have the same relationship with her oldest daughter as she did with her own mother.

She'd better get ready for Clint.

As if she ever would be.

Returning to the living room, she started putting firewood from the carrier into the cold fireplace, stacking the oak as her father had shown her years earlier. Before she lit the fire, Sarah rocked back on her heels and stared at the open grate, feeling the shadows in the house close in on her as they had so many times in the past. Though she loved it here, there was a melancholy to these ancient walls, a sadness that she'd told herself was all because of the tension and emotional drama that had played out here in her youth and probably long before.

With night having settled in, she was reminded of sitting in this very room in the dark, with only the fire as illumination, her father sleeping on the long couch, while her mother rocked in the chair nearest the flames, knitting as if by rote, never missing a stitch, her gaze glued to her work in the dim light, her needles clicking in an unending, staccato beat, the fire hissing. Red embers glowed. Hungry flames cast shifting, golden shadows. Her father's old hunting dog had usually been curled on the rug next to the couch and the discarded newspaper, and every now and again, Franklin, reading glasses still propped on his nose, would let his arm stretch down so that he could scratch Lady behind her ears.

Once when Sarah had been in grade school, she'd been walking from the kitchen to the stairs and heard her mother's voice, as clipped as the sounds of her knitting needles. "It's all your fault, you know," Arlene had said, and though her back was turned, Sarah sensed that her mother's lips were tight, suppressing the fury that was radiating from her thin body.

Her father hadn't responded to his wife, which, of course, infuriated Arlene all the more.

"That they're gone. Theresa and Roger. Both of them," she'd said tightly. "It's because you didn't love them enough, treated them differently. And it wasn't because they were older, like you always claim. It's because they weren't your blood and you had to punish me."

Silence.

Through her anger, she'd managed to keep knitting.

Click. Click. Click.

"I never should have married you, because it was a lie," she charged on. "You swore you'd take in my kids and love them like your own, but you didn't, did you? And . . . and . . ." Her voice had broken then, a quiet sob erupting. For a few long seconds all Sarah heard was the rapid click of the needles. Then, in a lower voice, Arlene added, "I hate you. You know that, don't you? For ruining my life and taking my children away from me."

Barefoot, Sarah sneaked closer, her heart pounding. Surely her father had something to say to those ugly accusations.

But he didn't say a word, and Sarah knew she should just sneak away, pad silently up to her room, and pretend she hadn't heard a word. Instead she bit her lip, her hand sweating over the glass of milk she'd retrieved from the fridge. Hardly daring to breathe, she peeked around the corner, her vision slightly impaired by one of the two pillars guarding the entrance to the room.

Mother was in the rocker, slowly swaying, her back to Sarah, but other than that the room was empty. Her father wasn't stretched on the couch, and Lady wasn't curled up on the floor.

Just her mother.

Alone.

Sarah's blood turned to ice.

Slowly, silently, she backed away from the darkened room to the staircase, where she planned to make good her escape. Her heels hit the riser of the first step, and she turned to dash up the flight of stairs.

"I know you're there, Sarah Jane."

Sarah froze.

"Don't you know it's impolite to eavesdrop?"

Sarah nearly dropped her glass.

"Get to bed before I get myself a switch!"

Sarah scurried up the stairs on her tiptoes, never making a sound, not taking so much as a sip from her glass, certain Arlene would follow after her and make good her threat.

Shivering under the covers, she'd waited.

Arlene hadn't followed.

The next morning, Sarah was convinced she hadn't slept a wink, but the full glass of milk that she'd set on the night table and left untouched was missing, and she didn't remember anyone removing it, so she must've dozed off. Or had her mother climbed up the old stairs to stand in the doorway, backlit by the hall fixture, her shadow long on the wall, a willow switch clenched in her hand? Had it been part of a distorted nightmare, or had Arlene stood in the doorway, eyes glowing like a demon, fingers twisting over the switch, rage contorting her beautiful features as she'd gazed down on her sleeping daughter?

When she'd finally gone downstairs, Sarah had found Arlene humming at the stove, bacon sizzling in a frying pan, a stack of pancakes warming in the oven, the smell of hot maple syrup filling the kitchen. Dressed in work clothes and reading the paper, Dad was seated at the table in his worn chair. He'd barely glanced up, but said, "Good morning, Sunshine. Runnin' a little late, aren't ya?"

"Oh, for the love of God, Frank. We've got plenty of time," Arlene declared, pouring batter carefully on a long griddle. "Come on now, Sarah, grab some hotcakes!" Her mother looked over her shoulder and offered Sarah a grin and a wink. Almost as if they held a private little secret. She then placed a stack of pancakes and a couple of slices of bacon on a plate in front of Sarah and handed her the syrup. "You slept so long this morning. You must've been exhausted."

"A little," Sarah said warily as she sat at the table where two empty plates, streaks of syrup evident, had been left. A couple of glasses stood empty as well. Obviously her brothers had already mowed through their breakfasts. "Bottomless pits" their father had often called the twins, and there had been a touch of pride in his voice.

Dee Linn's spot was bare. As always. Arlene had quit fighting outwardly about breakfast with the ever-dieting Dee Linn a year before, though Sarah suspected from the underlying tension between mother and daughter that the war was still ongoing but had morphed into a stony, simmering silence.

At least Arlene seemed in a good mood this morning, and Sarah relaxed a little. Cutting into the warm, buttery pancakes and tasting the sweetness of the syrup made the morning seem brighter. Arlene's off-key humming and her father's interest in the sports page convinced Sarah that things were back to as normal as they could be. She dug in eagerly, polishing off the stack. Once finished, she wiped her mouth with her napkin just as she heard the sound of Dee Linn's heels scurrying down the stairs.

"Hurry up!" her older sister called impatiently as she breezed past the kitchen to the anteroom off the back porch where the coats were hung. "I can't be late to first period," she called from somewhere near the back door. "Sister Annabelle will kill me if I'm tardy one more time!"

"Coming!" Sarah was feeling better. Dee Linn would take her to school and she could forget all about last night.

"Don't forget your milk," Arlene said as Sarah climbed off her chair.

Obediently, she grabbed the glass and realized it wasn't cold, that it had been sitting. But she couldn't be too concerned now, she had to get moving. Dee Linn was already bustling back through the kitchen and refusing any kind of food before it was even offered.

"I'm not hungry," she said, as she did every morning. "Are the boys ready? God, where *are* they?"

"Most important meal of the day," their father said, glancing over the tops of his reading glasses.

"That's just some radical scheme by the cereal companies to force people to choke down their overprocessed, sugary cardboard." She clomped her way to the staircase. "Jake! Joe!" then returned to the kitchen. "Can you get them going?"

"Yelling won't help," their father said and snapped the paper.

Arlene turned off the burners of the stove and glanced over her shoulder. "Want me to get my switch?"

"What? No!" Dee Linn stared at Arlene, but their mother wasn't looking at her older daughter, she was staring straight at Sarah, and for an instant Sarah thought of last night's nightmare, of seeing her mother, willow switch in hand, filling the doorway of her room.

At that moment frantic footsteps pounded from the upstairs, thundering down the staircase to herald the twins, pushing and yelling, backpacks flying, as they raced into the room. Their heads were wet, hair gelled into place, faces scrubbed until they were red. The smell of some kind of aftershave rolled in an invisible cloud around them.

"Take your plates to the sink!" Arlene ordered. "Both of you!"

The twins looked about to argue, and Sarah was grateful that the heat was off her, that Arlene's attention was turned to her rambunctious fourteen-year-old sons. "Oh, for the love of God, Joe, just how much cologne did you use? You can smell it from a mile off. You don't need to use a fire hose when you apply that stuff!"

"Listen to your mother," their father said.

"Let's get going!" Dee Linn was about to have a conniption fit.

Still wrestling a bit, the boys grabbed their plates, and Arlene lifted her brows at Sarah, who got the message and started chugging her warm milk.

Until something hit her tongue and the back of her throat, something that wasn't liquid and . . .

Quickly she spat the milk back into her glass and saw a black clot, with wings and legs . . . a dead fly floating on the surface. She met her mother's eyes just as her stomach bucked. Dropping the glass on the table, sloshing the remains of the milk and the fly, she raced out of the room to the downstairs bathroom, where she upchucked all of her breakfast into the toilet.

How had the fly gotten into her glass?

Had it just died there overnight, because Sarah was certain that was the same milk she'd poured the night before, that her mother had left it out to make a point. But the fly? Had it landed in the milk and been trapped, or had her mother actually . . .

Lifting her head, she caught her mother's reflection in the mirror over the sink. Arlene was just staring expressionlessly. "What happened?"

"You know what happened!" Sarah choked out. "You put it there!"

"Put what where?" Arlene asked.

"The fly, Mom. In my milk!" Grabbing the hand towel, Sarah wiped her face.

"There you go again," Arlene said on a sigh. "Imagining things."

"I did not imagine that fly!" Sarah's stomach roiled again, and she spat into the sink, then placed her head under the faucet and let the water run over her tongue and lips as she tried to get rid of the awful feeling that something was still stuck to the back of her mouth. She gagged several times and felt her mother standing behind her, probably smiling.

"Mom! Can you get her moving?" Dee Linn wailed over the sound of water rushing from the faucet. "Now I'm gonna be late for sure!"

"Your sister's sick. Maybe she should stay home and—"

"No!" Sarah straightened and wiped her face with the hand towel her mother was holding. "I'm going."

"Then you'd better run," Arlene said, her lips pursing. "We don't want your sister to drive too fast this morning."

Sarah flung the towel into the sink.

"It's just an insect, Sarah. Too bad it was in your milk, but it won't kill you, you know. It's not poison. Always the drama queen. Of course I didn't put it there. How could I? Why would I?"

"I heard you last night," Sarah whispered. "Talking to yourself. Blaming Dad for Theresa and Roger leaving."

"Oh, for the love of God!" Dee Linn appeared in the doorway. "I don't know what this is all about, but I'm leaving. With or without you!"

Sarah's stomach roiled again, and she turned quickly to dry-heave bile into the toilet. By the time she'd cleaned herself and grabbed her backpack, Dee Linn was furious.

"What's wrong with you?" she demanded, shepherding Sarah back through the kitchen and the pantry area, where their mother, one arm wrapped around her slim waist, was smoking a cigarette. She mouthed the words "Speak no evil," in a cloud of smoke, and Sarah ignored her. How many times had Arlene warned her of just that, to keep quiet? By the time Dee Linn had gathered their brothers together, forcing them to give up a quick game of catch with a football in the backyard, they were, indeed, late.

Sarah got a tardy slip at the elementary school, and according to the twins, they both had to do an extra set of push-ups in P.E., while Dee Linn had been "mortified" by Sister Annabelle in homeroom at Our Lady of the River.

Now, nearly a quarter of a century later, Sarah remembered that night and day vividly, the most indelible memory being her calm mother, watching her children leave as she smoked her cigarette on the back porch.

Her relationship with her mother had never recovered.

She'd sworn, when she'd given birth to Jade years later, that theirs would be a perfect mother/daughter relationship. That naïveté had worn off with the ensuing years, and she was convinced that perfection didn't exist, but at least she wanted a decent, fun-loving kinship with Jade, one that would last through the years.

But of course she'd lied.

Big-time.

So she could beat herself up about it, or somehow try to repair the damage. At least the truth was out.

"He's here!" Jade called from the dining room.

Sarah had been so caught up in the past, she hadn't seen her daughter slip into the foyer to stand by the windows near the door.

"Okay, let me handle this, and then you can talk to him—alone, or not. Or I'll be there."

"What about me?" Gracie asked. She'd pieced together what had transpired a few minutes earlier, and Sarah had been forced to confirm the truth.

"Can you and Xena hang out in the kitchen or dining room for a few minutes? Then we'll see how it goes. I'll probably join you."

Jade was shaking her head. "I don't want to be alone with him."

"I'll be right here. Don't worry. It's going to be okay," she said, though she didn't see how.

"This is a nightmare," Jade said under her breath as Sarah mentally counted to five, walked through the foyer to open the door, and realized her daughter was right: the night had taken a turn from bad to worse.

Clint Walsh wasn't standing under the harsh glare of the single porch light.

Nope.

The person waiting at the door was none other than Evan Tolliver, the man she'd told she'd never want to see again.

Apparently he hadn't gotten the message.

CHAPTER 20

Jade wanted to die.

Right here.

Right now.

If only God would take her, everything would be better, but now she had to face the truth and a father who probably hadn't wanted her way back when (or a mom who had told him the truth) and didn't need the inconvenience of a teenager right now.

As she hung back from the doorway, her heart jackhammering, her insides twisted into a billion knots, she saw not the man who was supposedly her father, but that jerkwad Evan Tolliver standing on the porch and trying to pour on the charm. Him being here would only make things worse.

How could her life get any more complicated?

She wasn't the only one who was feeling this way. Gracie, still as a stone, finally looked from the doorway to Jade, then took a step backward into the shadows, while the dog let out a low growl that sounded like a warning. Good! Jade hoped Evan heard it, got the message, and took the hell off.

Wrapping her arms around her middle, she thought of the man she now knew was her father. Why hadn't Mom had the guts to be honest when she'd first asked about her father? Why keep the secret? If everyone had been on page one from the get-go, there wouldn't be all this drama, all this angst. Everyone would understand the way things were. Maybe Jade would even have had a relationship with the man. But, oh, no, Sarah had bottled up the truth, and now Jade was faced with meeting a stranger and . . . what? Hope to form some kind of daddy-daughter bond with him?

Get real.

Mom had really fouled up, and not just in this instance. Jade was certain her mother had kept secrets about the family in general. Despite the fact that Sarah was working on this project with her siblings, there were obviously major rifts in the family, which wasn't much of a surprise.

Really, Mom was just plain weird, probably because the whole damned family was kind of out of some gothic novel. And the ghost thing was something else too. Was it real? Jade didn't know and certainly didn't care. She just knew her mother hadn't been truthful about her biological dad and hadn't been able to hold onto her adoptive one. Noel McAdams had walked out the door a few years back, and Jade had never forgiven Sarah for that bonehead move. Noel McAdams had treated her as if she were his own until Mom pissed him off and he split for good, taking off for the other side of the country and basically disappearing from their lives.

There were plenty of reasons to hate her mother, and now one of them was standing on the front porch, and from the looks of his country-boy smile, he was trying to wheedle his way back into Sarah's good graces.

The one *smart* thing her mother had done was break it off with Evan Tolliver. Too bad the jerk hadn't taken the hint.

He needed to leave now, before Walsh showed up and everything blew up. Oh, God, if she could just run away . . .

The thought had barely come into her head when she pulled her broken cell phone from her pocket to text Cody. She'd call him later, but right now, she needed him to be on alert, to help her make a plan.

She was going to leave this old monster of a house and her super-dysfunctional family as soon as she could.

Evan's eyes softened a little as his gaze met Sarah's. He was dressed down for him, in khakis, a sweater, and a jacket; he was a handsome, but heartless man. "Hi, Sarah," he said, offering up a smile, as if that would break any remaining ice from their last conversation. "Long time no see."

"What're you doing here, Evan?" Sarah asked. Could there be a worse time for him to land on her doorstep?

"I thought I'd surprise you."

"Mission accomplished," she said coolly.

He pretended he didn't understand as a cold wind blew from the east, scattering dry leaves and burrowing deep into her soul. "I just wanted to see you."

"I told you—"

"Shhh." He held up a hand, fingers splayed in front of her nose. "We need to talk." As if realizing how offensive the gesture was, he dropped his arm and took a step toward her, as if he intended to walk into her house. She blocked the doorway.

"I already told you I'm making a new life here for me and the girls. It doesn't include you." Her voice was firm. "I'm pretty sure I made myself clear on the phone."

"Well, that's a helluva thing."

Folding her arms over her chest, she tried to sound calm when she was actually anxious and angry inside. Who did he think he was? "Maybe so, but it's where we are." She felt rather than saw her children gathering behind her, then heard a low growl from Xena.

"What's with you?" His smile shifted to something hard and cruel. Half a foot taller than she, Evan Tolliver could be intimidating.

"Mom?" Gracie whispered.

"Not now, Grace." Sarah's gaze didn't so much as waver as she stared Evan down. "We don't need a scene. I'm asking you to leave now."

"I just want to talk things over. You know, face-to-face."

"I've said what I had to say, and this is a really bad time." It was even worse than he might think as she heard the low rumble of a truck's engine over the ever-present rush of the river. Clint's pickup, no doubt. Perfect. "Then again, there isn't a good time."

"Sarah—"

"Please leave. Don't make me call the police."

Her heart sank as she saw the flash of headlights through the trees. Talk about bad timing. If she didn't get rid of Evan—and fast—things were bound to get ugly. Or uglier.

"The cops?" He was more angry than wounded. "Are you kidding?"

"No." She yanked her cell from her pocket. As she started punching out 911, she asked, "What's it going to be?"

"For the love of . . ." Finally Evan heard the truck and saw the beams of headlights splash against the house. "Oh, wait . . . that's what this is all about? You're expecting someone?" He turned to spy Clint parking his old pickup near the garage. "What the hell?"

As the truck's engine died, Clint hopped from the cab, shouldered the door of the truck closed, and, hands in his jacket pockets, jogged toward the house.

"Of course," Evan muttered furiously as he skewered Sarah with a condemning look. "Bullshit, no one else."

No reason to argue. He wouldn't believe her anyway. "Just go."

"You played me for a fucking fool. Lying to me and cheating on me. Un-be-lieve-a-ble!" The skin over his face tightened. "You know, I could *smell* the stink of another man on you—"

"That's not what happened," she cut in.

"You moved back here because of *him.*" He jabbed an accusing finger toward Clint, who'd just reached the weak circle of light from the porch.

"It's not like that," she said, then caught herself. "Look, I don't have to explain myself. You just have to leave."

Clint took the stairs two at a time. "Something wrong?" he asked Sarah.

Evan bristled. "You tell me."

"Evan's just leaving." Sarah said tightly, "or I'm going to ask the police to escort him out of here."

"The police?" Clint's eyebrows raised.

Sarah glared at Evan as she introduced, "Clint Walsh, this is Evan Tolliver, my ex-boss at Tolliver Construction. He seems to think there was more to it than that. That our relationship was personal."

"Damned straight, there was." Evan's eyes narrowed to slits. "Who the hell are you?"

"Clint's my neighbor," Sarah told him flatly.

"And what else?" Evan demanded.

Wedging his body closer to Sarah, Clint said, "Looks like you'd better listen to the lady."

"Not just yet." Evan stood his ground, and Sarah wished they all could just disappear. "Sarah and I have unfinished business."

"No. We don't." Sarah wouldn't give him an inch.

"You heard her, Tolliver," Clint said crisply. "She wants you gone. And knowing Sarah, the call to the police isn't just a threat. She usually does what she says. She's a straight shooter."

"Is she?" Evan threw back, sizing up Clint while Sarah died inside. *A straight shooter? Not so much.* Clint would soon find out.

"What you're doing here is trespassing," Clint went on. "And if the cops come and maybe the press find out and do a little reporting, it wouldn't look all that good for your construction company, now, would it? Not exactly the kind of publicity you'd want."

A muscle worked in Evan's jaw, ticking off his rage under the bare bulb. He didn't like to lose. Ever. And he rarely backed down. Sarah knew. She'd seen construction projects go massively over budget, or have to be abandoned altogether because of Evan's inability to admit he was wrong or give up on something he wanted. But here, on her porch of the old manor house, with Clint calmly stating the facts, Evan actually took a step backward. When he hesitated, Clint advised, "It's time for you to go."

Evan's fists balled, and his lips flattened over his teeth. "Okay," he finally said between clenched teeth. "Okay," he finally ground out. "You and Sarah. That's the way it is." He made a disgusted sound, cold fury evident in his eyes as he slid his gaze to Sarah's face. "This isn't over," he warned.

"Yes, it is," she stated firmly.

"We'll see." He nearly tripped as he backed to the edge of the porch and half stumbled down the stairs, just catching himself before he could fall.

The muscles in the back of Clint's neck were tight, his rough-hewn features set as he waited tensely. If Evan didn't leave, it was clear he was ready to take matters into his own hands.

Evan hesitated, as if he were going to say something more, but, reading Clint's expression, thought better of it. Turning on his heel, he flung one last threatening glance in Sarah's direction, then stormed to his vehicle.

"Doesn't like to take no for an answer," Clint observed as Evan fired up his truck.

Sarah finally let out her breath and still held tight to her cell phone. "Evan lives in the land of yes, though I did go out with him a couple of times. Big mistake."

"Mmmm."

Behind the wheel, Evan hit the gas. His truck lurched forward and made a wide circle, nearly taking out the cherry tree, somehow managing to kick up practically nonexistent gravel.

"You haven't seen the last of him," Clint predicted as Evan's truck's taillights disappeared into the trees. "He the reason you called me over here?"

"Actually, no," she admitted, heart in her throat. Now that Evan and his threats were gone, the weight of what was about to go down settled over her shoulders. "There's something else. Come on in. We need to talk. You and me . . . and Jade." She hitched her head toward the foyer, where her daughters and the dog were waiting. With Clint following, she said to Jade, "Let's head to the living room. Clint, if you'll wait for me there?"

"All right." His brows were drawn together. He was clearly lost as to her cryptic comments, but he headed for the living room.

Placing her hands on Gracie's shoulders, Sarah steered her youngest down the corridor leading to the kitchen. "You might want to give us a few minutes. Once I tell him what's what, then I'll come back in here. He and Jade may need some time alone."

"You think it'll be that easy?"

"Not a chance."

"It's a little weird, Mom."

Sarah said with a humorless laugh, "It's a lot weird."

For reasons she couldn't name, Sarah felt guilty shutting Gracie out of this meeting, but she felt she owed Jade and Clint as much privacy as possible. "Okay. Fingers crossed this goes well," she said, turning back toward the living room.

"Good luck, Mom. I think you're gonna need it." Though Gracie and Xena were in the kitchen, Sarah was certain her youngest would hang near the living room archway so that she could eavesdrop.

Walking back into the living area, Sarah found two sets of eyes following her every move. Jade's were worried, almost scared. Clint's, as he stood near one of the pillars guarding the parlor, were filled with questions. "Okay, so what's going on that's so important?" he asked. Before she could answer, he smiled faintly and said, "You know, Sarah, you look like you've seen a ghost."

"She probably has," Jade said under her breath.

"Not now." Sarah cut off any chance of being derailed. "We've got more important issues to discuss right now."

"Issues?" Clint repeated. "But not with Tolliver?"

Sarah shook her head. "He just showed up, a few minutes before you. Bad timing."

"Super bad," Jade agreed.

"Are you in some kind of trouble?" Clint asked Jade.

Jade lowered herself to the hearth and visibly shrank as she pulled an afghan around her feet. "No . . ." Jade was tongue-tied for once. Rather than explain, she actually looked to her mother for help. "It's . . . it's . . . complicated."

"I'm the one in trouble," Sarah cut in.

Confusion pulled his thick eyebrows together. "How so?" He slid a supportive arm around Sarah's shoulders and squeezed her. For just a second, she remembered the smell of him, the easy way she talked to him, how safe she'd always felt when he was around. While life in this old house with her parents and siblings had been an emotional roller coaster, Clint had been rock-steady, an easy friend who had become a passionate lover. Even after they'd officially broken up, she'd found it impossible to resist him. Oh, Lord, this was going to be even harder than she had imagined. But it had to be done. She slid out of his embrace. "Maybe you'd better sit down."

"Heavy stuff?" he asked, half teasing.

"Very."

"Yep," Jade seconded.

He glanced at Jade, and his eyes narrowed a fraction, then, as he sat on the edge of the old couch, his hands clasped between his jean-clad knees, he eyed Sarah with a newfound suspicion. "Okay, go."

"This isn't going to be easy," Sarah said and felt her palms begin to sweat. She cleared her throat. "But I'll try to explain everything. Not just to you, but to your daughter too."

A beat.

He stared at her. The fire hissed and popped, and Jade seemed to shrink back.

"My what? My daughter?" He looked at Sarah as if he hadn't heard right, or that if he had, she'd lost her mind. "I don't . . ." His gaze moved from Sarah, standing near the pillar, to Jade, propped on the hearth and staring up at him with wide, worried eyes. Her fingers worked the edges of the afghan, and her face was as pale as death.

Trembling inside, Sarah tried to clear up the confusion. "Yes, Clint, Jade's your—"

"*What?*" he whispered, disbelief evident in the rough-hewn planes of his face. "What are you saying?" For half a beat he was quiet, thinking, doing the calculations in his head. Then the light dawned.

"Jade is yours," Sarah said before he could find his voice.

Jade closed her eyes and looked as if she wanted to melt through the floorboards.

Clint's jaw was rock-hard. "It's okay," he said to Jade, and when she didn't open her eyes, he added, "Give me a minute. Everything's going to be okay."

Sarah wasn't sure who he was trying to convince.

"No, it's not," Jade whispered, blinking hard against tears and ripping Sarah's heart in two.

"Goddamn," Clint said softly. He looked poleaxed, but it was clear he was trying to hold his emotions in check. But when his gaze met Sarah's, it was cold and hard. "Okay, Sarah. I'm listening."

CHAPTER 21

The night, as far as Rosalie could tell from her prison cell, was quiet, no sounds of wind in the rafters, no night birds calling. Completely and utterly alone, she lay on her tiny cot and held onto her bits of the nail clippers. All the while she plotted how she would use them.

If she got the chance.

If she hadn't been left here to die of starvation and thirst.

She hated how dependent she'd become on him.

Why, oh, why, hadn't her mother come? Did her dad even know she was missing? Had Sharon thought to call him? Had she gotten the police involved? Or was she so wrapped up in jerk-face Mel that she didn't care?

No, that wasn't right. Just her mind all turned around. She couldn't let the loneliness make her nuts. She had to have faith.

She looked up and saw a glint of light in the windows high above, then told herself she was probably hallucinating. No . . . wait. Was that the soft purr of an engine? Not the roar of a truck, but . . . oh, God, maybe someone had found her!

Leaping to her feet, she was about to shout, to scream for whoever it was, for her saviors to help her, but just before she said a word, she stopped suddenly. Maybe whoever had shown up wasn't a friend. So far, her captors hadn't harmed her, not really, though she knew their motives were sinister, but someone unknown might be worse.

Was that possible?

Poised to kick and pound on the door, to scream at the top of her lungs, she finally heard voices and footsteps crunching on gravel. All of her senses went into overdrive. *Please, please, please, let it be someone who has come to rescue me!*

The lock clicked and the door banged open.

Her heart pounded.

Snap! The lights came on, throwing an eerie glow over the open areas high above the stalls and along the tiny gap between the floor and the door to her cell.

Footsteps and muffled voices arrived.

Friend or foe?

Shrinking back into the corner, Rosalie hid the pieces of the clippers in her palm, just to be ready, as she recognized her captor's voice.

"Move it!" he yelled angrily, and she realized he wasn't alone.

What was he planning? What was he going to do to her? A cold sweat slid down her spine.

"Come on, come on!" he ordered. "We haven't got all night. Get her in here!"

Get who in where?

Was he talking about her? Was he ordering the other person to unlock the door and "get her" into the main area or . . . ?

She heard a second set of footsteps as another person entered and, over the uneven tread, the soft sobs of a woman or girl, she couldn't tell which.

Her heart sank. They'd captured another victim? For what? Yes, she'd heard them talking but hadn't believed it would actually happen. What the hell was their plan? Tiptoeing to her door, she tried to make out the muffled conversation.

"Give me a fuckin' break, man!" Scraggly Hair. She recognized the nasal tone of his voice. "She ain't no lightweight."

Rosalie bit her lip, and her mind whirled. Maybe this wasn't so bad. If there was another captive and they left her here, there was a chance that she and the girl could work together. Once alone, they could hatch a plot to escape. Unless . . . She froze as she considered the fact that now that the kidnappers had two victims, they might change their tactics. Maybe they wouldn't leave them alone together, or worse yet, maybe now, with the capture of the new girl, their plan for them might be put into motion. There was a chance they would be moved soon . . . or worse. Rosalie's mind spun with horrid, painful scenarios.

Don't borrow trouble. So far, so good, and now you have someone to help you. Swallowing back her new case of fear, she clenched her fingers around her minuscule weapon. *Please,* she thought desperately, *please let us find a way to escape.*

"Not there!" the man in charge yelled as the stall door next to hers creaked open. "We don't want them close to each other!"

"What?" Scraggly Hair said.

"Use your head, man. Take her down there, to the far end. Away from Star. She's Lucky."

"She's what?" Scraggly Hair asked. A Rhodes scholar, he wasn't.

"I said, she goes into Lucky's stall, there on the far end. See the name over the door? Yeah, that one!"

"Sheeeit." Scraggly Hair wasn't happy.

The door to the next stall was slammed shut, and Rosalie's heart fell to the floor. She'd hoped the girl would be closer so they wouldn't have to yell to communicate.

"Okay, okay, that's better. Yeah, as far away from Star as possible, and make it quick. I got more work to do tonight. Places to be. This just doesn't happen, y'know. It takes planning and working out details and timing. What the hell's wrong with you? You got shit for brains?"

Rosalie hated that he called her by a horse's name, but she didn't say anything. It was all she could do not to yell to the girl to fight, to get away, and unlock her stall door. If only "Lucky" could kick the bastard in his balls and nail the bigger man in his shins, then, while they were writhing and howling, somehow set her free, help her escape. They could make it to the car or the pickup or . . . or . . . *Stop it! That's not happening. Do you hear her? She's crying and sobbing like a baby. She's no help. Not now. Not until she realizes what she has to do. Bide your time, Rosalie. And hope God helps you and this girl is not a big wimp who will be more of a hindrance than a help. Oh, Jesus, that's not what you need.*

Suddenly there was another noise—weird techno music that she realized was the ring of a cell phone.

"Yeah?" her abductor nearly yelled into the phone. Then a pause while the girl who was headed to Lucky's stall sobbed and Scraggly Hair grunted. "Yeah, I know. I get it. Soon!" He sounded angry. Frustrated.

Rosalie kept her mouth shut, though it was nearly impossible. She wanted to yell and rage, to warn the girl not to let them shut and lock her door because then Rosalie would be in no better shape than she'd been before they had hauled the girl in. But she held her tongue because she'd already learned what her utter defiance had gotten her. At the thought of the bigger man's belt she shuddered. She tried to hear the conversation, though the commotion going on with the new girl made it difficult to make out the words. Closing her eyes, Rosalie concentrated.

"Yeah, I know what I promised . . . At least four, maybe five by next week."

Four or five what? Girls? Or was he talking about something else? Jesus, what was he planning?

"No, no! Not yet. I need the weekend . . . what? Monday? Yeah, that should work." Another pause. "Shit, I don't know. Seven?" Another pause. "Okay, okay. But we might have to wait until the next operation—"

And then the conversation was muffled as the new girl began to wail, and Rosalie thought maybe the call had ended.

The new girl was making a horrid racket, crying and wailing and shrieking.

"Jesus H. Christ, shut up!" Scraggly Hair yelled.

The other man snapped, "Do not use the Lord's name in vain!"

"Hey, butt-wipe, you swear."

"Fuck, yes, I swear, but I *never* use profanity with the Lord's name. We've been over this before."

He sounded royally pissed. Even the new girl's screams became softer.

"I just don't see the difference."

"Because you're a heathen. And a moron. And you damned well weren't raised right. No moral fiber to you."

"Bull*shit!* And you need me," Scraggly Hair argued angrily.

"I need someone. Not necessarily you."

"You'd do that? Dump me? After all I've done? Shit, man. Then I'd go to the cops. You hear me? Cut a deal. Get off scot-free. Roll the fuck over on you!"

"Would you?" The abductor's voice was stone cold. "Then you'd be a dead man."

Tense seconds ticked by. No one said anything. No sound of rats' claws scraped across the floor, no hint of bats stirring moved the air. Even the new captive was quiet. Rosalie prayed that the two bastards would go at each other. Maybe kill each other. Yes, definitely. Then the new girl, if the crier could get her damned wits about her, would be able to set Rosalie free from this god-awful stall and they could run out of here, take the truck, or that other car, and drive away. Escape! Finally.

Rosalie hardly dared breathe. *Please, please, please . . . kill each other.*

"Fuck, man," Scraggly Hair finally said, "let's just get the job done here and move on."

He was back to being the submissive one. His compatriot didn't respond, but Rosalie knew that for now, their chance of getting free was nil. But there was a wedge between the two men, and that might work to her advantage. Somehow. Trouble was, from the sound of the conversation she'd pieced together, they were running out of time. Whatever was going to happen to her and "Lucky," it was going down in a couple of days, and that scared her. It scared her to death.

The only good news was now she had another person on her side, one who presumably could help her and had a family or friends on the outside who could aid her mom or the cops or whoever in locating them. Maybe. If the girl didn't completely wuss out. Also, as far as she could tell, this old barn wasn't equipped with surveillance cameras or microphones, so once she and "Lucky" were alone, they could shout at the top of their lungs to communicate and make a plan to fight the bastards. Crossing her fingers, she waited, hoping to hear something from her new compatriot, but the girl didn't say a word, her sobs muffled.

Oh, God, please don't let her be a wimp.

That wouldn't work.

Not at all.

Maybe she was just traumatized or had been drugged or stunned with a stun gun so she couldn't communicate. Probably gagged too. Rosalie cringed as she thought of what they might have done to her, but she attempted to remain as positive as possible. At least now, she wouldn't be alone.

So she waited, her stall nearly dark.

Footsteps finally approached, just as she knew they would.

She slid backward and dropped soundlessly onto her cot. Quickly she flipped the top of the sleeping bag over her body and squeezed her eyes closed. Her fingers held the pieces of the clippers in a death grip, hidden beneath the musty cover.

The lock clicked.

She wanted to bolt.

Forced herself to stay where she was.

She heard the stall door swing open and even through her closed eyelids noticed a brightening. Still she remained motionless even though she heard his footsteps and knew he'd entered.

Touch me, freak, and I'll gouge your eyes out.

"I know you're not asleep, Star."

She didn't move, barely breathed.

"It's good you know your place, that you shouldn't fight."

God, she hated him. She itched to leap at him and kick and bite and claw at him, but she forced herself not to move.

"Yeah, that's a good girl," he whispered, as if she were an obedient puppy or a damned horse.

She heard him rustling around. "Got you some fresh water and a sandwich," he said, and she heard him exchange her used bucket for an empty one.

Sick bastard!

Finally the noise stopped, and she lifted her lids a fraction to see him standing in the doorway, his tall silhouette backlit.

He was staring right at her. "Cat got your tongue?"

She held her silence.

"Good. You were too mouthy as it was. You'll do much better knowing your place."

Dickhead!

Clamping her jaw shut, she didn't respond, wouldn't let him goad her.

"So now you're passive-aggressive?"

She was surprised he knew the term, but she made sure no emotion registered on her face.

"It won't work, you know. Your true colors are gonna show sooner or later, and that's a good thing. We want you to know your place, and you seem to be learning, but it's good that you've got that little bit of fire in you. You know what I'm talkin' about. That temper? Who you really are? That's gonna help too. He's gonna want to see that you'll give him a bit of a fight."

Who? Who was he talking about?

She felt sick inside as the wheels turned in her mind. They were giving her to someone. Or maybe selling her to him. A man who wanted "fire." Oh, that sounded bad. Real bad.

Still, she kept her thoughts to herself. It seemed that her not speaking caused him to open up a little. "Hey," he called to his partner, "look who's decided to give us the silent treatment."

"Beats all that screamin' and swearin'," the other guy said, and she heard some rustling and clanking of plastic and metal as, it seemed, they set the other girl up in her cell. Lovely. Rosalie wanted to rip both their faces off and then trample on them. All the while she heard the soft mewling of the other girl. Rosalie hoped to God that once she'd gotten over the shock of being captured, "Lucky" would show some backbone.

The bigger man said, "Come on, let's get a move on."

Should she take a chance? Leap on him? Cut him with the clipper? If he turned his back . . . But he didn't. Almost as if he'd read her mind, he backed out of the stall and shut the door, cutting off the bright source of light and her slim chance at freedom.

Be patient, she told herself. *There's still time.*

However, she didn't kid herself as she lay in the darkness, the smell of musty hay and horses an underlying odor in this dilapidated shell of a barn. No way did her captors plan to keep her in the old barn forever. No. They had a plan for her and for "Lucky" as well. She thought of the stories she'd heard of human trafficking, and prostitution rings with girls who'd been coerced into the life.

Whatever the two sickos had up their sleeves, it wasn't good; she was certain of that. Somehow, she and "Lucky" had to find a way to escape.

Soon.

While it was still an option.

CHAPTER 22

When Sarah hesitated, Clint had to tamp down his growing anger. "You had no right to leave me in the dark," he ground out, still struggling to process. He knew what it meant to raise a child, to have your life turned inside out for this little person, to love unconditionally. And then to lose the very object of your love and adoration.

His words seemed to snap her out of her frozen state. "I never told you because I didn't want to tie you down, to force you into doing something you didn't want out of some ridiculous sense of duty." She held up one hand, almost in surrender. Almost. "I should have told you and Jade long ago. I should have. I'm sorry I didn't. She just found out half an hour ago."

His gaze traveled to the seventeen-year-old huddled by the fire. Jade looked scared to death, and his heart twisted. "I didn't know," he told her, even though it was patently obvious.

She nodded jerkily, fighting emotion.

"I have no excuse," Sarah said in a nearly inaudible voice. "I thought it was the right decision at the time."

"You were selfish," Jade said.

Sarah nodded. "Afraid I'd lose you. And you," she said to Clint, her voice unsteady. "You were already with Andrea when you came home and . . . and we got together."

Jade squinched her eyes closed. "I don't want to hear this."

"I can't do any more than explain and say I'm sorry," Sarah said, ignoring Jade's attempt to derail her. "If that's not good enough, okay,

I even understand." She fastened Clint with that gaze that had singularly always made his breath catch in his throat. Then she began to tell her story in fits and starts. It took all his power of self-restraint to remain silent when emotions were waging a war inside him, but he managed . . . just . . . as Sarah rambled on about how she'd ended up pregnant after the one night they'd gotten back together, a rogue weekend after he and Andrea had split up for the third—or was it fourth?—time. Sarah assured him that she hadn't planned on getting pregnant. It had just happened, but when she found out she was with child, she'd been scared but excited for the baby growing inside her. Not having Jade or giving her up had been out of the question. Having Jade and being responsible for another human being had been a turning point in her life. Sarah, herself, had grown up quickly as she'd become a mother and understood unconditional love.

Clint listened over the thump of his heart and his crazily circling thoughts. The realization that he was a father, that he'd been a father for seventeen years and that he'd been denied the same responsibilities, joys, and heartaches that Sarah was extolling made him half crazy. Dear God, he'd been a father long before Brandon was even conceived.

"Why?" he asked when she wound down. "Why?"

She gazed at him helplessly. "Fear. Maybe because it seemed like the easier way out?" A moment later she shook her head and inched her chin up a fraction, almost daring him to set in on her, to tell her how angry he was. He nearly jumped at the chance. How could she have kept his daughter from him? What right did she have to lie with her silence? What if something had happened to this girl, the daughter he hadn't had the chance to know? A lock of hair fell over her face, and she pushed it away as if it were a bothersome insect, unaware how the brown strands showed red in the fire's glow, not knowing the battle that waged deep within him. Was he angry? Absolutely! Did he want to shake some sense into her? No doubt. And did he have the urge to pull her to him, kiss her, and make love to her until they were both breathless. Hell, yes.

Then he saw the girl, *his* daughter, Jade, staring at him.

"Don't you want to do some kind of paternity test?" she asked, a little attitude lacing the misery in her gaze.

"No," he said clearly. "Do you?"

She was startled, but almost smiled, showing off the hint of a dimple that was just like his mother's. He didn't doubt this girl was his for a second. He wondered now why he'd missed those dimples, or the shape of her eyes, or the barest hint of a bump in her nose, so like his, when he'd first seen her. How was it that he hadn't put two and two together before? How many times had he remembered that last night with Sarah, the magic of it, the guilt it involved? Warm, enticing sex that was somehow taboo as he'd been dating Andrea off and on for more than a year. It hadn't really mattered that they were "off" when he'd hooked up with Sarah again, because he'd suspected even then that they would get back together. "If you're not sure I'm your father, then I suppose I could get one," he said to Jade.

"That's not the way it works," she answered, staring at him. Before he could ask what she meant, she said, "You're supposed to rant and rage and yell at Mom, calling her a bitch and . . ."

"Jade," Sarah cut in.

He ignored her. "And?" he urged Jade as Sarah folded her arms across her chest.

". . . accusing her of being a gold digger and passing off someone else's kid as theirs . . . or . . . something?"

"Wow," Sarah whispered, clearly stung.

Clint said, "I think Sarah's telling the truth."

"And you're mad at her," Jade realized.

Clint didn't respond, but he knew his feelings were obvious. He didn't want to meet Sarah's eyes, knowing she would get to him without even trying, so he held Jade's gaze . . . his daughter's gaze . . .

"You never guessed?" Jade asked.

"Everyone thought you were Noel's," Sarah answered for him.

"Dad *adopted* me," Jade pointed out. "Everyone in the family knew that. Why would he adopt his own child?"

"Did he know?" Clint cut in, his gaze centered on Sarah. "Your husband, did he know that Jade was mine?"

Sarah shook her head. "No one knew but me. My mom guessed, of course, but she didn't tell anyone else about it, or at least not that I know of, and I'm sure Dee Linn would have confronted me if she'd found out."

"Your ex didn't ask?" Clint questioned.

"We, uh, we had an arrangement."

"God, what does that mean?" Jade asked under her breath.

"Whatever happened before we got together was just the past. Noel and I didn't keep secrets that would harm each other, but we let all the other stuff go."

"Very civilized," Clint stated flatly.

"At least Dad, er, Noel—God, what do I call him now? At least *he* was around," Jade declared. "Or he was until . . ." She looked to her mother.

"Until I started talking about returning here," Sarah continued. "He wasn't interested. We'd . . . oh, it sounds so trite, but we really had grown apart. We split, and the irony of it was that I didn't return here right away. I had to work things out with my siblings, and so I stuck it out in Vancouver."

"But he left the girls?" He tried to keep the censure out of his voice, but it came through anyway.

"That was the hard part," Sarah said. "For both of us. He was— is—a good father."

"Do you see him much?" Clint turned to Jade.

"He's in Savannah," Jade responded. "Clear across the country."

"Distance shouldn't matter," Clint swept that aside. He would have traveled the earth and back to see Brandon again, and now, he knew, he would do the same for Jade, and if given the chance, for the little girl, Gracie, as well. That's just the way it was.

Sarah said to Jade, "Maybe you two should talk while I go to the kitchen with Grace."

"No, Mom!" Jade was stricken.

"You don't have to go," Clint said to Sarah.

"I won't be far. Just around the corner." She visibly softened as she looked at her daughter. "You've been begging for this for years, right?" One side of her mouth lifted a bit, and he was reminded of the innocent girl she'd once been. Then, with a last, lingering look— a warning to be kind to her daughter—she walked out of the room, her jeans hugging her butt as she left him with his daughter.

For the love of Mike, he was a fool. Even with everything he now knew, she stirred his senses.

Turning to Jade, he opened his mouth to say something . . . what, he was not really sure. But she stopped him cold by staring at him in horror.

"Oh, my God," she said in disbelief. "You're still in love with her."

"Hey!" Rosalie shouted. She figured they were finally alone, the kidnappers having left a good five minutes earlier, the purr of the engine growing fainter and fainter before finally dying altogether. From the other side of the barn she heard the quiet sobs of the other girl. "Can you hear me?"

The sobs stopped suddenly. Then there was nothing, no noise over the sound of her own heartbeat.

"They brought me here a while ago. Last Friday night. My name is Rosalie Jamison." She was yelling at the top of her lungs, wondering if the other girl were scared spitless, or if she was deaf.

"The missing girl?" a faint voice asked.

"Well, yes. These cretins captured me and brought me here. I've been alone ever since. Until tonight. Until they brought you here."

"Oh. My. God." And then the girl began to cry again, sobbing and blubbering.

"Hey!" Rosalie yelled. "Stop it! We have to figure a way out of here."

Still the weeping continued.

Oh, this was going nowhere. "Who are you?"

"Wha—?"

Good Lord, the girl was a moron! "What's your name. I'm thinking it's not Star."

"Oh." Sniffle, sniffle. "C-Candy."

Rosalie inwardly groaned. That was just as bad.

"C-Can. Candice Fowler." Did the girl stutter, or was she just scared out of her mind? "You're . . . you're the girl on all the posters. I've seen 'em around town, and there was a safety assembly at school, but I . . . I didn't think . . . Oh, noooo." She was sobbing again, wailing and crying.

"Stop it!" Rosalie yelled. "Pull yourself together. We've got to find a way out of here. Tell me what happened. How you got taken. What they said. How they did it. If you heard their plans. We have to work together, you got it?" She was shouting at the top of her lungs over the partial walls of the stalls and Candice's crying jags.

Hesitantly, her voice sometimes fading, Candice finally explained that she'd been walking home from a friend's, taking a shortcut, not really paying attention to anything but her phone, when she'd been "squeezed" by the two men—one the driver of a Prius, she thought, some kind of hybrid car that was so quiet she hadn't heard it overtake her, and the other guy, smaller and wiry, who had subdued her. She'd freaked out and had no idea where she was, just wanted to go home.

Now she was crying again, bawling for her mother, swearing she was a "good" girl and this kind of thing shouldn't happen to her.

"I, uh, I uh, I can't have this happen. I want my mom!" she yelled and then squealed like a stuck pig. "Eeeeooow! Oh, God, I saw a rat. Swear to God. I've got to get out of here. Help! *Help!*" She pounded on the door and then started crying again.

"Calm down! This isn't going to work. You have to quit crying."

"But I saw a rat and I peed myself!"

Give me strength.

"Seriously, Candice, shut up and listen. We have to work together, and we might not have much time."

More wailing, including a horrible ear-piercing shriek that would certainly ensure all the rats in the area would run for cover, but that, unfortunately, no savior would hear. Wherever this barn was situated, Rosalie feared, it was too far from any kind of civilization for even a shriek like that to catch someone's attention.

Candice kept at it, screaming so loudly that Rosalie thought the remaining panes in the windows overhead would shatter and the dead in three counties would wake.

Too bad no live people would hear.

Flopping back on her cot, Rosalie decided to wait for Candice to give up or go hoarse. Because she was useless. That much was obvious. The new girl hadn't been in the barn for half an hour and already Rosalie realized Candy or Lucky or whatever Rosalie decided to call her was a pain in the backside. No doubt she'd turn out to be more of a hindrance than a help.

It was all Sarah could do to keep her legs steady. The confrontation she'd been dreading for seventeen years wasn't over, of course, but the worst part, the owning up to her secret, was out, and that was a relief.

Where would they all go from here?

Sarah had no idea, but she was determined to take one step at a time. Reaching the kitchen, she expected to find Gracie hovering near the archway, on one foot and the other, wanting to be a part of the action.

Instead she found her daughter seated on a stool at the kitchen counter. Her legs were swinging, and she was engrossed in what at first appeared to be homework. However, when Xena, the not-so-great watchdog, finally noticed Sarah's arrival and began thumping her tail on the floor, Gracie visibly jumped, and Sarah saw that the workbook was actually a leather missive that looked worn and about to fall apart.

"What's that?" Sarah asked.

Gracie looked up guiltily. "Nothing." Attempting to stuff the book into her backpack, she nearly fell off the stool. The book tumbled to the floor, where Sarah scooped it up.

She was still distracted by what was happening in the living room, but she forced herself to focus on her youngest. Turning the book over in her hands, she finally zeroed in on it. "What do you mean, 'nothing'?" She flipped through the yellowed pages of a smooth, faded script. "This looks like someone's diary."

"A journal," Gracie said.

"Whose?" she asked, but she felt the flesh on her arms raise. She knew even before Grace said, "Angelique Le Duc's. See the date." Grace pointed out a barely legible entry, but it didn't make sense.

"But the date is at the beginning of the journal and near the time she disappeared. How could she have written it?"

"*Allegedly* disappeared," Gracie corrected. "Maybe that was all a big lie. Maybe she was hiding out or being held prisoner or something."

"Where did you get this?"

Her eyes slid away.

"Grace?" Sarah prodded.

"In . . . the basement."

Sarah went cold inside, a visceral reaction that still attacked her from her time of being locked in the basement by her brothers—a prank that had lasting consequences. "What were you doing down there?"

"Just looking around." Her slim shoulders rose and fell in an "it really doesn't matter" shrug.

"She was snooping, like she always does." Her face pale, Jade appeared in the doorway.

"Where's Clint?" Sarah asked.

"In the living room. He wants to talk to you."

"How'd it go?" Sarah queried tentatively.

"How do you think it went? Just effin' perfect." She found the box of cocoa and began brewing herself a cup. "I wouldn't keep Daddy Dearest waiting too long if I were you," she warned as she opened a pack of instant mix with her teeth.

"Is he mad?" Grace asked.

Jade made a sound of disbelief. "Duh."

Girding her loins, Sarah handed Gracie the journal and warned, "We'll talk about this later. *Tu le sait, je parle français.*"

"What?" Grace asked.

"She said, 'You know, I speak French,' " Jade translated.

That caught Sarah up. "Wow."

"So, I learned something," Jade said.

As Sarah lifted her hands in surrender, Grace asked, "Can you translate this for me?"

"Yeah, maybe later. But in the meantime, don't go into the basement or the attic or anywhere until we know that it's safe."

Gracie tucked the diary into her bag again. "It's safe."

Sarah remembered the feeling that the house was being observed from the outside and occupied by the spirits of the dead on the inside.

But for now, she needed to talk with Clint. Putting all thoughts of ghosts and tragic ancestors aside, she headed to the living room.

CHAPTER 23

As he nosed his truck into the pockmarked parking lot of the Columbia Diner, he felt the urgency, the pressure of the operation, coming to a head. He had to step things up, and that took a helluva lot of planning.

Get in. Get out.

The whole operation depended on him and his partner—who was a moron at best and a complete idiot at worst.

Already, they had spent too much time between abductions, thereby giving the cops more time to investigate, and that was dangerous.

So now he had to be extra careful not to draw attention to himself. He needed to go about his business as he always had, keep to his routine and his cover, ensuring that no one would suspect he was the mastermind behind the kidnappings.

He pulled into his usual parking space on the access road side of the diner and, after locking his truck, strode inside. A couple of guys were standing outside in heavy jackets, their shoulders hunched against the wind gusting down the gorge as they smoked, the tips of their cigarettes glowing red in the night. Each nodded as he passed, and he returned the gesture, though he had no idea who they were. Probably regulars like himself.

Inside the diner smelled of overcooked coffee and grilled onions. Country music was audible over the sizzle of the deep fat fryer and general conversation in the brightly lit, narrow restaurant. He took a booth near the entrance, right across from the cashier's station and the case of "fresh-baked" delicacies that, at this time of night, consisted of a solitary piece of key lime pie, a few cookies, and half a coconut cake—not that he cared.

A few customers littered the booths and stools at the counter, none he recognized, some probably drivers of the big rigs parked outside. The waitress, Gloria of the ever-changing hair, hurried up to him, her usually harried expression doubly so.

"Hi," she said with a quick smile, her lipstick long faded, her mascara still thick. She handed him a plastic menu. "Anything to drink?"

"Beer. Whatever you got on tap."

"We have half a dozen," she said, and before she could start rattling them off, he held up a hand.

"Bud."

"You got it. Oh, and just so you know, we're out of the special, the salmon, but the cod's real nice tonight." And she was off, ostensibly in search of his beer. He glanced at the menu and didn't much care what he ate. Food was fuel. That was all. Especially at this stage of the game. He watched a couple truckers pay for their meals, then head outside, talking as they made their way to a semi parked on the river side of the diner.

A few minutes later, Gloria reappeared. "Here ya go!" She slid a beer onto the chipped Formica table. "You decided?"

"B.L.T. No tomato."

"So just a B.L.?" she said, forcing a smile as the joke fell flat. From the kitchen the sound of silverware crashing to the floor was followed by an audible "shit!"

Gloria rolled her eyes. "Fries with that?"

"Sure. That's all."

"You got it." Not bothering to write the order down, she started for the kitchen when something on the television screen mounted over the archway at the entrance caught her eye. She made a strangled little sound, her hands with their red-tipped nails covering those faded lips. "I'm sorry," she squeaked, and tears actually welled in her eyes.

He glanced at the television, and there, big as life, was a picture of the girl he'd come to think of as Star.

"Oh, my God, it's just so awful," she admitted. "No one knows what happened to her."

"She worked here, right? I remember her."

"Oh, yes. And such a sweet, sweet girl."

He didn't respond, but wondered if they were talking about the same person.

"She was here that night, and I should never have let her walk home. They think she was taken near here, on her way home." Gloria actually shuddered. "I can't sleep thinking about how if she'd just listened to me, and waited for me to take her home, she'd be here today, waiting tables and collecting tips." Another little squeak.

"They have any idea what happened?" he asked casually.

"Just that she was nabbed." She cleared her throat. "They haven't found a body."

"Any chance she just ran off?"

Gloria whipped her head around to stare at him, and he instantly regretted pushing it. Shit, he had to be careful. "What do you mean?"

"Sometimes teenagers just take off." He offered her what he hoped was an encouraging smile. "You'll see, she might come back."

"Well . . . we can only hope," she said, then took off again to take another order from a couple who had grabbed stools at the counter. He sipped his beer, watched the television, and reminded himself to not talk too much. *Loose lips sink ships.* How many times had he given his partner just that warning?

And yet he was anxious to hear more, to learn what the police might be thinking. The reporting on the case was spotty, in his opinion, so if the cops were anywhere close to figuring out what had happened to Star, they were keeping it to themselves. He needed inside info from the department, as the operation was going into overdrive this weekend and he couldn't afford to screw up. The pressure was on.

Gloria returned with his sandwich and, after again asking if he needed anything, was off to the kitchen. Catching glimpses of the television, he spread his sandwich with ketchup and listened to the news with half an ear. He learned from a reporter standing in front of the Sheriff's Department that there were "no new leads" in the case of the missing teen and saw nothing about the second girl. Apparently the authorities hadn't been contacted about Lucky; if they had been, the press hadn't gotten wind of it.

Only a matter of time, he thought, sipping from his beer as he watched the screen. He hadn't been kidding when he'd told his partner that it took a lot of planning to pull off a kidnapping, especially with the authorities and nervous parents on alert. And now the ante was upped. He'd figured on two, possibly three more. But five? He would have to be clever. And he'd have no time to maneuver. Grabbing Rosalie was easy, and he knew the authorities would think she was probably a runaway. Hadn't he ensured it with that fake boyfriend he'd conjured up? It had gone seamlessly, his alter ego Leo "meeting" her in the chat room she'd mentioned to him once while serving him a hamburger and french fries. He'd also learned that she longed to go to Colorado and connect with her "real" dad and that she hated the series of husbands and boyfriends her mother had hooked up with. So Leo had hailed from around Denver. The seed was planted, the flirting quick and sexual, and the rest had been easy. As someone who understood the Internet and computers and how to form an IP address that was virtually impossible to locate quickly, he'd been able to reel Rosalie in and create a reason why she might disappear off the face of the earth. The second girl wouldn't be considered a runaway, though, and as stupid as the police were, they could easily put two and two together and recognize both girls had been abducted.

And now *five more?*

He wasn't a fuckin' magician.

Grabbing a french fry, he dunked it in its little paper container of ketchup before taking a bite. Maybe he should move on; just use the two he'd picked up, maybe grab two more and haul them all across the border into Washington or, better yet, Idaho. Then find the next ones at a new location. But it would take time, money, and a new hideout he didn't have. Plus, his partner was right: he needed someone to help him. Unfortunately he'd chosen poorly, as his "friend" was an idiot.

First things first. He'd stake out the McAdams place again as soon as he finished here. The McAdams girls would be the final targets . . . or . . . *what about Sarah, the mother?* The thought wasn't new, but it was infinitely more attractive now that he needed so many. He could wipe out the whole damned family in one swoop. Sarah was old for what he had in mind; the younger girls were better choices. But she was pretty enough, and smart too. But odd. Well, that in itself set her apart and held its own appeal. He warmed to the idea as he took another swallow of beer. Would the authorities zero in on him if all three women disappeared?

Worth considering.

He'd been so lost in thought, he'd ignored his sandwich and the television, and as he took his first bite he nearly choked when he saw the image of Sheriff Cooke flash onto the screen. He steeled himself, but the news was only a recording, a tape of the one press conference the Sheriff's Department had held. Again, there appeared to be nothing new in the investigation into the disappearance of Rosalie Jamison.

Smiling, he licked the ketchup from his lip with his tongue and watched Jefferson Dade Cooke evade the questions while attempting to look authoritarian, as if he were indeed "the man" in charge.

He couldn't help but snort his disdain. An able adversary, the sheriff was not.

And that was just fine with him.

Sarah found Clint standing in front of the fire, warming the back of his legs, staring at the far wall, but viewing, she suspected, a place in the distance that only he could see. At the sound of her footsteps, he swung his gaze toward her.

If she'd hoped to find forgiveness in his eyes, she was disappointed.

If she'd thought she'd see understanding in his features, she was totally let down.

If she'd believed they could work things out now that he knew the truth, she'd been a fool.

"Jade said you told me the truth only because she figured it out," he greeted her.

"That's essentially correct. I was going to let you and her know when the time was right."

"And that would be when?" He made it sound like he didn't believe it would ever have happened.

"One of the reasons I came back here was to tell you," she said, trying not to sound defensive. "Jade needed to know and you did too, and now we all have to find a way to move forward."

"How do you intend to do that?"

"I don't know. Got any ideas?"

"I haven't exactly had time to work out a parenting plan," he pointed out, adding dryly, "give me a couple more minutes." Sarah couldn't think of how to respond, so she just stayed silent. After several tense moments, he said, "I guess we'll have to consult our lawyers."

That woke her up. "I'd like to keep lawyers and judges and social workers or whatever out of this. I was hoping that you and I—and Jade too, as she's seventeen—could work out some kind of arrangement."

"Arrangement?" he repeated with derision. "I had a son." He hooked a thumb at his chest. "I know what it's like to love a kid, to provide for him, to worry yourself sick over him. There was no 'arrangement'."

"Then come up with another word," she snapped, tired of being the bad guy. "I screwed up, okay? I know it. You know it. Jade knows it. Soon the whole damned world will know it. But I can't change it." She paced across the room, then walked up to him, the toes of her shoes a hairbreadth from the end of his boots. "And I'm not going to spend the rest of my life feeling bad about it. I did what I thought was best at the time, and if you don't like it, too bad. So sue me," she said before the weight of her words hit her full force. Would he? Would he actually sue her for custody?

"There are legalities that have to be dealt with."

"You want a paternity test? Get a paternity test." She was standing too close to him, but she wouldn't back down.

"Maybe I will." They stared at each other in challenge.

"Go ahead."

"I do believe you," he finally admitted. "Jade and I talked. I know her birth date, and I see the resemblance."

"Okay, so . . . what? You want to see a lawyer for partial custody?"

"I don't know, I—"

"Because if that's what you want, you need to consult with Jade. She's old enough to have some say in her future. I'm still her mother," she added, before he could speak, "so, yeah, you can be a part of this family, if you want, but that's it."

"That's where the lawyers come in. To ensure that—"

"Fine," she cut him off again. "Get your damn lawyer."

"Damn it, Sarah, let me finish."

"I know what you're going to say. Look, Clint, I've apologized. Up and down and sideways. I'm done with it. The apologies are over. If you need a lawyer to figure out what's next, so be it. I do want you and Jade to have a relationship, but I'm the primary parent and always will be." She just needed him to know the parameters.

"Got it," he said in a flinty voice. His eyes held hers for a second, then he turned his head and called, "Jade? Would you mind coming back in here a second?"

Sarah braced herself as her older daughter, carrying a cup of cocoa and looking wary, reentered the living room. Gracie and the dog were in her wake, but they hung back in the hallway.

"Come on in," Clint suggested, waving Sarah's youngest into the room. Gracie moved in cautiously, but Xena galloped into the living area and started circling near the fire, making a nest in the afghan and sleeping bags strewn near the hearth.

"Great guard dog," Jade said in an aside to Sarah. Then she explained to Clint, "For some reason Mom thought we needed one."

Sarah corrected, "I wanted an alarm dog or watchdog, and a pet. I'm glad Xena's a new member of the family."

"Getting a lot of those," Jade said beneath her breath.

Clint's stern expression relaxed some, and he almost smiled.

"We got the dog because of all the ghosts," Jade told him. "They see them, you know. Mom and Grace." Jade blew across her cup as she took a seat on the hearth. "Don't know what's wrong with me. Guess they don't like me."

"Jade," Sarah protested.

"You just don't look," Gracie told her. "Or maybe they don't want you to see them."

"You are seriously whacked," Jade retorted.

Clint rubbed his chin and said, "You know, I used to fight with my brother all the time too. Not just with words. We'd wrestle and kick holes in the wall and throw punches. My dad had a way of handling it, though. He would make us go out to the barn and the stable and shovel manure for hours."

"What does that mean?" Jade asked, making a face.

"Do I have to paint you a picture?" Now he did smile.

Gracie regarded him suspiciously. "You plan on disciplining us?" she asked in a tone that suggested he was out of his mind.

"He just means that bad behavior has consequences," Sarah intervened.

"You're not planning on moving in or anything, right?" Jade asked, not bothering to keep the horror from her voice.

Sarah was about to assure her daughter that nothing was further from the truth when Clint said dryly, "Not yet, but if I hear that you're giving your mom trouble or forever getting at each other, I might consider it."

He was lying, but Jade took him at his word. "Oh, God. I just wish I could get my car back from the shop and go home," she moaned.

"This is home," Sarah told her.

"No, it's not, and it never will be. And you—" She frowned at Clint. "Don't get all parental on me, cuz I don't even really know you."

"Deal. As long as you don't get all teenager on me," he said.

"I want my damn car," Jade said again. "How hard could it be to fix a Honda?"

Sarah could tell Clint was more amused at Jade than annoyed, which was a good thing, but his talk of lawyers made her feel cold inside nonetheless.

"I've got to run," Clint said. "Got a dog waiting for me and chores to do. Also have about fifty head of cattle and a few horses, so there's a lot of you-know-what to shovel at my place." He threw a smile at Jade, whose face was shuttered, as if she were seriously worried that Clint expected to jump in and start parenting both her and Grace right now. To Sarah, he added, "Why don't you walk me to the door?"

Sarah followed him out. As they circumvented a couple of boxes in the foyer, he said, loudly enough for Jade and Gracie to hear, "You have any trouble with them, just give me a call."

"You know they'd have a fit if you tried to tell them what to do," she pointed out, once they were on the porch and out of earshot.

"Oh, yeah. I was just joking with them."

She thought he would leave, and truthfully, she was feeling wrung out and ready to be alone, but he hesitated, then gave her a searching look. "Ghosts, Sarah?" he asked.

She shrugged, faintly embarrassed.

"I thought you got over that."

"Gracie's obsessed with Angelique Le Duc. She thinks she's seen her spirit and that she should help her pass to the other side."

"And you're buying that?"

"Not exactly, but something's going on. Earthly, unearthly . . . I don't want to completely shut her down and say there are no ghosts."

"You saw a ghost when you were about her age."

"That was a hallucination," Sarah said quickly, sorry she'd ever confided so much in him. "I was sick. Feverish."

"Jade said you accused her of being upstairs, in a room on the third floor, when she was downstairs."

Sarah gritted her teeth. She really didn't want to have this discussion with Clint, but there seemed no way around it. "Okay, I did think someone was upstairs. I guess I'm just nervous, what with the move and all." She glanced at the darkened acres surrounding the house. "Sometimes I think we're being watched. By something or someone."

"That's why you got the dog."

She nodded.

Clint's gaze held hers for an instant, and for one crazy second she thought he might kiss her, but all that changed as he stepped away. "I do have to get back, but this isn't finished."

"It's just beginning. You're Jade's father." She placed a hand on the doorknob.

He seemed to want to argue with her, but just said, "I'll talk to you soon."

"Good-bye." Sarah closed the door. She was weary of everything, especially of herself, because, though she wanted to deny it right down to the soles of her feet, the truth was she was still attracted to Clint Walsh. And Jade's father or not, Clint was off-limits. She couldn't, wouldn't get involved with him. All those fantasies she'd had as a girl when she'd found out she was carrying his child—that she and Clint would someday get together—had been pure fiction, the daydreams of a young, scared, and pregnant girl. She'd grown up and tucked those girlish thoughts into the mental closet of her youth, the one with the firmly locked door.

Clint was the last man on earth she should consider romantically.

It was going to be hard enough just navigating through their new family dynamics.

Hearing the rumble of his truck head down the drive, she had to force herself to keep from watching him leave through one of the windows.

Expelling a pent-up breath, she headed back to the living room. She just needed to keep reminding herself that, for her, Jade's father was off-limits.

CHAPTER 24

"For God's sake, pull yourself together!" Rosalie was nearly hoarse from yelling at the idiotic girl in the far stall, but Candy just kept sobbing and mewling and carrying on. "We have to find a way out of this place."

More sobs.

"Look, are you athletic? Can you, like, climb up over the stall walls and get out, then come and let me out?"

Sniffing and snorting. Oh, the girl was useless. "Come on. We have to find a way out of here. Do you like to play sports? Maybe swim?" Rosalie was wracking her brain and hoping beyond hope that she could get through to the girl.

"I—I'm a flautist."

"You mean like a gymnast?" For a second Rosalie's heart soared. Maybe this girl was the next Olympic contender and could jump, balance, do backflips, anything to get them out of here.

"I play a flute. In the band."

Rosalie slid down the wall, her legs giving way, and dropped her head into her hands. She wanted to scream obscenities, but took in a deep breath and yelled instead, "Can you try to climb over the wall?"

"How?"

At least she had the girl's attention, so she explained how she'd tried to climb over. "Look for anything mounted in the sides of the stall that you can grab onto, or step into, like a crack between the boards of the wall, so you can wedge your toe in and start climbing up and over."

"I don't think there is anything," she complained in a whining tone that suggested she was staring wide-eyed in the dark and wringing her flute-playing fingers.

Rosalie said, "You have to try!"

"Haven't you?"

"Yes, but my stall might be different. Nothing's worked so far. But I'm not giving up. And neither are you." *Oh, please, God.* "Come on, you can do it. You have to look for a way to get out."

"I just want to go home."

"Then you've got to find a way to get out of here!" Rosalie pointed out tautly.

"Okay . . . ," Candice finally agreed, sniffling loudly. "But it's so dark."

"I know. Do what you can tonight, feel around—"

"Ick! There could be rats and spiders and poop!"

All of the above. "When it starts to get light, look around. Everywhere. Examine the place, every nook and cranny. Just see if there's any way to get out of the stall." Trying to calm Candice down—to scream some sense into her, and get her motivated—was an uphill battle.

"I don't know . . ."

"So far, those two dickheads have never come back in the morning, so we'll have some time." Rosalie crossed her fingers and prayed she was right, but what did she know? It sounded as if the perv who'd abducted her was getting anxious and pressured, so things could change.

What was it he'd said about her temperament?

"It's good that you've got that little bit of fire in you. He's gonna want to see that you'll give him a bit of a fight."

She shivered.

Who the hell was "he," the guy pulling her abductor's strings? Worse yet, what was it *he* intended to do with her?

His night goggles in place, pistol strapped to his belt, he crept through the woods surrounding Blue Peacock Manor. Fortunately, the area was so vast there was little chance anyone would see him, and he'd parked his truck in an abandoned lane off a spur of the county road and then hiked along the deer trails, the same paths he'd used when hunting in his youth. Back then, he'd been convinced these woods were haunted and had seen ghosts and demons and even Satan himself flitting through the thickets of fir and pine, causing the skeletal branches of the deciduous trees to rattle, kicking up tufts of dry leaves, causing them to whirl and dance and blow their cold demon's breath through the gorge and down his spine.

Even now, as a grown man, he heard them whispering in the dark, the rush of the wind a cloak for their gravelly voices.

"You're evil," they murmured, causing his blood to run cold. "God knows and he will punish you." And at that moment a twig snapped, and he whipped around, peering through his goggles, and spied a skunk waddling off.

His heart was thudding crazily, and he closed his eyes for a second to ground himself. He didn't believe that these woods were haunted, he didn't. Those were just wild exaggerations, make-believe tales that had been passed down for generations to those who had lived around Stewart's Crossing. *Have faith,* he told himself and managed to bring his heartbeat down to a normal level and continued following the winding path, refusing to see the wraiths and phantoms he'd learned about so long ago. A coyote showed up in his range of vision, but as if realizing it could be seen, it quickly dodged behind a boulder and vanished.

Maybe it was a werewolf, his fertile imagination teased, and for just a second his skin crawled, and he imagined the beast reappearing, ten times its original size, as it lunged at him with snapping, bloody jaws.

Resolutely, he tamped down his fears. They were nothing, just the stupid ghost stories older kids told younger ones to keep them in line.

Thankfully, the forest gave way to brushy, unused farmland, though, of course, that damned cemetery was nearby, and being so near to grave sites set his teeth on edge.

He pushed his fears aside, told himself he was a fool, then started forward to the fallen log that had been so perfect for viewing the house before. This time he stopped.

Someone was there.

Someone or something!

A black figure stretched out on the ground.

The hairs on the back of his neck raised, and he reached for his pistol.

A demon?

Ghost?

Angelique Le Duc, her undead self?

Maybe even the Prince of Darkness.

Holy shit! His heart went into overdrive, and his fingers clasped around the grip of his Glock.

The figure, all in black, moved, starting to turn from its belly, gathering itself, ready to flip over and pounce.

Blam! He didn't think twice, just pulled the trigger.

The demon squealed, its body twitching.

The gunshot seemed to echo through the hills.

Blam! Blam! Blam!

Three more shots, and the figure stopped moving; only a long, gurgling moan issued from it. He was breathing hard, adrenaline firing his blood as he stared at the dark form. Vaguely, he became aware of a dog barking in the distance. Farther away yet, a train rolled on distant tracks.

Inhaling a deep breath, he waited for the unworldly specter to vanish, leaving no trace that it had ever existed.

But the being didn't disappear, didn't wither away into a netherworld mortals couldn't view. It just lay there, stone-still.

Because it's a person, you idiot! Why do you think the night goggles caught it? Because it was alive, jerkwad! You just killed a man! What the fuck were you thinking? Your damned imagination got the better of you. Thermal imaging, man. You know ghosts and demons don't emit heat! They're icy son of a bitches, their breath so cold it would freeze a man's skin. For the love of St. Peter, now what?

He was breathing hard. Sweating. Carefully approaching his target, he kept his Glock drawn, trained on the downed man . . . just in case he wasn't human. What if the demon had taken on the shape of a man, even going so far as to emit heat in order to fool anyone who came by? Then, when least expected, the beast could morph into its monstrous shape again and pounce.

The spit had dried in his mouth. He prodded one of his kill's legs with the toe of his boot.

Nothing.

He pushed a little harder.

Still the form seemed lifeless.

So he bent down to roll the thing over, had just flipped it onto its back when it let out a horrific groan, eyes staring wide, lips pulled into a hideous grimace as blood spurted from its mouth.

He dropped the body, stumbling backward, gun drawn, as if he expected the beast to rise into a grotesque creature of the night. Instead, the thing lay motionless again, and he told himself to grow some balls. Approaching once more, he studied the bloody victim and realized he'd seen the guy around town, maybe in the diner. No demon. No beast. No damned ghost. A man. Now a very dead man.

What the hell had he been doing here?

Now that he realized his victim wasn't unworldly, he began looking around and noticed a pair of high-powered binoculars that had fallen to the ground on the far side of the log. So the guy had been spying, just as he'd intended to do.

With rapid speed, he searched the guy's pockets, pulled out his wallet, cell phone, and keys—where the hell was his vehicle?—then decided it was time to get the hell out. He couldn't risk surveillance tonight.

Suddenly he was aware of a dog's agitated barks, coming from the damned house.

Not good.

Not good at all.

He thought about dragging the body into the woods and hoping the coyote he'd spied earlier, or some of the canine's friends, would feast on the man's remains, but as he heard the dog barking, he knew he couldn't be slowed down with his victim. Nor did he want to leave a bloody trail leading toward the place where he parked his vehicle.

And he was running out of time if anyone got concerned about the idiot dog barking its fool head off.

Spurred into action, he drew on all of his courage, lifted the body, and carried it to the overgrown cemetery with its bleached white headstones poking through the brambles. Here, he speculated, is where the dead man belonged. He tossed the unlucky voyeur over the uneven pickets of the fence, and as the corpse landed with a soft thud, he took off at a jog for his truck. He'd change into the fresh set of clothes he kept in the van, then stop by a local watering hole, establishing a bit of an alibi.

The night had turned into a fuckin' disaster.

Sarah was in the kitchen, lost in thought, when Xena first started barking. She'd let the dog outside for a few minutes, and now she hurried to the front door to find Xena on the porch, hairs on her back and neck standing on end, eyes fixed on the dark distance. Stiff-legged, tail up, she was growling and barking.

Opening the door, Sarah said, "What is it?"

Another spate of wild barking ensued, as if she were even more excited at Sarah's presence.

"Xena! No! Come on inside!" Sarah was beginning to think Xena was still too much of a puppy to be effective.

Whining slightly, head lowered, and tail at half-mast, the dog followed but still let out a low, unhappy growl as Sarah locked the door behind them.

"I know," she said, patting Xena on her head. "Come on." The dog padded after her to the kitchen, and Sarah assured herself there was nothing outside, no one watching the house. Nonetheless, she was certain she'd feel safer next week when the guesthouse was finished with its two doors, new windows, and state-of-the-art dead bolts.

It's not the house, she reminded herself, but couldn't help feeling vulnerable here. That ticked her off. The truth of the matter was that when Clint was around, she felt safer. Yes, another adult helped, and yeah, a man provided a different kind of presence, but she wasn't going to fall into the trap of being a helpless female. Not at this point in her life. And as for Clint Walsh, she wasn't going to be intimidated by him just because he was Jade's father, nor would she go running to him just because he lived close by.

Pop!

She heard the sound of a car backfiring, she thought, though it was far away, of course, as there were no roads close by.

Xena scrambled toward the back door, barking furiously.

"Stop! Good grief. No more!" She quickly found a dog biscuit in a box on the counter and gave the dog a couple. Xena chomped loudly. "There ya go," Sarah said and heard another faint series of far-off pops.

Car backfiring?
Firecrackers?
Or gunshots?

Grabbing her phone, she went to the back door and opened it, so that if the sounds repeated she could pinpoint them.

Xena scrambled after her, and Sarah had to grab her collar to restrain her from taking off. "It's nothing," she told the dog and considered calling the police. *And say what? That you think you might have heard the report of a rifle being shot, when you know in your gut that's not what it sounded like?* Maybe it was local hunters, out late at night with scopes, or stupid teenagers, like her brothers when they were younger, "out plinkin' in the woods," as their father used to say. Or maybe a car backfiring. She could call and complain about trespassers, but she wasn't sure the noises, whatever they were, had originated on her property. Nervously, she bit her lip. Xena kept up her whining and barking, and no amount of shushing seemed to settle her down.

"Gracie!" she called when Xena wouldn't stop.

"Come on," she said to the dog, dragging her back inside again and locking the door behind them.

"Grace?" she called as she headed toward the dining room, where Gracie had all kinds of papers spread out on the table. Phone to her ear, she was eyeing the pages.

". . . yeah, you too . . . uh, I will . . ." Gracie was smiling and twiddling a pen in one hand. "She's . . . um . . . I don't know. Just a minute." She turned the phone to her chest and yelled, "Jade! It's Dad!"

Great. Sarah shook her head, and Gracie got the message. "Sorry," she said into the phone as she held her mother's gaze. "Jade's not around . . . I will. Uh-huh. Promise . . . okay . . . Love you too." She hung up and said, "Sorry, guess it's kind of weird for her now. With two dads."

"Didn't you hear Xena?"

"Yeah." She shrugged. "Did she see a squirrel or something?"

Xena pushed her big head between them, still whining. "Grace, it's night," Sarah said. "She didn't see a squirrel."

Gracie rubbed Xena's ears. "What're you barking at, huh?"

"I know you were on the phone, but did you hear anything?" Sarah asked. "Like a car backfiring?"

"Nope." She shook her head and pulled some of the papers that she'd scattered over the table closer. Sarah wondered if she was overreacting again, her nerves frayed from all her conflicting emotions. Oblivious, Grace said, "Look at what I found on the Internet. I forgot to show you earlier. This is Angelique Le Duc and her family. Check it out." She slid a page across the old table.

Sarah stared down at a copy of an old-time photograph in black and white and tried to tamp down her annoyance at Gracie's obsession with all things related to Angelique. Taking a deep, calming breath, she struggled to put her feelings aside as Gracie pointed to the picture of a stern-looking man with a mustache. "Okay, so this is Maxim, and this is Angelique." Her finger moved to the image of a petite woman with large eyes, straight nose, rosebud mouth, and dark hair pulled away from her face. A widow's peak gave her face a heart-shaped appearance that was accentuated by a strong, pointed chin. She was holding a boy who wasn't quite a toddler in her arms. "She was Maxim's second wife, so that's why some of the kids are almost her age. This is George, the oldest. He's probably about seventeen." The boy standing next to Angelique was as tall as his father and just as grim, though no mustache was visible, "Then there's Helen." She pointed to a slim waif of a girl whose expression was blank. "I think she's maybe a year or two older than me, then Ruth, she's the blonde in the apron—"

"Pinafore."

"Oh. Well, she was around nine, I think, which would make Louis five."

Sarah nodded.

"The baby's Jacques," Gracie said, as if she knew them all intimately.

"He looks around two," Sarah said. "Where did you get these?"

"I did the research during study hall and printed it out at school."

"You work fast," Sarah observed.

"Nah. That was just the last part, most of the stuff I got online here on the iPad."

Sarah had seen her daughter tuned into the tablet for hours. Now she knew why. "Shouldn't you have been doing your homework in study hall?"

"Yeah, but this is important, Mom. This is *Angelique Le Duc,* and see what she's wearing, *the white dress*. That's the same dress she's wearing when I see her. Like on the stairs."

Sarah's mind was still on the backfiring noises, but she dragged her attention to the photo. Something was off here. "You recognize her?" she asked Grace.

"This is the woman on the stairs, the one who can't pass over, she's trying to get me to help her! I told you that already."

"But—"

"You don't believe me, either."

"No, honey, I do. I know you see something."

"Her! I see *her!*" Gracie left in a huff, and Xena, taking her cue, followed. What Sarah wanted to explain, but didn't know how, was that although the woman in the photograph might well be Angelique Le Duc—and she was maybe the ghost that Gracie was convinced she'd seen—she wasn't the woman in white that Sarah had seen as a child. Nor had she been wearing the old-fashioned dress that Angelique was wearing in the picture. Sarah's personal specter, though she might have resembled Angelique, was another woman altogether.

What the hell did that mean?

In a second of insight, she remembered being in the attic, barefoot, cold . . . wet? Shivering, she'd looked toward the cupola, certain she'd heard footsteps on the widow's walk, though no one was supposed to be up there. So why the noise? Were those voices carried on the wind?

Heart in her throat, she'd started for the few stairs leading to the roof when she'd seen it, a flash in her peripheral vision. A woman.

She'd nearly screamed, then realized she was looking into an old full-length mirror that had been shoved to a spot near the stairs, its dust cloth puddled beside it on the attic floor.

Walking closer, and feeling foolish, she had smiled at her own silly reflection.

But it hadn't smiled back at her.

Her face remained somber and thin, nearly sheer, as if she were seeing an image over her own, like one of those old double-exposed photographs, two images caught in one picture frame. The clothes weren't what she was wearing; a dress was superimposed over her nightgown.

Horrified, she backed up a step, and as the girl in the mirror opened her mouth to say something, Sarah had let out a strangled scream.

The image vanished quickly.

She was alone in the attic, her hand over her mouth, her heart thundering in her ears, the feeling that she'd just had a face-to-face with a ghost indelibly etched in her brain.

"Sarah?" her mother had called from somewhere down below, and Sarah had fled the attic, unsure of the noise on the roof, unsure that she'd seen anything in the weak light, unsure that she wasn't losing her sanity.

Now as that memory came to the surface, she realized that her "ghost" wasn't Gracie's. "Terrific," she said under her breath. Now instead of being haunted by one ghost, there were two.

Or, very possibly, none whatsoever, and what did that say about herself and her youngest daughter?

CHAPTER 25

"I'll take care of you, don't worry." Sarah was lying naked by the side of a stream, the scent of the water heavy in her nostrils, Clint's muscular body was stretched atop hers, the tip of his nose touching hers, the sweat on his forehead shimmering from the heat of the summer day. The sky above him was as blue as a mountain lake, no clouds visible, a jet's vapor trail dissipating. He kissed her, his beard stubble scraping her skin, his tongue supple and strong, playing with hers, running along the inside of her teeth.

Heat rose within her. She wanted him, oh, God, she wanted him, and as her mind swirled and the smell of sex tinged the summer air, she knew she would do anything he asked.

Anything.

He leaned down and breathed across her naked breast.

Her nipple puckered in anticipation, her insides aching with need. "Make love to me," she begged.

"Oh, darlin', you know it." Big hands splayed across her spine, pulling her closer still. Eager lips slid silkily over her skin.

Sarah melted inside.

His mouth encased her nipple, and she cried out, fingers delving into his hair, holding him close, his tongue flicking over her skin.

"Love me," she whispered, clinging to him.

"I do."

If only she could believe him, could trust those simple two words. But there was something wrong, a darkness that was coming, she could feel it.

His tongue ran hot circles around her breast. His teeth bit, just enough to make her inhale sharply with desire. Her back bowed, and he touched her lower, fingertips running a quick, light trail down her abdomen and to the juncture of her legs.

As he explored her, feeling the liquid warmth of her longing, he smiled, that crooked cowboy grin that she'd found so endearing, though sometimes she didn't know what it meant. Did he really love her? Was he playing with her?

"Oh . . ." His fingers probed deeper, and she was suddenly breathing hard and fast, wanting more, dragging him closer, sensing the darkness descend, the sun and sky disappearing to a darkening landscape. "Clint," she whispered.

He pushed her back onto the dry, suddenly brittle grass and nudged her knees apart with his own.

She loved him. She'd always loved him!

Groaning, his own breathing ragged, he thrust into her. "Sarah, oh . . . oh, God, Sarah . . ." His hands moved upward and seemed to tangle in her hair in desperation. "If you would just trust me."

She closed her eyes. "I do."

"No."

"Of course I do," she said, but he'd stopped moving, the lovemaking ceasing, heat and desire recoiling.

"I will keep you safe." Cool drops hit her face. One, then another and another. Tears? Sweat? "I promise."

His voice had changed.

Opening her eyes, she saw that it was night, and no longer was Clint making love to her, but Roger was holding her in his arms, rain pouring over them as he started to carry her across the roof to the cupola.

Fear tore through her.

"I won't let him hurt you," Roger said tenderly, and she saw that he was crying. "I won't . . . I promised her. I promised . . ." And for the tiniest of heartbeats, she saw the image of her sister, Theresa, floating above them, only to disappear into the roiling storm clouds overhead. "I promised."

Sarah sat bolt upright in her sleeping bag.

Gray morning light was filtering through the windows of the living room where she and her daughters were sprawled in front of the now-dead fire. Her heart was pounding, her skin damp with sweat, the memory of the dream crystal clear. One second she'd been making love to Clint on a hot summer day; the next it was night, dark and stormy, and through the rain Roger was carrying her naked body to the cupola.

Shivering, she told herself it was just a dream, nothing more; there was nothing to be read into the disturbing images. Of course she would have a restless night with dreams of Clint after she'd finally revealed her secret. The image of her sister and brother probably resulted from all the weird feelings she had tied to this monstrosity of a house that she hoped to turn back into its original, beautiful form.

"There's a metaphor in there somewhere," she told herself as she scooted out of her bag and felt the morning's chill. She wouldn't let a stupid dream screw her up. She could do that easily enough when she was wide-awake, thank you very much. "Coffee," she whispered, and headed to the kitchen, where she'd make a pot before tackling the whole process of rebuilding the fire.

Her muscles ached, and her mind was still clouded by a night of worrying about Jade and Clint and how the new father-daughter dynamic would play out. She went through the motions of measuring coffee and water before hitting a button and hearing Mr. Coffee gurgle to life. Then before the machine was finished brewing the pot, she poured herself half a cup and walked barefoot to the back porch.

The dog followed, to wander down the long porch steps and sniff around the backyard, searching for squirrels or other creatures of the morning. After relieving herself near a hydrangea that had lost its color, Xena picked her way through Arlene's once-loved garden, then stopped suddenly. Nose in the air, the dog stared past the garage, guesthouse, and barns to a spot only she could see.

Mourning doves?

Bats?

A coyote or rabbit moving through the underbrush?

Or just nothing? So far, the dog hadn't shown herself to be all that brilliant.

As if hearing Sarah's thoughts, Xena let out a quiet whimper and pranced nervously, looking upriver toward the fields that were butted by the forest and the family plot, where many of Sarah's ancestors had found their final resting place.

Again, Xena whined, a little more loudly.

"You're okay," she assured the dog and sipped the strong coffee with its shot of caffeine, a little boost she needed this morning. She hoped the hot drink would clear her head and chase away the cobwebs in her mind that still held onto pieces of her disturbing dream. Rotating her neck to stretch out a kink, she watched the sun rise in the east, a brilliant orb muted by a layer of thin fog lying on the back of the river. Wispy tendrils crawled through the cracks in the cliff face hanging low, like the nightmare that lingered. "Finished?" she said to the dog. "Let's go. Come."

As Xena returned, wet feet bounding up the stairs, Sarah forced the nightmare back into the dark corners of her mind, where it belonged.

"Screw the whole 'being missing for twenty-four hours' thing!" Len Fowler was leaning over Lucy Bellisario's desk, his face red, his graying hair disheveled. "Candice is a good girl who never once gave us any trouble, and she didn't come home last night!"

"Mr. Fowler, please, have a seat," Bellisario suggested, motioning to one of the chairs on the other side of the desk. The clock mounted on the wall of her office indicated that it was barely eight o'clock in the morning. Len Fowler looked as if he hadn't slept in a week, though it was probably the very twenty-four hours he was discussing. Discreetly, so that he wouldn't see any information about Rosalie, she turned her computer monitor away from his line of sight. "You can certainly file a Missing Persons Report."

"I was already down there," he said, raking fingers through graying hair that was already standing on end. "Did that." But he did sit in the nearest chair, all of his intensity seeming to drain away, leaving him an emotional shell of a man, his rumpled clothes suddenly looking much too big for his body. "I left my wife there with . . . with . . ." Confusion clouded his features.

"Officer Turner?" she supplied.

"The black woman? With glasses and short hair?" Before Bellisario could respond that, yes, he'd described the Missing Person's Officer, he went on, "I left my wife with her, giving her more information, but it's not good enough, don't you see? Whoever took that Jamison girl must've gotten Candy too. That's why I came up here, I heard you were the detective who was trying to find her and thought maybe you could help us. Oh, God." He dropped his face into his open palms and fought the urge to break down.

"Why don't you tell me about where your daughter was last night?" she suggested, pushing a box of tissues across her desk, just in case he broke down completely.

Trying to pull himself together, Len said, "Candy was at her friend Tiffany's in the late afternoon. They're in the school band together, and they've been friends forever, so they were going to have pizza and whatever it is teenage girls do."

"Tiffany—?"

"Monroe. We, well, actually Reggie called." He cleared his throat and explained that Reggie—Regina—was his wife of twenty years, then gave a blow by blow of what he knew about his daughter's whereabouts, which wasn't much. "The girls just hung out, as I understand it, and then Candy must've gotten a wild hair and decided to walk home. Reggie was running late, I guess," he said, lines creasing his face. "We called all her friends, relatives, acquaintances, everyone we could think of, even the hospitals, and no one's seen her."

"I'll need a list of all her friends, anyone you can think of, and your neighbors and relatives. Does she have a boyfriend?"

"She's only fifteen!"

"Fifteen-year-olds have boyfriends."

"I told you she was a good girl!"

Bellisario nodded. "What about Tiffany's friends? Were there any other girls or boys at her house?"

"Not that I know of, but she's got an older brother . . . oh, what's his name, it escapes me right now. Seth! That's it. Goes to a community college around here, I think, I don't really know."

"Seth lives around here?"

"I don't . . . yeah, maybe. Seems that I saw his car when I dropped Candice off." His expression darkened. "You don't think . . . that the boy?"

"I'm just gathering information, Mr. Fowler," she said. "Did your daughter know Rosalie Jamison?"

"Of course not. That girl was bad news." Then he heard himself and said more quietly. "At least that's what I'd heard, but no, I don't think Candice had ever met her. She certainly didn't say so. I never heard her name until she went missing, and then, of course, we talked to both our girls . . ." His voice faded to nothing, and he bit his lip as if the severity of the situation was too much to handle. "These kind of things don't happen to good people. We go to church! We give to charity! We . . ." He looked to Bellisario for reassurance, but she could give him none.

"What you can do to help me is give me a list of the people she knows and is in contact with, and especially if she had any trouble with other kids or at school."

"No, I told you, she's a . . ." He stopped himself and, with a sigh, began writing down the names of friends and acquaintances, checking his cell phone's contact list for numbers. As he was writing, a woman appeared in the doorway. Tall and thin, her ashen face a mask of sorrow, she stared at Bellisario with stricken eyes. At her side was a girl of about ten, and the woman was clutching the kid's shoulders as if she were afraid the girl was about to be pried away from her.

Bellisario stood and offered her hand across the desk with its piles of folders and two empty coffee cups. "Detective Lucy Bellisario."

The woman's grip was limp, as if even finding the strength to shake hands was impossible. "I'm Reggie," she said in a monotone, "and this is Emily."

"Nice to meet you," Bellisario said. "Would you like to take a seat?" she invited, taking the girl's smaller hand in her own and giving it what she hoped was a reassuring shake. She indicated the other guest chair, but Mrs. Fowler shook her head.

"I'd—I'd rather stand," she said, still clutching her daughter.

Though she thought it would be better if the young girl weren't included in the conversations, Bellisario understood the parents' desperate need to hold her close. "Does Candice have a cell phone or any kind of mobile device on her?" she asked.

"What fifteen-year-old kid today doesn't?" Fowler glowered at the list he'd been writing as if somewhere in the names of people he barely knew was a kidnapper. "But she's not answering, and we've called the cell phone company, she's on our plan, but . . ." He shook his head sadly, rolling his eyes upward to look at his wife. "She's not answering," he said again in a softer voice.

His wife dropped a hand on his shoulder. "I know." Tears filled her eyes.

For the next hour, Candice Fowler's parents held themselves together enough to answer the rest of Bellisario's questions. Len Fowler sold insurance, was an independent agent who had "no enemies, none!" Reggie worked part-time keeping her husband's books and volunteered at the school and at Second Chance Animal Shelter, or S.C.A.R., which Bellisario had always thought was a weird acronym, but kept her opinions to herself. Candice had been active in the school band and wanted to become a nurse someday, they said, Reggie dabbing at her eyes. They gave Bellisario everything they knew about Candice's routine, her teachers, her extracurricular activities, her friends, her enemies, her social media accounts. Bellisario asked if Candice had been acting strangely, if there was any trouble at home or at school. Of course not, in both cases, they assured her. Did she know Bobby Monroe, who had been a boyfriend of Rosalie Jamison's? Candice's parents shook their heads, but met each other's gazes as if they were each silently asking the other about the name.

"I've never heard of him," Len said.

"She never mentioned anyone named Bobby or Bob or Robert that I can remember," Reggie agreed, then lifted her shoulders, "These days, there's so much online stuff going on that I might not know." She swallowed hard at the realization there could be so much about her daughter and her acquaintances she might be unaware of.

"How about someone named Leo? You mentioned online. Maybe a chat room or Facebook or something?"

Mrs. Fowler shook her head, then glanced down at her younger daughter. "Emily, did Candice ever mention anyone by those names, Leo or Bobby?"

The younger Fowler girl, hanging close to her mother, shook her head slowly side to side.

"Candice doesn't know anyone associated with Rosalie Jamison!" Len insisted, getting more defensive by the second. He acted as if Bellisario were trying to put the blame on him and his wife for their daughter's disappearance. Fortunately, Reggie, the calmer of the two, laid a hand on her husband's and reminded him that the police were "only trying to help."

Some of the starch left Len's spine, and he slid back down in his chair again. He asked about the investigation into the disappearance of Rosalie Jamison, but Bellisario was tight-lipped, not wanting to jeopardize or compromise the case they were building, though there wasn't much, and even bringing up Bobby Morris's name was a shot in the dark. All that Bellisario had found on Morris was that he might be a small-time marijuana dealer, though there was no real proof of that either, just unsubstantiated rumors. None of the leads in the Jamison case had panned out. The area where the detectives thought she may have been abducted showed no disturbance, no sign of any kind of struggle. In fact, the entire distance between the Columbia Diner and Rosalie's home gave no clues as to the where-abouts of the missing girl.

Even dogs had been unable to track her off her beaten path. It was as if she had found a secret portal and stepped into another universe.

Or, more likely, a vehicle being driven by someone she knew.

That was the kicker. Though Bellisario's theory was unproven, she believed in her gut that Rosalie knew her kidnapper, that she'd somehow gotten into that vehicle willingly. Hence the mention of Bobby Morris. The boyfriend in Denver had yet to be identified, and Bellisario believed he might not even exist. She'd begun to think of him as Leo the Illusion.

But if Rosalie knew her abductor, maybe Candice did as well, and that could work in their favor, help narrow their net.

Either way, it looked as if Candice Fowler could be another victim. Bellisario did what she could for the panicked Fowler family, and, once they'd left, she coordinated with Turner in Missing Persons, who had already put out an AMBER Alert. She only hoped that America's Missing Broadcast Emergency Response would help and that someone would call in with information on Candice and/or Rosalie, and kick-start the investigation.

"There's nothing!" Candice, in that little girl's voice that grated on Rosalie's nerves, yelled. It had been light for a few hours, and still the captive in Lucky's box was as useless as ever.

"You've looked all over the stall?"

"I already told you!" she whined.

Rosalie's head was pounding from trying to deal with this . . . this *girl*, for lack of a better term. They'd been shouting back and forth, time ticking by, as Rosalie had tried to cajole, instruct, and wheedle Candice into some kind of action. She rubbed her side where she'd hurt it in her last unproductive attempt at escape. "There's got to be something. A hook? Uh, a nail? Maybe a loose board?"

"I already told you. There's nothing." Sniffling again. "I'm cold."

"Wrap the sleeping bag around you."

"It's dirty."

Rosalie sighed, realizing the girl needed time to adjust, to understand the gravity of her, of *their* situation, but they just didn't have that luxury.

"I'm hungry."

"Didn't they leave you food?"

"I hate sandwiches! It looks like it's from a convenience store case. All wrapped in plastic. It is!" She sounded positively mortified, and Rosalie closed her eyes as she leaned against the wall trying to think, to find a way to break out of this damned cell. "It's past its pull date!"

"He probably got it on sale."

"Ick!" she said, her voice high again, signaling she was about to break down once more. "I want—"

Don't say "My mommy." Please, just don't!

"—to go home."

"Me too," Rosalie said, surprised at how warm and fuzzy life with Mom and big-bellied Number Four appeared now that she was locked in this drafty old barn with Candice. "The only way we can go home is to escape. They're not going to let us go. Don't you watch any cop shows? They never let the victims go once they've seen the killer's faces."

"Killer?" Candice squeaked.

"The bad dude. Killer. Robber. Whatever." Rosalie was thinking fast, trying not to panic the weaker girl, who was her only hope to break free. "So even if they don't kill them, they never let the victims escape. They can't. Or else they would be ID'ed and the police would catch them."

"Oh, no . . ."

"So we *have* to outsmart them."

"Do you think we can?"

"Yes, but we'll have to be clever . . . and really brave."

"I don't know if I can."

"If you want to go home, then you have to work with me. That's the only chance you've got." Rosalie's patience was wearing thin, and her throat was raw from screaming. Dear God, if the bastard had hidden a camera or microphone anywhere in here, they were dead meat. But, she figured, they were already, and if there had been a camera or any kind of security device, she was pretty sure she would know it by now. "So, the big guy, he doesn't trust me anymore."

"Why?"

"Well, he never did." She really didn't want to explain about her failed attempt to escape, because she didn't want to scare the girl any further, didn't want her to consider the fact that whatever they attempted had a slim chance of working, but she figured it might come up. The big guy and Scraggly Hair might talk about it, so she hastily explained what she'd done and how she'd ended up back in her stall. "So you have to lure him in. Okay? He thinks you're"—*wimpy; he thinks she's a wuss. And he's right*—"meek, so use that to your advantage, and when he's not looking, make a run for it, but, here's the important part, you need to lock him in there, so he can't catch you, and then you can set me free."

"I don't know . . . I don't know . . . what about his friend?"

Oh, geez, was she going for it? Rosalie couldn't believe it. "Well, of course you can only do it if whoever shows up is alone. So far the littler guy, he's never come by himself, but the big guy has."

"So—you want me to trick him and lock him in."

"That's right, but we'll have to be fast. He has a cell phone, so he'll get help soon." Rosalie already knew there were others involved, like some kind of conspiracy, it seemed. So timing was everything . . . well, and getting one of the men into the stall alone. "And you'll have to play your part. Act scared."

"I won't have to act."

"Okay. Good. You can do it, Candice. If you get the chance." But Rosalie wasn't so sure; she just knew she couldn't come up with another option. "So start with a weapon. Anything that will do damage." What were the chances of her being able to pull this off, a captured girl concerned about expiration dates on the jail food she was offered?

She fingered the pieces of the nail clippers and thought about tossing them to Candice, but she might miss, and really, what were the chances that the meek girl in the far stall could really gouge out a guy's eyes or try to puncture his jugular or kick him in his balls?

She didn't even answer herself. She already knew the odds were infinitesimal.

"So buying me a beer was just a ruse to get some free legal advice," Tom Yamashita said as he shrugged into his jacket. He was seated across the table at Clipper's, a local pub that featured a bevy of microbrews indigenous to the area on tap and was decorated with pictures, sculptures, and models of all kinds of sailing vessels. Located on the crest of one of the town's hills, the tavern smelled of beer and was outfitted with floor-to-ceiling windows that overlooked the roofs of buildings built lower down on the hillside, offering up a panoramic view of the wide Columbia River and its northern shore in Washington State.

"Not free advice," Clint said, scraping his chair away from the table. "Bill me." He downed the last of his pale ale and fished in his pants for his wallet. "I just wanted some advice—and fast. This kind of blindsided me."

"I'll bet."

"So, thanks."

"Any time." Tom stood and zipped up his jacket. The son of a farmer in the area, he was a couple of years older than Clint, had gotten a scholarship to Stanford, become a lawyer, joined a prestigious firm in San Francisco, and then decided big-city life wasn't for him. His wife, the mother of his two young sons, had agreed. So he'd hauled his family back to Stewart's Crossing and hung up his shingle while still managing the family orchards, becoming the town's favorite farmer/lawyer. Squaring a trucker's cap onto his head, he joked, "You remember that I charge double on Saturdays, right?"

"And you remember that the next time your tractor breaks down and you need to borrow mine, it'll cost ya triple?"

Tom's smile stretched a little wider, showing even, white teeth, with a hint of gold near the back of his mouth. "Fair enough, man." They shook hands across the table littered with empty glasses and the remains of what had been burgers and fries in plastic baskets. "I don't think I told you anything you didn't already know. If this kid is yours and you want to claim her, you're going to want a paternity test and to file for at least partial custody. Father's rights and all that. It's best if Sarah's on board, of course, costs less if we don't have to have a lot of court appearances. Work it out with her, if possible, and it should be smooth sailing."

"Okay."

"I'll start putting things together Monday," Tom promised and sketched a good-bye.

"Thanks," Clint said, but Tom was already gone.

After leaving enough cash for the meals, beers, and tip, Clint made his way to the wide front door, which was swinging open again. Four men that he didn't recognize wearing jeans, plaid shirts, and jackets shoved their way inside. There had been a time when he'd known most of the citizens of Stewart's Crossing, but those days had long passed, he reflected, as the men—a couple of them older than he was, the others maybe his age—bellied up to the bar. He shouldered open the door once more, and a cold wind from the east hit him as he headed out.

The day had turned wintry. A light mist was falling, puddles forming on the sidewalk and streets, the temperature dropping. The Beast was parked a couple of blocks down the hill, wedged between other vehicles that ranged from motorcycles and small sedans to a huge van hauling Idaho plates.

Windsurfers, he thought; the area was one of the best in the world for a sport that used large sailboards for skimming across the water, propelled only by the wind racing through the gorge. The van, equipped with racks, would be able to carry all the paraphernalia sailboarders needed. They were a fast-growing segment of the population in an area once known mainly for its fertile farmland.

And so it goes, he thought, things change all the time. Wasn't he experiencing a major alteration in his life? A day ago he didn't know he had a daughter. Now, once again he was a father, this time to a near-grown woman he didn't know. Sarah was right. He needed to change that fact, and fast. He'd taken the first step of setting up the

legal boundaries of custody and responsibility with Tom. He wondered how Sarah would take the information that he'd gotten a
lawyer involved and decided, as he yanked open the door of his
truck, that he didn't give a damn. He'd unwittingly waited seventeen
years; now things were going to be done his way.

Or not? Were Sarah's reasons for not telling him about Jade valid,
or just excuses? He'd been so into her when she was in high school,
the out-of-step girl who was funny, beautiful, and smart. But things
had moved too fast, and he'd had issues at the time about being tied
down, so he'd dated others, gotten involved with Andrea, and, other
than the brief affair with Sarah during a period when he and Andrea
had broken up, never looked back.

Or so he'd tried to convince himself.

Now, as his breath fogged in the cold air, he second-guessed himself. Maybe he didn't know about Jade because he hadn't wanted to
admit he had a daughter. Maybe he'd convinced himself Jade was
McAdams's kid because he hadn't wanted the responsibility of a
child.

Would it have been better if he'd known the truth?

Would he have embraced fatherhood and marriage or, as Sarah
had suspected, felt trapped and bitter and ended up resenting his
family?

"Damn it all to hell," he said as he neared his truck.

It wasn't just cut-and-dried, and his feelings for Sarah were a
mess. One second he wanted to throttle her, the next pull her to him
and kiss her so hard that the rest of the world faded away. She had always gotten under his skin in a very sexual way, but they'd been
young and randy, and now . . . now he was already fantasizing about
her. He'd watched the way she handled her daughters and that jerk
of an ex-boss or boyfriend or whatever Evan Tolliver was, and he'd
liked what he'd seen.

Then there was the way she handled him, standing up for herself,
apologizing, but not groveling, insisting they move forward. She had
a maturity and wit about her that he sure hadn't noticed all those
years ago. Maybe those qualities hadn't existed half a lifetime ago, or
maybe he'd just been too blind and self-centered to notice.

So now he had a problem.

He had to fight the urge to "step in" and "be a man," not only insist he was Jade's father, but get closer to Sarah as well. It sounded archaic, and no doubt Sarah wouldn't want him inserting himself into her life too much, especially when she learned that he'd already contacted a lawyer about his parental rights.

No, he'd have to play it cool, he thought, as he stopped at the corner before he jaywalked across the street to his truck. There, on a light post, was a poster of the missing girl, Rosalie Jamison. He gazed at the picture for a second and remembered her waiting on him at the Columbia Diner a few weeks earlier. She was probably about Jade's age, though she'd seemed older, a little brassy and flirty, and now she was missing, perhaps dead.

His jaw clenched hard at the thought, and for a quick second he remembered Brandon and the pain of losing his boy. Rosalie's parents had to be devastated. He hoped that the girl was found safely, that she had just run away to be with a boyfriend, or whatever local gossip intimated.

He waited for a car to pass, a Volkswagen filled to the gills with teenagers, then jogged across the street to find Tex waiting for him as usual, his tail end wriggling as Clint shooed him from the driver's seat to his spot on the passenger side.

A daughter. He had a seventeen-year-old daughter.

Man, oh, man.

Life was full of surprises.

Starting the engine and switching off the emergency brake, he looked over his shoulder, then pulled into nearly nonexistent traffic on this side street. All the while, he was thinking of Sarah and Jade and wondering what the hell he was going to do with the rest of his life.

CHAPTER 26

Sarah spent most of Saturday morning forcing herself not to think about Clint Walsh, nightmares about Roger, missing teenagers, or ghosts haunting the old house. She used her time to organize the guesthouse, wishing they could move in immediately. "Soon," she told herself, walking through the upper floor with its two small bedrooms.

"I can't share a room," Jade had announced, seeing the small space.

"Sure you can. It's just for a while."

"But—"

"No, 'buts.' You'll have your own room again, when we move back into the big house after the renovation."

"Until you sell it."

There was always that. No way would she be able to keep the house herself, and her siblings would rightfully want the return on their investment in Blue Peacock Manor.

As she left the guesthouse, she told herself that was a bridge she'd cross later. She had enough on her plate for the time being and was contemplating how she was going to get through Dee Linn's bash when, just as she was entering the main house, her sister called.

Speak of the devil, she thought as she saw Dee Linn's name and number and picked up. "Hey, I thought you'd be too busy doing last-minute things to call," Sarah greeted her.

"I know, I know, and thankfully it looks like everyone's still planning on coming. I was afraid that with the missing girls, people might not attend, but it turns out things are just the opposite. People want to get out and kick up their heels."

"Missing girls?" Sarah repeated, hoping she'd heard wrong. "As in more than one?"

"Oh, my yes, haven't you heard? Becky actually told me. She saw it on Facebook or something . . . maybe Twitter or whatever she does now. But another girl in town has disappeared. Candice Fowler, she's a classmate of Becky's. They don't hang in the same circles, but I've heard her name."

"What happened?" Sarah had asked.

"No one knows. I think she was walking home from a friend's house . . . oh . . . what's that girl's name? I know it. Dear Lord, I hate when this happens. Oh! Tiffany. Yes, Tiffany Monroe, that's the name of the friend. Her father is a lawyer who plays golf with Walter once in a while, belongs to the same club. Walter doesn't much like him, but you know Doctor . . . ," she said as if Walter were just so quirky and cute.

Sarah didn't say anything. She was still too shocked. Another girl? Gone missing?

"Then there's Tiffany's mother, well, she's a little out there. A psychologist or psychiatrist, I think."

"What about the Fowlers?"

"It was the younger daughter who made the original post," Dee Linn said, "You know how kids tweet about everything, and then I just saw on the noon news that there's an AMBER Alert out for both girls. Once I saw that I started calling around, to see that people were still coming. You are, right?"

"Oh. Yes," Sarah said, her thoughts on the missing teens. She leaned against the wall for support. "Those poor parents. What they must be going through, and the girls . . ." Her throat tightened as she wondered if either teenager were even alive.

"I know," Dee Linn said without a whole lot of empathy. It was as if she were calling to spread the word and check on her party, but really wasn't overly concerned about the victims or their families. "A shame. I don't know the Fowlers. The father, he's an accountant or sells insurance, I think, but that could be wrong. Not that it matters."

"Right." Sarah shook her head, hoping to dispel the terrible images suddenly circling her mind. Purposely, she changed the subject, "Have you seen Mom lately?"

"Yesterday."

"How is she?"

"The same. In and out of it, I think. She kept talking about Theresa and saying she was safe. With Luke, I think. As far as I know there's no Luke in the family, and how would Mom know anyway?"

"She said the same thing to me, but she didn't mention any Luke. I think she said John and Matthew."

"What? Like in the Bible?" Dee Linn asked. "Matthew, Luke, and John. Where's Mark, I wonder?" She sighed. "Just goes to show you, we're losing her. Mrs. Malone wants to bring in hospice."

Sarah was silent. Of course it would come to this. They'd all known it, but the finality of it all was coming too fast. She remembered her mother thinking she was her older sister, not remembering her. Dee Linn was right. Arlene probably didn't have a lot of time, and for that Sarah was sad.

Dee Linn seemed to understand. "Look, Sarah, I know you carry around some guilt about leaving Stewart's Crossing and not returning and never getting along with Mom, but the truth is, it wasn't your fault. I know I was all wrapped up in myself when you were a kid, but I saw it, the way she treated you. One minute she was overprotective, the next almost cruel. Face it, Mom was never in the running for mother of the year."

"She's old now."

"And cranky as hell and still nasty. You know, I don't know why she had so many of us. Six! Can you imagine? What was she thinking? To tell you the truth, I never understood why Dad didn't divorce her. He married her because of me, I was on the way. And, knowing her, she probably got pregnant on purpose to trap him."

Sarah winced inwardly, thinking of her own situation as a teenager.

"Okay, so that was that. And I'm sure she wanted him. Dad was a catch, had a lot of money for the times, and the big house and all. You know, a descendant of the original forefathers of the town, which isn't really anything to brag about, but there it is. And she needed a father for her kids. The way I hear it, Hugh Anderson didn't have a dime to his name when he died and just a pittance of life insurance, so what was she to do?"

"Marry Dad."

"No. Get pregnant, *then* marry Dad. Swear to God, she planned it all. I bet if Theresa were alive she'd confirm it."

"You know that she's dead?" Sarah asked.

"Oh. No. I just think she *must* be, y'know. Wouldn't she have come back, I mean, if she'd just taken off? Why not let anyone know she was alive? Mom was probably bad enough before she left, but then, wow, Arlene really went around the bend, and that doesn't begin to touch what happened to Roger. And, by the way, has Lucy Bellisario called you? She's a detective with the Sheriff's Department now."

"No, why?"

"She's looking for Roger. Big surprise. There's trouble in Stewart's Crossing, a couple of girls missing, and our brother ends up on the police's radar."

"I don't have any idea where he is."

"I know. None of us do . . . Oh, dear, look at the time! I've got to run. I'll see you later."

i'm not going to make it

Jade stared at the shattered screen of her phone and wanted to scream as she read Cody's text. Was he out of his mind? It had been so long already, she couldn't stand another day of not seeing him. Didn't he love her? She sat on the lowest step of the house's staircase and started texting him back. Her life was going to pieces, and there was nothing she could do about it. Her damned car was still in the shop, that Sam kid from Algebra wasn't taking the hint, Liam Longstreet apparently wanted to be her "friend," whatever that meant, her weird mom and sister were seeing ghosts and now decoding some old diary, and Jade had to deal with a father she'd learned of only twelve hours earlier. Now, Cody was backing out? *Now?* After she'd waited all this time to see him?

Why? she demanded. This was cruel and unusual punishment. She felt her old insecurities rise, that he didn't love her as much as she loved him, that he, older, was too good for her or, maybe, as

Mom had intimated, just using her. Oh, it was all such a mess. Ever since they'd moved to this godforsaken place! *Le Paon Bleu,* my ass!

work

How could work interfere? She wasn't buying it.

have to close

Since when? He'd been employed at a local convenience store for about six months, and his hours had been part-time and erratic, but now, the very day he was supposed to come visit, he had to close the place for the night?

Can't someone else do it? she typed. My car's in the shop or I would come to you.

k was the reply. Seriously? Cody was okay with them not being together? That was *so* wrong.

Miss you she typed swiftly, before her anger took control of her fingertips.

me 2 got 2 go

Luv u she texted.

me 2

And then she was left staring at the phone, her heart as shattered as the screen. She hated to admit it, but ever since Cody had learned she was moving, he'd changed, and she suspected she knew why. Twice before she'd left she'd caught him flirting with a girl he knew from high school. Sasha Driscoll attended the local community college but lived in the same apartment complex where Cody and his roommate, Ted, resided. It didn't help that Ted, who was going with Sasha's roommate, practically lived at her place, and Sasha, of course, spent a lot of her time at Cody's. Of course, Jade's mother had forbidden her from hanging out there with the same old complaint—"You're too young to be there without an adult." Jade knew why, of course. Sarah had gotten pregnant before she'd taken off for college, and she was desperate to save her daughter from the same fate. What Sarah didn't know was that Jade had no intention of falling into that trap. She had friends who talked about marriage and babies, not necessarily in that order, but Jade had bigger dreams. Of course, she wanted to go to school, to have some kind of career. She just wasn't sure what yet, and she didn't see why it couldn't involve Cody.

God, she loved him.

Even though he wasn't as true to her as he should be. And right now she thought he was a big, fat loser, but as she scrolled through the pictures of him on her cell, her heart melted, and though the pictures were marred by the cracked screen, she remembered what it was like to stare into his blue eyes and see her future. She knew he would go back to school and become a philosophy professor or something. His job at Lakeside Cash and Carry was just temporary, until he could fix up his car and figure out his next move.

As she stared at the pictures she'd taken of Cody, she heard the click of nails on the hardwood floor before Xena appeared and, as if sensing Jade was distraught, trotted up to her and placed her cold nose against Jade's cheek. "Hey," Jade said and petted the dog's wide head. She was rewarded with a "kiss" that was a little on the sloppy side. When the dog started washing her face, she'd had enough. "Okay, I get it," she said, giving Xena a final pet and walking into the dining room, where her mother and sister were huddled over the old diary that Gracie had found in the basement. Like who cared?

Well, they did. All of Mom's architectural plans for the house, along with a couple of coffee cups, pens, and a tape measure, had been pushed to the far end of the old table, and they were seated near the archway to the foyer, side by side, the journal spread out before them, a legal pad at Mom's side, the iPad glowing in front of Gracie. Gray daylight was streaming through the dirty windows, and, Jade noted, Longstreet's van was parked near the guesthouse, from which the sound of hammering emanated. She wondered if Liam was with his father, then quickly closed her mind to that uncomfortable line of thinking because the truth was that she found Liam interesting. He was cute as hell, and smart, and she knew deep down that because he was supposed to be going with Mary-Alice Eklund, he was taboo, which made him all the more fascinating.

But she loved Cody—the jerk.

"Find anything juicy?" Jade asked, feigning interest.

"Um-hm." Sarah didn't bother looking up. She was into it, turning the pages, scribbling on a notepad, squinting at the faded pages, and spelling out words she didn't understand so that Gracie could type them into the iPad, which had a translation app that converted the French word or phrase into English.

In a way, it was kinda cool the way Mom had jumped in on this, as

Gracie was so damned obsessed with the first mistress of Blue Peacock Manor.

"Have you decided what you're wearing tonight?" Sarah asked, glancing up.

"Do I have to—?"

"Yes. You're going. We're *all* going to Dee Linn's extravaganza."

"Maybe I can dress up like a crazy person," Jade said. "But I'll need to borrow some of your clothes."

"Funny," Sarah said.

Gracie sighed. "Why do you always have to be so mean? You're like a bully or something around here."

Jade snorted.

"Positive attitude, Jade, that's all it takes." Mom rattled off another French phrase and then spelled it. Jade was impressed with her command of the language.

"I'm going as a ghost. Angelique Le Duc," Grace announced.

"Mom, can you make her stop?" Jade said. "This obsession isn't healthy."

"It's for Halloween," Grace said, then under her breath, "Positive, Jade," in that little innocent voice that grated on Jade's nerves.

"Here's a phrase with *Mama* in it . . . ," Sarah said. "And I thought I saw . . ." She flipped through several pages. "Yes, here it is . . . another one with *mère*." Her eyebrows knitted in concentration. "Where's the family Bible?"

"Family Bible?" Jade repeated.

"The big Bible . . . it should list Angelique's parents. I thought her mother was dead. Maybe even died giving birth to her. I can't remember, but it was a bit of lore that's a part of Blue Peacock Manor."

"So maybe," Gracie suggested, "Angelique did communicate with her mother anyway."

"You mean after she was dead." Jade's voice dripped sarcasm.

"The Bible is more than a hundred years old, and it was here forever, in this room, on that shelf." Sarah pointed to a built-in corner cabinet with glass doors that was now empty.

"Whatever." Jade was fast losing interest.

Sarah was still staring at the empty shelf, her brows drawn into a line. "It's important for the family history it holds. Not only is it an heirloom, it also contained the family tree. There were pages in the front where people wrote in it. Generation to generation, someone took the time to list all the births, marriages, and deaths in the family. Divorces too, though there weren't many early on. Anyway, the Bible was the old-time version of genealogy, as it held all the family records, and it had been passed on for generations."

"So Angelique would be in it?" Gracie asked.

"And Maxim and his first wife . . . I don't remember her name."

"Myrtle," Gracie supplied.

"I'm outta here," Jade said, though she didn't immediately move.

"Grandma kept it in that cupboard for years. I remember seeing it there." Biting her lip, Sarah glanced around the dining room as if she expected to see the book appear, which of course it didn't. To Gracie, she said, "Hold on a sec, okay?" Then she scraped her chair back to run up the stairs.

The dog, sensing adventure, followed.

Once their mother was out of earshot, Jade asked her sister, "What is it with you? Sometimes you act like you're a ghost whisperer or something. I mean, how old are you? Like seven?" she added, hoping to shame her sister into smarting up.

Her ploy backfired. Gracie's back stiffened, and she turned on Jade. "Why don't you grow up?" she said, her eyes narrowing. "You act like a lovesick ten-year-old. It's ridiculous."

"What do you know?"

"Enough," Gracie said, and the way she said it gave Jade goose bumps.

Why was her sister such a freak? Before she could ask just that question, she heard a text come into her phone and her heart leaped. Cody had come to his senses and found a way to pass off his shift so he could come up and see her. Surely that was it! Turning on her heel, she left Gracie with her damned journal and whipped out her phone, only to feel bitter disappointment when she realized the text was from Becky.

Her cousin was okay, but she didn't need to deal with her now. The text read:

Tried to call. What about tonight?

What? Jade checked, and she saw no evidence that any calls had come in. Great. It looked like her phone had been damaged more than she'd realized.

Phone is jacked, Jade wrote. **See you at your house?**

K was the quick response.

Awesome, she thought as her phone jangled in her hand. Another night with the crazy Stewart clan and her cell wasn't working for shit.

Tracking down the friend of Lars Blonski, one of Stewart's Crossing's illustrious ex-cons, wasn't easy, and when Jay Aberdeen was finally brought into the station he, and his alibi, were as slippery as a proverbial eel. Bellisario talked to the guy in the interrogation room, but Aberdeen couldn't keep his story straight.

"Yeah, I was with Lars," he said. He was seated on one end of a small table pressed against the wall, she on the other side, cameras rolling, microphones turned on, the sheriff himself on the opposite side of the "mirror" that allowed other people in the department to view the interview as it went down.

"Where?"

"At The Cavern. Y' know." He shrugged and reached into the pocket of his T-shirt for a nonexistent pack of cigarettes, then frowned at the realization there was no pack.

"When did you get there?"

" 'Bout eleven, maybe, eleven fifteen."

They were talking about the night Rosalie Jamison had disappeared.

"You're sure of the time?"

"I didn't check my watch, if that's what you mean," he said, with a bit of hostility.

"And on this Friday, around five or six?"

"Lars was with me. At my house."

"The apartment you share with your mother?" Bellisario said.

"Yeah. But she wasn't there."

Of course.

"Where was she?"

"I dunno. Out. Shoppin', I think." He pulled a face, his lips turning downward within his thin goatee. "You'd have to ask her."

"I will," Bellisario promised and asked more questions that Aberdeen answered or dodged. She felt he was lying, but since he was of no help, she had to let him go.

So far, the day had been fruitless. She and several deputies had interviewed all the members of Candice Fowler's family, as well as Tiffany Monroe and her parents. As luck would have it, Tiffany's father was a defense attorney and her mother was a psychologist who was often used as an expert witness for defendants in criminal trials, so they'd been cooperative, but suspicious, which hadn't helped things. The brother had yet to be located, but Bellisario intended to talk with Seth Monroe. None of the neighbors had noticed anything out of the ordinary, and there were no surveillance cameras anywhere near the Monroes' street.

The FBI were now involved, and as much as Bellisario didn't like anyone butting their noses into her case, she was relieved the feds, with their expertise, equipment, and extensive databases, were a part of the kidnapping investigation. Time was critical. If the girls were still alive, they needed to be freed before they were harmed. She didn't want to think the girls, on the threshold of their adult lives, had been killed, but she knew that it was a distinct possibility, and if they were dead, finding their bodies could be hell. Not only was the river huge and deep—a perfect place to dump a body beneath the lowest dam, so it could be carried out to sea—but the forests and hills surrounding Stewart's Crossing were dense, sometimes, in winter, nearly impossible to search.

Her thoughts grim, she escorted Aberdeen out of the building, then stopped for a refill of coffee before making her way to her office. Now it seemed a slim possibility that Rosalie Jamison was a runaway. In a usually sleepy little town like Stewart's Crossing, it was highly unlikely that two girls would run off separately within a week, and even though Candice's father was convinced his daughter was just about perfect and unwilling to do anything but walk the straight and narrow, Bellisario didn't believe it. She'd been fifteen before, a passable student, considered a "good" girl too by her family, but she'd had a wild side that she'd hidden from her parents. It was just human nature and a part of growing up.

In the hallway to her office, she blew on her coffee and dodged a deputy walking a suspect in handcuffs in the other direction. Shackles too, she noticed, hearing them rattle as the would-be prisoner was led into the interrogation room she'd just vacated. With graying hair that reached his shoulders and a beard that hadn't been near a pair of shears in a long while, he snarled, "You don't have the right to do this, y' know. I'm gettin' me a lawyer."

"Do that," the deputy, Officer Mendoza, said in a bored tone. Santiago Mendoza had been with the department longer than Bellisario and had the attitude that he'd seen it all. Today was no exception. He shot Bellisario a "can you believe this guy?" look. "Let him explain why you need an arsenal of unregistered assault rifles."

"I hunt!"

Mendoza said, "Herds of elephants apparently."

"It's a damned free country!"

"So they say," Mendoza said, opening the door for the suspect to walk inside.

The prisoner, eyes glittering, paused in the doorway. "Maybe you should listen to 'them' or go back to where you came from."

"L.A.?" Mendoza gave his head a quick little shake. "I thought you were against the government. Isn't that what you and your friends are all about? Kind of like those guys from Ruby Ridge about twenty years ago. Some new kind of mountain men?"

"*Bastardo!*" the suspect spat.

"Hey, Bellisario, did you hear that?" Mendoza said, cracking a smile. "Mr. Dodds, here, is bilingual."

Bellisario nodded. "*Perfecto.*"

What was it with the recent infusion of antigovernment types? Why here, why now? She had to leave that line of questioning to Mendoza.

Back at her desk, she tried to find, once again, a connection between the two missing girls, but other than that they were female, teenagers, and lived in the area, they had little in common. Taking a sip of her coffee, she stared at her computer screen, now split, with two images showing—one, Rosalie Jamison's driver's license photograph, the other a picture of a smiling Candice Fowler that her parents had given the department.

"Where are you?" Bellisario asked, as if the girls could hear her. Together? Probably. Or maybe not. There could be a copycat on the loose. Sick as it sounded, with all the publicity surrounding Rosalie Jamison's disappearance, a new whack job might have had the sudden inspiration and opportunity to abduct Candice Fowler.

But who?

She glanced down at her desktop at an open file on Roger Anderson. He was a long shot, she thought, had no connection to either family. But he had grown up in Stewart's Crossing and had spent some of his adult years in the area, as well as in prison. Now he'd submerged and was avoiding the law, in violation of his parole. And he had a history of violence against women.

"Three strikes and you're out, Roger," she said, picking up the thick manila folder and skimming through several arrest and evidence reports. He was not exactly a stellar citizen, and part of a family that wasn't the most stable, if local gossip were to be believed. He'd left his last known address and, according to his parole officer, hadn't contacted any of his family; the officer had made calls, and Bellisario had followed up on them. So far, she hadn't located him and would have assumed he was long gone except for the rumors floating around town that he was nearby.

Yeah, Roger Anderson was certainly someone worth checking out again. Before another unlucky girl didn't make it home.

CHAPTER 27

*What're you doing in here? You know you're not supposed to
come into this room. Not ever. Mom will kill you if she finds out.*

Sarah refused to listen to the nagging voice in her head. It
sounded a lot like Dee Linn's, and she knew that years before, her
older sister had warned her about stepping across the threshold to
her parents' suite. She had gone into the room, of course, not only
then, but recently when she'd first gone through the house room by
room, taking note of the repairs that were to be made, and she'd told
herself to get past all the rules and paranoia of her childhood. She
was in charge. This was just a house, and she could go anywhere she
damned well pleased.

That proved more difficult than it sounded, however. Even now,
walking through the bedroom, she felt as if her mother were watching, and she heard bits and pieces of old fights between her parents,
harsh words that emanated through the closed doors.

". . . I mean it, Franklin, you touch her, and I'll make sure it's the
last time you ever look at another woman!" Arlene had screamed,
while, on the other side of the door, twelve-year-old Sarah had
cringed and Dee Linn, walking past, had rolled her eyes.

"What's that all about?" Sarah had whispered.

"Mom thinks Dad has a girlfriend."

"Does he?" Sarah hadn't liked the thought of her father with anyone other than their mother.

"What do you think? Mom . . . you know . . ." And Dee Linn, ushering Sarah back down the stairs, had rotated an index finger beside her head to indicate that their mother was crazy.

"But maybe he does."

"Who else would want him?" Dee Linn had wrinkled her nose. "Face it, Sarah, Mom and Dad are weirdos, and so they're perfect for each other. And you"—she'd pointed a long finger at Sarah's nose—"shouldn't be hanging around closed doors and listening to private conversations."

"You heard it too," Sarah had charged, knowing full well that Dee Linn was a master eavesdropper, learning secrets and using those secrets to her advantage.

"But I wasn't trying."

"Bullcrap, Dee!" Sarah had said and seen her sister's eyes flare. For the briefest of seconds Sarah thought Dee Linn might actually slap her. Instead, Dee Linn had grabbed her by the upper arm, so hard that her fingernails had actually made deep impressions in Sarah's skin.

"Don't," Dee had warned through lips that had barely moved. "Don't insinuate that you know what I'm doing because you don't. You don't know anything about me."

Now, as she stepped through the nearly vacant, darkened rooms, Sarah wondered about a lot of things in her family. There had been rumors of her father's infidelity for years before his death. Women he'd met on business trips, women in town, women whom Sarah had never seen but who had haunted the hallways of Blue Peacock Manor, if only in Arlene's twisted mind.

And Dee Linn, a vindictive soul as a teenager, had mellowed with age and marriage to a man whom she'd let dominate her. Or had she changed all that much? Was it possible that Dee Linn's nicey-nice, obedient wife persona was just an act? Who knew?

Running her finger through the dust on her mother's old vanity, she looked to the broad bay window, where one of the matching side tables still stood; the bed and other nightstand were now missing. The carpet showed a shadow of more vibrant colors where a bed had once stood, saving the fibers from fading. Sarah remembered her parents' four-poster bed. More often than she wanted to recall, she'd heard the rhythmic creak of mattress springs and the accompaniment of low, almost anguished moans.

Caught up in memories, Sarah searched the suite for the family Bible, in which she hoped to find answers to the past, but all she uncovered was the same disturbing feeling that had been a part of her childhood.

Sarah had hoped that, upon returning to Stewart's Crossing, she would finally be able to lay to rest the demons of her past. But on this gray afternoon, with a chill in the air and so many unanswered questions hiding within the walls of Blue Peacock Manor, she wasn't sure those very same demons would ever let her out of their grasp.

"I tell ya, I haven't seen Anderson in a while," Hardy Jones insisted from the chair at Bellisario's desk. He was a twitchy man, always rubbing his faded jean pant legs or glancing furtively, his eyes a little on the wild side. Today he was nervous as hell—jumpier than Bellisario remembered, rubbing one arm with his opposing hand. "I avoid him."

"But he's in Stewart's Crossing?" Bellisario persisted, thinking that Jones, as one of Roger Anderson's former cell mates, might be of help in locating the missing parolee. "People have reported seeing him around town." But when pressured, no one so far could come up with solid information on Anderson. Bellisario hoped Hardy could change all that.

Hardy glanced out the window to the gray day. "Maybe. Probably. The guy is weird."

This from the funny little guy across the desk. "Close to his family?"

"Nah. Don't think he talks to any of 'em."

"Not even his brothers?"

"Beats me, but nah, don't think so."

"Jacob Stewart didn't visit him?" she asked and heard the fax machine down the hall click and clack to life. "Or his sister and her husband, Dee Linn and Walter Bigelow?"

"Not that I know of." Hardy shrugged. He was an affable guy, with a nervous tic under one eye.

And he was lying. According to the prison records that had been e-mailed to her earlier in the day, Jacob Stewart had visited his brother twice; Dee Linn, once, with her hubby the dentist.

"What about his cousins? Did they see him?"

"Don't know who they are." Hardy's suspicious gaze had returned from the window to focus on Bellisario again, as if he were sizing her up. "Hell, he could have had a million of 'em for all I know. There's Stewarts and Andersons and whatever up and down this whole county, but I wouldn't know 'em."

"How about Clark Valente?" she asked. Valente, who was close to Anderson's age, was one of the few people who had visited Anderson during his latest incarceration.

"It wasn't like I was overseein' his fuckin' social calendar." Glowering at her, he slouched lower in his chair.

"So you don't know if Valente visited?"

"He could've had the fuckin' president come and I wouldn't have known it. But nah, I never heard of . . . what'd you say his name was?"

"Clark Valente."

"Nah."

Another lie. Hardy was racking them up.

She glanced at the computer screen. One other name had come up as a visitor: Cameron Collins, a father of four who owned the feed store in town.

"What about Anderson's friends?"

Pretending to mull that one over, Hardy shook his head slowly. "He didn't have any."

"Not even Cameron Collins?"

"Who?" Hardy said, then stopped short. "He the religious nut who came in with his Bible and quoted verses or something? Owns a store in town."

Possibly. Bellisario made a mental note to check that out. "Don't know."

"That guy came by once or twice."

But his tone made her think he wasn't sure. This was getting them nowhere and becoming a big waste of time, when time was of the essence if they were to find the two girls unharmed. As if to reinforce her own thoughts, her cell phone vibrated on the desk, and she saw Rosalie Jamison's mother's phone number flash onto the display. Because of their loose connection—Lucy's sister was in the same class as Rosalie—Sharon wasn't afraid to call Bellisario's cell at any time, day or night.

She switched her phone off and tried another tack with Roger Anderson's ex-cell mate. "You know, Hardy, it strikes me as strange, this lack of knowledge you profess. Here you share a cell for what? Two, two and a half years?"

"Twenty-three months," he replied. "Time off. Good behavior."

"Yet you don't know one person your cell mate was close to, don't remember anyone who visited him. Is that what you're telling me?" She stared at him hard, then leaned back in her chair as a phone rang in a nearby office and the furnace hummed. "So, tell me, what have you been up to lately? You know, aside from keeping the cutlery spotless down at The Cavern."

"What'd'ya mean?" Suspicion crawled into his voice.

"You're keeping your nose clean, I assume."

Hardy ran a hand through his unruly hair.

"So, what can you tell me about the missing girls?"

"The what?"

"You've heard the news. Seen the flyers. Rosalie Jamison and Candice Fowler have disappeared."

"What's that got to do with me?" He stared down at the pictures on the desk, then back at Bellisario. Finally, she'd caught his attention. "You know that's not my thing. Roger, yeah, he got in some trouble with the ladies, but me, no. Not my deal."

Which was true. Hardy's crimes had all revolved around drugs and check fraud. He wasn't much good at either—hence, his rather lengthy rap sheet. "If I called your parole officer, I'd get a stellar report, right?" Actually she'd already phoned the guy. Hardy was clean.

"What the hell do you want from me?" He seemed worried now, and blinked rapidly.

"Any and all information about Roger Anderson."

"There ain't any. I mean, I don't have none. Anderson's a loner, okay? And weird as a three-dollar bill. Always goin' on and on about his sister, the one that took off. Theresa, that was her name. I heard about her over and over, about how he loved her."

"Loved her?" she repeated.

"Yeah, and I'm not talkin' about brotherly love here, if ya know what I mean." He slid Bellisario a sly look. "He *loved* her. Felt it was his fault or somethin' that she took off. Always talkin' about the big house, how great it was and how weird his mother was. It was fucked up, the way he was about his family," he said, and for the first time since the interview started, Bellisario sensed some truth was flowing past Hardy Jones's lips. "You know what he did? Do you? Anderson and her?"

"Why don't you tell me?"

"They hung out in some fuckin' graveyard on the Stewart place, that fuckin' Blue Parrot or whatever it's called."

"Peacock."

"They'd spend time alone up by a damned crypt or something. Him and Theresa." Hardy was smiling now, finding some sick humor in the situation, but all the while shaking his head. "It was fucked up, I tell ya."

"You're saying they were sexually involved?" she asked, cutting to the heart of it. "Theresa and Roger Anderson?"

"Well, from the way he talked, I'd say if he wasn't doin' her, he sure as hell wanted to. Probably the reason she took off, I'm thinkin'. It was freaky, man, the way he talked 'bout her." He paused then, and as if he realized he'd said too much, he suddenly clammed up.

"Anything else you remember about him?"

"Look, we were cell mates for a while. That's all. We both got out, and that was that." He leaned closer, over the desk. "I try not to hang out with ex-cons, y'know. It just don't look good."

"To whom?" she asked.

"Everyone. Cops 'specially. Why do you think I'm here talkin' to you? It's not cuz of anything I've done." He was a little hostile, his voice whiny. And he was still lying. Bellisario felt it in her gut. Maybe it was the way he tried to stare her down, or how his arms folded defensively over his chest, stretching his jean jacket over his shoulders. He wasn't a big man to begin with, but he sure as hell was trying to puff himself up.

"You're a mechanic by trade."

"Well, yeah, but who'll hire an ex-con? That's why I'm washing dishes."

"Roger Anderson was spotted down at The Cavern." The tip wasn't confirmed, a wino had "thought" he'd spied Anderson when shown a picture of him, but she decided to see what kind of reaction she got. "A patron saw him."

"He wasn't in the kitchen." Hardy was emphatic.

"But he was there?"

"I heard that he hangs out there, but it's got nothin' to do with me. Shirley, the bartender, she's seen him a couple of times."

"He didn't come around to the back?" she asked. "Strike up a conversation?"

"We ain't friends. Why are you pushin' me? I told you I haven't seen Anderson, and that's that. Now, you want to charge me with something?"

"All we're doing is talking here. At my desk." She hadn't taken him into the interrogation room as she figured he might freak out or seal his lips. Here, in her office, it was more of a "we're just friends" atmosphere, or so she hoped. But Hardy wasn't buying it.

"Well, then, we're done," he said. "I ain't done nothin', and I don't know why you dragged me down here in the first place." He stood as if to leave.

"Okay, fine, but if you hear from Anderson, you let me know."

"It'll be a cold day in hell when that happens."

"You had a falling out?"

"I already told you, there wasn't nothin' to fall out. We were never friends to begin with."

"You don't know where he lives."

"Haven't you been listening? I told you every damned thing I know about the dude!" Hardy was really fired up now, but she wasn't quite finished.

"He left the house in The Dalles. The woman he rented from said he just up and left, took everything with him." Bellisario leaned forward a little. "We checked, he was gone, the room clean as a whistle. As if he hadn't been there." *A ghost,* she thought.

"So?" Hardy was unimpressed.

"And he hasn't kept in touch with his parole officer. Made no contact in a couple of months."

Hardy didn't say a word.

She plowed on, "He's always done what's required, you know. Walks the straight and narrow every time he gets out, but this time, all of a sudden, Roger Anderson's not playing by the rules."

"Happens all the time. Why do you think he keeps landing his ass in jail? Look, I already told you I don't know where he's livin' or what he's doin' or who he's doin' it with. I don't hang out with the dude. That's it. I ain't sayin' another word."

"Fine," Bellisario said, but she was talking to herself. Hardy had already turned on his heel and was marching down the hallway, leaving her with nothing except the lingering feeling that Hardy Jones, the ex-con who insisted he didn't hang out with other felons, was hiding something.

Something important.

CHAPTER 28

Her parents' bedroom was a bust.

She'd stirred up some old memories she'd rather forget, but Sarah found nothing in the suite or anywhere else on the third floor. She'd even ventured into Theresa's room, her heart hammering, half expecting the Madonna statue to have moved again, but no. The figurine was just where she'd left it, and she told herself, after examining the room, that the Madonna was not smirking at her as she closed the door.

"All in your head, Sarah. All in your head." In the hallway, she hesitated at the doorway to the attic, hearing footsteps on the steps from the second floor.

"Mom?" Gracie called up as Xena bounded into view and came galloping along the hallway. "You said you'd be right down."

"Yeah. Sorry. Thought I could lay my hands on that Bible. Mom wouldn't have gotten rid of it." She glanced at the attic door, but she hadn't noticed the Bible when she'd been through the garret earlier. The only place she hadn't really examined was, of course, the basement.

"You didn't see it when you found the journal?" she asked Grace.

"No."

"You looked all around, right?" Sarah said, remembering what Jade had said about Gracie snooping. "Even in the basement?"

"You told me I wasn't supposed to go down there."

"But you did, didn't you? That's where you found the journal. So the question is, while you were down there, did you notice the Bible? It's big, so I don't think you'd miss it."

"I didn't see it," Gracie said. "Sorry."

"Too bad. If we find it, we might just be able to make more sense out of the journal, why it's in French and what it all means."

"Why do you want the Bible? Can't you just translate it?"

"Yes, but that's the weird thing. I don't think you've found the diary of Angelique Le Duc."

"What do you mean?"

"From what I've translated, this journal was written by someone else, probably her daughter, Helen. She keeps talking about her mother, and I don't think Angelique would be doing that."

Gracie's disappointment was palpable. "Then it won't help."

"We don't know that. But to be sure, we need to find the Bible."

"You think it's in the basement?"

"Maybe." Sarah forced a smile and tamped down her twenty-year-old phobias. "Let's go look."

Gathering her courage, Sarah followed her daughter to the door of the basement, but as she swung it open, her cell phone rang and she recognized Clint's number on the screen. Her stomach tightened, and she hesitated at the top step. "Hello?"

Gracie was already halfway down the stairs.

"Hey," he said, his voice neutral. "How're you doing?"

"Okay." *Aside from the fact that I'm stepping into the place I've feared all my life.* "What about you?" She started down the steps.

"Doin' okay, I guess. I'd like to spend more time with her, y'know. Really get to know her."

"I'm sure we can work that out. But you should be talking to her, don't you think?"

"I texted her, but she hasn't gotten back to me yet. I figured she would, but I'd give her a little space. Let her get used to the idea. It's a lot for a kid to take in."

She nearly tripped on one of the uneven stairs but grabbed hold of the rail and somehow managed not to drop her cell phone in the process. "A lot for an adult too."

"I wanted you to know that I contacted a lawyer today. Tom Yamashita. Local guy. I've known him for years. He'll be calling you; probably want to talk to Jade too."

"You did?" Her chest suddenly constricted.

"Don't worry. I'm not going to do anything you don't like. I just need to know my rights, and Jade needs to understand hers as well. Not to mention McAdams."

"Okay. I'll—I'll talk to your attorney," she said reluctantly.

"Your ex adopted Jade, right?"

"Yes, soon after we were married, but—" she'd wondered how Noel would handle the news. Probably not all that well. "I'll take care of it. He's a . . . reasonable man."

There was a pause, and she wondered if he were going to ask her about the divorce and the reasons she and Noel had split up. Her stomach tightened.

"If you say so," Clint agreed. "Sarah—?"

"Yeah."

"We've got a lot of talking to do."

"I know." One quick conversation was just the tip of the iceberg. "And maybe we should do that talking before we start hiring attorneys."

"It's nothing against you. I swear."

She was trying not to be threatened. "Do I need my own attorney?"

"Your call. But as I explained, I'm not trying to cause any trouble." A pause, then he asked, "So where do you and I go from here?"

"What do you mean?" she asked, but it was an automatic question. She knew. When he waited for an answer, she finally said in a low voice so Gracie wouldn't overhear, "You and I . . . were over a long time ago."

"Maybe we should work on that."

Her heart squeezed. *Don't do this, Clint. Don't be attractive.* "How?" she asked tentatively.

"That's what I'm asking," he admitted. "Look, there's the legal thing, yes. But there's more to this, Sarah, a lot more."

"One step at a time," she said automatically, as she glanced down to the cracked floor of the basement and gave herself that same piece of advice.

"You're going to Dee Linn and Walter's party?"

Clint was invited? She shouldn't be surprised, she guessed. Aunt Marge had mentioned that Dee Linn was throwing a really big bash, her brothers had said as much when they'd visited, and since it had proved to be her older sister's MO in the past, why would tonight's "get-together" be any different. "Yeah, I'll be there. At least for a little while. Big parties. Not my thing."

"I remember." There was almost a smile in his voice. Almost. "Then, you're not a thing like your sister." He said it as if he still knew her, understood how different she was from Dee Linn, the sister who didn't resemble her in looks or personality.

"So I'll see you tonight, I guess." She hung up and realized her lungs were tight, her pulse elevated, her heart rate unsteady, even though she'd made it over the first hurdle of explaining to Clint and Jade that they were father and daughter. As hard as that had been, it wasn't over. All of her family would soon learn the truth, and in a town the size of Stewart's Crossing, an item of gossip was like a stone thrown into water, the ripples of any kind of scandal making ever-wider circles within the community.

She could handle it, deal with the questions and probably more than one set of raised eyebrows or cutting comments, but what about Jade? Her daughter was already having trouble fitting in at Our Lady of the River. Her new status as the love child of Sarah Stewart and Clint Walsh wouldn't help things.

Bolstering herself, Sarah made her way down the final stairs.

Grace was already snooping through the junk that had collected for several generations. Only one lightbulb in the whole area still worked, its illumination shadowy at best, so they used flashlights, and Sarah saw objects from her youth that she'd forgotten. An old bike—Jacob's, she thought—was propped against one wall; empty canning jars were stacked in wooden shelves; the old milk-separating station, complete with stainless steel discs and a drum, had been left idle for dozens of years. Now cobwebs covered the equipment, and cracks were visible throughout the concrete floor.

Yeah, Sarah thought, she'd need to come down here with a foundation specialist; several of the posts holding up the building appeared to be rotting, and who knew how long they would last. Jacob's teasing words about getting a bulldozer came to mind, but she refused to consider taking down this old house.

Her skin crawled as she walked through the area where dust and debris and old artifacts had collected. "This is worse than the attic," she said to Gracie, "and guess who gets to clean it all up?"

"Me?" Gracie asked.

"You can help, but I think it's my job. I wonder if Dee Linn or the twins want any of this."

"Isn't it still Grandma's?"

"I don't know, honey, but we won't sell or get rid of anything she wants." They began looking through boxes and moving old vases and books on shelves, pushing aside furniture.

"This will take forever," Gracie complained.

"No . . . it's not that much. Just disorganized." It was as if Arlene, as she was starting her battle with dementia, had used the basement as a holding cell for things she couldn't quite part with. An old radio, a broken dresser, a cracked mirror, and a television that looked like it was from the sixties—a lifetime of treasures turned to trash. Strangely, Sarah had calmed down; being in this underground space with items from her youth wasn't frightening at all. Plastic toys and a hula hoop, her father's pipe collection, and finally, tucked on a shelf near the old root cellar, behind some cookbooks with broken spines and stained pages, the Bible.

"Here we go," Sarah said. "Let's take this upstairs."

It wasn't easy, as the Bible was heavy and a little difficult to carry, and they tried not to trip on the uneven stairs, but soon they were in the dining room again. It was late afternoon, and daylight was fading as Sarah flipped open the tome to the page where, for nearly a century, the family births, deaths, marriages, christenings, and divorces had been recorded.

"Am I in here?" Gracie asked, and Sarah said, "I don't know. I don't think my mother kept this up. Oh . . . look, I was wrong." She flipped the page, found the most recent listings, and ran her finger down the list of names. Dee Linn and the twins' names had been entered in Arlene's fluid scroll, but that's where it ended, with Joseph's name and time of birth, ten minutes after Jacob's.

"That's odd," she said aloud when she realized that nothing had been posted after Joseph had come into the world. No more marriages, nor the twins' christenings, which maybe they didn't have. Seeing the family tree end with her siblings, with no mention of her, was difficult, and it stung a little. Had her mother had too much to do with six children, one an infant, two troubled teenagers, to list her?

Oh, wait, now she understood. She had been born around the

time that Theresa had gone missing. Of course, Roger and Theresa weren't listed in the Bible as they weren't Franklin's children, but had been taken in by him when he married Arlene. That union was recorded, the date of the wedding clear, the children listed below. Except for one.

"It looks like Grandma quit making entries. See, I'm not listed, nor you or Jade, and there are no further marriages written down either." Not hers, of course, because she didn't exist in the family Bible, but neither Dee Linn's nor Jacob's wedding was jotted into the page and Becky, Dee Linn's daughter, wasn't listed. It was as if from the moment Theresa disappeared, a light in Arlene had died, her enthusiasm for life, if she'd ever had it, had withered away.

"Let's not worry about that just now," she said to Gracie. "You know, if we want, we can always add the names."

"It's kinda weird, though. Look at all these names."

She was right. There were nearly six pages of names and notes, more than a hundred years of Stewart lives and deaths, the branches of the family tree long and sometimes crooked.

"Are all of these people, the ones that have died, I mean, buried in the graveyard?"

"You mean the family plot?"

"Yeah, the one out there." She pointed to a window and beyond.

"The family stopped using that plot years ago. You know, Grandpa's not in it. He's in the community cemetery with a lot of other people who lived around here."

"Then who is?"

"Mostly people who died more than eighty years ago. I don't really know when the plot was given up, but sometime in the early nineteen hundreds."

As much to stem her daughter's interest in the old cemetery as well as to get her back to the point, Sarah flipped the pages of the Bible. "Here we go." Angelique Le Duc's information was complete, written in, no doubt, after she married Maxim, the date of her wedding not six months after the death of Myrtle, Maxim's first wife. Great-great-great-grandpa worked fast. Myrtle had been forty when she'd died, and Angelique was still in her teens when she'd tied the knot with Maxim.

"Angelique must've added her own information because her own mother's death is listed as the day after her birth," Sarah said. "That happened a lot back then, women dying in childbirth."

"So she never knew her mom?" Gracie said. "That's sad."

"Uh-huh." There was a lot of sadness in the pages of this old Bible, Sarah thought. "So that means the journal belongs to Helen."

"Or it's Ruth's," Gracie ventured. "Or even Monica's."

"No . . . look, at the date Helen was born." Sarah pointed out the faded record. "April eighteenth, nineteen ten. That would have been about right. She would have been about the right age, fourteen, when Angelique disappeared. And look," she flipped a few pages of the journal, "you can see where she names all of her siblings. Here's Ruth and baby Jacques, Monica, and Louis. *Papa* would have been Maxim, *Mama* Angelique, even though technically she was Helen's stepmother. The only person whom she doesn't mention is herself, Helen."

"Because she's writing in the first person."

Sarah smiled. "Someone's been paying attention in English."

"I learned that a long time ago," Gracie said. "Mrs. Stillman in the third grade was really big on it."

"Fine, so Helen is 'I' in this journal," she said, tapping a finger on the diary.

"They called Angelique Mama even though she was their stepmother."

"I guess. Helen and George would remember their real mother, of course, but the little ones might not remember Myrtle. Angelique, as their father's wife, was their mother, the only one they'd ever known." As she said the words aloud, they resonated within her—like a guitar string plucked and trembling nearly invisibly, barely moving, but causing a ripple of sound that toyed with her memory, eliciting images that caused her heart to pound a double cadence.

Why?

Was it all the talk of ghosts? Of the mystery of Angelique Le Duc and what had happened to the beautiful mistress of Blue Peacock Manor?

Or was it something deeper, a chord that touched her own soul in this house, on the very rooftop from which Angelique supposedly plunged to her death? In her mind's eye, she saw her half brother, Roger, rain plastering his hair and running down his face, his shirt flapping open, his chest bare and dripping, as he cradled her in his arms on the widow's walk.

Was he crying? Was that regret in his eyes? Or was it the onslaught from the heavens, rain from the midnight storm dripping from his nose?

The memory played at her mind, causing her pulse to elevate and the same question to flit through her brain. Why couldn't she remember? And why couldn't she completely forget?

"Mom?" Gracie's voice brought Sarah back to the present.

She blinked and stared down at the open journal. What had happened a hundred years earlier had nothing to do with today. So why did she let it bother her?

"Are you okay?"

Clearing her throat, she nodded. "I'm fine," she said, still quivering inside, but managing to keep her voice steady. "Sorry. I kind of spaced out."

"Why?"

"I, um, I was thinking about Angelique and what happened to her," she said quickly, then slid the diary closer to them, so she had a better view. "Come on, Gracie, let's figure this out."

CHAPTER 29

He was back!

Rosalie heard the truck's engine, then the quiet, after which the lock clicked and the door banged open. Lights snapped on; the interior of her cell was somewhat illuminated as she bit her lip and listened, hoping to learn if he was alone.

One set of heavy footsteps entered.

She waited.

No conversation ensued, no second set of boots ringing against the floorboards. Just one person, walking confidently on the other side of the locked stall door.

Good!

Was it possible? Could they get so lucky? For a second, she wondered if perhaps it was someone other than her captor, and she nearly called out, then stopped short. She needed to size up the situation.

But there was a possibility that finally there would be a chance of escape. If the girl in Lucky's stall held up her end of the bargain.

So far Candice had been completely useless, and their escape plans had fizzled into nothing—or, Rosalie thought, *her* escape plans. Candice hadn't been able to climb the wall of the stall or find anything to aid in the escape or do anything much more than cry and whimper. But now they had a tentative plot, if the idiotic girl would just remember and act on it. Rosalie crossed her fingers and silently prayed this was their chance.

Oh, please, please, please.

The footsteps passed by the door of her stall on their way to the other side of the barn.

Rosalie crept to her side of the door and hovered as close to it as possible while holding her breath and straining to hear even the tiniest sound.

A lock clicked, and the door scraped open. "Lucky?" their abductor called, his voice surprisingly even, his tone smooth. The same way he'd talked to Rosalie when she'd waited on him at the Columbia Diner, which seemed like eons ago. "How're you doing?" he asked.

Uh-oh. He was acting concerned for Candice? Would she fall for it? Or maybe his actions, his worry about Lucky could unwittingly work in their favor, if it lulled him into a false sense of security.

He didn't get a response.

"You need to eat something," he said. "Keep your strength up." He sounded worried, and she was reminded of how easily he'd duped her, how she'd believed that he was giving her a ride home as an act of kindness when in actuality he had planned to kidnap her all along.

Candice didn't say a word.

Maybe that was good. Rosalie clutched the nail file. She was tense, afraid that down in Lucky's stall he'd get suspicious and yank the door closed behind him, as he now always did when he entered her small cell. But now, as far as she could tell, the stall to Lucky's door was still ajar.

C'mon, Candice. Just lure the perv in, and when he's least expecting it, race past him and slam the door shut. Throw the dead bolt! Lock his sorry ass in the damned box. Squeezing her eyes shut, Rosalie willed her thoughts to reach the other girl. *Remember the plan!* This was their chance. No way would he expect shy, wussy Lucky to get the drop on him, to bolt. *Do it, Candice. What are you waiting for?*

Silent seconds ticked by. She heard noise on the roof, a branch or a squirrel, and the sough of the wind, but nothing from the stall down the row.

Rosalie wanted to yell at the girl, but she didn't want to ruin any chances of the plot working, so she bit her tongue, her heart pounding, adrenaline coursing through her blood. If she had the chance, she'd blind the bastard, then slit his damned throat, but she was dependent on the other girl.

Come on! Her fists were clenched so tightly, the impression of the nail file was imbedding itself on her palm.

"Lucky?" he said softly, then began talking in a low voice. Soothing. Cajoling.

NOW! Make a run for it! Lock the son of a bitch in his own prison cell! Do it, Candice! COME ON!

But the girl was softly crying again, talking in murmured, broken tones. Rosalie couldn't hear the conversation, but hopefully . . .

Scrape! Thud! Click!

What? The door was closed?

Just like that?

No!

Rosalie couldn't believe it.

But she heard him stalking down the main area of the barn again, this time in her direction.

That coward, Candice, had done nothing. *Nothing!* This had been their chance, when the abductor was alone. So upset she nearly cried out, she had to scramble back to her cot as she heard his footsteps approaching her stall. He came in, didn't say a word to her, just took care of the business of giving her fresh water and food and replacing her "toilet." She watched him with sullen eyes, her pulse pounding in her brain, hate and despair warring within her. Ready to leap between him and the door, she never got the chance. He was on to her because of her previous escape attempt and made sure that now, as ever, his body was between her and her escape route.

She considered leaping at him, flinging her body through the air with her tiny weapon ready to maim and disfigure. She was afraid this would be her last chance, that he would never come back to this awful, smelly barn alone.

But she was afraid to risk it.

Why? What are you waiting for! Go for it!

Too late. He was in and out of her stall before she'd screwed up her courage and gathered her strength.

Almost as if he could read her thoughts, he was out the door, the lock engaged behind him.

She dropped the nail file and grabbed at her hair, pulling at it in frustration, silently wailing to the rafters. *What were you waiting for? You're no better than she is! Both of you are fucking chickens!*

Moments later, she bent down and picked up the nail file again, glad it had made barely a sound when it hit the dirt. She was still railing at herself and wondering how she could rectify the situation, turn it around, maybe call out to him and pounce when he entered, when she heard his voice again.

"Yeah. It's me . . ."

He must've dialed his cell phone.

". . . that's right," he said. "I know, you wanted seven, but it may be fewer." There was a pause, when whoever was on the other end spoke loudly enough that she heard a male voice, his words indistinguishable.

"Hey!" her abductor cut in. "I can only do what I can . . . I'm the one sticking my neck out here for you." Another pause, and then he was calmer. "Okay, just so you and I are both on the same page. I find the girls, you come and get 'em. Look, I've got a plan. I'll wrap up the collection tonight. We're running out of time. The cops are nosing around." Another pause, then, "We can't risk a preview. What the hell are you thinking? There's no damned time. Just come tomorrow night with the others. This needs to be over."

Rosalie's heart began to pound as she considered what he was talking about.

". . . Of course I've got an alibi, but let's not have it come to that." Another tense few moments, and then, "No, no. Don't show up that late. If anyone sees five or six vans heading up here in the middle of the morning . . . Come late enough so there's not much traffic, early enough that no one thinks anything about a few extra rigs . . . Midnight'll work." There was another pause, the man on the other end talking. Finally, her captor barked out a laugh. "No, you don't have to worry about him. He might not be the brightest bulb in the refrigerator, but he knows how to keep his mouth shut."

Who? Who would keep his mouth shut? Scraggly Hair? Or someone else, a silent partner?

"Yeah, sure." Her captor sounded a little tense. "I know. Let's do this thing!"

He was already walking across the old floorboards toward the outer door, his boots ringing a quick tattoo as if he were in a hurry.

That was a problem.

Once the meeting or whatever it was went down, Rosalie's and Candice's slim chances of escape would peter to nothing.

What were the man who'd captured her and his accomplices planning? Who were the other victims—as yet, it seemed, not caught. Another thought crossed her mind. If, in an attempt at another abduction, her kidnapper and Scraggly Hair were involved in some kind of shootout and were killed, how would they ever be found? Would she and Candice end up dying here from dehydration or starvation?

Oh, man, this was bad. Rosalie's heart was a drum as she slid down the wall to sit on the floor, where there were still flecks of hay along with the spiderwebs and, no doubt, mice. Everything was going down tomorrow night, and she knew it wouldn't be good. Oh, Lord.

She bit her lip and thought of her dad and Leo, the guy she'd met online, both a million miles away in Colorado. It had all seemed so perfect a little more than a week ago. All she'd had to do was work as much as she could and save enough money for a car, then drive south to get away from Sharon and Number Four.

Now, she worried it would never happen.

Whatever her abductor had in store for her, it certainly didn't include visiting her father or meeting up with Leo.

"I—I'm sorry," a weak voice called from the other side of the barn. Candice was starting to cry again. "I just couldn't do it. I was too scared. I, uh, I peed myself again."

"It's okay," Rosalie lied as tears slid down her cheeks and the gloom of the barn seemed to sink into her bones. Going off on the weaker girl wouldn't help. "Don't worry about it. Clean yourself up. I'll think of something else. We'll get another chance."

"But you heard him. He talked about tomorrow night."

"But he might come back before that. He's got to get other girls . . ." Swiping her nose with her sleeve, Rosalie clenched her teeth to keep from breaking down and sobbing like a little girl, like Candice was doing.

Swallowing hard, she tried to think, to come up with another plan to free them. The trouble was, she was out of ideas, out of options, and soon, she knew, she would be out of time.

Where the hell was Liam? Mary-Alice wondered as she paced in the parking lot, turning her collar up against a wet cold that seemed to seep into her bones.

And why was he texting from a weird phone number?

Waiting near the back of the gym of Our Lady of the River, in the spot where she and Liam usually met, she tried to tamp down her fury. It was Saturday, finally, but it had been a horrible week. Horrible! First her mother had found her cigarettes. Big deal. So she smoked? It wasn't as if she was using weed or meth or whatever. But her mom had hit the roof, reminded Mary-Alice that Aunt Sally was currently battling cancer, and wrenched a promise from Mary-Alice that she would stop her cigarette habit immediately.

Mary-Alice had broken the promise the next day because she was so stressed. How could she quit smoking when she was having the worst week of her life? Being assigned as an angel to that awful Jade McAdams was bad enough, but she felt as if she'd blown the SATs again. Her first scores had been little better than mediocre, and though she didn't yet have the results for her second attempt, she knew they wouldn't be up to her father's expectations. Despite her good grades, she'd have to take the tests again after the new year if she wanted to get into University of Washington, "U-Dub," her dad's alma mater, which was a real reach anyway, or Gonzaga, in Spokane, where her mother was pushing her to attend. Not that she cared about either of those schools, as she planned to follow Liam wherever he ended up. The trouble was, he was brilliant in science and a stellar athlete to boot, and was being recruited by both Oregon and Oregon State. Again, she might have trouble being admitted to the school he ultimately chose. But at least she could attend one of the community colleges near the universities. One way or another, she was going to be close to him, whether he wanted her to or not.

He just didn't seem to care if they attended the same college, which really ticked her off. Lately Liam had been distant, not even interested in sneaking away and being alone with her, which he'd always wanted. He usually couldn't keep his hands off her, was always trying to cop a feel, but lately he'd been distracted, caught up in his own thoughts, whatever they were. Until recently he'd shared everything with her. Now, not so much. Another reason to be angry.

Worse yet, he'd actually shown some interest in Jade McAdams and was even worried that somehow he'd broken her phone or something. Why the hell did he have her phone to begin with? The girl was a loser with a capital L, and Mary-Alice wished she'd just drop dead.

Isn't that what people in that old house where Jade lived usually did, anyway? According to Mary-Alice's mother, more than a couple Stewarts had died in that horrible old house on the gorge. So, fine, Jade could vanish and the world would be a better place.

She shivered at her own thoughts and anxiously looked around the area. At least she wasn't completely alone. There was a heavy woman in one of those puffy jackets walking her dog around the track. For the love of God, lady, you do *not* have the body type to pull off that look! Also, there was a guy jogging, lapping the woman with her little Pomeranian or whatever it was; with the fog it was hard to tell. From about midfield on, the track was obscured, the bleachers rising ghostlike and shadowy in the mist.

She considered getting into her car, parked in a spot that obscured it from the road, not that anyone could see anything in this soup. But she was too keyed up, too worried, too irritated with Liam.

Cinching the belt of her long coat, she thought she saw a solitary man sitting on one of the benches, but when she squinted, looking more closely, his shadowy image was gone or had become veiled by the thick, ground-hugging clouds.

Talk about creepy.

Don't let your nerves get the better of you. You're here, at school. This is your playing field. Where you belong. If not the most popular girl, you're in the top five. But today, with no one in attendance, not even athletes practicing on the soccer field, the school looked bleak, its white walls seeming a dingy gray, the stained-glass windows appearing like a multitude of eyes, dark and ominous as they stared down on the school grounds. She didn't feel that she belonged at all.

"Don't be a goose," she said, repeating words her mother had spoken on more than one occasion.

She thrust her hands deep into the pockets of her coat, but even though she was wearing gloves, her fingers were cold. In fact, her whole damned body felt like it was fast becoming an icicle. "Come on, Liam," she said, her breath fogging in the already cloudy air. The whole scenario was weird, and the campus seemed strangely isolated now, even with the dog walker and runner.

This area was a little remote and private; that's why she and Liam had picked it—a spot where they could meet on the sly, a place where the only security camera, above the back door of the gym, was broken.

Rubbing her arms, she wished that he'd just show up as he said he would. Waiting here in the foggy afternoon made her uneasy.

She'd seen on Facebook that another girl, Candice-Something-or-other had gone missing. Not that Mary-Alice really cared, she didn't know the victim, had never heard of her; Candice attended public school, while Mary-Alice had been in the Catholic school system since she'd turned five.

Mary-Alice paced the pockmarked asphalt lot with its ever-growing potholes. She wasn't going to wait all day! She checked her phone for the twentieth time. Liam hadn't texted or called, and he was five minutes late. He was *never* late.

As the fog thickened, turning day to night, she grew more nervous. Eyeing the track again, she'd lost sight of the guy on the bleacher and the woman with her little dog, but the jogger, a small man in a stocking cap, sweatshirt and tights under his shorts, was still doing laps. She wasn't completely alone.

She texted Liam, then remembered he had that new number. What a pain! Everything was changing. She started to text the new number just as she heard a truck's engine roar up the street.

Maybe he was finally here!

The truck's engine slowed, as if to turn onto the access road that led to the back of the school.

About damned time.

Headlights cut through the rising mist, and a pickup she didn't recognize slid around the corner.

Not Liam's truck.

She was all set to be pissed again when she saw the magnetic sign on the driver's door, one with the logo and phone number of Longstreet Construction.

So Liam was driving one of his father's vehicles. She breathed a sigh of relief. Keith Longstreet was always swapping out one of his company vehicles for another, the removable signs making it easy for him to add or subtract a truck, van, or car from his company's fleet. Liam, when he could, drove some of the vehicles as his own truck wasn't all that reliable.

The truck slid to a stop only a few feet from Mary-Alice.

"I was about to give up!" she said, starting in on him as the door opened and she realized that the driver wasn't Liam.

She slid to a stop. "Hey . . ."

The man who jumped from the cab was big and angry-looking, a man she swore she'd seen before—and he had a gun in one hand, aimed at her chest.

She screamed, a loud piercing wail, and turned to flee, hoping the jogger or the dog walker or anyone would hear her.

He was on her in an instant, a huge hand with a work glove covering her mouth and nose, his brute strength drawing her hard against him. She couldn't let this happen! No, no, no! Biting hard into the leather glove, she tasted deer hide and oil.

Her assailant didn't so much as flinch. "Don't' move!" he ground out against her ear, and her skin crawled with the heat of his breath on her skin. This couldn't be happening! Not to her!

Struggling, she ignored him and desperately tried to wrench away.

And then she saw her savior. The jogger was running toward her, his face red, his wiry hair poking out of his cap. *Help me!* She tried to yell, but the sound that emitted from her throat was a strangled scream. Beseeching him with her eyes, kicking and flailing at her attacker, she hoped the jogger would stop the attack.

Instead he whipped off his cap, his straggly hair held in place by a headband. "Ah, she's a nice one," he said, grinning lewdly.

The big man ordered, "Get the cuffs on her!"

What? No!

"With pleasure." With a twisted grin, the smaller man tried to put handcuffs over Mary-Alice's wrists, and though she fought and squirmed, believing that any minute the guy holding her would put the gun to her temple and shoot her dead, she was no match for the two of them. The little guy whipped off his headband, his hair unleashed as he used the sweaty rag to gag her. Unable to stop the knot from being tightened at the back of her head, she nearly threw up with the stench of his sweat on her lips and in her nostrils.

She couldn't let this happen!

Frantically she fought, but it was no use.

Who were these psychos? What did they want? But she knew. Deep down, she knew, and her heart nearly stopped. They were taking her, as they'd already taken two other girls. Her blood froze at the thought of what they might do to her, the torture she might endure, so she fought harder, trying to scream. Where was the woman in the puffy coat? Where was anyone? This was a school, for the love of God; the parsonage was nearby.

But no one appeared through the rising mist to save her.

"Get her inside." The bigger man said, breathing hard while his partner, the jogger, wheezed and coughed, all the while propelling her toward the open door of the truck.

Mary-Alice bucked and twisted, but she was no match for the two, and within minutes of the truck's arrival, she was unceremoniously tossed into the back, the jogger taking the time to grab her purse and gym bag from her car. Once he'd robbed her, he climbed into the cab and slammed his door shut. The bigger man was behind the wheel, and he shoved the idling truck into gear, then punched it. In a spray of gravel, the big rig took off.

Please, God, help me.

Mary-Alice felt sick and was shivering inside, afraid to think what these horrid men might do to her. As she rolled over and got her bearings, she realized she wasn't alone on the long bench seat.

Dana Rickert, a girl in her trig class, was already hogtied in the backseat, her big eyes round, her mouth gagged, fear emanating from her. The big man drove fast, through the lot, up the access road, and away from the school with its tall spires and large cross. Mary-Alice tried the back doors with her cuffed hands. Locked. She thought about flinging herself into the front seat, to cause an accident, but she saw the jogger in the front passenger seat half turn to stare her down and point the gun at her again.

"Don't even think about it," he warned and cocked the gun.

Click.

Oh, shit!

For the first time in a long, long while, Mary-Alice didn't just repeat a prayer, she sent up a plea to God, a soulful request asking Him to please, please, please spare her.

CHAPTER 30

At the dining room table, the journal spread out in front of her, Sarah read over the translation. It didn't make any sense. If she was right, and she'd double-checked herself, Helen was on the roof the night that her mother, Angelique Le Duc, was supposed to have fallen to her death nearly a hundred years before.

The account loosely translated was, *I found Mother on the roof with George.*

But that couldn't be right. Maxim was Angelique Le Duc's husband, the man who was supposed to have killed her, one of Sarah's ancestors and the man who had built this very house. For his wife.

"What the devil?" she whispered.

"What, Mom?" Gracie was all ears as she looked at the script in French, Helen's second language, the one she'd learned from her stepmother. "What are you reading?"

"This diary entry is Helen's account of the night Angelique disappeared," Sarah explained, her gaze skimming the thin pages. "If she's telling the truth, Helen was on the widow's walk that night. She saw her stepmother and George fighting near the railing."

"George?" Gracie repeated.

"I know, there's no mention of Maxim." Sarah read through the faint handwritten passage again; Helen's picture of that stormy night was clear. George was attacking his stepmother with an axe, trying to kill her and the child she was carrying, while she sought to fend off his blows with a candlestick.

"What happened?"

"Helen claims that they were fighting and George accused her of being . . . all sorts of not nice things," she said when the direct translation was "whore." According to Helen, George was furious that his stepmother had been sleeping with someone, having an affair . . . no, that wasn't right. As she read further, Sarah realized that George, Maxim's oldest son, was actually Angelique's lover. George was furious, out of his mind, according to Helen, that Angelique was carrying a child he thought was his father's, the man to whom Angelique was married.

"What're you saying?" Grace asked, when Sarah stopped trying to explain the translation.

"According to Helen, George and Angelique were having an affair," Sarah went on reluctantly. "They were close in age, you know."

"Oh . . . ," Gracie made a face. "But he was like her son."

"I know, but he'd been raised by his mother, Myrtle, Maxim's first wife. Angelique married Maxim when George was almost a man. Not that that's an excuse."

Gracie nodded, soft curls bouncing around her face. "Did Angelique die?"

"Angelique and George were apparently locked in some kind of macabre embrace, intent on doing bodily harm and struggling, before they fell over the railing, together." Sarah stared down at the confession of a young girl who had witnessed the horrid battle and demise of her stepmother and brother from the cupola.

"And then?"

"The section just stops with the fight on the rooftop that night." She shivered as she thought about it. No wonder Angelique's soul had found no peace. Quickly, Sarah flipped through the following pages, but the rooftop was where Angelique's story had ended. After Helen witnessed the fall of the lovers in their death throes, she wrote more sporadically and talked of taking charge of the family. Sarah imagined Helen trying to be a mother to Maxim's brood. She would have been so young—about Gracie's age, the others younger still. It seemed nearly impossible. "If she's telling the truth, then . . . then all three of them—George, Maxim, and Angelique—disappeared on the same night."

"So, if George and Angelique fell into the river and drowned, what happened to Maxim?" Gracie asked. "Where was he? Why didn't he return?"

"She doesn't know . . ." She studied the pages. "Twice Helen adds a lonely note at the end of her entry: Where's Papa?"

"Maybe he left when he found out about George and Angelique."

"Maybe . . . but to leave his children? The house? The diary continues for only another couple of weeks, but wait a minute . . ." She read the faint words twice, and her world shifted. Was it possible? Here in this decades-old journal of a young girl, was the mystery of Blue Peacock Manor, finally solved? If so, everything Sarah had thought was her family history had been upended, and her stomach churned uncomfortably. "It says here," she said reluctantly, "that Helen believed Jacques, the baby in the picture we saw, my great-great-grandfather, was George's son with Angelique, not Maxim's. She'd overheard arguments to that effect."

"Freaky." Gracie thought hard. "So, he was still a Stewart. Oh . . . wait . . . What does that mean?"

That Jacques's half brother was his father, that Maxim was his grandfather, that everything I believed about my lineage is really messed up. "It means it's complicated."

"That's what you always say when you don't want me to know the truth."

"Until I can read this entire diary and authenticate it, I don't know what the truth is."

"I believe Helen," Grace defended. "Angelique had a son from her husband's son. It's incest. That's what you're saying."

"Not technically, but yes, that's what I'm saying. In any event, it wasn't healthy." She cleared her throat. "But we're here to find out the truth, not judge them, right?"

"I just want to help Angelique pass."

"I know." From the corner of her eye, Sarah caught sight of a vehicle rolling up the drive—a Jeep, one she didn't recognize. "Looks like we've got company," she said, almost glad to change the subject. As she scooted back her chair, she slammed the journal shut. Through the window she watched as the Jeep slid to a stop next to her Explorer, which was parked near the garage.

Belatedly, Xena caught wind that someone had arrived. On her feet in an instant, the dog began barking like mad, turning circles, going out of her mind, the hairs on the back of her neck standing on end.

"Great watchdog," Jade said as she strode into the dining area. "I heard the car before she did." She had been in the other room, sorting through some of her boxes before they moved into the guest-house at the beginning of the week. "Who's here?"

Sarah recognized Lucy Bellisario, someone she'd gone to school with, as she climbed out of the Jeep. According to Dee Linn, Lucy, never married as far as Sarah knew, was now a detective with the Sheriff's Department. "The police," she stated flatly.

"Why would they come here?" Jade asked, staring out the window.

"Good question," Sarah thought aloud as she watched Lucy push the Jeep's door shut and start up the walk. Her hair, still a vibrant red, was clipped away from her face, her eyebrows were knit, her expression stern on a face devoid of makeup. "Guess I'll find out. Someone deal with Xena, okay?"

"Got her," Gracie said, grabbing the dog's collar. "Hush, girl," she commanded, and surprisingly Xena's fierce barking was reduced to a soft whining sound that, once Sarah stepped through the front door, became silent.

"Lucy," she greeted her.

"Hi, Sarah." She flipped open her badge. "I'm Detective Bellisario now. With the Sheriff's Department."

"I heard you were with them," Sarah said, feeling the chill of the afternoon pierce through her sweater and jeans. "Dee Linn. She keeps me informed." She wrapped her arms around her to ward off the cold. "So, this isn't a social call?"

"No." Lucy shook her head. "I'll cut right to the chase. We've had some girls who've gone missing, and we're checking out everyone associated with them as well as looking at known predators."

A cold knot twisted in Sarah's stomach. She had a sense where this might be going.

"May I come in?"

"Sure." Without hesitation she swung the door wide. "Excuse the mess," she said automatically. "We just moved here from Vancouver, and all our stuff is everywhere until we can settle into the guesthouse." Why she felt she needed to explain or make excuses she didn't really understand, so she ended with, "We've got a lot of work left in fixing this old place up."

"I heard you were planning to restore it."

"Easier said than done," Sarah admitted, guiding Lucy around stacks of boxes and crates to the living room. To her credit, the detective took in the mess inside the house but didn't comment. No doubt she'd seen lots worse.

"Known predators, you said," Sarah prompted when they were in the parlor, where the fire was still glowing, embers bright, flames crackling. The sleeping bags were folded but piled with their pillows in a corner. "That's why you're here." No reason to beat around the bush when they both understood whom Lucy was looking for.

"Roger Anderson's name came up."

"It always does." The knot in her gut cinched a little tighter, and she noticed her girls walking in from the dining room. Great. They would get to hear about their uncle again. "These are my daughters," Sarah introduced, waving them into the living room/parlor. "Jade's my oldest, and this is Gracie. Girls, this is Detective Bellisario. She and I went to school together. Yes, Jade, the dreaded Our Lady." To Lucy, she said, "Jade's not a fan."

For the first time Lucy really smiled. "Nice to meet you," she said as the girls murmured hellos. Gracie was holding onto Xena's collar with a death grip, though the dog was wagging her tail. "I hated the school when I went there too," Lucy confessed, "but it turned out okay." She patted the dog on her head and said to Jade, "The way I heard it, most of the really mean nuns retired."

Suspicious as ever, Jade said, "Remains to be seen."

"You're here about the missing girls," Gracie said as Xena trotted to a rug she'd claimed in the corner by the fireplace.

"She's looking for your Uncle Roger," Sarah answered, then said to Lucy, "I haven't seen him in years."

"Not even when you visited your parents?"

"Roger left home for the first time when I was very young, an infant. I don't remember it, of course, but according to my sister, Dee Linn, who must've heard it from Mother, Roger had a major falling out with my dad, the whole power struggle between a stepfather and stepson, or something like that," she said, and for a second she thought of what she'd read in Helen's diary about the struggle over Angelique between Maxim and his son, George.

"You didn't grow up with him?" Bellisario clarified.

"No, though he came back off and on," Sarah said. "But Roger and my parents, even my mother, didn't get along. So he never stayed very long." *But long enough to be with you in the rain on the widow's walk and to carry you, traumatized, down the stairs to your shrieking, panic-stricken mother. His mother.*

Her throat went dry as the memory played with her, rising up but never quite breaking the surface of her conscious mind. Her skin was suddenly clammy, and she felt Lucy's gaze upon her, as if the cop were reading her mind.

"When was the last time he lived here?" Bellisario asked, and the question seemed to come from a distance, the words echoing.

"Uh . . . I don't really know. He could have returned after I left home at eighteen. The time before that, the last time that I saw him I was . . . twelve maybe?" She swallowed hard, remembering Roger's strong arms, his wet face. *I won't let him hurt you. I won't . . . I promised her. I promised. I'll save you.*

Whom had he promised?

Save her from *what?*

Lucy was looking at the fire, watching as the flames licked at a mossy piece of oak. "So you haven't seen him recently?"

"No."

"You never visited him when he was incarcerated?"

"No," she said as within the grate the moss sizzled, shriveling and blackening as it caught fire.

"And he hasn't come to the house?"

"No. I already told you. Not since we've moved here."

"I'm just double-checking, because we have information that he's back; he's been seen in town but is flying under the radar. I thought he might want to come home."

"This isn't his home anymore," Sarah pointed out firmly. "Dee Linn said he lives in The Dalles."

"The room he rented there has been vacated for a while. The woman who leased him the place said he just up and left. Paid for another month, then disappeared without a word." Lucy's expression shifted. "Do you know how your brother took his sister Theresa's disappearance? I understand they were close."

Sarah wasn't sure what she thought about the change of topic. "I heard it bothered him a lot. From what I understand, that's when he left home."

Lucy glanced at the girls as if weighing what she was about to say, then asked, "Do you know if Roger and Theresa were . . . romantically involved?"

"They were full brother and sister," Sarah pointed out coldly.

Lucy inclined her head in agreement. "Could it have been—"

"No."

"All right. I just needed to follow up on a rumor. If he comes by, will you call me? Tell him I want to talk to him."

"He won't," Sarah assured her, unnerved. Roger and Theresa? No . . . no way. Roger might be a lot of things, some of them not very good, but . . . Her mind spun with images from her dream. *I'll keep you safe. I promised her.* Her lungs tightened. Was the *her* Theresa? Had he promised Theresa that he'd keep Sarah safe? But why?

A distant chord thrummed through her. Maxim, George, and Angelique, a love triangle that had ended in murder and death . . . and *Theresa and Roger?*

"Are you all right?" Lucy asked, and Sarah could feel that her face had drained of color.

"Yes . . . yes . . . just fine," she lied, trying to sound calm and together when it felt as if her whole life was turning on its head.

"Mom?" Gracie was staring at her and Sarah forced a smile.

"I said nothing's wrong."

Lucy's phone rang, and she pulled it from her pocket and checked the number, little lines forming between her eyebrows before she replaced it. "Okay, good. That's it for now," she said with finality.

Thank God.

"Thanks for your time, Sarah," Lucy said.

Just like that, the interview was over, as quickly as it had begun.

Still shaken, Sarah walked the detective to the door.

"Call me if you hear from him," Lucy requested again. "I would really like to talk to your brother and clear up some questions." She pressed a business card into her palm.

Clutching the card, Sarah watched Lucy walk swiftly to her Jeep, then take off, taillights winking red before disappearing into the thickening fog.

"What's the deal with Uncle Roger?" Jade asked, coming up behind her.

"I don't know," Sarah answered, but the police obviously thought he was involved with something.

The interior of the barn was barely illuminated, fog obscuring the late-afternoon sun, night stalking the day, when Rosalie heard the roar of a truck's engine, far away but getting closer by the second. "Candice!" she yelled. "Get ready! He's back."

From the far stall came a quiet whimper, as if Candice was going to fall into a million pieces again.

No! She couldn't! She had to play her part this time and fool the bastard. This might be their last chance to set themselves free. "Just do what you did before," Rosalie yelled, hoping to convey her urgency. "When he comes in to change out your water and bucket, pretend you're going to do what he says and—"

Outside, gravel crunched under heavy tires, and the loud engine died.

Rosalie figured that if she could hear what was going on outside, through the barn's wooden walls, there was a good chance he would hear her screaming at Candice, so she lowered her voice. "You know what to do," she stage-whispered and prayed the girl would pull herself together.

"I don't know . . ."

Fists clenched, her ridiculous little weapon clutched tight, Rosalie hovered near the door to her stall, waiting. It didn't take long. Within minutes, she heard footsteps and muted conversation.

Her spirits tumbled.

He wasn't alone.

Now what?

Would idiotic Candice remember to watch out for the second

man? To adjust the plan, to make her move at the right time? To not mess up? What were the chances of that happening?

Click!

The exterior door was unlocked, and Rosalie heard the door creak open, then bang loudly against the wall.

"Watch it!" her captor shouted.

"For fuck's sake, I'm tryin' to get her in. She ain't exactly cooperatin', y'know." Scraggly Hair.

"Just get her inside!" her abductor barked.

Another girl. They'd kidnapped another girl!

Snap!

Overhead lights blinked to life, chasing the shadows to the corners.

"Bring 'em in. Hurry," he yelled.

Them? More than one?

Muffled moaning and shuffling footsteps confirmed her worst fears. This was bad news for the new girls and for them all; the simple fact was that the more women he caught, the closer they were to the time when whoever was on the other end of the phone would come for them. Leaning close to the door, Rosalie closed her eyes, concentrating, trying to figure out what was happening on the other side.

She couldn't tell how many captives were involved, but she knew the exterior door was open, from the rush of fresh air sweeping high overhead, above the walls and doorways of her prison cell, confirming that she hadn't heard it shut.

"The blonde," her abductor said. "She's Princess!"

Rosalie heard a surprised, muted response. The girl, probably gagged, but realizing she was going to be locked up, was stirring up a fuss, feet dragging, trying to scream as she was forced into the adjoining stall.

"Shut up!" her abductor yelled, obviously irritated at his latest victim. "Go on, get her in there!"

Rosalie leaned closer to the wall separating the next stall from hers, the cell she already knew had been labeled "Princess." Scrapes and thumps and a loud humming emanated, the girl, struggling, yelling through a gag at her attackers.

"Cut that shit out!" Scraggly Hair.

"Be good and we'll take off the cuffs," the abductor said, his voice calmer. "I don't want to bruise your wrists. And the gag will be removed too, but you have to sit there, on that cot and not move. Do you hear me? Screaming won't do you any good. You can ask Star, she's in that stall next door. Yelled her damned lungs out, but no one heard. You know why. You saw where we are. No one can hear you." There was rustling on the other side of the wall, familiar sounds of pails and water bottles being left, but the girl was either obeying or the fight was out of her.

The abductor continued, talking to his partner. "We'll put the pudgy one in Whiskey's stall. And if Princess does what she's told and doesn't give us any trouble, then we'll come back and take off the cuffs and gag. If not, you"—he must've been looking at his latest victim—"can stay in here just as you are. Your choice."

It sounded as if they left the stall, the door swung shut, and Rosalie's new cell mate gave a muffled squeal of distress before going silent.

Outside the main area of the barn, Scraggly Hair said, "Why the hell Whiskey?" Not the most brilliant accomplice.

"Because we're running out of stalls!" was the quick, agitated answer. "Get her in there, fast. I don't have a lot of time."

Within five minutes, after a similar ritual, "Whiskey" was ensconced inside her new home. She hadn't put up near the fight as the girl next to her, the blonde now referred to as Princess.

So now there were four.

The wheels were turning in Rosalie's mind as she listened, hearing that both new inmates were, as promised, uncuffed, their gags removed.

"You let me out of here!" the girl in the next stall blasted the second, Rosalie assumed, the gag was removed. "Right now!" She was furious and ready to disobey. Good. "You can't keep me here!"

The abductor disagreed. "You don't have a choice."

"I'm telling you, I won't be left in this sty."

Stall, Rosalie silently corrected.

The door closed, and the click of a lock sealed Princess's fate.

"No! Let me out!" A heavy thud and accompanying "oof" suggested she'd launched herself at the door. "No, no! *No!*" She started pounding and shrieking so loudly that Rosalie couldn't hear what was happening in Whiskey's stall. Hopefully that girl had more brains.

"Keep it up," the big guy yelled again, "and see what happens. Remember what I said?"

She quieted for a second, then tried a new tact. "Please, you can't leave me in here. My dad . . . he'll pay you. Whatever you ask. Seriously . . . and I won't identify you. The police won't—"

"Shut up."

"No, please, just listen, you have to listen," she begged, while, farther down the line, the other girl was crying too. And, of course, Candice had joined in the sobbing. Oh, God, how were they ever going to get out of here?

"Just shut. The fuck. Up," the abductor snapped out.

"But—"

He yelled, "You want the handcuffs again? Is that it? The gag? Fine."

"Nooooo!" And then Princess went quiet.

But she'd touched a raw nerve. The abductor was losing it. "I've got other girls," he yelled. "I don't really need you, so go ahead and work yourself into a lather, bang your damned fists raw, but it's not going to do any good. None whatsoever."

He was lying, Rosalie knew. True, escaping was nearly impossible, but the guy did need Princess and Whiskey, and a few more, if she'd understood his end of the conversation with his coconspirator correctly. Princess didn't know the half of it. Someone was pulling this jerkwad's strings. It was his assignment to find the other man more girls. She'd had a lot of hours to think, and she suspected they were going to be forced into prostitution, some kind of white slavery, used as some sicko's partner in sadistic sexual acts, even torture. Bile climbed up her throat. The thought of what might happen to her, to all of them, scared the hell out of her.

So far, the two men hadn't hurt either her or Candice. Keeping them bruise-free seemed important—for now, until she and the others were distributed, sold, she figured, to the highest bidder. She imagined an auction in her mind, where the girls would be paraded, naked possibly, in front of those who would bid on them.

Her stomach revolted. Gagging, she held the vomit back, as much to stay quiet as anything. She didn't want to call attention to herself today, didn't want to deal with the bastard. But what was to come frightened her to the core. She and the other girls were vulnerable to the whims and desires of the men on the other side of these doors, much like the horses who had once occupied these stalls.

But unlike the animals, she understood what was happening, how awful the future might be.

Once she and the others were alone, she would get all of their attention and organize a plot to get the hell out of here. Of course, there first would be that ridiculous time of disbelief when each of the other girls would weep, and scream, and be completely useless.

Somehow, she'd find a way to cut that short. Princess and Whiskey didn't have the luxury of feeling sorry for themselves.

If they wanted to escape, it was now or never.

She swallowed back another bit of vomit, her mouth sour, her throat burning, as she heard a stall door swing shut, then a lock snap into place. Damn, but she wished that just once the lock would fail and not quite latch.

"Okay, I'm outta here," the big man said, and for a second Rosalie thought he might leave Scraggly Hair to guard them. She wondered if she could lure Scraggly into her stall, then somehow lock him inside, but her plotting was in vain. Her abductor said, "Quit fiddle-farting around. Let's go."

"Fine, fine. I'm comin'. Shit, I was just makin' sure the doors were latched. For the love of—okay, okay." More footsteps and muttering.

A second later the light was snapped off, and the barn fell into a murky half darkness.

CHAPTER 31

Outside the barn, the big man and his partner split up, getting into separate vehicles. The first order of business was to dump the pickup he'd used in nabbing the latest two girls. There was a chance that someone might have seen him—for example, the woman at the track who'd been walking her little dog as he'd waited on the bleachers to make sure the girl had arrived. Or possibly one of the school's security cameras had caught his image or that of the truck as he'd pulled into the lot. Yeah, he had to ditch this vehicle pronto.

No problem.

He didn't own it.

He'd actually lucked out with it. The registered owner was the voyeur he'd capped at the Stewart house. After taking the guy's keys, wallet, cell phone, and money clip, he'd used the keyless remote to find the vehicle. As he'd hit the unlock button, the big truck had chirped and flashed its headlights, making it easy for him, with the aid of his partner, to take it and use it for this job. He'd also been able to leave his own truck in town, in full view of one of the few traffic cameras in Stewart's Crossing.

A stroke of genius.

As was the magnetic sign he'd slapped to the driver's side. Driving into the mountains, he smiled at how easily that ploy had worked. From his research of the schoolgirls via their social media connections, he'd learned that "Princess," aka Mary-Alice Eklund, was "in a relationship" with the star soccer player for the Catholic school's team. By luck, he'd come across the Longstreet Construction advertising panel on a van that was in Hal's shop for repair. It was almost as if God were helping him. He'd stolen the sign easily and attached it to this rig, worrying slightly about the truck's out-of-state plates, but he decided that by the time anyone noticed the discrepancy, his mission would be completed.

He'd even used the rig when he'd cast his victims' IDs over the bridge at The Dalles. Yeah, he thought, easing off the gas at a hairpin turn, he was golden.

But he couldn't get cocky, and now the pickup was just too visible. He had to wipe it down and get rid of it so that it had no connection whatsoever to him. No problem. He predicted that the vehicle, when discovered, would lead the cops in a different direction by distracting them with the mystery of the missing owner. He only needed a little breathing room. A couple of days. Then he'd be free and clear, across more than one border, before the cops put two and two together.

As he drove across a narrow bridge, he checked his rearview and saw his partner behind the wheel of the hybrid and following at a safe distance, barely visible in the fog. He climbed upward into the surrounding hills, through the forest, until he found an unused logging road that was overgrown with weeds and brush. Slowing to make certain his partner followed, he pulled the truck as far off the county road as was possible, then quickly cleaned the interior, though he'd been wearing gloves to make certain he hadn't left any prints or DNA evidence. Satisfied, he locked the vehicle and, after removing the sign for Longstreet Construction, made his way to the Prius idling a few yards behind.

"Is all this really necessary?" the dumb shit asked as he backed out, long grass scraping the undercarriage of the hybrid, over the rocks in the ruts of this overgrown road, jostling the tires.

"The more time we can buy, the better."

Once he'd backed onto the county road again, his partner rammed the Prius into gear. On smooth pavement again, he'd gunned the engine, causing the car to switch automatically from its quiet electric engine mode to gas.

Their plan was set. They didn't need to discuss the details another time, and soon they were driving through the city limits of Stewart's Crossing, and within forty minutes of the time they'd dropped the truck, he was delivered two blocks from where his truck was parked near The Cavern.

He walked inside through the alley, just as he'd exited, then returned to the bar, to the very spot he'd vacated nearly two hours earlier. Between the abductions, he'd made a show of being on the premises, ordering another beer, leaving his credit card, then going outside for a smoke.

"Wondered if someone was coming back," the cute bartender said, swiping the smooth wood of the bar as she glanced up at him. "Since you left your jacket and Carla, she said you still had to pay up." The shift had changed while he was gone, Carla had left, and this new girl was now tending to him, all of which should aid his alibi as both girls had seen him.

"Went outside for a cigarette, came across some old friends and lost track of time."

She didn't argue the fact as he ordered another draft and picked up a conversation with a guy who was dressed in a green sweatshirt with a yellow O emblazoned across his chest. Watching the football game on the screen mounted over the bar, the man barely touched his dark beer.

The barmaid left a fresh beer in front of him. Sipping, he checked the score, making a note of it, as if he cared. Oregon was struggling against Stanford in a tight game of the Pac-12 North.

The fan in the green sweatshirt scowled. "Damn it," he said to anyone who was listening. "I can't believe they aren't wiping the floor with these guys."

"Stanford's not only good," someone down the bar said. "They're smart."

"So are the Ducks!"

Another person snorted. "Without Phil Knight and Nike, they wouldn't be worth a damn."

"Go screw yourself," the fan muttered under his breath before burying his nose into his drink just as Oregon intercepted the ball and ran it back for a quick score. The fan's mood visibly brightened. "That's what I'm talking about!"

"Nice," he said, clinking his glass with the fan's, making eye contact, establishing his alibi, should he need one. Yeah, there was a big hole in his afternoon, but his truck hadn't moved, if any cameras were watching, and the bartending shift had changed, so the staff's recollection of when he actually left and came back would be shaky, more open to interpretation. Even if there were security cameras inside the place, he and his partner would provide backup alibis to fill in the gaps.

He thought he was covered.

He just needed to return the construction sign he'd "borrowed" from the van that had been left at Hal's Auto Repair.

Piece of cake.

"Yeah, Miss McAdams?" the gravelly voice asked as Jade answered her cell. Her phone was hard to read, but it showed a number she didn't recognize on its tiny, mutilated screen. "Uh, this is Hal from Hal's Auto Repair." As if there were another Hal in this Podunk town. "I've been calling you all afternoon. Your car's done."

"I thought it wasn't going to be fixed until next week."

"The part came in, and you seemed pretty anxious to have it back."

"I am! Great."

"We'll be lockin' up in about twenty minutes, and the shop's closed on Sunday, so if you want it for the rest of the weekend, you might want to come and get it."

"I will! Please wait!" Jade said, feeling her spirits lift a little as she hung up. She was about to run up the stairs, only to find her mother looking over the plans for the house, while Gracie was still poring over the damned journal again, as if it held the secrets of the universe.

Since the cop had left, her mother had been distracted, and now Jade could tell she wasn't really seeing the plans.

It was clear something was going on with Uncle Roger, and what the cop had intimated was just plain sick, but her mom didn't want to talk about it. She'd lost interest in what was going on around her, lost to some weird world where only God knew what she saw. Again, Jade thought she'd definitely been born into the wrong family. The whole group was a bunch of fucking ghost-whispering oddballs. Maybe being related to Clint Walsh was a good thing, a way to dilute the freaky Stewart genes.

But there was no reason to dwell on it now, not when her damned car was finally repaired.

"We have to leave right now and pick up my car," she announced. "It's done, and Hal's like leaving in twenty minutes!"

Mom looked up from her plans. "Sure," she said, though she sounded anything but. "Okay . . . I guess we can make it."

"We *have* to make it," Jade insisted. There was no "guessing" about it. "I'm driving to Aunt Dee Linn's party."

"We're all going together," Sarah said.

"Then I'll follow you there," Jade said, already reaching for her coat. She couldn't believe that finally, after what seemed an eternity, she'd be able to drive her own car again. *Freedom! Finally!*

"We'll go get your car, okay, but we're going together to the party. There's a second girl from around here who's gone missing, and I want us to stay close."

"This is not how I want to spend my Saturday night! I'm not a baby," Jade argued hotly.

"Neither were the two girls who were taken."

"No one knows if they were kidnapped, Mom. Maybe they just decided to take off for a while," Jade declared.

"And not tell anyone, including their friends or parents?" Sarah slung the strap of her purse over her shoulder. "The police are worried, and so am I."

"Mom—"

"You're not going alone. Come on, Gracie!"

"But I don't want to go pick up the car," Gracie protested, and their mother actually sighed.

"Really? Didn't you hear what I just said? Come on. Get your jacket."

"I could stay here with Xena," Gracie protested.

Mom wasn't buying it. "Move it."

Hurrying out the front door and sprinting across the grass to her mother's Explorer, Jade glanced over her shoulder and confirmed that Sarah, Gracie in tow, was only a few steps behind.

The dog romped after them and bounced into the backseat. Well, fine.

In an ironic twist of fate, Jade thought, as their mother got into the car and started toward town, Gracie was now the one who was pouting, pissed off that she had to give up her research on the ghost of Blue Peacock Manor or whatever. It all sounded *so* Nancy Drew.

But Jade didn't care. She was getting her Civic back, and by the end of the weekend she intended to see Cody. One way or another. If he couldn't, or wouldn't, drive to Stewart's Crossing to visit her, maybe it was time to visit him at his apartment in Vancouver.

A drip of dread slid into her heart, and she reminded herself that she might not like what she found when she surprised him.

Too bad. Either he loved her or he didn't.

She deserved to know the truth.

Bellisario felt as if she were onto something as she drove into the parking lot of the Sheriff's Department. Most of the way back from the Stewart place, she'd been caught up in her thoughts about the case, and they had come full circle back to Roger Anderson. No matter how many times she tried to convince herself he wasn't involved, she couldn't shake the idea that he had a part in this.

If not Anderson, then who?

You have nothing on him. Just your gut instinct. Not exactly first-class detective work, Lucy. You need a helluva lot more.

Halfway to Stewart's Crossing, she'd called her sister back, the call she'd missed when she'd been at the Stewart house. Lauren was worried, explaining that their mother had taken a fall. Mom was okay, Lauren assured her, but she sounded overwhelmed. Dealing with a parent with Parkinson's disease was tough on a seventeen-year-old. Hell, it was tough on Bellisario, and she was thirty-five. After being assured that the part-time nurse was on hand, and that her mother was indeed resting and comfortable, just feeling more embarrassed than anything, Lucy told her sister she'd be home as soon as she could after work. She sometimes felt guilty that her job took up so much of her time, but it was the nature of the beast, and she really wouldn't change things.

Anyway, she knew what would happen when she got to Mom's. She and Lauren would have another discussion about their mother, who was only sixty-four but already needed full-time care. Lucy knew it, and Lauren was definitely on board, but Landon, their brother, the middle child—who conveniently lived in Tacoma, far enough away that he didn't have to deal with the situation except a few times a year—was certain Mom was "fine."

If Mom remained stable, they'd all probably let it go again and get by, but any way you cut it, the day was coming when their mother would need a lot more help.

Parkinson's was a bitch.

She parked in her favorite space near the department's rear door, her thoughts turning back to the case. Heading inside the brick edifice, she felt her stomach rumbling. She'd missed lunch and had picked up a prepackaged sandwich and Diet Coke at a deli on the outskirts of town, which she figured she'd eat at her desk.

Inside, the building was bright, the glow of fluorescent lights reflecting off floor tiles that had recently been polished, light coming through arched windows that had stood the test of time and paint so new there were few scrapes or scuff marks visible.

Yet.

Hundred-year-old buildings tended to show their age, no matter how recent the paint job.

Past the lockers and lunchroom, she headed into the wing housing the detective unit. In her office she peeled off her jacket and kicked out her desk chair. She still wondered if she were on the wrong track, if her obsession with Roger Anderson was completely unfounded. So he was skipping out of meetings with his parole officer. So he hadn't shown up at the family home. So there were "sightings" of him in town. He had a record. Yeah. But never for kidnapping.

Muttering under her breath, she unwrapped her sandwich with one hand and scrolled through her e-mail with the other. Without really thinking about it, she opened the ham and cheese, scraped off the excess mayo with the plastic wrap the sandwich had come in, and read through her messages. Maybe a security camera somewhere had found something, or a witness was finally coming forward or some damn thing.

Nothing.

In fact, she discovered that after further investigation by an assistant detective, the alibis of the other suspects had now all checked out. Even Lars Blonski could prove he wasn't anywhere near either of the two girls. Her stomach burned a bit as it did when she was super-stressed, so she popped a couple of Tums with her diet soda and took a bite of her sandwich.

Where the hell were they?

Who the hell had taken the girls?

She looked up when she heard footsteps approaching and saw Cooke walking into her office. "Could be we have more of a problem than we think," he said.

"More?" She swiped at the edge of her mouth with the napkin that had come wrapped with her sandwich.

"Got a call from Turner in Missing Persons. Two more girls are missing."

"What?" She nearly came out of her chair, but Cooke held out his hands, fingers spread, indicating she should sit.

"They've only been gone for a few hours, but their parents are terrified, panicking, probably overreacting." But his eyes were dark, his lower lip protruding, worry evident in the lines of his face.

"Let's hope," she said.

"They'll probably show up later at a friend's house or something." He didn't believe it, she could tell.

"They were together?"

"No."

Bellisario didn't like the sound of that.

"But they do know each other; both go to Our Lady. The first, Dana Rickert, was shopping. Didn't return. The parents found her car in the parking lot of the outlet stores down in Troutdale. Purse and cell missing."

"Probably with her," Bellisario said. The outlet mall was about an hour west on I-84.

"She left this morning. Was supposed to be home by noon."

Bellisario glanced at the clock on her desk, where the digital readout glowed a bright 4:47. "Alone?"

"Apparently. She wasn't even going to meet friends."

"Really?"

"When she didn't answer her phone, they drove out to the stores to investigate, thought maybe she had car trouble and the battery on her phone was dead or something. Found her car, talked to Security, and pushed the panic button. She was supposed to be home for her sister's birthday party—a big deal, I guess. She'd been excited about it. Had some special present planned."

"Shit." Bellisario leaned back in her chair, her sandwich forgotten. "GPS chip in the phone?"

"There was. No more. She's kind of a techie. Didn't like her parents snooping. Disabled it."

"What about security tapes from the shopping mall?"

"Getting 'em now."

Bellisario had hoped this was a false report, that the worried parents were, as Cooke had suggested, pushing the panic button before it was time. "Is she a friend of Rosalie Jamison or Candice Fowler?"

He shook his head. "Not according to her parents." Cooke frowned, suddenly looking older than his years as he stood in the doorway, one shoulder shoved against the frame. "The second girl, Mary-Alice Eklund, said she was meeting her boyfriend, a kid by the name of Liam Longstreet."

Bellisario nodded. "Soccer player," she said. "For Our Lady. I've seen his name in the papers."

"There's the problem. The kid said they had no plans to meet up, but her car was found parked behind the school, in a place where Longstreet said they'd get together sometimes. You know, to be alone."

"Let me guess. No purse. Not answering her phone."

"You got it. Longstreet got a weird text from her, but he was working for his dad, didn't notice it for a couple of hours as the old man is death on texting and cell phones in general, especially when he's on the job."

"And the text was?"

"Why are you contacting me from this number?"

"You're saying someone was using another phone and claiming it was Longstreet?"

"Looks like it. The good news is that her old man called the phone company and read them the riot act. He got the number of the phone that had called his daughter and dialed it, but no one answered."

"Shit. Tipped the guy off."

"Maybe. Anyway, Eklund gave us the info, and we got the name of the registered owner. A guy by the name of Evan Tolliver."

"Who's he?"

"Owns Tolliver Construction. Out of Vancouver, Washington."

"Vancouver," she repeated. "Where Sarah McAdams came from," she said, her thought synapses snapping as she remembered Sarah saying as much, and Bellisario had taken notice of the Washington plates on her Explorer. "What the hell does Evan Tolliver have to do with this?"

"Beats me."

She made a note. "I'll talk to Sarah again."

"Good. Because there is a connection between Mary-Alice Eklund and Jade McAdams. Seems the McAdams girl was Mary-Alice's charge. As a new kid, Jade was put under the wing of an upperclassman—in this case, Mary-Alice Eklund. But things weren't going smoothly, according to Mrs. Eklund. The girls didn't like each other, and Mary-Alice complained to her mother that Jade had threatened her, said she wished her dead or something like that."

"Kid stuff, probably. I met Jade McAdams today."

"Maybe, but there was also a jealousy thing going on. Mary-Alice was convinced the Longstreet boy was interested in Jade. He denied it when her parents asked him about it and said he only knew Jade from being a TA in one of her classes."

So two girls didn't get along. That wasn't exactly breaking news.

"Do Mary-Alice Eklund's parents have a GPS locator chip on their kid's phone?"

"Oh yeah." Cooke didn't seem too excited about it. "According to the last coordinates, the cell is somewhere in the Columbia River."

"Oh, Jesus," Bellisario said, and it was more a prayer than a curse. Could it be that the missing girls had been killed and tossed into the huge span of water separating Oregon and Washington? Would their bodies have been weighted down to sink to the bottom, or carried westward to wash up on the shores or batter against the huge dam downriver?

"FBI's all over it," Cooke went on. "The Eklund girl was last seen sometime this afternoon. Her mother left the house around eleven, and Mary-Alice was still in her bedroom. Asleep probably. That's when the timing gets a little iffy, as no one was home when she left, but when Mrs. Eklund got home around two, her daughter was already gone. The parents are worried sick she's been abducted."

"It's early for an AMBER Alert."

"Who the hell cares?" Cooke said. "Worst thing that happens, the kids show up and the department looks like it was quick to pull the trigger. A little egg on our face. FBI agrees."

"You're right," she said, tossing the remains of her late lunch into the trash. Her bad feeling had just gotten worse. "I'm on it."

Her first stop? A place she'd been not two hours earlier: Blue Peacock Manor, that god-awful monstrosity of a house, to talk again with Sarah McAdams and her daughter Jade, just to cover all her bases.

And, oh yeah, she planned on having another face-to-face with Hardy Jones, the scumbag who had lied to her earlier. It was time for Hardy to come clean.

CHAPTER 32

As Sarah pulled the Explorer into the parking area of Hal's Auto Repair, Gracie, still in a bit of a snit, said, "I'll wait in the car."

Her immediate response was *no,* because of the missing girls, but Sarah realized she'd have a full view of her vehicle for the few minutes she'd be inside the shop. She pulled under the awning that stretched to a spot where gasoline pumps had once stood and was right next to the door and wall of glass that formed the front of Hal's building—unconventional for the town, as there wasn't anything the least bit Western decorating this glass-and-concrete building. "Fine." Gracie could sit in the SUV and stew, she thought, yanking her keys from the ignition. "This shouldn't take long."

The second Sarah cut the engine, Jade was already out of the car and walking through the front door. "I'll be right back," she said to Gracie, then followed after her oldest, leaving Gracie to pout and in plain sight through the plate-glass windows that lined the front of the building where the reception area was located.

Hal, seventy-five if he was a day, was waiting for them, though she could see through another set of windows two men still working on a pickup in one of the bays. The hood was open, a light suspended over the engine, one man on a creeper that he slid underneath the truck, the other peering into the open engine cavity from above. Antique signs selling anything from Nehi Soda to Lucky Strike cigarettes adorned the walls.

"There ya are; should be good as new!" Hal said as he took Sarah's credit card, swiped it, then slid a receipt across the worn counter, where an antique cash register actually dinged as the drawer opened. Hal's snow-white hair peeked from beneath an oil-stained baseball cap that was probably as old as the vintage cigarette machine standing against the back wall.

"Thanks," Sarah said as she tucked the receipt and the card into her purse. Jade snagged the keys that glinted under the fluorescent lights mounted high overhead, reminding Sarah of something . . . what was it, a niggling little thought that she couldn't quite recall.

"I'm going to stop at the store, get some things I need and a Coke," her daughter sang on the way out.

"Wait, Jade, I don't think—"

"Mom, please. It's no big deal. It'll take ten minutes. Then I'll come straight home. I promise."

Sarah wanted to argue. To remind Jade that girls had gone missing, but they'd been over it a million times already. "Just be careful and really, 'straight home'."

"Yeah, yeah! I know."

"Your car's in the lot out back," Hal called to Jade and hooked a thumb at an exit near the back "Through that door."

Jade stopped and switched direction, the key swinging from her fingers as she headed out the door he'd pointed to. Sarah watched her go, her gaze trained on Jade's key ring. What the hell was she trying to remember?

"Good to have you back, Sarah," Hal said, snapping Sarah to reality.

"Good to be back."

"You gotta let 'em go, a little," he said. "Kids. It's hard. You worry yourself sick. But you gotta remember what you were like at her age." His eyes glinted. "I do. You never wanted your wings clipped."

"I know, but, the missing girls . . ." She stared at the doorway.

"And what? They don't have crime in Vancouver?" He offered her an encouraging smile. "Raising kids isn't for sissies, I know. See my hair? From my kids. All five of 'em. Trouble." He chuckled at a memory, "But they survived, grew up to be fine people, gave me twelve grandkids, with another on the way."

"Congratulations," she said, and wished she could take his advice.

"Sorry about your mom." Hal had serviced cars for everyone in the family, including Arlene. "Heard about her from Dee Linn."

Of course.

"Give her my best."

"I will," she promised before pushing her way out the front door.

Gracie sat quietly in the backseat, absently petting Xena's head and playing a game on her phone.

Sarah opened the door and asked her daughter, "Gonna join me up here, or pretend I'm your chauffeur?"

"Funny, Mom," Gracie said, but switched seats to the front. "Sorry," she mumbled.

"It's okay, we all have bad days."

And they were piling up.

Since arriving in Stewart's Crossing, she couldn't remember a good one.

Not a great start for that new beginning she was hoping to find.

Traffic was practically nonexistent as she pulled from under the awning and into the side street. The fog was thinning a bit, and she caught a glimpse of Jade sitting behind the wheel of her parked Civic as they passed the open gates of the area where the cars that were finished were kept. Sarah waved, but Jade, concentrating on her cell phone, didn't bother looking up.

Some things never change, she thought, starting the drive home. There was still a party to attend tonight, she thought, and inwardly groaned. She had no costume, and unless she wanted to rustle through some of her mother's, and probably grandmother's old trunks in the attic to come up with something, she'd have to attend without so much as a mask.

Which was just fine. As she understood it, costumes were "optional," though it was obvious that Dee Linn was hoping everyone would dress up.

Too bad, she thought, driving past the animal shelter where they'd adopted Xena, then turning up the hill. She'd attend Dee's party, fine, even put up with the insufferable Walter and their friends, along with the rest of the family, but she'd go as herself, the harried, single mother.

And you'll see Clint there.

Perfect, she thought, and held back a long-suffering sigh.

Clint's jaw grew rock-hard as he flipped on the local news. The reporter, a thin woman with a wide smile and impossibly white teeth, was standing on a tree-lined street he recognized and pointing out that there weren't many streetlights in that particular area of town.

". . . though the police aren't confirming, we believe this is the most likely spot where Candice Fowler was abducted."

He listened to the rest of the newscast and the serious discussion between the reporter and anchor on a split screen, in which the reporter hesitated before answering the slick-haired anchor's questions because of a delay in the audio feed. What Clint learned chilled him to the bone. Another girl missing, possibly taken. Worse yet, the anchor mentioned that there were "unconfirmed" reports of two other girls who hadn't come home, though the police and FBI weren't commenting.

He stared at the screen.

What the hell was going on in his sleepy little town?

He thought of Jade, his newfound daughter, and Gracie, the younger one. Were they safe? Probably not. Even Sarah. No one was secure when a freak was loose. He picked up the phone to call Sarah, then thought better of it and decided to visit her face-to-face. Maybe he was overreacting, but he'd rather err on the side of caution in this case.

Tex whined to go outside, so Clint walked through the back door to the porch and, leaning against a post supporting the overhang, peered through the fog in the direction of Blue Peacock Manor as the dog hurried down the steps.

From this vantage point on a clear day in winter, he could look across the sprawling acres of his property, to the forest separating his land from the Stewarts'. After the leaves fell and left the branches bare, he could glimpse the old house with its widow's walk and cupola.

Today, the air was thick and soupy, the low clouds obscuring any visibility. He'd always liked the change of seasons, the different weather patterns that were a part of the gorge, but he was rapidly changing his opinion. He felt a need to see Sarah's house, to catch a peek at a window burning in the night, to know that she and the girls were safe.

Besides that, he rationalized, it was his right.

* * *

All the way home, Sarah's thoughts were jumbled. While Gracie was content to play whatever game had caught her fascination on her iPhone, Sarah drove and considered the fact that the new life she'd envisioned, her fresh start in Stewart's Crossing, was a complete and utter disaster.

Little more than a week ago, she was worried about renovating the old house, about relocating away from Evan and Tolliver Construction, and about settling her girls into a new life here in Stewart's Crossing.

Now, those considerations seemed small. She had Clint to deal with, a man whom she still found attractive, a man she also wanted to keep at arm's length, one who'd lost his son and now realized he had a teenaged daughter. Complicated.

And that wasn't the end of it. Sarah had to somehow deal with the recent soul-jarring discoveries about her family. What she'd thought was her heritage, her beliefs about her ancestral line, had turned out to be false, with possible incest and murder, and maybe suicide, in the mix. This was her family's legacy, if Helen's journal could be believed.

Then there was the fact that her own birth had been deliberately omitted from the family Bible's genealogical records. All her brothers and sisters were listed, so why did the notations stop at her name? Just one more entry? Surely her mother hadn't been that busy. She understood why Roger and Theresa hadn't been listed; they hadn't been Stewarts by blood. Their father was Hugh Anderson. But worse than all of her other worries was the fact that there was a predator on the prowl in Stewart's Crossing. Two girls were confirmed missing, two more feared abducted, and her older half brother was, at the least, a person of interest and, at the most, the primary suspect.

Roger . . . fathered by Hugh Anderson.

She glanced in her rearview mirror and wished she had insisted Jade come straight home. Maybe she was overreacting about the missing girls and being overprotective—well, tough. Despite Hal's unsolicited advice, Sarah had to be the best mother she could be, and if she and Jade ended up on separate psychiatrists' couches one day because of it, so be it.

But she would take her worries down a notch or two. The kid did need her own life. She took the corner into the lane a little too fast and hit the brakes, slowing a little, driving through the mist-shrouded trees and telling herself that things would get better.

They had to.

Got my car back, Jade typed into her phone. **I can come to Vanc. Meet at your place?** She sent the text to Cody and wondered how she'd convince her mother to let her leave. Sarah would have a fit if she thought Jade was going to stay at Cody's apartment, so she had to text some of her other friends in Vancouver to see if she could use them as cover.

It's not like she was going to spend the whole night at Cody's, though that would be cool, but if her mother ever got wind of it, she'd be dead meat, so she needed Brittany to work it out with her mom, who was single too, but whom Sarah had met a couple of times.

She nosed her Honda onto the street and liked the feel of the steering wheel in her hands, and the return of the familiar sense of freedom. She couldn't go back to Blue Peacock Manor, that dreary monstrosity of a house. Not quite yet. In fact, she refused to think of the decrepit place as home. She'd drive around a while, then stop by that diner off the freeway, grab some french fries and a Diet Coke, wait there until she heard from Cody and Brittany, figure out exactly what her next move would be, then head up to the *Psycho* house.

Hopefully, Brittany would text her back quickly. Driving through the center of town, she looked for the road that ran parallel to I-84, but she kept driving in circles. For a small town, Stewart's Crossing was kind of confusing. Hadn't she driven by the feed store and The Cavern twice now? Crap. Still thinking about how she could get together with Cody, she found a map app on her phone and typed in the name of the diner. If it turned out she couldn't stay with Brittany, there was always Plan B, which included sneaking out of the house and just taking off, but she'd rather go the more legit route.

She didn't really want to go as far as sneaking out if she didn't have to. And then there was the new wrinkle in the plan, her new-found father. She didn't know what to think about him. He seemed okay, maybe even could be a little cool, but she didn't like the idea of *another* parent butting into her life right now. As much as she'd wanted to know who her real father was, she didn't need another adult laying down the law. Besides, she had a dad—Noel McAdams, the man who'd adopted her. Oh, crap. Was that even legal? Since Clint Walsh hadn't known about her, hadn't given up his parental rights? She'd read about something like this online, about a celebrity kid whom the mom claimed was the daughter of one dude and it turned out that had been a lie. A big lawsuit had ensued.

Clint had tried to call her, though he hadn't left a message, maybe showing he cared and giving her some space all at once. She hadn't responded. Was still deciding what to do. It was all pretty hard to digest. And the fact that he was into Mom—Jade recognized the signs—that was weird. She supposed it was cool, in a way, but she just wasn't sure. It was all more than she wanted to deal with.

With a voice from the map app guiding her, she was finally able to turn onto the road leading to the diner. She parked outside the long, low building and walked inside to take a corner booth. A waitress with overbleached hair took her order, then left her alone.

And that's when she realized just how lonely she really was. In the brightly lit diner, with the lights gleaming off the harsh white walls and black-and-white tiled floor, she was all by herself in a booth that could easily hold four. There were a few other patrons—an old man in a brimmed hat, eating a piece of pie at the counter, and a woman doing a crossword puzzle while she sipped on a soda and ignored her half-eaten burger.

To top it all off, the music coming through the speakers mounted near the ceiling was some old Beatles tune that Cody loved. He liked everything from rap to country to old stuff from the sixties and seventies. "Eleanor Rigby" was one of his favorites.

The haunting lyrics about isolated people resonated with Jade, touched a deep, unhappy part of her soul. She had two fathers now, neither of whom knew her, an overprotective mother who thought she saw ghosts, a sister who was as weird as all get-out but whom she loved, and a boyfriend she felt was slipping away.

Get over yourself, she thought as the song went on. For the love of God, was this the long version? She didn't need to be reminded that she was by herself.

As the waitress brought her drink, she took a sip and checked her phone. No response from either Brittany or Cody.

"Come on," she said out loud, then shut up. She thought about texting Cody again, but didn't want to be *that* girlfriend, the needy one begging for his attention.

But she was.

Gracie was right. She was obsessed with Cody, and he didn't care for her. Kind of like Gracie's damned ghosts, always just out of reach, real or not. Wasn't that how Cody's love for her was? Didn't she know he was really into Sasha, the college girl who probably even had that damned Beatles song, which, thankfully, finally ended, its last note dragging out.

Her fries came, but she wasn't really hungry and her excitement about getting her car back disintegrated as she stared at her phone and faced the heart-wrenching truth that Cody didn't love her. Probably never had.

Disconsolate, she dragged a french fry through some ranch dressing and took a bite. She had two choices. Either she could run off to Vancouver to have things out with Cody, meanwhile trying to beg a friend to take her in so she could leave this stupid little town, or she could face the fact that her boyfriend was a jerk-face who didn't care enough for her and make it official—break up with him and do what Mom wanted: make a new life for herself here with her oddball family, horrible school, and scary, old, supposedly haunted house.

There were some good things about staying. The girl whose locker was next to hers had been friendly, and that Sam dude in Algebra was really kind of funny, and then there was Liam Longstreet. Although his friend was a total dick, Liam was nice enough, had even offered to help her get a new phone, and he would be around at the house while the renovations were being completed. Except that he was going with Mary-Alice, who was a total nightmare.

Her phone buzzed, indicating a text had come in. She read it quickly, her heart doing a quick little kick at the thought that Cody was answering.

Of course she was disappointed.

Again.

It was Mom. Worried about her as usual.

Home soon? was the text.

She responded. **Ya. On my way.** That was a bit of a lie, but it bought her some time.

"Can I get you anything else?" the waitress asked. Her name tag read "Gloria," and she seemed worried, for some reason, her eyebrows drawn together, her lips turned downward. Not exactly great for business, Jade thought.

"I'm fine," she said, not meaning it.

"Well, thanks, then," Gloria said, and paused as if she were about to add something, then offered an unconvincing smile and headed to the counter, where the man in the hat was starting to put on his jacket.

Jade took another long swallow of soda and looked outside, through the long bank of windows at the parking lot and farther out, to the traffic rushing along the interstate, headlights appearing out of the fog, taillights fading quickly.

Her own reflection was visible, pale and watery, like one of Gracie's damned ghosts. She did look sad. Troubled. Even haunted.

God, this was ridiculous.

She wasn't going to let anyone, including Cody Russell, make her feel miserable.

With a newfound insight, she decided no boy was worth all this misery.

She was done with him.

But she couldn't break up with him in a text. The next time he called, she'd tell him.

And if he didn't phone her?

His loss.

CHAPTER 33

"You have to calm down! Everyone!" Rosalie was shouting again, her voice raw from screaming over the yelling and crying and shrieking that was happening in the nearby stalls. "Shut up! Everyone!"

A break. They actually stopped making noise to listen.

"Look," she said desperately, hands against the wall closest to her. "You have to all pull yourselves together. We don't have a lot of time, and we need to find a way out of here!"

"How?" the girl in the next stall said.

"I'm not sure. But we *have* to figure it out!"

"Again, I said, 'how?' " A little snobby-sounding. Who cared. "Who are you?"

"I'm Rosalie. The one he calls Star."

"I knew it!" the girl next door said harshly. "Rosalie Jamison. I thought you were dead!"

"Is that what everyone thinks?" Rosalie asked, panicked. Had her mother given up on her? Candice, of course, started to wail again.

"Do they think I'm dead too?" Candice cried. "I'm Candice . . . Candice Fowler."

"Not everyone," Princess clarified. "It's just that you've been gone for so long, it seemed likely. At least to me. I don't know what they think about you, Candice."

"I want to go home." Candice was crying again.

"Oh, God! How do you stand that?" Princess said. "Can she please stop whining!"

Never, Rosalie thought, but yelled in the direction of Candice's stall. "Cut that crying shit out. Candice, we don't have a lot of time, so pull yourself together."

The crying was reduced to an irritating sniveling, but at least Rosalie could hear herself think again. More important, she could communicate with the new girls. "Okay, now that we don't have to yell. Who are you?" she asked, throwing the question out to both girls.

The two new girls started talking at once.

"Wait. Hold it. One at a time. You, Princess."

"Don't call me that! It's demeaning," she snapped, and Rosalie wondered if, because of her obviously superior attitude, for once the name was apt. "My name is Mary-Alice Eklund." She paused, as if the name should mean something. When Rosalie didn't respond, Mary-Alice—a little miffed, it seemed—explained that she attended the private, Catholic school in town, that her father was some big deal, and she was tricked into thinking she was meeting her boyfriend when she was taken. She sounded like she was holding herself together, but her words trembled a little. Rosalie could hear she was scared, just not falling apart like Candice. "There was this lady walking a little dog at the school where they attacked me. I hoped she would help, and maybe she did. Maybe she called the police. But I can't be sure. She was there one minute and gone the next. The same with the man in the bleachers. Oh, God, what if they were all part of the plot."

Maybe, Rosalie thought. She knew there was someone in the background, someone pulling the strings.

"Maybe the woman will call the police. Maybe she got the license plate of the car," Candice said. For once she was thinking beyond her own misery. God, was there hope for her?

Mary-Alice continued, "But my mom and dad, they'll find me."

Oh, yeah, how? Rosalie thought, but didn't say it while the second girl, "Whiskey," said that she was Dana Rickert, also a student at Our Lady of the River. Dana's story was a little different; she'd been caught at a shopping mall and had thought it was a random abduction until she was driven to the school and Mary-Alice was captured.

"Did anyone see you being forced into the truck in the parking lot of the mall?" Rosalie said, hoping beyond hope.

"There were some people there," she said, sniffling, as if fighting tears, "but no one close."

"What about security cameras. At the school? They have them, and at the outlet stores?" Rosalie's mind was spinning. There was an outside chance that someone had seen it happening, could ID the kidnappers, and would call the police.

"I think so," Dana said.

Mary-Alice wasn't so confident. "I know at least one of the cameras is broken. That why Liam and I meet there . . . or did." A sadness tinged her voice, but Rosalie ignored it. At least both girls seemed to be willing to do something, and though she heard the terror in their voices, neither had fallen into the same emotional, self-pitying puddle as Candice had.

Rosalie grilled them, trying to think of questions that would help.

Neither girl could identify their abductors. Rosalie had had the most personal contact with the big guy, though Dana, who worked part-time at the local pharmacy, thought she'd seen each of the abductors at one time or another in the store, but she wasn't sure and couldn't name them.

Neither had overheard what the two losers had planned for them, but they'd both known about Rosalie going missing; it had been all over the news. Candice's name hadn't been mentioned, as far as they knew, probably because she'd been captured more recently, and neither girl had caught the news or heard about it on Facebook or Twitter. That bit of information, of course, caused Candice to start sobbing again.

Perfect, Rosalie thought, but didn't reprimand her as she was crying quietly.

As both girls had been forced out of the truck, they'd seen the barn and a lean-to with a car parked in it and a little cabin, but it had been foggy. There had been some fields, maybe, but no animals that they'd seen, and they each said they'd driven through the forests.

"It's in the hills, above the river," Mary-Alice said. "I think we passed that old tavern. The Elbow Room."

Rosalie had missed that when she'd been hauled up here.

"I didn't see it," Dana said, "but I was so freaked."

Mary-Alice hesitated. "Me too, but . . . but my uncle used to go there years ago, when my grandpa was alive. They both worked in the woods, and my mom said they hung out there after work. It's not too far from that old wreck of a house, you know the famous one,

Blue Peacock Manor, or whatever it is. Where that new girl lives." The sneer in her voice returned. "Jade McAdams."

"We're close to her house?" Dana said, and Rosalie was at a bit of a loss. These new girls had lived here most of their lives, it seemed, and that would help. Rosalie was a newcomer, didn't know the old landmarks.

"Yeah. It's around here." Mary-Alice seemed sure.

"How far from town?" Rosalie asked. "Or the tavern, or another farmhouse, or something?"

Neither girl was certain, but their impressions helped. At least they had some idea of where they were and the direction of the nearest road. That was something. For a few seconds Rosalie felt a sliver of hope. Until she reminded herself that the only reason the captives would be allowed to view their surroundings, as well as the faces of their kidnappers, was that this barn was temporary. Either they were going to be taken to another location, probably far away, or they were going to be killed.

An icy dread stole through her, but she tried like hell to keep it at bay. She had to fight whatever sick fate the kidnappers had planned.

Once she'd learned as much as she could, and the girls were starting to repeat themselves or worry aloud, she said, "We have to work fast," and took heart that both Mary-Alice and Dana seemed to have more backbone than Candice. As she had with Candice, Rosalie instructed the new girls to search their stalls inch by inch and look for anything that could be used as a weapon. Surprisingly Mary-Alice came up with the buckets that were used for their toilets and said, "I'll swing mine at his ugly head."

"Me too, but I'm gonna make sure it's full first," Dana added bitterly, clearing her throat. Though she was obviously scared spitless and sniffed back tears, she was willing to get on board with the escape plan. Dana said that she'd been a gymnast until last year, when she'd suffered an ankle injury. Now, she admitted, she'd gained weight and was really out of practice, but she was willing to try scaling the walls. Better yet, Mary-Alice claimed she was a cheerleader, used to doing human pyramids and being thrown into the air to land on her feet and was, she informed Rosalie, in great shape. The snooty girl at least seemed game.

"Then go for it," Rosalie said. "But listen up. I'm not kidding when

I say we're out of time. Don't freak out, but tomorrow night, things are gonna get worse."

"How?" Dana asked, and Rosalie launched into what she'd overheard, leaving out nothing.

"An auction?" Mary-Alice whispered, horrified.

"I'm not sure. But whatever it is, it isn't good."

"Fuckers!" Dana declared over Candice's sniffling.

Mary-Alice's snooty tone disintegrated. "Let's get out of here. Now!"

Finally, Rosalie thought, someone who understood. Felt the urgency. Was willing to help in trying to get free.

Now, maybe, just maybe, they had a real chance to escape.

He drove past the diner, still not believing his good luck.

Twenty minutes earlier, he'd parked in an alley near Hal's Auto Repair. Knowing it was about closing time, he'd decided to wait until the last grease monkey left, and then he'd hop the fence and return the magnetic sign he'd "borrowed" to its rightful place on the Longstreet van. Hal was an old-school businessman, a guy who'd lived and worked in Stewart's Crossing for all of his near-eighty years, a man whose word was as good as his handshake, and a man who had avoided computers and everything he considered high-tech. Including security cameras.

So he'd felt safe in his plan to jump the fence and return the sign.

But, as it had turned out, his course of action had changed the second he'd spied a Honda Civic pull out of the lot with none other than Jade McAdams at the wheel.

He'd fired up his truck and followed her at a safe distance as she'd driven around town to finally land here, at the Columbia Diner, where he'd first met Star and later abducted her. It was amazing, he thought, how easily the girls' new names had stuck. Once he had them rounded up and locked in their stalls, he immediately made the transition, and they'd literally lost their identities, become nothing more than flesh to be traded. He smiled at that, thinking about how much money they would fetch. The bidding, if he played it right, would go well into the tens of thousands for each ripe, young woman. That's why he hadn't touched them himself, hadn't so much as run a finger down their soft cheeks, or stripped off their bras to feel a tit. He didn't want to damage the goods, though he'd love to experience at least one of those tight little pussies around his cock.

Or force one to give him head. That would be nice. A hot wet mouth, slick tongue and . . . shit, he felt his damned body respond to his fantasies, his cock growing rock-hard.

That wouldn't do.

Not yet.

As he watched Jade enter the restaurant, he'd considered going inside himself but hadn't wanted to press his luck. He'd driven to a wide spot in the road and kept his eye on the rearview mirror. The fog made it tricky, but with few vehicles on the road, he could wait, his truck idling.

Now, after smoking two cigarettes, he was getting impatient. What the hell was she doing? He figured Jade's mother wouldn't let her daughter out of her sight for long, so he told himself to be patient. But the fog was getting thicker, and he could no longer distinguish her car from the others in the diner's lot.

That worried him.

He couldn't blow this God-given opportunity.

Reaching for a third smoke, he saw taillights glow red through the growing darkness as a vehicle backed out of a parking slot.

The car turned around, headlights heading his direction, reflecting in the side-view mirror.

He waited to put his truck into drive, not wanting to alert the driver by flashing his tail or backup lights until the car had passed.

But it was a lumbering old Cadillac that drove by slowly, an older man in a hat at the wheel.

Damn. He watched the old guy roll past, red taillights glowing brightly as he stopped to enter the side street leading into town.

"Son of a bitch." He couldn't wait much longer. People were expecting him. If he didn't show, it would raise suspicion, and he couldn't afford that, any more than he could afford not to grab Jade McAdams. He had to remind himself that in about thirty hours his mission would be over, the transaction complete, and he would be gone, away from this small town with its small-minded citizens, away from the claws of Stewart's Crossing. Just the name of the town curdled his stomach. But he wouldn't have to be here long. He had his escape plan plotted, a new ID tucked away, a new life just hours away. He planned to drive into Canada to begin with, using his current ID; then in Vancouver he'd get on a plane bound for Mexico, but he would stop there for only a couple of days, pay a local fisherman to boat him from Cabo to Mazatlan and then fly south to San Paulo. He'd get lost in Brazil, find a small village where, he hoped, he could live like a king.

And never think of Stewart's Fucking Crossing again.

Another glance in the rearview mirror as a set of headlights blazed toward him. "Come on, baby," he whispered, and this time, he got lucky. He recognized Jade's Honda. Ramming his truck into gear as she passed, he left his headlights off and hit the gas. The trouble was that she flew by, doing nearly forty in a twenty-five. What was she thinking? Didn't she notice the damned fog? If she drew a cop's attention for speeding, he'd be shit out of luck.

"Slow down," he warned aloud as he watched her take a corner much too fast. The Civic slid a bit. He hit the gas. Once she'd turned onto a busier street, he switched on his lights and tried to gain on her, but that proved impossible when she barely paused at a stop sign, then hit the gas, shooting across the intersection and forcing him to run the stop. A Volkswagen van nearly clipped the rear end of his truck, but the driver swerved at the last second, honking loudly and, he saw in his rearview, flipping him off.

"Fuck you too!"

What was wrong with her, driving like a maniac?

For a second he thought she'd seen him. That's why she was speeding; she was trying to outrun him. But a moment later he decided that was giving her too much credit.

Nope, she was just a teenager in a hurry.

He had to keep up with her without getting a ticket.

Fortunately, Stewart's Crossing was a small town, and it wasn't three more minutes before he was out of the city limits, the traffic thin as he kept her taillights in his field of vision. He followed her as she drove upward, into the hills, not knowing that she was heading right where he wanted her to go, closer and closer to the spot where he'd hidden the others, a barn that would become her new, temporary home, a place, ironically, very close to the damned Blue Peacock Manor.

Bellisario had gotten hung up at the station.

First, her sister had called with another report on Mom, then the security tape from the mall where Dana Rickert had last been seen had arrived, so she had taken the time to view it. As she watched, she felt sick. Sure enough, two men had approached Dana as she was getting into her car, her hands full of packages; while one had distracted her, the other had urged her forward, no doubt with some kind of small, hidden weapon, probably a pistol or knife, though it wasn't visible on the tape. The men's faces were obscured by the fog, but the camera had caught a clear shot of the vehicle and its Washington license plates. The out-of-state plates weren't a big deal. Every day, thousands of Washington residents drove across the bridges into Oregon, where they worked and/or shopped. Since Washington had a state sales tax and Oregon didn't, shopping centers and malls had sprung up on the south side of the Columbia to lure the out-of-staters and their shopping dollars.

A check with the Washington DMV and Bellisario discovered that the truck captured in the security camera's lens was registered to Evan Tolliver, the same guy whose cell phone was used to text Mary-Alice Eklund.

To top it all off, she'd discovered that Tolliver too was MIA.

His father had filed a Missing Persons report in Vancouver. The Vancouver PD had interviewed him, and he'd said his son had told him he was going to their vacation home in Sun River, Oregon. But according to the management service that maintained the home, he had never arrived. Nor had Evan Tolliver shown up for an appointment with a client who lived in The Dalles.

The other kink in the story was that Tolliver's old man had told the Washington cops who interviewed him that his son had been infatuated with Sarah McAdams, but that the relationship had died before it got started. He'd even speculated that Sarah's departure from Tolliver Construction, and ultimately Vancouver, had been sparked because of Evan's advances. "That boy is like a dog with a bone," the father had said, "won't give something up until he's damned well ready."

"We'll see about that," Bellisario said to herself after she'd talked to the cops who had interviewed the old man. Was Evan Tolliver the abductor? Had he flipped out and started taking girls off the streets of the town where the woman who had rejected him had taken up residence? That didn't make any sense whatsoever, not that people couldn't be strange. The images from the camera weren't clear, but they were being compared to pictures of Evan Tolliver and other known criminals. Bellisario wasn't certain, of course, but the smaller guy looked familiar, a lot like Hardy Jones. She'd already put out a call to bring Jones back in because she wanted to see what he had to say, find out if he knew Tolliver, and rattle his goddamned cage.

Stuffing her arms into the sleeves of her jacket, she marched through the station to the back exit and shouldered open the door. Outside, feeling a sense of urgency, she jogged to her Jeep.

What did Evan Tolliver, a man who'd never been arrested in his life, have to do with the girls who'd disappeared from Stewart's Crossing?

She damned well was going to find out, and she knew where to start—back at Blue Peacock Manor.

The house was cold.

Outside, night threatened, the fog still hanging low.

And something pulled at Sarah's mind, irritating her, something she should now remember. She dropped her keys onto the dining room table, where they clattered onto an open, coffee-ringed copy of the architectural plans for the house; she spent the next five minutes feeding the fire, trying to warm up the first floor. With a poker she prodded the charred logs, exposing glowing embers, then placed a chunk of mossy wood in the firebox. As the coals touched the dry wood, the fire began to crackle hungrily, throwing off the beginnings of heat and casting flickering shadows against the far wall.

What was it?

Rocking back on her heels, she studied the flames, but her thoughts were turned inward. Beyond Clint Walsh and what to do with him, and the continual worry over her daughters, there was something else toying with her, teasing at the corners of her brain.

Try as she might, she couldn't urge whatever it was from its hiding spot.

Straightening, she dropped the poker into its stand, then walked back to the dining room, where Gracie, her iPad at hand, was once again poring over the pages of Helen's journal. The tablet was propped against the family Bible, once again open to the mess that was the Stewart family history.

In her mind's eye Sarah envisioned a skeletal tree with naked branches all tangled and twisted by the intricate lies of generations.

"I just don't get why Grandma left you out," Gracie said.

"Me neither."

"It's as if you don't exist. Me or Jade either."

"I know." No more lying. No more excuses. Maybe Arlene had been busy when Sarah had been born, maybe her hands had been full, but sometime in the last thirty-odd years, she could have taken the time to write down the name and birth date of her daughter and her granddaughters . . . unless . . .

Unless you're not Arlene and Franklin's child.

"No," she said aloud.

"No what?" Gracie asked.

"Nothing," Sarah said, her mind spinning. That wasn't right. She'd been raised by her mother and father, and she looked like her siblings and . . .

And she confused you with Theresa when you visited her, didn't she? What if you've been living a lie all your life, Sarah? What if you're not who you think you are?

"Mom?" Gracie was staring up at her with wide, worried eyes.

"I'm fine, honey. It's all just a little weird."

"I know."

Anxious inside, she tried to concentrate. To calm down, she took the time to reheat a cup of coffee in the microwave and carried it into the dining room, where she promptly left it, untouched, on the table. How could she find out the truth, whatever it was, and really, did she even want to know? She glanced at the house plans, the reason she'd come here in the first place. Of course, there was no answer in the old drawings; there couldn't be. But she shoved her keys away from the scrolls of the plans and flattened the wide pages, her gaze skimming each one, searching for something, but not quite knowing what. Pages were labeled with different dates, showing the additions she'd displayed for her brothers the last time they'd come by. Drawings of roof lines and footings, walls and plumbing lines, rooms and walls, and finally, the last page, a map of the original homestead that included all the surrounding acres, including the legal description and the lot lines denoting ownership.

A creek wandered through the property, and a pond was located on Stewart land, near where it abutted the Walsh property. Somewhere along the line, someone had penciled in the existing buildings and landmarks, including the house, pump house, machine shed, and barns. There were notes elsewhere on the property where an old bunkhouse had once existed, complete with a stable; close to the Walsh property line, near the creek, was the old cemetery.

For the love of God, what was she doing? Searching house plans for a secret to her identity? Frowning, she walked to the window and looked out. Where the hell was Jade? She'd texted half an hour ago. Her teeth on edge, she decided to call. If they were going to make the party, they'd have to get going soon and—

Thud!

The sound echoed in Sarah's ears. Echoed through her heart. She looked upward, to the ceiling; the noise had come from an upper story.

Theresa's room.

Gracie didn't look up.

The dog, lying on the floor at Gracie's feet, didn't so much as move.

"Did you hear that?" Sarah asked, the hairs on the back of her neck prickling. No one else was in the house. At least no one was supposed to be.

Gracie placed a finger on the open page of Helen's journal, marking the place she'd been reading and shook her head. "No."

"Probably nothing," Sarah said, to keep her child calm, though she couldn't imagine how Gracie and the dog hadn't reacted. "But I'll check anyway."

Gracie's attention had already returned to the journal.

Sarah took the stairs two at a time and didn't pause on the second landing. She headed straight to Theresa's room; despite that tinge of trepidation that always touched her when she was near her older sister's part of the house, she flung open the door.

Sure enough, the Madonna statue was on the floor, having somehow fallen off the mantel and rolled to the window, where cold air seeped into the room. "What is this?" Sarah said aloud, and before she picked up the ceramic idol, she did a slow spin around the room. "Are you here?" she demanded in a low voice. "Angelique? We know what happened to you, so please, just . . . go. Cross over. Do whatever you need to find peace."

She sounded like a crazy person, and catching her reflection in the cracked mirror over the fireplace, she thought she looked like one too.

In an instant, she felt the temperature in the room drop.

Sarah froze, and the spit dried in her mouth.

Oh, Jesus . . .

Goose bumps broke out on her flesh. Murmured voices seemed to swirl around her, whispering in quick, short sentences she couldn't understand. No. The sound was just a breeze seeping in through the window that wouldn't close, or rushing past in choppy, noisy gusts from within the chimney's flue.

Right?

It's all in my mind. This is just nuts . . .

The air seemed to swirl around her.

What the hell?

She remembered her mother telling her that she should never enter this room, that it was still Theresa's, and that these things all belonged to her. *Don't you ever go inside, Sarah, don't you touch any of Theresa's belongings. You've done enough damage as it is. I won't have you harming her things.*

What damage?

Why did her mother seem to blame her for something she couldn't remember? Turning, Sarah stared at the statue. What had Mother said recently, when Sarah and her daughters had visited Arlene at Pleasant Pines?

"Don't you know that the Madonna is the key to your salvation? The Holy Mother? She's the key! Are you a heathen?"

It had sounded like incoherent babbling at the time, her mother's dementia and deep faith ruling her tongue, but now the little figurine of Mary was so close, staring at her, smirking at her. The statuette seemed to mock her somehow.

Without another thought, Sarah spun and grabbed the figurine, her finger curling around the cold ceramic as if she were clutching the tiny religious icon for . . . for what? Strength? Guidance? Peace? A renewed faith?

Or answers?

"What is it?" she demanded, talking to the ceramic doll as if it could hear, as if it would actually talk to her. "If you're the key, then . . ." She caught a glimpse of herself again in the mirror, a raving lunatic talking to an inanimate statuette.

"Oh for the love of God!" she cried and hurled the figurine at the mirror, at the lunatic of a woman she'd suddenly become.

Crash!

Reflective glass shattered, cracking into a thousand shards, jagged pieces flying through the air.

Instinctively she turned, arms up, protecting her face and head. Splintered shards rained over her, tiny pieces catching in her hair, slicing her arms, littering onto the floor.

Sarah was shaking, taking in one breath after another, trying to pull herself together. What had she been thinking? What the hell had she done?

The room went eerily quiet, only her own ragged breathing and the frantic beating of her heart disturbing the silence. Slowly she turned, glass clinking as it fell from her shoulders.

There on the mantel, in front of what remained of the mirror, the tiny statue stood.

Sarah's heart nearly stopped. No way could the figurine have survived unmarred, balanced on its base, staring serenely at her, saintly smile in place.

Oh, God. Oh, God. Oh God!

Sarah's heart clutched.

What was this? What *was* this?

The statue should have hit the mirror and shattered, or bounced back onto the floor, gravity pulling it downward to smash against the floorboards, but no, it stood motionless on the mantel.

Swallowing back her terror, her breathing coming in short, sharp breaths, Sarah stumbled back a step. Again, the now-familiar noise, the whispers were hissing and whirling around her. Words barely intelligible . . . "daughter . . . baby . . . mama . . . no . . . no! . . . father . . . don't . . . kill."

"Who are you?" she whispered, her heart thudding, the room feeling as if it were closing in on her. Cold. Tight. The atmosphere thick. "What do you want from me?" Her breath fogged as she started to back up toward the door, her shoe crunching on the glass, her gaze fixed on that small painted figurine.

"I'm not leaving," she whispered, while inside she wanted to run like hell. "We're staying." She sounded like a fool! "So . . . so you can damned well deal with it."

At that moment the statuette seemed to shiver, teetering a bit on the edge of the mantel, then jerkily tumbled, end over end, almost in slow motion, and hit the floor with the same loud thud she'd heard earlier.

Sarah gasped, watching as it rolled to a stop. *Craaack.* With a sound as dry as a demon's hiss, the ceramic Madonna slowly split apart, separating into perfect halves.

Terror sizzled down Sarah's spine as the front side of the little woman rolled away from the back piece, turning over and over, crunching over glass to end faceup, eyes open wide, peaceful expression intact, not one chip evident.

Sarah backed away. This wasn't happening. It couldn't be. This was all part of a weird dream, a strange hallucination. It had to be.

Her gaze swept to the back half of the figurine, which hadn't rolled at all, but had landed, painted side down, near the window. Cavity exposed, that perfect half of the Virgin's replica lay motionless.

Within the hollow figurine, nestled upon a bed of cotton batting, rested an ancient-looking key. Tarnished, obviously crafted in an earlier century, the key glinted even though the light in the room was faint.

In an instant, Sarah remembered the keys glinting as they'd swung from Jade's fingers, the image that had bothered her.

Heart pounding, perspiration suddenly beading over her face, she forced herself not to flee down the stairs, grab her kid, and jump into her SUV to drive as far away as was possible. Instead, she inched closer to the broken statuette.

Nothing happened.

No angry, shrieking apparition sprang up at her.

Her throat as dry as sand, she plucked the key from its nest and quickly stepped backward toward the door.

Heavy and inscribed, and icy to the touch, the key was one she'd never seen before. Squinting, she made out the tiny names etched into the metal:

Matthew, Mark, Luke, and John.

The first books in the New Testament.

With her next breath, Sarah knew which door this key would open.

She stood in silence, terrified to the very pit of her soul.

CHAPTER 34

Driving home, with the radio blasting a tortured love song by Adele, Jade thought for a second about Cody, then reminded herself how over it was. She should be concentrating on Liam Longstreet. He'd been nice to her even as she'd been nasty to him. True, he kept lousy company with Miles Prentice and Mary-Alice Eklund, but maybe she could trust him . . . even that Sam in Algebra. Whereas Liam was serious, Sam could be funny, in a geeky kind of way.

So what?

Right now both of them beat Cody Russell hands down.

She squinted and turned on her brights. Didn't help. The fog was getting soupy, but she wasn't far from home. She only hoped she would recognize the turnoff.

She had to be close. Yeah, she thought she'd passed the mailbox for the Walsh property that their mom had pointed out when they'd first arrived. It seemed like a lifetime ago, now that she knew Clint Walsh was her father. She still wasn't sure how she felt about that. "Conflicted" seemed to be the word of the day when it came to warring emotions, so, yeah, conflicted would work. She certainly wasn't doing handsprings over the knowledge, but she didn't hate the idea. Yet. Time would tell how he dealt, or didn't deal, with her.

She'd have some say in the matter because it wasn't like she was a kid, for crying out loud. And Walsh better respect her relationship with her adoptive dad. If he didn't? Too bad. For a large part of her life Noel McAdams had been the only father she'd ever known. She was pretty sure he would be cool with the fact that she now knew her biological father, or at least be able to deal with it. After all, he had bailed on the family, hadn't he? Even if Mom, with all her craziness, had driven him away, he hadn't bartered for his children to come and live with him.

It said a lot.

So now, everything depended on Walsh, whether he was big enough to accept the fact that Jade had another father who, if not bound by blood, was by years. Glancing at her rearview, she noticed a set of headlights approaching fast, like the glowing eyes of some big beast appearing out of the mist.

Her cell phone chirped, indicating a text had come in, and she was distracted, her attention drawn to the cup holder in her car's console, where the phone was resting.

Without a thought, she caught a glimpse of the screen and noted that Cody had texted her. The heat of satisfaction stole through her heart.

"About time," she said, reminding herself that she was over him. She peered through the windshield, searching for the entrance to the lane. Wasn't it around here? Slowing a bit, she searched the area with her eyes, but her mind was half on Cody's text. What had he written? Was he sorry? Or was it worse? Maybe *he* wanted to break up with her.

Her fingers itched to grab the phone.

He doesn't love you, he doesn't. It's over!

Determined not to think about him, she forced her fingers to curl over the steering wheel as she tried to find the turnoff. *He's not worth it, Jade. You know it. Really, you've always known it. That's why you've been so insecure.* Setting her jaw, she tried like crazy not to pick up the phone, but she just couldn't help herself as her curiosity got the better of her. She reached for it, clicking on the text, and—

Bam!

The whole car shook.

Her phone flew out of her hand and hit the windshield.

Her body started forward, stopped only by the sudden hard jerk of her seat belt.

What the hell?

Automatically, she hit the brakes and glanced into her rearview, where those massive headlights loomed. The idiot behind her had rear-ended her! "Son of a bitch," she said, shaken and instantly furious. Cody was forgotten. Swearing, she managed to get the car under control and ease it to the side of the road, her tires sliding a little in the gravel. For the love of God, the Honda hadn't been out of the shop for *an hour* and now . . . now it was *wrecked,* compliments of this stupid driver!

What kind of idiot follows so closely in the fog?

She glanced at the vehicle that was pulling over, fog surrounding the large truck. At least the guy behind the wheel of the pickup had the decency to pull over behind her, but it was small comfort.

This was not what she needed right now! He'd probably ruined her bumper! Maybe popped the damned trunk and creased the entire back of her car. Asshole!

Flinging open her door, she was ready to read the jerk the riot act. He climbed out of the cab of the truck, his face still obscured in the night. "Are you blind, or something?" Jade demanded. "Didn't you see that I was slowing down?"

He didn't answer, just walked to the front of the rig, its engine thrumming, smoky tendrils of fog wisping over the headlights.

"Did you hear me?" She began closing the gap between them before her white-hot anger started to shred a bit and she felt the first tremor of fear. Hadn't her mother mentioned several ways human predators caught their prey? One was the lost-puppy scam, another asking for directions they didn't need, a third intentionally rear-ending a victim to get her to leave her car. And now there were girls missing in Stewart's Crossing.

She slowed. "You . . . you've got insurance?" she asked and wished to high heaven that she'd brought her cell with her. "What is this?"

"The best day of your life." And then he raised his hand, and she saw the gun, a sleek pistol, backlit by his headlights.

Oh, shit! No way was she going to let this happen. She turned on her heel and scrambled for her car, where the door was still open, the interior light blazing, a warning bell rhythmically beating.

She'd taken one step when he attacked, his heavy body colliding with hers, the two of them landing facedown on the pavement. Her chin hit the asphalt first and split, blood pouring from the wound. Still, she squirmed and wriggled, fighting him, trying to buck him off, but his weight pinned her against the pavement, and he didn't bother intimidating her with his gun, just pulled one arm behind her back, then the other, and cuffed her wrists.

She screamed, as loud as she could while kicking and fighting. But he jerked her to her feet and pressed his pistol against her temple. "Let's go," he said, and still she fought, letting out a shriek that she hoped someone would hear.

"You little bitch." He jerked her toward the car, and she kicked, landing the toe of her boot hard against his shin. With a wrench of her arm, he dropped her to her knees and leveled the gun at her temple.

"You won't kill me," she said with false bravado.

"You're right." His eyes gleamed through the fog. "But I'll hurt you, Jade," he said with a heart-stopping depravity she believed, pulling her face close to his, so close that his nose nearly touched hers. "And I'll hurt you in ways that you'll carry with you to the grave," he promised.

Before she could respond, he whipped out a gag, tied the rubberized piece of cloth so tightly over her mouth that she nearly threw up. Then he picked her up as easily as if she weighed nothing, and slammed her into the backseat of his truck.

A few seconds later, he was behind the wheel, pressing down on the accelerator. The truck peeled out, spraying gravel as he passed her disabled car and sped into the coming night.

"Let's go!" Sarah said as she flew down the stairs. She found Gracie in the living room, phone to her ear; Xena was resting on an open sleeping bag near the fire.

"Go where?" Gracie asked, but Sarah was too freaked out to explain. Had she really been in the presence of a ghost or some kind of unseen being who could move figurines and cause the temperature in the room to suddenly go cold?

"Out." Sarah grabbed her kid's arm and tugged, pulling Gracie to her feet. "Bring the phone."

"Mom! Stop! You're acting crazy!" Gracie declared. "Scottie, I'll call you back," she said into the phone as Sarah, her breathing still coming in short bursts, tried to calm herself. As Gracie pocketed her phone and her fear lessened, Sarah said, "I think . . . I think . . . oh, God, it's impossible . . . to explain."

"Try." Gracie was immobile, gazing at Sarah hard as she picked up on her panic. Then, "You saw her, didn't you? Angelique?"

"No, no, I didn't see anything." And that stopped her short. While Gracie "saw" the ghost of Angelique Le Duc, Sarah had not. And the ghost she had seen when she was young wasn't the same woman Gracie had shown her in the pictures. She glanced anxiously at the stairs. "Didn't you hear the mirror crash?" Oh, God, had she imagined it all? But, no, she was holding the key, the cold metal still clutched in her hand.

"I heard something," Gracie said slowly, "but I was talking to Scottie, and I thought you knocked over a vase or something."

"It was a little more than a vase," Sarah said, looking around for the dog, panic still swelling inside her. "Xena! Come!"

"Wait, Mom," Gracie pleaded. They were standing between the pillars guarding the living room. "Are you scared?"

"Petrified! Come on." Tugging on her daughter's arm, she started for the kitchen.

"She's not going to hurt you." Gracie was keeping up with her but wasn't moving as fast as she needed to.

"Angelique?" Sarah asked with a gasp, the sense of urgency to get away from the house overwhelming. "How do you know?"

"That's not how it works," she said simply, as if everyone understood the rules that governed relations between this world and the next.

"So, now you know how the ghost thing works? After I found you shivering on the stairs the other night?"

"I didn't get it then," Gracie said.

"But you do now? Well, I don't." They reached the kitchen, and Sarah quickly searched through the drawers for a flashlight, patting her pocket to make certain she had her phone, wishing for the first time in her life that she owned a gun. She settled for a jackknife that was in the same drawer where she finally found a flashlight.

"If she was going to hurt us, wouldn't she have done it by now? We've been living here for long enough that if she wanted to levitate a knife and slit our throats, or electrocute us while we were showering, or put some of that old rat poison in our drinks, she would have, don't you think?"

"Knives? Rat poison? Electrocution?" Sarah shook her head and took a deep breath. Seeing how her own panic could infect her child, she tried like hell to be rational. "I don't really know how it works, but see this?" She held up the key. "It was hidden in a statue upstairs, the little Madonna . . . And somehow that inanimate figurine just, all by itself, mind you, hurtled off the mantel and split open. Perfectly. Down the middle, as if sliced by an unseen . . ." Oh, sweet Jesus, she sounded like a raving madwoman. "Come on." She headed out of the kitchen.

"She wanted you to find it!" Gracie said, following Sarah down the hallway to the foyer. "Don't you see?"

No, Sarah didn't see. She didn't see at all.

"So what's it open?" Gracie asked. "The key."

"My guess?" Sarah said, her pulse still throbbing in her temples. "Angelique Le Duc's tomb."

Gracie nearly gasped. "You're kidding."

"Nope."

"How do you know?"

"I don't know."

"But you're going to try to open it? Now?"

"I'm sure going to try," Sarah stated tautly.

"Really?" There was awe in her tone as Gracie moved past Sarah and shot out the front door ahead of her. Sarah second-guessed the wisdom of engaging Gracie in her mad need to open the vault, but she damned well wasn't going to leave her daughter alone in the house with the angry, statuette-tipping specter.

"He's here!" Rosalie announced, as she heard the whine of the truck's engine fast approaching. Never before had he returned only a few hours after leaving. But that was probably because they were getting ready for tomorrow night. "Shhh. No one say anything. Don't let him know we've got a plan."

So far, they didn't have much of one. Mary-Alice had made a half-hearted attempt to climb the stall walls, but she, like Rosalie, had crumpled the frame of the cot with her efforts and hadn't been able to reach the top. Dana hadn't fared any better. Rosalie had heard her trying to leap upward, only to land hard and swear loudly. And Candice . . . well, nothing had changed there.

Rosalie figured they had a chance of beating one of the abductors, maybe both, by their sheer numbers. One girl could distract while another attacked. If they got the chance. If they were *all* free. If the fuckers who held them didn't have weapons.

All pretty big ifs.

Mary-Alice had found a horseshoe nail in her stall, while Dana had come up with nothing. However, they had to escape before the other man, or men, showed up for whatever meeting it was that the abductor had planned. In her mind's eye, Rosalie saw a huge orgy where the men, drunk or hyped on drugs, took turns raping the girls. Her insides shriveled, but she wouldn't go there, wouldn't let her imagination run wild.

There would be time enough for that later.

For now, just as it had been from the minute he'd locked her inside his truck when she'd stupidly been walking home that night, her mission was to escape and, while she was at it, do as much damage as possible to the son of a bitch who'd tricked her. If she could, for once, get the upper hand.

The engine died, and the girls went silent.

Seconds later the big man arrived, the door flying open, light flooding the area, making Rosalie squint against the flash of brilliance.

Please fuck up. Just once, fuck up, Rosalie thought, clenching the clippers.

"Okay, that's enough!" he said, his breathing heavy, his tread shuffling as if he were struggling. The lights snapped on. "You get in here."

He had another one!

Rosalie heard the girl trying to scream through her gag, and from the sounds of his movements, she was struggling, fighting him, dragging her feet.

That was good. Now, if she was smart and figured out that the rest of them were in nearby stalls, she might come up with a way to let them out. "Hey!" Rosalie called. "What's going on?"

As if on cue, Candice let out a broken sob.

"You got another girl?" Rosalie baited.

"Shut the fuck up, Star!"

"My name's Rosalie!"

"No more. *Ooof!*" More struggling. "You little bitch!" *Slap!* The sound of flesh meeting flesh ricocheted through the barn, and the girl let out a muted shriek of rage. "Quit your fighting, Rebel," he said. "Or you'll get no food or water or pail. You can go hungry and thirsty and defecate all over yourself for all I care!"

More muffled shrieking.

Smack!

God, he was hitting her. Unfazed about leaving a mark. Never before had he seemed so angry, so out of control, at least not since Rosalie's last thwarted attempt at escape.

"You see that, do ya, Rebel?" he yelled. "No, I'm not talkin' about my cock, you little whore, but this belt. I'll use it on you, I will. Ask Star; she knows all about it."

Some other girl gasped, Dana maybe, and Candice crumpled completely; soft sobs emanated from her stall.

The new girl shut up, which was probably smart, but Rosalie hated that she'd given up so quickly. True, the bastard who was holding them had all the power, but Rosalie would have liked to have heard a little more fight from their new cell mate. In order for any plan to work, they had to be strong, united, and willing to do whatever it took to break free.

Familiar noises came from the stall, the addition of a pail and water bottles.

Finally, things went quiet, and Rosalie imagined the bastard squaring off with his new victim. Tense seconds passed, and she heard a bat fly overhead. Next door Mary-Alice shrieked, and then the barn went silent again.

He must have removed the new girl's gag, because suddenly the barn was filled with a new voice. "What the hell do you think you're doing?" she yelled. "You fucker! Let me go!"

Thud!

A stall door slammed shut, and with the click of a lock, the newest victim was bolted inside.

"You can't do this!" she screamed, and sounds of her throwing herself at the door echoed through the barn.

He wasted no time and snapped off the lights before slamming the door. With a click, the lock was latched. "You damned freaking fuck! Let me out!" the new girl screamed at the top of her lungs. "You can't do this!" She was beating on the door as if she thought she could break it down with her fists.

The truck's engine sparked to life, rumbling loudly.

"No!" she cried, but the sound of the engine was already fading as he drove off. "Oh, God, no . . ."

"Hey!" Rosalie said.

"What?" the new girl said, sounding startled.

"There are four of us locked in here besides you."

"What is this? What the hell's going on?"

Of course she was confused. She'd just suffered the trauma of her capture and then what sounded like a beating. "I'm Rosalie Jamison, the one he called Star."

"Oh God, I was afraid of this. I just didn't want to believe it," she said.

"Believe it."

"Who else?"

Rosalie said, "Candice, they call her 'Lucky'."

"Candice . . . wait, 'they'?" the new girl said.

"There's more than one guy." Rosalie explained about Scraggly Hair, then introduced Dana as Whiskey. "Finally there's Mary-Alice. She's Princess."

She moaned, "Jesus, this is worse than I thought."

"Jade," the snooty girl said as if the word tasted bad.

"Mary-A," Jade's voice was dismal.

"Hold it," Rosalie barked, sensing a fight. "I don't know what's going on with the two of you, if you know each other or not, but we really don't have time for any petty girl-bitch shit."

The two stopped talking to each other, thank God. Rosalie then laid out everything to Jade, the entire, dire situation, including telling her about the meeting planned for the next night and what her fears were about the future. "These bastards aren't screwing around," she said, "So our best bet is to get out of here before the rest of the posse of perverts shows up."

No one said a word for a few seconds, and the bat took another turn around the rafters.

"Okay," Jade said. "How?"

"First of all, look for anything on you, or in that stall, that will help.

We need weapons. You can't see anything now, I know, but the second it starts to get light, or if he comes back and turns on the lights, look around, see what you can find, and get ready to use it."

"How can you be so calm?" she asked.

Rosalie wasn't calm, not inside. She was scared and angry and a whole shitload of emotions that just wouldn't help the situation. "I don't know about you, but I don't like being called by a horse's name, and I don't like some freak kidnapping me and selling me off to a prostitution ring or whatever, so I'm going to try to get the hell out of here any way I can."

Jade said with hard resolve, "I'm in."

CHAPTER 35

Sarah jogged down the path leading to the cemetery. With Gracie beside her, the dog somewhere in the nearby fields, she followed the weak, bobbing light from her flashlight. Night was falling rapidly, and the beam did little to pierce the surrounding umbra.

Years before, she'd followed this same path. First sneaking out of the house, then running across the fields, her heart light, her feet swift, moonlight her guide as she ran to meet Clint near the pond.

Oh, how long ago that seemed. A summer of hot days and passionate nights, of sunlight, and swimming and sex.

Now, instead of anticipation, she felt a burgeoning sense of dread steal over her. Rather than turn to the right, to circumvent the pond, she took a hard left, veering toward the graveyard she'd explored as a child and mostly avoided during her teen years, when she'd started to understand the malevolency of the undead, a notion fostered by her brothers, who gleefully told her ghost stories and scared the crap out of her. Of course, those tales had been silly attempts to scare her, and her brothers' imaginations, though vivid, could conjure nothing that compared to the nightmare she was now living, whatever the hell it was.

As they topped a small hill, the cemetery loomed before them, grave markers seeming to rise out of the surrounding mist, brambles growing over the decrepit, broken fence that had once surrounded the plot. Angelique Le Duc's tomb was taller than all the surrounding headstones.

"Wow," Gracie said, in awe.

Sarah found the gate that had tumbled into the enclosure, where grave markers poked through the tall grass and weeds.

She didn't wait, but cut across the graveyard to the vault built squarely in the center of the cemetery. A large marble edifice engraved with angels and scriptures, it had once been surrounded by a rose garden, but now, when she passed the beam from her flashlight over them, the plants that remained were leggy and leafless, winter-dead.

Making her way to the front of the tomb, Sarah shined her light over the doorway and beneath the carved angels, where a bit of scripture from the book of Matthew had been etched into the stone.

She moved to one side and swept the beam over the long, south-facing exterior wall. where a line of scripture attributed to the Gospel of Mark had been carved.

"What're you doing?" Gracie asked as the dog bounded over the fence and began sniffing the headstone. "Let's go inside."

"We will." *Or I will,* she amended as she wasn't certain she'd let Gracie step inside the tomb if she were able to open it. Not until she'd viewed it first.

She walked around to the rear of the vault to view another piece of scripture, this one from Saint Luke, and then finally, on the last wall, a verse from the Gospel of John.

A tingle of dread slid down her spine.

What was it Mother had said? That Theresa was safe with Matthew and John, and then, at another time, she'd mentioned her oldest daughter was safe with Luke? Dee Linn had even joked about Mark, wondering where he was.

"Right here," Sarah whispered and wondered about what she would find inside. A dusty, empty vault? Or the final resting place of the sister she'd never met?

Sarah's heart beat faster. Was it possible? Would she find Theresa in this very tomb? No . . . If Mother had known where she was, she wouldn't have been so haunted, so hopeful that Theresa would return. But that cryptic bit of conversation that she and her siblings had considered just a part of her mother's dementia . . . what did it mean?

A gust of wind blew by, chasing the fog, chilling the air.

She rounded the final corner that led to the front of the vault and again ran the beam of her light over the angels carved above the door. The cherubic faces were marred, streaks of dirt running down their cheeks like black tears.

"Okay, let's do this, but, Gracie, I'm going first. If I get in there and it's safe, you can come on down the steps." She slid a glance at her daughter. "I don't know what I'll find, if there are bodies down there . . ."

"I can handle it, Mom. What else would you expect to find in a grave?"

God only knows, Sarah thought, training the light with one hand and sliding the key into the lock. "I'll be right back."

To hell with the party. Clint didn't give a damn about Dee Linn or Walter Bigelow and the event he'd planned to attend. His reason for saying yes to the invitation was because he'd known Sarah would be there and he wanted to see her again. Of course, he'd told himself it was just to break the ice because they were neighbors and he'd be inspecting the work on her house and . . . well, it had all been bullshit. He strode to his truck and, because Tex was putting up a fuss about leaving, whistled and opened the driver's side. The black-and-white dog was a streak as he leaped inside, as always, thrilled to be a part of any adventure, even if it was running to the store for a box of batteries. Every trip was an occasion to stand with his legs on the armrest and put his nose to the wind when Clint cracked his window, which he did before he fired up the Beast and took off. He didn't know how he'd explain his presence to Sarah, and didn't really care.

He was a part of her family, whether she liked it or not, and after a day of coming to terms with the fact that he was Jade's father, he'd decided to quit acting like a fool and take command of the situation, not just with the lawyer but with actions. They were neighbors, for God's sake. They could make this work.

There were rough times ahead, he saw that, but if he'd learned anything in the past few years, it was that life was short and a person had to do what he wanted to do or lose the opportunity. Sarah had taken the bull by the horns and come home to Stewart's Crossing, even taking up residence in that old wreck of a house she'd sworn she hated. Well, hell, if she could fight her fears and inner demons, so could he. The plain, hard fact of the matter was that he'd turned his back on Sarah years ago because she was a complicated woman, different and intriguing, a woman to whom he knew he could lose his heart and soul. Loving her wasn't easy then, and it sure as hell wouldn't be easy now.

Love?

He glanced into the rearview mirror to look himself in the eye.

Slow down, pardner. It's far too soon to be thinking in those terms.

Yeah, well, what the hell good would waiting do? He knew it half a lifetime ago, and he knew it now: Sarah Stewart McAdams was the single most fascinating woman he'd ever met.

At the county road, he eased off the gas until the Beast nearly stopped; then, seeing there was no traffic, he cranked the wheel and took off again. He wanted to see Sarah and Jade and even little Gracie right now. Ridiculous? Probably. But now that he'd made up his mind to work things out with Sarah, he couldn't wait.

A sense of urgency that was way out of proportion to the moment overtook him, though he couldn't say why.

He rounded the final corner, looking for the lane leading to Blue Peacock Manor, when he saw headlights aimed at him. Easing off the throttle, waiting for the car to pass before he crossed in front of it, he squinted through the fog and sensed that something was off about the vehicle. It wasn't completely on the road, and the driver's side door was open.

Frowning, he slowed down. It looked like someone had slid off the road in the fog or had suffered a flat, but whoever it was hadn't had the sense to close the door. He rolled past the entrance to Sarah's house and drove the extra hundred yards. To the car. The import seemed almost abandoned—though, in the fog, who knew? He nosed up to it, hit his emergency flashers, and cut the engine.

"Stay," he told a whining Tex. It was too dangerous with the low visibility for the dog to be out of the truck.

He climbed out, his boots hitting the gravel on the side of the road, while a bad vibe stole over him. The car, interior light glowing, was empty, the engine running. "Hey!" he called out. "Need any help?" Only silence reached his ears. "Hello?" he tried again, turning slowly and squinting, eyes searching the surrounding forest on Sarah's side of the road and, on the other, a wide field. Walking around the car, he saw that the back bumper had been bashed in, hard enough to crease the trunk, but no one was around. He thought he'd call it in himself when he noticed that the license plates were from Washington.

Sarah drove an Explorer, so this wasn't hers, but . . .

For a second the world seemed to stop. Hadn't Jade said something about her car, a Honda, being in the shop? The breath stopped in his lungs. Dread spiked through his blood. For a second he flashed on the accident scene where his son had lost his life. A mangled car. His wife at the wheel . . . But this was different. What the hell had happened here? The car was still running, so Jade hadn't just left it by the side of the road and walked home. He checked inside it. Sure enough, her phone was on the floor in front of the passenger seat, her bag next to it. He looked for her wallet and found it. Cash and a credit card, her Washington driver's license . . . all left in the car.

His heart dropped.

No woman left her purse unattended.

No teenager was ever without her phone.

Oh, sweet Jesus.

A dark thought started deep in the back of his mind. He'd read about intentional accidents, in which the criminal rammed into the back of a vehicle in order to force the victim from the car and—

He saw the blood. Deep red, a small pool near the side of the road, at the edge of the asphalt. *God, please, don't let it be Jade's,* he thought frantically, knowing his prayer was for naught. This was Jade's car, and no doubt the pooling red stain on the dark asphalt was her blood.

Yanking the phone from his pocket, he intended to call Sarah . . . maybe Jade was only hurt, taken to a hospital. If not, he'd dial the police. He hadn't gained a daughter just to lose her again.

He started to punch out Sarah's number when he heard the thrum of a car's engine rounding the corner; a second later, blue and red lights strobed the night.

Somehow, the police had arrived.

He only hoped they weren't too late.

Bellisario slammed on her brakes. What the hell was this? An accident? Cars at the side of the road, headlights on, doors open, one man leaning against the fender of a Honda. "Look, I gotta go," she said into her headset. "Got a situation, but run Hardy Jones in. If that isn't his ugly mug on the shot of Dana Rickert being abducted, I don't know what is."

"Got it," Mendoza said. "And while I'm at it, I'm gonna ask him about his association with our friend, Josh Dodds, now that we've got him in for his cache of illegal weapons. The FBI is leaning on him, and it looks like he might know more about these missing girls than we thought."

"Seriously?" The guy by the Honda was now running at her car, waving his arms.

"That's what he's saying. But he wants a lawyer; wants to strike a deal. If Dodds is involved, we'll have leverage, play one against the other."

"Where does Roger Anderson figure into this?"

"That's what I aim to find out."

"See if Jones and Dodds will roll on Anderson. He must be the guy in the security cam shot with Hardy. About the right size." But something was off about it, something not quite right. There was something about the second man in the picture that didn't fit. "Accident here. Send backup to the curve just before Rocky Point, about a mile south of The Elbow Room, close to the turnoff to Blue Peacock Manor. In this soup, we need traffic control at the least and probably more."

"You got it."

He hung up as Bellisario pulled onto the shoulder, parked, and drew her sidearm from its holster. "Stand back!" she ordered, opening her car door. "Hands over your head." She didn't like anyone running at her.

The guy raised his hands over his head. "You have to help," he said. "I'm Clint Walsh, and I've discovered my daughter's car, but she's not inside." He stood in the middle of the road, and as Bellisario approached, she saw that his features were drawn, worry in his eyes. He looked familiar, but she didn't know him.

"What happened?"

"I was driving to my neighbor's house to see my daughter."

"She was visiting?"

"She lives there," he said. "My daughter is Jade McAdams, this is her car, and I found it just as you see it. Empty. Her purse, ID, and cell phone are inside. There's blood on the pavement." A muscle worked in his jaw. "We need to contact Sarah Stewart, her mother, see if Jade's at the house and just left her car out here," he said, but Bellisario, her weapon trained on him, knew he didn't believe it for a second.

"I think my daughter's been kidnapped," he added. "We have to find her. Now!"

Jade was scared and pissed and couldn't believe she was caught with these other girls, locked in a stall in a darkened, smelly barn so that, according to the Rosalie chick, these dirtbags could auction them off. For what? Prostitution, Rosalie had guessed, but Jade refused to think that would happen.

If any one of them touched her, she'd kill them first.

She rubbed her arms. The drafty barn wasn't insulated, cold fog seemed to seep through the wooden walls, so old the knot holes had fallen away, allowing more frigid air inside.

Rosalie had mentioned finding a weapon, and in the time that the lights had been turned on, Jade had seen something—a horseshoe, she thought—mounted over the inside of the door, high over her head but, she hoped, reachable.

It wasn't much, but damn it, it was something. And if she could bash the creep who'd hauled her in here over the head, she'd do it in a heartbeat. She'd watched a lot of crime shows, and she knew how to kill a person, in theory. Go for the throat, bite out the fucker's Adam's apple, shove his nose up into his brain with the flat of her hand, go for the eyes and the balls.

She'd try them all.

Rosalie's plan was simple, to try and get the drop on whoever showed up next. Lure the guy into the stall, then escape and lock him in his own prison. After which, the freed prisoner would unlock all the other cages and the girls would either take the vehicle parked outside, or run through the woods to freedom.

Simple.

Neat.

And it most likely wouldn't work.

She rubbed her cheek where the loser had slapped her. Twice. She bet, if she had a mirror and could see her face, she'd see a welt there.

"I think I know where we are," Jade ventured after listening to all their stories and piecing the information together.

"Where?" Mary-Alice asked, and Jade's stomach turned. Of all the people she hated to be caught with, it was supercilious, self-righteous Mary-A. *She's a victim too. Your ally.* It ground Jade's guts to think so. But, fine.

"I think we're on our property."

" 'Our' property?" Dana said.

"My mom's or my family's." She remembered looking over the maps and plot plans that Mom had scattered over the table when Jade's uncles had come over. At the time, Jade had only been concerned with leaving the damned Blue Peacock or having Cody visit her, and she'd been looking for spots where she could sneak off and meet him. "If I'm right, this place is an old stable that's near a bunkhouse on the east end of the property. The house isn't that far away. It's west, along the river."

"Isn't that all kind of, I don't know, convenient?" Mary-Alice wasn't buying it. "To be on the same land as the Blue Pigeon or whatever you call it."

Jade didn't bother correcting her. Who cared? Rosalie was right. Whether she liked it or not, Mary-Alice was on their side. *Strength in numbers. Remember: the more of you there are, the better the odds of getting free.* "It seems like a coincidence, but maybe it's not. Maybe these guys are connected to Blue Peacock Manor."

"How?" Mary-Alice again.

"I don't know." She thought about her family tree, how recently it had changed. If the long-dead girl Helen could be believed, then Angelique had borne a child with her stepson, who had eventually killed her. But there was also that business with Theresa and Roger, two people who were related to Jade on her mother's side, but who weren't Stewarts. And what about herself? The girl who'd had an unnamed biological father for most of her life? "Look, I'm telling you, that I think this is my mom's place, and if we get out of here—"

"When we get out of here," Rosalie corrected.

"When we get out of here, we need to go west to the house. It's the closest place."

"Then that's the plan," Rosalie said. "It's dark, and we split up, run in the direction the river flows."

"How—how will we know?" Candice asked.

"You need to run so that your right shoulder is facing the river, then you'll be heading west, toward the house," Jade said, and didn't add that the place was supposed to be haunted. Whether the spirits in the house were real or all in her mother's and Gracie's imagination, they still had to be a hell of a lot better to deal with than the flesh-and-blood lowlifes willing to sell them to the highest bidder.

Would the door really open? Hardly daring to breathe, Sarah twisted the long key.

It didn't move.

She tried again.

Nothing.

No latch clicking, no locks tumbling, just sheer, utter silence.

"Doesn't look good," she confided to her daughter.

Gracie was deflated. "If it isn't for this, what's it for?"

Good question, Sarah thought, as she knew of no other places on the property that were old enough to require this key to open them. She'd looked through every room in the house, including the basement and attic. There were no other obvious locked rooms.

It didn't make sense. Well, really, nothing did. *Not when ghosts chase you out of your own home, for crying out loud.*

"Where's the dog?"

"Around." Gracie swiveled her head and whistled, but Xena didn't come bounding from the shadows.

"Hold this." After handing the flashlight to her daughter, Sarah tried the key once more, putting a little more pressure on the shaft and—

Click!

The key suddenly turned in her hand as if greased. She held her breath. With a bit of a shove, the door creaked as it swung inward.

Her heart thudded with dread. *Showtime,* she thought, as the fog moved in closer, seeming to encase the tomb where Angelique Le Duc was to have been laid to rest, had her life and death gone according to plan.

But whose ever did?

She took her flashlight back and shined its skinny little beam inside and down a short flight of stone steps leading deeper into the darkened vault.

"Stay here," she told Gracie again. "I mean, right here." She pointed to the ground in front of the tomb. "And keep Xena with you."

"Mom, I'll be okay. Just because you're freaked out and—"

"The dog. Right here. Right now. With you." Sarah brooked no argument, and Gracie got the hint.

"Fine." She whistled softly, and a few seconds later the big, blond dog appeared, springing from the darkness to sit, her whole back end wiggling. "Stay." Xena whined, but Gracie was firm. "Lie down." Xena didn't. The dog's response to commands was limited, but Sarah was as satisfied that Grace was safe with her mutt.

Drawing a steadying breath, she held the flashlight in a death grip and started down the stairs.

Her throat tight, the muscles in her neck so tense they ached, every horror film she'd ever watched running through her brain, she followed the flashlight's pale beam ever downward. *This is certifiable, Sarah. As crazy as anything you've ever done. Shattering mirrors, being terrorized by a miniature statue, and now exploring a tomb in the dark.*

She reached the final step. The air was thin and dry, and the scent of dust and an odor she didn't want to name hit her nostrils.

Eerily quiet, the tomb was larger than she expected, seemingly separate from the rest of the world.

"Gracie?" she called over her shoulder, her voice echoing.

"Right here, Mom."

Good.

Slowly, nerves as tight as bowstrings, she swept the weakening beam across the floor. Heart racing, ready to bolt, she tried to convince herself there was no one in the vault, no one but her and her own pounding pulse.

She was wrong.

A skeleton lay stretched upon a slab—a woman, she guessed, from its small size and the rotting nightgown and dark clumps of hair. "Oh, dear God." The corpse had been here a while—teeth long and visible, hollow eye sockets, bony hands devoid of flesh folded over her empty chest.

Sarah felt woozy, as if she might faint.

After all these years, the mystery was solved. Sarah was certain she'd found her sister.

But Theresa wasn't alone.

CHAPTER 36

"Dear God," Sarah said, her heart nearly stopping, her skin suddenly clammy, the sturdy walls of the shadowy vault seeming to draw in on her. Hands quivering, she shined her flashlight to a corner of the tomb, where the yellowish beam slid over the body of another person, a man, she guessed, as she backed up a step. Dressed in clothing from another era, in shirt and pants that were disintegrating, he was propped into a corner, his ghoulish face devoid of flesh, the bones white, his mouth set into what appeared to be a grotesque grin. Several teeth were missing, and above the empty eye socket was a huge gash where his skull had cracked, a deep fissure in the bone that had splintered away from the gaping hole.

This man had been murdered long ago, his skull bashed in by something hard and sharp and . . .

She swallowed, her heart pounding in her ears. Gooseflesh raised on her skin. This man had to be Maxim Stewart, the first owner of this property, the cuckolded husband of Angelique Le Duc. "Father in heaven," Sarah whispered, thinking of Helen's account of the night that Maxim, Angelique, and George went missing. In a vision of stunning clarity, Sarah saw a bloody axe, wielded high over Angelique's head as they struggled on the widow's walk.

Was Maxim already dead, his body hidden in the vault meant for his wife? Had his own son murdered him in a jealous rage over the woman in their fatal threesome? Had George, after sealing his dead or dying father in the vault, carried his bloody weapon of death across the fields to the house, taking the very trail that Sarah herself had used again and again when she'd met Clint on the sly, and just now as she'd jogged here to enter this tomb?

On the floor, visible beneath what was left of the man, was a dark stain where, she surmised his blood had pooled as he'd bled out, his heart still pumping after he'd been locked here.

She imagined the night of terror so many years ago, and then she took another look at Theresa, if that's who she really was. How had she died? Had she died in here, resting as if she were in a coffin, her hands folded meekly over her chest?

Sarah stared at the remains of what once had been a vibrant body. Someone knew Theresa was here.

Someone had carried her into this vault and locked the door behind her, then hid the key in the little Madonna statue.

Who? Why?

Outside, Gracie stood on one foot and then the other. It pissed her off that Mom wouldn't let her go into the vault. After all, it was her idea to explore the cemetery, and she could deal with ghosts better than her mother.

If anything proved it, Sarah's reaction to seeing the ghost of Angelique Le Duc in Theresa's room tonight did.

It wasn't fair, she thought, wrapping her arms around herself. She noticed that Xena was going a little nuts, whining and pointing, ears and tail raised, as if she wanted to chase after a possum or raccoon or, worse, maybe a skunk. Gracie was in no mood to get sprayed, and it was kind of freaking her out, the way Xena stared into the darkness, her skin quivering anxiously, her high-pitched whimpers creeping through the night.

"Hush!" Gracie ordered. Then, "Okay. Fine. Show me." Using the flashlight app on her phone, she lit the area around her feet and walked a little farther into the darkness, away from the tomb. She only hoped that whatever had caught the dog's attention wasn't a predator ready to leap out at them. Cougars and coyotes lived in the surrounding woods. Gracie felt a little tremor of fear but ignored it. Graveyards didn't scare her; cemeteries didn't freak her out.

But still . . . she didn't like the way Xena was going mad, shooting forward in the dark, being swallowed by the fog, her bark sharp and piercing. *Don't let every creepy ghost story you ever heard get the better of you.*

Where the hell had the dog gone?

Walking carefully, she shined the light over the uneven ground, where long grass and molehills were visible. *This is ridiculous. There's nothing out here.* But she was nervous as she moved past a small headstone covered in vines, the ancient grave of a long-buried child.

Gracie's heart twisted a bit as she looked around. All these dead people. Related to her, buried beneath her feet.

Where was the dog?

She turned in the direction of the barking, but didn't see Xena in the fog and twilight. "Come on, girl," she said, trying to ignore the weird feeling that prickled her spine as she shined her light on the ground, illuminating the uneven turf of long grass and weeds, mole-hills and ferns. "What is it?" she said as the dog stopped barking suddenly. "Xena—?"

A low growl sounded.

Her dog?

Or?

Unnerved, Gracie turned, searching the mist, the flashlight's beam providing weak illumination. She was still near enough to the tomb to call her mother if there was any problem and—

Another growl came just as the light caught a glimmer, a glint of something metallic. A watch? Out here? She leaned forward, and her insides turned to ice. The watch was strapped to the wrist of an un-moving hand, big fingers spread wide.

What!

Heart galloping, she ran the light up the attached arm, over a shoulder, and across a jacketed chest stained dark. "Oh, God," she said, stumbling backward, as the beam crept up the man's neck to land full on the bluish, very dead, face of Evan Tolliver.

Oh, God, oh, God, oh God.

Terror riddled her body, and she willed her legs to move when she heard a deep, warning growl and turned to spy Xena, the fur on the back of the dog's neck raised, her head low, her eyes focused not on the dead man, but on Gracie herself. No, that wasn't quite right. Xena was looking past her, as if she saw something over Gracie's shoulder, as if—

In a heartbeat, big hands grabbed her and yanked her from her feet.

She screamed!

"Don't!" a deep male voice warned, his breath hot and foul against her ear. "Don't make a sound." Arms as strong as steel bands surrounded her, hauling her, kicking and shrieking, away from the dead body.

"Shh!" he warned. "I'll protect you. I'll keep you safe. I promise."

Like hell! She kicked him hard. Her heel slammed into his shin, but he only sucked in his breath through his teeth.

In her peripheral vision she saw Xena, bunching to spring.

The dog launched just as Gracie screamed again at the top of her lungs.

As the back of Sarah's foot hit the lowest step, a bloodcurdling shriek echoed through the tomb, reverberating in its terror.

Gracie!

Sarah ran up the uneven steps, yelling back, "Gracie!"

Thud!

The door to the vault was slammed shut.

No!

Sarah threw herself against the old wooden panels, screaming, pushing hard, trying to get out, to reach her child.

The damned door wouldn't budge.

She dropped her flashlight, tried again, shouting and shoving, pounding on the rough wood with her fists. "Gracie!" she yelled. "Grace!"

The door didn't budge.

She tried again, throwing all her weight against the door just as she heard the familiar and final sound of a lock being turned.

"I'm telling you, Jade's my daughter," Clint insisted, frustrated and worried sick, feeling the seconds of his life ticking by. "Maybe she's at the house. Got rear-ended and walked home."

"But the car's still running," Bellisario said, eyeing him as if he were stark, raving mad at the very least, some kind of criminal at the worst. "She could have just driven."

"Let's call Sarah." He pulled out his phone when a terrified scream rippled over the surrounding fields.

Whipping around instinctively, he faced the direction of the sound, west toward the Stewart family's holdings; the old house was nearly a quarter mile downriver from this point.

The shriek came again. A female scream filled with terror.

"I don't know," Bellisario said. She stared in the direction of the house, one hand on her pistol, her gaze searching the gloomy landscape. "I don't like it."

He was already sprinting for his truck and wasn't about to wait for a response. Someone, a woman, needed help. Dread propelled him, and if the cop wasn't ready to investigate, too damned bad.

He jumped into the cab, and Tex, sensing his anxiety, moved quickly to the passenger seat. "Hey! Hold up!" the cop called after him, but he ignored her, slammed his door shut and took off with a chirp of tires. He'd already explained everything he could about Jade and her car, and the fact that he'd just learned he was her father. Now Bellisario could deal with it. In his rearview, he caught sight of the detective talking rapidly into her phone as she dashed to her car.

Rolling his window down, squinting into the coming dark, he listened for another scream but heard only the distant wail of sirens. Hand tight over the steering wheel, he prayed they were cops heading this way, responding to Bellisario's request for backup.

He took the corner into the lane for Blue Peacock Manor a little too fast, and the empty back end of his truck slid a bit. "Get down!" he ordered the dog as he eased off the throttle. Tex hopped to the floor in front of the passenger seat just as the wheels found purchase again and Clint hit the gas.

What the hell was happening?

His heart was racing, his mind spinning.

It looked like Jade was already in serious danger.

Was she the one who was screaming? Or had the shriek come from Sarah or Gracie?

"Son of a bitch," he ground out as his truck bounced and shimmied down the lane, mist swirling in the headlight's beams, a startled deer bounding into the woods.

The sirens drew closer.

"Just get here!" he shouted, as if the damned police could hear. He was clutching the wheel in a death grip, his knuckles showing white, every muscle in his body clenched. He tried like hell to be rational, to think, but the sound of that horrified scream tumbled through his mind, while the image of Jade's abandoned car, door open, burned through his soul.

The stands of pine and fir parted as he rounded a final curve, then drove across the clearing where the old house stood. On this gloomy afternoon, with twilight fast approaching, the once-grand manor looked evil and stark, its cupola and roof shrouded in the mist.

He slammed on the brakes and slid to a stop near the front yard. No more screaming. Just silence, and that somehow was worse. Sarah's Explorer was parked in its usual spot, no other vehicle was around. Good or bad? A few dim lights glowed from the windows of the first floor. "Be home," he whispered, throwing himself out of the cab. "Be home."

He raced up the walk and porch steps to the front door. It hung open a bit, not quite latched, as if someone had been in a hurry to get out. "Sarah!" he yelled at the top of his lungs as he barreled into the foyer. "Jade!" He stalked through the rooms, his boots ringing on the floorboards, his fear mounting as he searched.

A fire burned in the hearth, a coffee cup was left on the dining room table with Sarah's keys. He touched the cup—still warm—then spied her purse on a nearby chair. He found a kid's backpack left on the pile of sleeping bags in the living room. "Sarah!" he yelled again, his voice thundering.

No answer.

But he didn't stop looking. Up the first flight he ran, opening doors, calling their names. "Sarah! Jade! Gracie!" Empty rooms greeted him, silent chambers devoid of furniture, of life.

For the love of God, where were they?

And where the hell was the damned dog?

Leaving closet doors open, he dialed Sarah on his cell and ran upward again, phone to his ear, boots thudding on the steps.

The phone started to ring, then stopped, suddenly going dead.

Call fail flashed on the screen.

"Shit!"

He reached the third floor and, breathing hard, stalked through each room, still yelling their names, dread mounting. In a blur, he checked the suite where her parents had slept, the huge closet and two baths, then ended up at the corner room with the fireplace, the missing older sister's room. Its door hung open, and as he looked inside he saw evidence of some kind of a struggle. A new fear shot through his blood as he surveyed the scene. Hundreds of pieces of glass glittered on the floor, the mirror that had been mounted over the fireplace now showing only the backing, a few clinging shards looking like reflective teeth dangling over a yawning hole. Near the hearth, half of a little statue of the Virgin Mary lay, face turned upward, its serene expression at odds with the mayhem in this room.

What in God's name had happened here?

Broken glass, he told himself. No blood. And, of course, no one.

Where the hell were they?

Jaw clenched, he dialed Sarah again. Waited.

Call failed.

"Damn it all to hell!"

Where were the cops?

He backed out of the empty room and twisted open the last door on this level, the one that led to the attic. He didn't think twice, just pulled it open and ran up the narrow, dark staircase. "Jade!" he called, his voice echoing. "Sarah!"

Bats, disturbed as they roosted, flapped and squeaked. Heart in his throat, he shined the light from his cell phone over the interior of the garret. Beneath the sharp gables and rafters he saw only decades of discarded furniture and boxes, crates and baskets, dust-covered, long-forgotten treasures of another generation.

No one was here, nor, he supposed, were they on the roof overhead, but he climbed those spiraling stairs anyway and forced open the door of the glass cupola to step onto the widow's walk. He'd

been here before, of course, with Sarah. She'd showed him all the
nooks and crannies of the old house, excluding the basement, and
they'd even made love on this rooftop, though that night, he remembered now, she'd shivered in his arms, her naked body respon-
sive but colder than usual, her eyes never closing when he'd kissed
her, as if something were troubling her, something, when he'd
asked, she'd been unable or unwilling to name.

Now he hurried across the tiles and peered past the chimneys,
hearing the river, far below, rush through the gorge.

He tried to call from here, but, as it had before, the cell went dead
in his hands.

Yelling again, his voice smothered by the rush of the river, the
sirens finally sounding closer, he felt a dark, mind-numbing fear.
They were gone. The house was empty. Just as he feared it would be.
A kaleidoscope of images spun through his mind in horrifying detail.
Don't go there. Do not go there! Find them, Walsh. Just find them.

Hands gripping the short rail, he leaned forward, searching the
coming night. From this point he had a three-hundred-and-sixty-degree
view, acres upon acres of the surrounding property, if the fog would
rise faster, if the night weren't approaching.

Where are you? He thought, just as he caught a glimpse of red
and blue lights blinking through the thinning mist.

The cops.

Too little, too late, he thought, but started back down to the first
floor, trying to piece together what had happened here, forcing himself not to panic.

He knew that Sarah had been here and very recently.

The fire in the living room grate was bright, some of the logs
barely burned.

Her vehicle was parked near the garage. No other car or truck had
been driven out of the lane in the past fifteen minutes or he would
have seen its lights, heard its engine.

No, she was here, he sensed.

The basement.

Quickly, he rounded the staircase to the doorway to the basement
stairs and flung open the door. Down a rickety staircase he raced, land-

ing in a vast underground storage space where artifacts from another lifetime had been stacked. He scanned the shelves, a milk-separating station, a clothesline from ages before, everything gathering dust.

Nothing that would help him locate his family.

No one hiding in the shadows.

A complete bust.

They weren't here. Just as he'd feared. Boots pounding a quick, desperate tattoo, he ran back up to the first floor and beelined for the open front door.

How long had it been since he'd heard that soul-rending scream?

Five minutes?

Ten?

Too damned many.

Hitting redial again, he leaped down the porch steps, only to stop short when he heard the sharp but distant sound of staccato barking. The dog was going out of its mind, sending up an alarm.

Breathing hard, Clint sensed the frantic barking was coming from the direction of the pond, on that piece of property that butted up to the fence line. For the love of Christ, what were they doing out there?

He ran to his truck, threw open the door, grabbed a flashlight he kept in the glove box, and whistled to his dog. "Come, Tex!" he commanded just as Bellisario's Jeep roared through the trees.

He didn't wait.

Tex sprang from the truck, and Clint, already running in the direction of the other dog's barks, commanded, "Sic 'em!"

Her phone died in her hand. Again. Clint was trying to reach her, and each time his number showed on her cell's screen, it faded out completely. "Come on, come on," Sarah sobbed, pounding on the door, her skin seeming to shrink over her muscles whenever she thought about being locked in this vault with two long-dead bodies. "Gracie!" she cried, her fists raw from beating on the old panels, her shoulder aching from trying to wedge the damned door open. "Gracie! Open this door!"

Fear jetted through her bloodstream. What had happened? Why had Gracie screamed? Oh, dear God, had the twisted pervert who'd kidnapped those other girls somehow find Gracie? Was that possible? "Gracie!" she screamed frantically, beating wildly on the old wood.

Muted sounds reached her ears. The dog barking, a siren screaming, but not a sound from her daughter.

Please, please, please, God, if you're listening, keep her safe.

"Gracie!"

"Walsh! Stop!"

Bellisario's voice chased after him.

"Stand down!"

To hell with her. He was running for all he was worth, his feet traveling the familiar path of his youth, fear propelling him. God, why
hadn't he brought his rifle?

Hopefully the police were at his heels, weapons drawn, but he
couldn't count on them now, as he was in the lead, sprinting through
dry grass and brush, catching a glimpse of the dark water of the
pond. Footsteps pounded behind him: the cops.

He'd lost sight of Tex, but heard the other dog barking like he'd
treed a bear. The sound wasn't coming from the pond, no . . . he
veered to the left as he realized the dog was farther toward the river
and . . . Oh, Jesus! The old cemetery? The place where he and the
Stewart boys had shot BB guns? What the devil was the dog doing
there? Breathing hard, at the top of the rise where the graveyard appeared, he saw what was left of the Stewart family plot: graying headstones listing badly, others completely tumbled over. He leaped over
the fence and headed toward the center, to the single tomb in the
enclosure, pointing the flashlight at the old vault with its weird carvings.

The dog had something or someone cornered. Snarling and snapping, Xena pinned a dark, writhing figure against the front of the
vault.

He forced his beam onto the odd-shaped figure.

A tall man was holding a twisting, frantic Gracie McAdams hard
against his chest, his face screened by her wildly moving head, as if
he were using her smaller body as a human shield.

"Help!" Gracie cried, terrified. "Help!"

"Put her down!" Clint ordered. The bastard blinked rapidly against
the harsh illumination of Clint's flashlight, but didn't release her.

In a heartbeat, Clint recognized the man and his insides turned to
water.

"Police! Let her go!" Bellisario's voice ordered from somewhere behind Clint, just as Clint sprang forward. "Walsh! Stand the hell down!"

From the corner of his eye, Clint caught sight of the detective, weapon drawn, advancing upon the abductor and his squirming, frightened captive.

"Police!" Bellisario snapped loudly. "Roger Anderson, release the girl and put your hands in the air."

CHAPTER 37

The door opened suddenly, a rush of fresh air racing into the vault. "Sarah!" Clint's voice called anxiously.

She stumbled upward, over the tomb's threshold, to fall into his waiting arms, tumbling with him to the ground in front of the vault. "Thank God, you're safe!" he said, and his voice cracked a little. He kissed her forehead, and she was surrounded by the smell and feel of him, warm and safe, but she pulled back.

"Gracie?"

"Safe. Here," he told her.

Her insides melted, and tears raced down her cheeks as her youngest daughter came rushing to them, and Sarah, still in Clint's embrace, held her daughter close. "Thank God, you're safe," she said, sniffing. "I was trapped. The door . . ." And then she noticed the crowd that had gathered, three men and Bellisario and—

"He did it!" Gracie said, pointing to a tall man standing near one of the officers. A beard covered the lower half of his face, his hands were cuffed behind his back, and his eyes, when he stared back at her, flared with recognition.

"Roger," she whispered. Mixed emotions clogged her throat as she stared into the sharp-featured face of her half brother, Roger Anderson. "What . . . ?" She clutched her daughter tight to her and felt something in her mind start to click, the tumblers of an old, broken lock falling suddenly into place.

She remembered being with him on the roof as a storm raged. He was holding her close, his body against her wet, shivering skin. "I'll keep you safe," he vowed, water dripping from his face onto her naked flesh as rain lashed the cupola and slickened the roof tiles. Gently, he carried her into the little glass room at the top of the winding stairs.

Her heart had been beating painfully, shame and disgust roiling inside her as she looked over his shoulder and through the rain-drizzled glass to the widow's walk, where another man stood. Her queasy stomach released, and she threw up over Roger's shoulder at the sight of her father, rain darkening the sagging shoulders of his jacket, his belt undone.

"Daddy?" she whispered, remembering him taking her to the rooftop, holding her close, sliding the buttons of her nightgown through the little slits of buttonholes. "I love you, Sarah girl," he'd said, lifting the hem of her gown and pulling the wet fabric over her head. "I just want to touch you a little, honey, because I love you so, so much." His breathing had been shallow and swift, and she'd tried to pull away. "This will be our secret. Our place." And then a big, rough hand had slid down her shoulder to graze her flat, undeveloped breasts.

"Oh, God," she whispered now, her stomach quivering, even though Clint's arms were surrounding her and she was holding her own daughter. Wrenching free of them both, she leaned forward, hands on the ground, and vomited, her body heaving violently. Disgrace and shame swallowed her, and, as if her father were still looming over her, still threatening to violate her, she whispered, "Don't. Don't you ever touch me again!" Her body convulsed once more, and she spit, blinking, coming back to the moment, realizing where she was again: in the cemetery with Clint and Gracie and . . .

Roger. Staring up at him, the memory fresh and clear, she forced herself to her feet.

"Okay, Anderson," Bellisario said, "Let's go."

"No—It's not . . . he didn't . . ." She pulled herself together with an effort, realizing that Roger was in custody, that the police thought he was behind the recent attacks . . . "No, wait. You're arresting him?" she asked Bellisario, feeling Clint tense beside her and Gracie once again slip under her arms. "No . . . he didn't . . ." She could barely draw a breath when she finally blurted out, "Theresa, my sister. She's down there," and weakly motioned to the vault. "I mean, her body."

Gracie looked up at her. "Really?"

"Roger," Sarah said to her brother, "you put her there? You knew?"

He frowned, but some of the tension left his shoulders, and he nodded. The cop beside him was staring at him as if he expected the ex-con to flee. "I failed her." Roger's voice was raw, filled with emotion, his face twisted in guilt. "I failed my sister."

Sarah tried to understand. He seemed to have shrunk two inches with the admission. "How?" she asked.

"This man was trying to abduct your daughter," Bellisario said.

"No," Sarah and Roger said at the same time.

Then Roger said to Sarah, "It was your father. He . . . he and Theresa. He wouldn't leave her alone. Oh, Jesus! I should have done something."

The cops and Clint and Gracie all were silent, listening as his face hardened in hate for the man who had sired Sarah.

Shaken, Sarah had to be certain she understood. "My father killed Theresa?" The thought was a cold stake in her heart.

"It was his fault. Because of what he did to her, because . . . because after the baby was born Theresa was never the same. Because of him, she died."

"Because of him?" she repeated, trepidation taking hold of her, a piece of his story not fitting. Clint's arms tightened over her shoulders, and a cold wind blew from the east, racing through the gorge, chasing away the fog.

"Let's go." Bellisario had heard enough.

"No, wait!" Sarah insisted, holding her brother's gaze. "How did she die?"

"By ending it," he said simply, his Adam's apple working. "She took her own life. To end the torment. By him. She hung herself in the guesthouse."

Sarah felt as if she'd lived her life on quicksand, the truth and lies always shifting, never really knowing from one moment to the next what was the solid truth and what was a dark, guarded secret.

"I found her and cut her down." His expression was tortured, filled with the regret of a lifetime. "I, um, I cleaned up the mess. It was all I could do and then . . . and then I brought her here, so she could rest in peace."

There was a frightening thread of truth here running through the fabric of lies that had been her life, or what she'd thought was her life. "And you didn't tell Mother?"

"I didn't have to. She knew." He said it with conviction, and Sarah remembered the anguished wails that had risen up the stairs as Roger had carried her down from the attic. All too vividly she recalled their white-faced, stricken mother and how she had crumpled in the hallway. "Bastard! No, no, no!" she'd cried, her fingers laced over the small statue of the Madonna as she'd pounded the floor. The little serene statue hadn't shattered, had remained intact as even Arlene had cracked, weeping and swearing, tears raining from her eyes. "I'm so sorry," she'd said to Sarah, but hadn't offered to hold her, had clutched the figurine, Theresa's little statue, as if the last bits of her sanity had depended upon it. Roger said, "Mother took care of the problem."

Sarah's chest squeezed tight. Memories flooded through her. The pieces of her life tumbling together rapidly as a cold, Canadian wind blew fast and hard to the west, chasing away the fog, Sarah Stewart McAdams saw the pictures of her past come into focus. "The baby . . . it was the problem?" she asked, but knew the answer before it passed his lips.

"No, Sarah, the baby was you."

She stumbled back, wanting to deny it, but she remembered her mother's reaction at the retirement home when Mrs. Malone had introduced Sarah to her mother, reminding the older woman of a simple truth, but Arlene wasn't about to be fooled. "My daughter is Theresa," Arlene had sworn, mistaking Sarah for the woman Sarah had believed was her older half sister. Now, if what Roger was saying were true, that simple fact too was a lie, a secret Arlene had hidden for more than thirty years.

"Theresa was my mother." Sarah said the words, hardly believing them, but realizing how many questions they answered.

Roger didn't have to respond.

"And my father . . . ?" she whispered, but in a heart-stopping instant, she understood that sickening truth as well. It was all so clear now: Sarah was the child of the man she had always known to be her father, Franklin Stewart, but her mother was Theresa. Arlene had raised Sarah as her own child, somehow making the family and friends believe she'd been pregnant, perhaps becoming a recluse, who knew? Then, years later, when the same perverted man who had sired her had been sick enough to try it again, to intimately touch and sexually caress his own flesh and blood, Roger had intervened. Her breathing was shallow, her pulse uneven, her stomach filled with acid and hate.

"Sarah," Clint said, his voice a rough whisper as he wrapped his arms around her again. "Sweetheart, it's okay . . ."

"No!" she cried. "It is not okay."

To Roger, she said, "How did Mother think she fixed things? By adopting me? But there's more, isn't there? You said 'she took care of the problem'," Sarah repeated, taking a step closer to her criminal of a half brother to stare him in the eyes. "What did you mean?"

"That she killed him, Sarah."

For a second no one said a word.

"Explain that." This time it was Clint.

"My mother killed her husbands." Roger's words were without inflection. "Both of them. First my father, so she could marry Franklin, and when she couldn't take any more of Franklin's incest, when she saw that he would never change, she began poisoning him, as she had my father, watching him die, inch by inch, day by day."

"And you know this how?" Bellisario demanded.

"I bought the rat poison for her. Not for my father, of course, I didn't really understand at the time what she'd done. But when she asked me to pick it up at the feed store, I did, then I knew that it was for Franklin, and I just let her." He looked off into the distance, his expression blank. "It was justice. For Theresa."

"Sarah, I've heard a lot of bullshit stories from cons," Bellisario began.

"No." Sarah cut her off. She was remembering her mother's satisfaction when she'd nearly drunk the fly in her milk, so many years ago, and then recently, she'd been accused of lacing a diabetic man's drink with sugar at the retirement home. "I believe him." Sarah's mother was really her grandmother, a murderess, her father a sexual predator who'd raped her older sister and nearly done the same to her.

"This is some tale you're telling," Bellisario said, unconvinced, as she motioned for the deputy to start hauling Roger away. "Why the hell were you here with the kid?"

"I told you," Roger said, "I was saving her."

"From what? Or whom?" Sarah demanded, then scanned the stern faces of everyone who had collected in the old graveyard near the open door of Angelique Le Duc's tomb. A new fear struck her. Why were they all here? How did they all know to come and save her when they should be out searching for the madman who was stealing girls from the streets of Stewart's Crossing?

No!

"Where is she?" she demanded, turning to Cliff, her worst fears congealing when she read the pain in his eyes. "Oh . . . God! Where's Jade?"

Bellisario glared across the interrogation table at Roger Anderson. Pale, with light eyes, unkempt beard, and a high forehead, he sat in clothes that hadn't seen the inside of a washing machine in a month. His legs were shackled, and his cuffed hands were clasped atop the table as if he were about to pray. Overhead, the fluorescents were harsh, giving him a sickly, beleaguered appearance.

"Let's start over," she suggested, as they'd been at the interrogation for nearly an hour and she wasn't buying his story. "Where's Jade McAdams?"

"I'm telling you, I don't know. Ask Hardy Jones."

"We have. He says he doesn't know anything."

"He's lying."

"That's what he says about you," Bellisario said, knowing that the interview was being watched through the "mirror" on the wall, as well as every word and nuance videotaped.

"I was there to save them."

"Sarah and her daughters? The way you saved Rosalie Jamison?"

"I don't know her."

"What about Candice Fowler?"

"I told you—no."

He was calm. Too calm. "I failed with Sarah," he said for the fourth time, "but I wanted to help her girls. Make certain they were safe."

"But Franklin Stewart is long dead. Your mother took care of that, according to you."

"True."

"Why did you think the McAdams girls were in danger?"

"They always are," he said simply, and Bellisario fought back a desire to throttle the man with his cryptic answers. It had all been so bizarre, almost surreal. Finding Anderson at the tomb had been the first surprise; the second was Sarah McAdams and the dead bodies inside. Anderson swore he didn't know who the skeleton of the man was, though Sarah McAdams was certain the corpse was Maxim Stewart, the first of the line and the man who'd built Blue Peacock Manor for his wife Angelique Le Duc, a woman who had apparently cheated on him with his son, her stepson. Anderson had admitted to locking Sarah in the vault, to "keep her safe," that he was planning to find a way to put her and her daughters somewhere outside the kidnapper's range, but Sarah had found the key to the vault and he'd seen her leave the house—he'd been watching it ever since they'd returned—and he'd followed her to the cemetery. In his deluded mind, he thought that the vault had become a safe house of opportunity. Which was all a little too convenient, another part of the Stewart family mess, in Bellisario's opinion.

The kicker was that the other corpse, that of a woman, was supposedly Theresa Anderson, Roger's full sister, who was pushed over the edge of sanity when she was raped by her father. All of that was conjecture at this point, but time would tell. Anderson also swore he'd stayed under the radar and away from his parole officer because he'd sensed, from Hardy Jones, that something was up as Jones, after drinking too much at The Cavern after his shift, had bragged to Roger that he was in for a major score. Though Hardy had played coy and hadn't said exactly what the scam was that he was running, he had mentioned how valuable "girls" were, how men would pay big money for them, use them as slaves or whores or even wives, if the situation were right. Anderson had gone on alert, knowing that Sarah and her girls were moving to Stewart's Crossing. He vowed to himself to protect them because of his broken promise to Theresa to keep Sarah, her baby, safe all those years ago. He included Sarah's children, Theresa's grandchildren, as well. He'd been living in the woods since their return to Stewart's Crossing, moving his camp every few nights, staying close

Bellisario had trouble believing the story Anderson was peddling, but there was a ring of truth in there somewhere, she just wasn't sure what was fact and what was fiction. The trouble was, if Roger Anderson wasn't in cahoots with Hardy Jones, then who the hell was?

Things were unraveling fast.

Sweating, he parked in an empty lot near the center of town. He knew he had to keep calm, force a smooth exterior, not alert anyone around him about his secret life.

He'd heard that Dodds was in lockup and Hardy Jones was already at the station house, being interrogated. Both men knew the drill, if they stuck to the plan. Dodds was solid, Hardy Jones a bit of a wild card. He rued bringing Jones to his first serious meeting with the "mountain men," as they called themselves, a handful of rogues who lived in Idaho, lived by their own rules, and defied the government. Their homes were fortresses, complete with underground shelters, stashes of food, water, and weapons, and booby traps if a trespasser, the "enemy," should ever dare step onto their properties.

They liked their women strong, beautiful, maybe a little sassy, but in the end, obedient to their "husbands."

Fortunately, they were willing to pay. Munitions sales were lucrative, and they weren't afraid to pay a high price for the right "wives," as they called them, married by their own ministers, in their own small fundamentalist sect.

The deal was dangerous, but oh so lucrative.

So he had to play it cool for a few more hours.

He made one quick call, heard it ring, then a distinctive click as the phone on the other end was connected. Before the mountain man could utter a word, he said, "We're moving the operation up. Twenty-four hours. Midnight tonight. There won't be seven girls, only five, but we have to move them. Now."

There was hesitation on the other end, and he wanted to scream at the man, *It's now or never, cocksucker,* but apparently the guy understood. "All right, then. We'll be there," he said with finality.

"With the cash," he reminded his client.

"Of course," the man responded, then hung up.

He let out his breath, lit a cigarette, rolled down his window, and drove through town to a house on a high point above the city where Dr. Bigelow and his wife lived. As if thumbing its nose at the little town below with its rustic, Western decor, this home was sleek and modern, with walls of glass and an "open-concept interior," which seemed to be all the rage these days. Built on one level, it boasted commanding views of the river and the Washington shore, as upscale a Stewart's Crossing address as one could pay for. Dr. Bigelow and his gossip of a wife and all their damned money, a lot of it inherited . . . such a fucking travesty.

From the number of vehicles lining the winding driveway and parked on the street, the party looked to be in full swing.

Good. He hadn't worn a costume, wanted everyone at the party to see that he was there, in attendance, though it wouldn't matter in twenty-four hours. But for now, he needed a little breathing room, a bit of an alibi that would at least pass at a cursory level. Also, he wanted to be certain that the dirt from his operation was sloughed onto someone the police would more likely suspect; then he'd be on his way.

Tossing his half-smoked filter tip through the window, he grabbed a bottle of Merlot from the front seat and walked up a slate walkway to the huge glass door. He rapped lightly on the panels, and Dee Linn, herself, dressed as Marie Antoinette, a white wig piled high, answered. "Oh, dear," she said, deflated. "Another one in street clothes. I suppose you didn't get the memo that this was to be a costume party."

"Sorry," he said and handed her the bottle of wine. "Been busy."

"Hmmm." She eyed the label, one eyebrow rising. "Nice. Thank you."

Walter Bigelow, DDS, deigned to join his wife at the door. Despite "the memo," he was dressed in the uniform he wore at the office: scrubs, lab coat, and superior expression. "Glad you could come. Your mother and sister are already here. You know how Marge is. Always punctual."

"That she is," he agreed, holding up his hand, spying Joseph, in jeans and an open-collared shirt, drink in hand, surveying a table laden with appetizers and decorated with pumpkins, black cats, and a witch's hat. The caterers were in the kitchen, all dressed in white shirts, black slacks, and long, orange aprons. He mingled with those dressed in street clothes, along with three women who were supposed to be kittens, a witch or two, a husband and wife who were ancient Egyptians, Rambo, and Indiana Jones.

He refused to look at his watch, hoped he appeared relaxed, felt the seconds click by in slow motion.

Just a few more hours, he reminded himself as he snagged a beer from a passing waiter, and then, finally, freedom.

Jade's hands were bleeding and raw. She couldn't see them, it was much too dark, but she felt them throbbing, knew her fingernails had split, the flesh beneath her fingertips and palms exposed.

She heard the other girls, shuffling in their stalls, lying on a creaking cot, gurgling down water, or occasionally peeing, the sound of urine hitting the bottom of a bucket.

God, this was miserable.

In-fucking-humane!

She'd spent all the daylight hours trying to climb the damned wall of the stall and get over it, to find a way to escape, but she'd failed. Over and over, she'd scaled the rough siding, forcing her toes into knot holes or spots where the boards didn't quite fit together, but each time she'd neared the top, she'd lost her balance or couldn't find a foothold and had ended up sliding down to land on the floor again. Her only triumph had been knocking the horseshoe down and catching it deftly.

The other girls hadn't fared any better. Dana, who claimed to be a gymnast, hadn't been able to vault over the doors (no big surprise there, the girl was a braggart), and Mary-A, still a pain in the butt, proclaimed that she'd found a tool stuck in the corner of her stall, something she thought was used to clean a horse's hoof. Jade didn't trust the girl, not even now. She was probably lying. Candice had no weapon, but Rosalie said she'd found something that might cause damage, part of a nail clipper or something that sounded incredibly small and useless. No, her horseshoe was the only weapon she'd trust.

She only hoped that, with another day before this supposed slave auction or whatever it was, the police or some of the parents or the damned FBI would locate them. Jade had checked; no one had their phones on them, nor had the jerkwads kept them. Nothing electronic, no ID, to help.

She felt her insides shredding at the thought of what her abductors planned to do to her, but she knew she wouldn't go down without a fight. Rosalie's plan wasn't brilliant, but it was all they had, if Candice, the whiner, could play her part. Only then, if she could lull the dirtbags into thinking she was ill and letting down their guard, would they have any chance at all.

Jade didn't like the odds. She paced the stall, where odors of horseflesh and urine still lingered, and wished she had just one nail, something she could step on, to lift her up a little higher, a bit of wood or metal that she could wedge between the boards and that was strong enough to bear her weight long enough that she could push herself up, pull herself over, and drop onto the other side. She'd open all the stalls and they could run, ever westward, to the house and her mother.

Her heart cracked a little at the thought of Sarah and Gracie, so near, but so damned far. Would she ever see them again? And what about the father she'd just met? Would she even get the chance to get to know him?

Not if you let these sickos determine your fate!

She plopped down on the edge of her cot.

Someone would come for them, surely. They weren't that far off the grid. Weren't there FBI helicopters or something reserved just for the purpose of saving hostages? On television there were always battalions of ace sharpshooters, all dressed in black, with helmets and assault rifles.

But that was in the city.

No, she reminded herself, that was in Hollywood.

"Hey!" Rosalie shouted. "Listen up! Hear that? Someone's coming."

The barn went silent. Jade hardly dared breathe, and sure enough, the sound of a engine whining as it climbed a hill reached her ears. Her muscles tensed. Did he have another girl? More than one? Was he coming just to check on them?

"Just remember the plan," Rosalie shouted as the engine—a truck, Jade thought—rumbled closer. "If we can get him tonight, before there are others, even if it's both of them, we need to go for it. Candice? Do you hear me?"

"Yes," was the dispirited reply, and Jade's heart sank. Having their whole plan resting on the shoulders of a girl who was obviously the weakest link seemed ridiculous. But at least Candice had quit crying and sobbing and moaning. That was something. Could she pull it off?

Jade doubted it. She couldn't allow her fate to be in Candice Fowler's hands.

"Let me do it!" Jade shouted. "I'll pretend to be sick. I can do it, I know I can."

"No. Stick to the plan," Rosalie hissed.

"Yeah, Jade, don't screw things up." Mary-Alice, of course.

"But she can't . . ." she stopped, not wanting to denigrate the girl, then thought, oh, to hell with Candice's feelings. This was Jade's life they were playing with! "She's too wimpy. She'll never be able to dupe them. I can make it work!"

"He won't believe you. He'll expect a trick." Rosalie was desperate. "You defied him earlier and he hit you, right? He won't fall for it. What we've got going will work. So. Everyone. Stick to the plan." Usually calm Rosalie was definitely losing it, her voice rising an octave. "We might not get the chance, but we have to try. No matter who walks through the door, Candice, you're on!"

Frustrated, Jade banged a fist against the wall and swore. "Okay, fine," she said, then shut up and held tight to the horseshoe.

"I'll do it," Candice, in her little Minnie Mouse voice, insisted.

Jade closed her eyes. *God help us.*

CHAPTER 38

Hardy Jones, with his mop of shaggy, thin hair and perpetual sneer, was defiant, almost cocky, as he sat in the interrogation room. Bellisario didn't like him. *A worm,* she thought, *that's what he is.* A useless piece of human flesh in a beat-up jean jacket and worn Levis.

She was tired, getting nowhere fast, and the clock on the wall said it was eleven-thirty. They'd been at this for hours.

"I don't know what you're talkin' about," he insisted, having taken the chair so recently vacated by Roger Anderson.

"I'm talking about your life and your freedom," Bellisario said succinctly. "Either you tell us what you know, where the girls are, or you're going away for a long, long time."

"I don't know nothing about any girls." But there was a spark in his eye, as if he had something on her.

"That's not what Roger Anderson says."

"He's a liar. Ex-con."

"So are you."

"But I never did nothin' to no women. That's his deal. Not mine."

Hardy had a point. And yet . . . "Well, then, let's look at it this way," she said calmly, hoping to somehow get the worm to turn. "It's not what Dodds is saying either."

"Who?"

"Joss Dodds. You know him."

"Nah." Jones's Adam's apple wobbled, and a sweat began forming above his sideburns.

"Sure you do. He's the guy who lives in the mountains of Idaho, just across the border in the panhandle. Antigovernment type. Always gettin' into trouble. You met him a couple of times down at The Cavern." She was bluffing here, but pushed it a little, realizing that finally the smug grin on his grizzled face was slipping a bit. "We're just waiting on the security tapes to confirm, but Dodds says he knows you."

"Lyin' son of a bitch!" Jones leaned back in his chair and folded his arms over his scrawny chest. "I'm tellin' ya, I don't know him. And I'm not into dealin' guns, er ammo—" He shut up. Real quick.

"I didn't say he dealt weapons."

"You said he was antigovernment. What else do they do?"

"A lot, Hardy. Most of it illegal," she said, with a knowing smile. "And some of them, they're not very nice to their women, always looking for someone who might want to be a servant. Or a slave." She pushed a little harder, remembering something she'd read. "Or maybe even a wife. Or two."

Hardy Jones snorted. But Bellisario knew he was thinking, trying to figure a way out of this. In the past, he was quick to point fingers, to shuffle off blame.

"Roger Anderson says he thinks you keep the girls nearby, that way you could scoop one up and take her to a hiding spot until you got the next. Now, it's not your apartment, we checked, so I'm thinking it might be somewhere in the hills. A secluded spot. So if your captives yelled—"

"I ain't got no captives! No girls!"

"No one could hear them."

The Adam's apple was really rocking now, but Hardy had shut up, and that was the problem. She'd hit a nerve talking about hiding the girls nearby, but that didn't help a lot. The town was small, but the area around Stewart's Crossing was vast, a steep wilderness abutting the river.

She figured there was another culprit involved. Jones wasn't smart enough to be the brains of the operation, so it had to be someone a little slicker. Someone who knew the area. Someone girls might trust. Someone, she thought, that Rosalie Jamison, at the very least, had known. And if Bellisario was reading this right, Hardy was trying to pin the crime on his old cell mate, Roger Anderson.

Was making Anderson the fall guy Hardy's idea? She stared at him hard. Probably not. The man was a soldier, not a leader, and a weak soldier at that.

Then who was behind it all?

She thought about anyone close enough to Roger Anderson to know how to paint him as a criminal. Someone who knew him? Maybe someone he trusted and had hung out with? A few names sprang to mind, those who had visited Anderson, in particular. Was it possible that the man she was thinking of had visited not only Roger Anderson, but our boy Hardy Jones as well?

She was about to spring the guy's name on Hardy, when, as luck would have it, he saved her the trouble.

"Look, I've got an alibi," he said hurriedly, obviously trying to think on his feet and stumbling badly. "Anytime one of those girls was taken, you know I got an alibi. And . . . and if you don't believe me, call Clark Valente, he'll tell you. I was with him. He'll tell you! I think he was goin' to that party the dentist and his wife are throwin'. You know, Dr. Bigelow."

"Roger's brother-in-law?" she asked, the thrum of knowing she'd hit on something valuable propelling her on. "You know, I think I will." *And fast,* she silently added as she left the room.

"Hey!" Hardy cried. "You can't just leave me here!"

Sure she could. She saw a deputy in the hallway. "Hold him," she pointed to the interrogation room. "Don't let him near a phone." And then she was running.

Sarah paced the living room. As tired as she was after enduring her ordeal in the tomb and then giving a statement to the police, she was too keyed up to sleep. A blanket wrapped around her, Clint stoking the fire, Gracie and the dogs huddled on the couch, Sarah was heartsick and anxious and wished to high heaven she knew what to do. She and Clint had talked, and she'd even told him about the Madonna statue and the damned ghost, but all the while, no matter what the conversation was, they thought about Jade, where she was, who she was with, and if . . . if . . . Oh, God, if she were still alive.

"We'll find her," Clint said, but his words sounded hollow rather than reassuring.

"How?"

"The police. Bellisario."

She shook her head in despair.

"FBI."

"We need to do something," she said, and he nodded, feeling it too. She saw the restless energy in him, knew that he was staying calm for her. "Okay, I can't stand this a second more." She felt trapped in the house, as if the ancient walls were closing in. "I'm going to the roof."

"Why?"

"Because these walls are closing in on me."

He glanced at his watch but didn't tell her it was almost midnight. She knew. She knew every second that Jade had been missing. "I'll come with you."

"Me too." Gracie said, and for that, she was grateful. She didn't want her youngest child out of her sight for an instant and was still blaming herself for letting Jade drive home on her own. That had been her mistake, one that Clint hadn't called her on. He was too busy feeling guilty himself to blame her.

Needing to get out, to breathe, to think and clear her mind, she headed for the stairs.

As she climbed, she held onto the rail, but she didn't falter. The knowledge that she now had, the truth she'd heard from Roger Anderson, pushed her ever upward. She wanted to settle an old score, one she had with her father. She'd step out onto that widow's walk and never again fear the darkness and fear of that night so long ago. With Clint and Gracie at her heels, she climbed two flights and passed by the room on the third floor where her parents had slept and fought. Now she understood why. *Not your parents,* she reminded herself, *your father and your grandmother.*

Her head ached from all she'd learned, all the secrets that Roger had kept. He'd sworn to protect his mother too, despite the fact that Arlene was a murderess. As she passed Theresa's room, she forced herself not to look inside, not to even glance at the broken statuette or the shattered mirror. Through the attic door they filed, up the stairs and across the floor to the final staircase that curved upward through the cupola. She felt that same clamminess cover her skin, the same fear toy with her mind, but now she remembered the source of it, and, at least she could try to banish it forever.

Once on the widow's walk, she sucked in deep lungfuls of air. Finally the fog had lifted, the full moon without its shroud a bright disk casting a silvery glow over the land. The night was quiet, even the river hushed, no sounds of trains rolling on distant tracks or owls hooting in the surrounding woods.

She shivered, and Clint draped a strong arm over her shoulders, holding her tight, while she wrapped her arms around her daughter's slim frame, and Gracie leaned back against her, a family of three staring into the night and thinking of Jade.

"We will find her," Clint promised, leaning a comforting cheek against the top of her head.

"God, I hope so." She tried to feel secure, but as she stared to the east, upriver, she wondered if she'd ever see her daughter again.

Clint squeezed her just as she caught the glimmer of something in the distance. Headlights, she realized, and started to look away. Until she saw more headlights, a string of them. Not a big deal, generally, but it seemed the vehicles were closer than they should be, inside the county road, snaking through the trees . . . where? In her mind's eye she saw the plot map for the property, remembering landmarks, and the old logging road . . .

"Clint?" she said, her insides tightening. "Why would anyone be going up to the old logging cabin?"

"Don't know," he said, turning his attention in that direction.

"All that's up there is what?"

"The cabin, if it still stands. And a stable, if I remember right."

"No one's been up there in years," she said. *Until now.* "Trespassers?"

"Don't know." They looked at each other, and Clint said grimly, "Let's find out."

The door of the stable banged open, and the lights snapped on.

Here we go, Jade thought nervously.

"Okay, girls. Tonight's the night," he announced.

"Tonight?" Rosalie asked, sounding alarmed.

So far he was alone. The little man who was his partner in crime, the one the others had talked about, wasn't with him, or at least wasn't in the barn. Maybe he was guarding the perimeter, Jade thought, and tucked the horseshoe under her sweatshirt.

"Your new husbands are coming, and I want you all to behave," their abductor told them.

"Husbands?" Mary-Alice repeated.

"That's right, Princess. Husbands. Men who are looking for obedient wives."

"What?" Mary-Alice again. Horrified.

Stop it, stick to the script! Jade thought. *You're the one who wanted to go along with depending on Candice.*

Shaken, Mary-Alice murmured, "Jesus, what the hell are you talking about?"

"Do not use His name in vain!" He was snapping, his voice rising. "And yes, you'll be obedient!"

"You're selling us to be wives?" Now Dana was chipping in, showing her disgust. "I think that's illegal!" and then caught herself as she belatedly realized that everything the scumbag did was outside of the law.

"But I thought it was tomorrow night." Rosalie again.

"Things have changed, so pull yourselves together."

Oh, shit!

"Trust me, it will go better for all of you if you behave. The boys, they like a little fire, but they want wives who will serve them. The nicer you are to them, the more you do what they want, the better your lives will be."

No effin' way, Jade thought, wishing she could kick this pervert in his balls just as she heard another engine, a second vehicle, fast approaching. They were coming—the men who planned to buy them. There was no more time. None!

Come on, Candice, she silently thought. *Now's the time.*

But the girl in Lucky's stall didn't do anything.

Jade was sweating, pacing, trying not to panic and failing badly. Didn't the twit of a girl hear them? Dear God, there was a second engine and maybe a third.

From down the line, Rosalie cleared her throat, an obvious attempt to signal Candice to get the ball rolling.

Still nothing.

Come on!

Frantic, Jade decided she should just take the bull by the horns and pretend to be sick herself. Candice wasn't coming through; she wasn't doing anything. Jade opened her mouth, ready to moan, when she heard the first whimper, a soft, low moan.

"Ooohhh." Then coughing. "I—I think I'm going to be sick," Candice groaned as if in agony, and she was so effective Jade was certain it wasn't an act.

The kidnapper said, "You're fine."

"No . . . No . . . I'm so sorry," she said in that little mouse of a voice. "Ooooh. Oh, God," Candice said and began making retching noises so loud that Jade was sure she was losing the contents of her stomach.

"Stop it!" he snarled, losing control.

More retching, and then the sound of upchucking, liquid hitting the bottom of the pail.

"Oh, for fuck's sake. Not now!" he declared furiously. Then, as if he heard the sound of the approaching vehicles, he added quickly, "Listen up, Lucky, you need to clean yourself up. You too . . . you other girls."

"Ooooohhhh." Candice wasn't giving up. Her moan was louder, reaching the rafters, and Jade held her breath, her teeth sinking into her lower lip.

"Crap!" A lock clicked and a door squeaked open. "Okay, Lucky," he said, angrily. "What's the prob—"

Bam!

The sound of a pail cracking against a skull, and the slosh of liquid as the bucket spilled. He cried out at the same time frantic footsteps peppered the floor.

"You little bitch!" he roared, but it sounded as if Candice had escaped.

She dashed to the next stall and threw the bolt.

Thud.

Another hit, probably from Dana, hitting him with the stall door. He let out a strangled yell, but he kept coming, his heavy tread hard on the floorboards. Dana squealed, and then there was the sound of a scuffle, Dana screaming, him swearing. "Get back in there, cunt!" he cried, and the stall door slammed shut, the bolt thrown.

Jade's heart sank.

Candice couldn't fight him alone, and there were others who would join him soon! The engines were roaring. Close. So damned close. Oh, God.

She heard the sound of tires crunching on gravel, men's voices over the thrum of idling engines.

"Let me out!" Dana yelled, locked up again and hurtling her body against the door to no avail.

Damn it.

"Come here, you," he yelled, and Candice let out a frightened little mewl.

No!

Click! The dead bolt on her stall slipped.

The door flew open.

Under the overhead light, Candice—frightened, appearing about to pee her pants—took one look at Jade, then dashed away as Jade rushed into the open area of the stable.

He was there. In a heartbeat. One huge hand caught her by the throat and lifted her off her feet. Damn! "Get back in there!" he ordered, his eyes wild, his face a vibrant shade of red. She didn't think twice, just reached into her blouse and yanked out the horseshoe, swinging it hard and slamming it against his skull.

His legs wobbled, and he lost his grip as Candice opened another stall door. Rosalie burst out and wasted no time. As Jade struggled with the bastard and the sounds of more vehicles arriving reached her ears, Rosalie threw open the other doors, letting the girls into the common area. God, how many men were coming here to bid on them? Sick, sick, sick!

"What's goin' on?" A man shouted from outside the building. "Valente!"

Valente? Jade had heard the name before. Oh, shit was this jerkface a *relative?* She struggled to get away from him, but though he was dazed, he flung himself at her as she scrambled to get free. She went down hard, her chin slamming against the floor. Pain exploded through her jaw, her skin splitting open again.

Blood poured from the wound.

She kicked at him again as he dragged her backward. Twisting around, she shook off his grip with several hard kicks and stumbled to her feet. He was up too, but staggering backward. She saw his phone, peeking out of the pocket of his slacks, and leaped at it, yanking it from his pocket just as Rosalie, from out of nowhere, sprang onto his back, one arm around his neck. He spun around, trying to knock her off, as Jade frantically dialed 911.

"Help!" she cried as the operator came onto the line, and Rosalie, reaching around the bastard, swung hard and rammed the small weapon she had in her fist into the monster's eye. Blood spurted. He yowled, a shriek of agony, and fell to his knees, while she clung to him like a burr. She pulled her bloody fist back, then jabbed it even harder into his eye socket. Again. His scream of pain was a blood-curdling shriek that streaked to the heavens. Crazily he reeled, howling and trying to dislodge her, but Rosalie hung on with a vengeance.

Boots rang outside. Men shouted at each other.

"What the hell's going on?"

"Let's get out of here!" The male voice was panicked. Gravel crunched. Engines roared to life. Too late!

Sirens suddenly began screeching and finally the interior of the stable pulsed in vibrant red and blue.

"Oh, shit, cops!" one of the men yelled.

The police were here? Jade staggered to her feet. *Thank God!*

Boots crunched outside. Men shouted.

Finally, swearing, the bastard flung Rosalie off him. Blood poured from the socket where his eye had been, and he yowled in desperation. "Help!" he cried, but Rosalie didn't wait.

"Die, fucker," she said, and jabbed what she had in her fist into his throat just as the cops, weapons drawn, burst through the door.

"Stay back!" the lead cop, the woman detective, yelled, but one man following behind her, didn't listen. Clint Walsh raced inside, one step behind Bellisario. His expression was tense, dread in his eyes until his gaze landed on Jade.

Then without saying a word, ran forward, reached Jade and scooped her into his arms as if he would never let her go.

"Oh, God, are you all right? Are you?" he said, his voice cracking.

Nodding, unable to speak, she clung to him, her nose buried in his shoulder.

"Oh, honey," he said.

Jade's tears flowed, filling her eyes but as she peered over his shoulder, she saw her mother and Gracie, huddled together in the doorway, their eyes round, anxiety and relief evident in their strained faces.

Jade let out a shuddering sob and buried her face in the warmth of his neck, realizing she was finally safe.

EPILOGUE

The next summer
Blue Peacock Manor

A wild shriek rose to the heavens, and Sarah, standing on the widow's walk, looked down to the yard, where, she saw, the new peacock was showing off for the hens that were with him. She smiled and thought about the past nine months and all that had changed.

The sun, reflecting off the swift waters of the Columbia far below, was warm and promised another bright day. Her life had finally stabilized, and for the first time in years, she felt a well of happiness. At the sound of a truck's engine, she looked up and grinned, watching as Clint drove that awful old pickup of his up to the house.

They'd decided to move in together and were even discussing marriage and the possibility of another child, but they were taking things slowly. For her girls. Gracie had blossomed over the past year, looking less like a girl and more like a teenager who was interested in makeup and boys, along with her fascination with ghosts and now, it seemed, after the ordeal of the previous autumn, criminal investigation.

Sarah walked through the cupola, glad that she no longer feared the upper floors of the house, nor even the basement, though it still was far from her favorite place on the property.

Slowly, Clint was moving in as the house was nearly finished— plumbing and electricity repaired, old wallboard and rotten boards removed, new walls in place. The kitchen was still a mess but workable, and all the bathrooms had been upgraded. She and the girls had already staked out their rooms—she, with Clint, hopefully, in the master, Jade in Dee Linn's old room, and Gracie, predictably, insisting on the corner bedroom that had once belonged to Theresa. Gracie still believed it was inhabited by her ghost, the spirit that Sarah had seen, though she also was certain the ghost of Angelique Le Duc was no longer on the premises.

"She's passed over, Mom," Gracie had informed her.

Perhaps.

They'd moved into the guesthouse soon after the horrible events that had finally ended when Jade was rescued from Clark. Apparently he'd always been jealous of the "Stewart side" of the family. He'd never done anything worth a damn, had never married, and then had finally fallen upon a grand scheme to start searching for girls as potential "wives" for men who had no respect for women or the law. It was a bizarre plot, to be sure, but it had apparently been potentially very lucrative for Clark, who'd lost an eye at Rosalie Jamison's hands and was awaiting trial along with the mountain men. In an ironic twist, it seemed that Clark might be in line for some serious new money by selling his story to Hollywood. Negotiations were being pursued, if the court allowed, which was still much in doubt.

As far as Sarah was concerned, he should be locked up for life and never receive a nickel for the horror and pain he'd caused. Even though she'd reminded herself the ordeal could have turned out much worse, she would never forgive Clark. Not ever. She hoped he lived a long and wretched life within the walls of the penitentiary.

Jade, luckily, had been only slightly scarred from the ordeal, and though she swore she hated going to school at Our Lady of the River, she had begun dating Liam Longstreet, who'd been around the house a lot, helping his father, over the winter. Cody Russell had never once set foot in Stewart's Crossing, and that particular romance seemed to have petered out. Mary-Alice Eklund was still considered a mortal enemy despite the fact that they'd been held captive together, but who knew how that would eventually play out as Mary-Alice was heading off to school somewhere back East, according to Liam, whose own college career would be in state.

Sarah had come to terms with the part her parents had played in raising her. Her father, bastard that he was, had deserved an even worse fate than the one Arlene had dished out. Arlene, frail and dis-oriented, was locked away, awaiting a trial she would never under-stand. She'd murdered two men, it seemed, and she'd regretted nothing, though it was difficult to say in her distant state. Aunt Marge was "devastated" and swore never to speak to Sarah again, though Caroline didn't seem to care; she and her brother had never been close.

Clark had resided in a tiny apartment, not far from his mother, and had made his living buying and selling via the Internet, but he'd never made much money. It was while he was dabbling in guns that he'd hooked up with Josh Dodds and the mountain men. He'd met Rosalie Jamison at the diner where she'd worked and she'd become his first victim. Now, Sarah heard, Rosalie had moved to Denver to be with her father and was going to enroll in a community college in Colorado. According to Rosalie's mother, the girl was finally on the right track, ready to put the horror of her captivity behind her and start over.

So it was a time of new beginnings for everyone.

Sarah reached the first floor of the house and marveled that her siblings, after all the trouble, had decided to sell it to her. She hadn't been able to swing the deal on her own, of course, but Clint had sug-gested they put his place on the market and live together in hers. A deal had been struck, and now there was talk of the two of them turning Blue Peacock Manor into a bed-and-breakfast, though Sarah wasn't certain exactly what would happen.

She walked outside, where Clint was parking the truck. When he opened the door, the two dogs bounded outside and ran up to the peacock, which gave them the evil eye and another bloodcurdling wail. Tex and Xena lost interest, and Clint gave the fowl wide berth as he climbed the stairs to the porch.

"Not a great idea," he said about the bird.

"Tell that to Gracie."

"I know, but—" He shrugged, then swept her into his arms. "I missed you."

"You've been gone three hours."

"I know, I was trying to be romantic."

"Make another stab at it," she suggested, and a wicked light flared in his eyes.

"All right." He grabbed her then and kissed her, hard, bowing her back, causing one of her feet to come off the porch so that she had to cling to him. Her bones melted, and she felt that same cocoon of safety wrap around her that she always felt when he was nearby. His tongue flicked against hers with more than a little bit of promise. "How was that?" he asked, finally lifting his head but still holding her in his tenuous embrace.

"Better." She laughed. "Marginally."

"You're impossible!" Righting them both, he grinned.

"I try to be."

Chuckling, he said, "So where are the girls?"

"Gracie's at Scottie's and Jade is—"

"With Liam."

"You got it."

"So we're alone?"

"Most assuredly."

"Good," he said, the glint in his eyes growing positively devilish. When he scooped her up, she let out a startled cry, clinging to him as he strode to the front door and said, "Let's give this romance thing another go."

Her answer was to kiss him hard, and with that, he walked across the threshold, pulled the door shut behind them, and carried her up the stairs.

You've turned the last page.

But it doesn't have to end there . . .

If you're looking for more first-class, action-packed, nail-biting suspense, join us at **Facebook.com/MulhollandUncovered** for news, competitions, and behind-the-scenes access to Mulholland Books.

For regular updates about our books and authors as well as what's going on in the world of crime and thrillers, follow us on **Twitter@MulhollandUK**.

There are many more twists to come.

MULHOLLAND:
You never know what's coming around the curve.

HODDER